Dear John

AUTHOR'S NOTE

Living Apart Together is a series.
Dear John is the third book.

Dear John

Living Apart Together

Book III

ELISE DARCY

Penny Lane Press

For Grandma Pat, with my love.

1

Sylvie was busy getting ready when she heard the sound of a car draw up outside. She opened the curtains in the lounge and glanced at the London taxi cab waiting at the kerb, its engine idly turning over. Sylvie checked the time. She was late. She knew who she had to thank for that – her neighbour upstairs. Sylvie glanced up at the ceiling and frowned.

Sylvie turned from the window and caught her reflection in the wall-hung mirror over the mantel shelf; she hardly recognised the woman staring back at her. Gone were the tweed skirts and woollen jumpers that made her appear older than her years. Gone was the excess weight she had carried around since having children and starting the yo-yo diets. Today she was wearing a brand-new Ralph Lauren trouser suit which complimented her svelte figure. And her new hairstyle – shorter, softer and layered with highlights – had, to Sylvie's surprise, given her an instant facelift. She now spent time applying makeup which she had never bothered with in the past.

Sylvie stared at her reflection. She looked like somebody who'd had a makeover. But it wasn't just her appearance that had changed; it was much more than that. Over the last few months, as she approached sixty, her life had changed beyond all recognition. Sylvie had taken voluntary redundancy from her secretarial job. Spurred on by her mother passing away, and the thought that she wasn't getting any younger, Sylvie wanted to do something different with her life before it was too late. When she left her job, she had no clue what that something might be. That something turned out to be the realisation of a long-cherished dream to be a writer. What was even more surprising was that it was in no small part down to her husband, John, that she was where she was today; a successful writer and columnist working for a prominent women's magazine.

It all started with his idea to convert their five-bedroom four-storey townhouse into two separate apartments, in order to live in one and rent out the other. John had been forced to take early retirement five years ahead of plan at the age of sixty. It seemed like a good idea to downsize and have an additional source of income without having to move house. However, what John didn't expect was that his wife would move downstairs into the rental apartment – and stay there. Sylvie didn't foresee that either but she was desperately unhappy with her life and needed some space to sort out the cause of her unhappiness; was it simply that she was unfulfilled as a person and needed to find herself? Or was it something more – was it John?

It wasn't long after she moved downstairs that, by chance, Sylvie rediscovered her childhood diaries. They had been packed away in boxes and stored in the landing cupboard for decades until John used the storage space during the conversion. Sylvie had forgotten all about them, along with the dreams she once had before she met John. Finding her diaries stirred up those dreams of the past. That's when she started writing again. Her youngest daughter, Chloe, bought her a laptop and suggested that instead of writing diaries she could start an online blog.

Chloe convinced her that it would be fun, allaying Sylvie's fears about putting her private life out there. According to Chloe, it would be highly unlikely anybody would read her blog. How wrong she had been. Sylvie had John to thank for that. Or was it to blame? Sylvie was still undecided.

It was soon after Sylvie started her blog that John surprised her by taking her out for restaurant meals and romantic walks in Regent's Park. He even bought her flowers. Her husband was paying her attention for the first time in years. Sylvie had written all about it in her blog. She assumed that living apart had made John stop and think about their relationship.

Living apart together had certainly put a spark back in their marriage and brought the romance back into their lives. That's when the interest in her blog had gone stratospheric, and Sylvie's new career took off. She became hot property. A magazine offered her a weekly column all about the phenomenon LAT living and the positive impact it had on her relationship. However, Sylvie soon discovered her new column was built on a lie. She thought her husband's romantic gestures were genuine until she found out the truth by way of the postman and an unpaid bill.

The truth was John was in over his head financially because he had underestimated the final cost of the conversion. He had to re-mortgage the house and take on an additional loan to pay the builder. He desperately needed the rental income to cover his outgoings.

Sylvie had no idea what John was hiding. As far as she was concerned the additional income from renting out the garden apartment – the apartment Sylvie was living in – was meant to provide a more comfortable retirement, even though they could live quite adequately on John's pension.

It wasn't Sylvie's idea to convert their house, the home she had lived in with John most of their married lives and in which they had brought up their three daughters. But it was Sylvie's idea to spend as much time as she needed in the garden apartment downstairs. She wanted to work out what the future held for her and whether that future included John. What she didn't know was that John needed her to move out of that apartment ASAP.

John had always been very conservative and careful when it came to money. He couldn't admit that he had made a mistake. Rather than being honest and telling her the truth, John had hatched a plan to get his wife to move back in with him so he could rent out the apartment and pay off his mounting debts. Sylvie would be none the wiser. That plan backfired spectacularly when she discovered John had been sabotaging her apartment. Sylvie dug her heels in and refused to move out.

He even suggested that if she didn't want to move back in with him – he was well aware she had made herself at home in the garden apartment – that he could move in with her. Sylvie wasn't having any of it. She liked her autonomy and didn't want to move back upstairs and certainly didn't want John moving in with her. Not after finding out about John's little deception. Although Sylvie was shocked when she discovered how financial-ly irresponsible John had been, what upset her the most was when she realised John wasn't romancing her to save their marriage. The romantic gestures were all about saving his precious house. Sylvie was still reeling from that.

Once she found out the truth, everything changed. Sylvie had no intention of moving back upstairs. That's when things went from bad to worse. Her neighbour started playing up because she wouldn't budge, still refusing to let him rent out the garden apartment. He held parties in the apartment upstairs, disturbing her sleep. This went on for several weeks to the point where she considered moving out and checking into a hotel. Until one morning she finally flipped.

Sylvie thought back to last week. It was the morning after yet another party upstairs and another disturbed night's sleep. She couldn't take much more of it. Sylvie was working hard in her new career to try and get them out of this financial mess. She didn't tell John this. Hardly a word had passed between them since she found out what he had been hiding from her. But she did confront him on that Tuesday morning and told him just what she thought of him.

She had stormed up to his apartment and got the shock of her life when she found a slob sleeping it off on the sofa. Sylvie had stood there staring down at him in wide-eyed amazement. His flat looked like a train wreck. John used to be so meticulously clean and tidy that he would drive her up the wall to the point where she felt she couldn't relax in her own home.

Sylvie remembered all too well what it was like living with John. When he converted the house, what she didn't account for were the consequences of living together in a compact two-bedroomed apartment on the top two floors of the house. After forty years of married life, mostly spent living in a spacious five-bedroomed four-storey townhouse, living in such close quarters with her infuriatingly tidy husband was not a recipe for the relaxed, enjoyable retirement together she had envisaged. On the contrary, John was driving her to distraction. It didn't help that he had been forced into early retirement. With nothing to do all day, few friends, and no hobbies, Sylvie imagined this had only served to accentuate John's excessive cleaning habits at home. It was certainly a factor in Sylvie moving downstairs.

In the space of a few weeks, since Sylvie upped and moved downstairs, she couldn't believe how much John had changed. He never used to drink. He didn't like parties and would never have let himself, or his home, get in such a state. Sylvie had stared at her husband, lying crumpled and depleted on the sofa, and for a split second, she'd felt sorry for him. Sylvie had also felt a tinge of guilt that she could have saved them both a lot of grief if she just did as he asked and vacated the garden apartment, so they could rent it out. But she didn't. Instead, she called him a slob and gave him a piece of her mind. It seemed to have done the trick because the parties stopped. However, she wasn't about to thank him for it. While she was busy working hard, and paying the bills, he didn't lift a finger.

John didn't ask her to move back upstairs again. They had barely spoken a word to each other since last week. But the issue was bound to raise its head sooner or later. Not that it would make much difference to their immediate situation. John didn't realise that renting out the garden apartment wasn't going to get him out of this financial mess. Unlike her husband, who buried his head in the sand, Sylvie had sat down with all the red reminder letters and actually worked out their finances. There were urgent bills they needed to pay immediately, not two or three months down the road when they found a tenant and the rental money started rolling in.

Sylvie concluded that it wouldn't make any difference if they started looking for a tenant now; that opportunity had long gone. Which was just as well because Sylvie wasn't interested in moving back upstairs at the moment. What was at the forefront of her mind was her new life as a writer and columnist. Sylvie was relishing her newfound freedom, pursuing a career and living in her own apartment. She didn't want John pestering her to put a stop to all this nonsense as he called it – Sylvie called it a trial separation – and move back upstairs. Sylvie was enjoying her independence. She didn't want to think beyond that to where all this was leading, living apart together, and what it would mean for their future.

Sylvie turned away from the mirror. It was time she left for work. She could work from home, but Sylvie enjoyed the camaraderie of the office. This was so unlike her previous life as a secretary; she couldn't wait to get to the end of a working day and leave it all behind. Now her work was her life, and she looked forward to seeing her fellow journalists. Sylvie loved the buzz it gave her to be among like-minded people. It beat sitting at home wondering if her upstairs neighbour, John, would knock on her door and start on about their living arrangements.

Sylvie walked out of her flat into the communal hall and locked her door. She slipped the key into her handbag and glanced upstairs at the entrance to John's apartment. There was no sign of him. Sylvie sighed in relief.

'Come on, Alfie.' Sylvie smiled at her black cocker spaniel puppy. Now almost fully grown, he had been a moving-in present from her best friend, Julia.

'It's time for walkies.'

Alfie yapped excitedly and wagged his tail before darting up the stairs.

Sylvie stood at the bottom of the stairs and watched Alfie sit outside John's door, wagging his tail.

'Good boy. I'll see you after work.'

Sylvie quickly crossed the hall, her heels click-clacking on the parquet flooring. She opened the front door and nearly careered into her husband who was standing on the doorstep fumbling with his key. Sylvie looked at him in surprise and then gave him a disapproving glare as she stepped aside. She watched him walk into the house, avoiding her gaze, and upstairs to his apartment with the morning paper tucked under his arm. He was met halfway up the stairs by Alfie bounding towards him.

'Ah, there you are.' John glanced at his watch. 'I suspect someone is late for work.' John surreptitiously glanced over his shoulder at Sylvie.

She scowled at him and shut the door. Sylvie had overslept. That wasn't really John's fault, but after weeks of house parties the lack of sleep had finally caught up with her. Sylvie had slept through her alarm. Thankfully, she didn't have to walk her dog before setting off for work. They had an unspoken agreement of sorts. It all started on Sylvie's first day at her new job. Never having had a pet before, Sylvie had forgotten to make arrangements to have him looked after while she was out of the house all day. Sylvie had no choice but to leave him outside John's door with a little note stuck in his collar, on which she had simply written, *walk me*. She just hoped John didn't walk him to the nearest animal shelter.

That evening Sylvie had returned home to find Alfie sitting outside her door. There was a little note, tucked in his collar, which simply said, *feed me*. John had not kicked up a fuss about it. This took Sylvie by surprise considering John was not an animal lover – to put it mildly. He didn't get "the pet thing" as he called it. House-proud, John couldn't abide animals indoors.

Sylvie always imagined buying a puppy for their daughters, when they were growing up, but it wasn't to be. It was only when Sylvie moved into the garden apartment, on her own, that something magical happened; she started doing all the things she couldn't do with John and his infernal plans.

Unfortunately, since getting Alfie, her circumstances had changed. Lucky for Sylvie this arrangement with John had stuck. She still left a little note tucked in his collar with the words, *walk me*. And she always got her dog back at the end of the day, along with a little note in his collar from John – *feed me*. Surprised that John had not complained about looking after her dog practically every day of the week, it occurred to Sylvie that perhaps Alfie was a welcome diversion from being stuck at home all day with nothing to do and nowhere to go.

Sylvie climbed into the waiting taxi. Nearly bumping into John reminded Sylvie of the last run-in she'd had with her husband. Sylvie recalled that after she found out they were drowning in debt, she had asked John if he really wanted her to move back in with him, or was it just about the money? His silence said it all. That's when she had consulted her best friend, Julia, to ask her advice. Julia told her that if she wanted to stay in the apartment, then she had better take any and every opportunity that passed her way to earn money.

It was a brave new world for Sylvie because she had only ever worked part-time. Throughout their marriage, she had always depended on John to be the main breadwinner and pay all the bills. He was an accountant. The one constant throughout their marriage was that John was responsible with money. What had happened as a result of the conversion knocked Sylvie for six. She couldn't depend on John anymore – that much was obvious. So, she had taken her best friend's advice, accepted the job as a columnist and never looked back. It wasn't just about the money. Sylvie was living her dream.

There were times Sylvie could pinch herself to be sure she wasn't dreaming, and she really was a successful writer and magazine columnist. The only thing she had to blot out of her mind was that it was all built on a lie; she was still writing about how living apart together had brought the romance back into her life even though that episode with John had ended weeks ago. It was what had made her blog so successful and led to a new career, at the age of sixty.

To keep her job, she knew she had to give her readers what they want. And what her readers wanted was to hear all about how the writer calling herself Love on the Rooftop had found romance again through living apart together. Fortunately, she was writing under a pseudonym, so nobody knew who she was. They weren't out of the woods yet, financially speaking. Sylvie needed to keep hold of her lucrative column. Nothing could jeopardise that.

Sylvie opened her handbag, to find her purse for the taxi fare, and spotted a mobile phone at the bottom of her bag. 'So that's where I left it,' Sylvie mumbled to herself. She'd been looking for it all week but hadn't thought to look for it in the most obvious place. Sylvie sighed and picked up the phone. She supposed she should call the magazine and tell them she'd be late.

Sylvie switched on the phone and was just tapping in her work number when it started to vibrate in her hand. That was unusual, thought Sylvie staring at the phone in bemusement. It was a voice message. Perhaps it was her editor, Marcia Hunt, concerned that she hadn't turned up for work. She knew it wasn't from John; this was a new mobile phone, and Sylvie refused to give him this number. She didn't want any chance he would disturb her at work. Throughout the past week, since Sylvie had confronted John over the parties, she came home each evening to another message on her answerphone. She refused to play them because she knew who it was.

Sylvie dialled the number to retrieve the message. There were five messages, all left in the past week, all from her eldest daughter, Harriet.

'Oh.' Sylvie's heart leapt in her mouth. Her first thought was that something had happened to Gertie, their two-year-old grandchild. She didn't hear the words *Gertie* or *A&E*. Instead, Harriet had left a rather cryptic message saying she had called round each morning to find she was out. Apparently, Harriet had something urgent to discuss with Mum and Dad. It made Sylvie wonder if those answerphone messages she refused to play weren't from John after all.

Harriet finished the message with the words, "This time you better be in, Mum."

Sylvie's shoulders sagged. She was already on her way to work. Pity, she hadn't checked her answerphone first. It wasn't as though she could text Harriet and let her know she was at work today. Harriet knew nothing about her new career as a writer and columnist. Sylvie wanted to keep it that way.

Harriet, a journalist herself and part-time editor of a prominent women's magazine, had already made her opinion crystal clear when it came to people Sylvie's age pursuing second careers. Sylvie had attempted to enter a magazine competition for new writers run by the magazine Harriet worked for. She recalled that excruciatingly embarrassing episode when she turned up at the office to personally hand in her competition entry, only to discover Harriet, the editor, wouldn't read anything submitted from anybody over the age of forty-five. Thank goodness Sylvie hadn't got around to handing Harriet her submission before she found this out. For this reason, Sylvie didn't think Harriet would take her new writing career seriously. Especially when she found out Sylvie's blog and column were complete lies; Mum and Dad were not enjoying a second honeymoon, and well she knew that.

Sylvie looked at her phone and sighed. As far as Harriet was concerned her mum had nothing better to do than sit at home all day waiting for her daughter to pop round when she felt like it. Harriet hadn't even asked if it was convenient. It was as though she didn't have a life. Sylvie debated whether to phone Harriet back and let her know that it wasn't convenient. However, she had a feeling in the pit of her stomach – call it mother's intuition – that something was up.

Sylvie picked up the phone and dialled the magazine's office. They would not be expecting a call from their star writer to say she can't make it into work. Unlike some of her colleagues, Sylvie did not have any commitments or responsibilities to interfere with work. The days of looking after young children were long gone; her youngest child, Chloe, was almost thirty. Even so, no matter how old her children were, they still expected her to drop everything as if the world revolved around them.

Sylvie sighed and leaned forward in her seat to speak to the taxi driver. 'I'm so sorry, but there's been a change of plan. Please can you turn around and take me home to Holland Park.' Fortunately, Sylvie didn't have to be in the office today; she was only popping in to answer fan mail. In this instance, her fans would have to wait.

Sylvie listened to the telephone message once more. Harriet had some important news. She didn't elaborate any further. This left Sylvie sitting in the back of the taxi, waiting anxiously to get home, worrying about what could be so important that she had to see Mum and Dad as a matter of urgency – together.

2

Sylvie paid the taxi driver a generous tip for putting his foot down and using The Knowledge to cut down numerous back streets avoiding commuter traffic. If Sylvie hadn't been so preoccupied, she might have enjoyed seeing the picturesque London side streets and alleyways straight out of a Dickens novel. Instead, she gazed out of the window, the journey passing in an anxious blur.

Sylvie left the taxi and hurried through the front gate and along the garden path. As she unlocked the front door, she could see through the obscured pane of frosted glass that someone was waiting in the communal hall. Sylvie opened the door.

John turned around looking as anxious as Sylvie felt. He was holding a mobile phone in his hand. Sylvie presumed he had got the same message.

He held up his phone. 'Harriet left me a message.'

'Me too,' said Sylvie, fishing in her purse to find the key to her apartment.

'What do you think is going on?'

'Honestly John, I don't know,' said Sylvie as she unlocked the door. She was about to step inside her apartment when she did an about-turn and glanced at the floor by John's feet. She looked up at John. 'Where's Alfie?'

'I was doing a circuit of the park,' explained John, 'when I got Harriet's text and came straight home.'

'You didn't leave my dog over the—'

'Relax. Alfie is upstairs as we speak demolishing some dog biscuits.' John frowned. He'd never left Alfie alone in his apartment before. He left him up there, on the spur of the moment, because he didn't think Harriet would appreciate an excitable spaniel demanding her attention as soon as she walked through the door. Now John was regretting that decision. He hoped Alfie wasn't demolishing his flat too. He could just imagine what that little mutt was getting up to now he had the run of the place: spreading dog biscuits around his kitchen floor; drinking out of the toilet bowl; making himself comfortable on John's white sofa and chewing the television controls to his new flat screen TV.

'I'll go and fetch him,' said John, about to dart upstairs.

'No, don't do that. We could do without Alfie getting under our feet when Harriet arrives. You know what a naughty dog he can be sometimes.'

John cast his eyes heavenward and tried not to think about what Alfie was getting up to at this moment.

Sylvie walked into her apartment and straight through the lounge, aiming for the door at the far end of the room that led into the inner hallway. A little way along the hall Sylvie stepped into her bedroom. She deposited her coat and briefcase on the double bed and paused for a moment to switch on the bedside table lamp. Sylvie cast her eyes around the room. There was dirty laundry on the floor where Sylvie had cast off her work attire yesterday evening and forgotten to pick it up. There were women's magazines, and notepads full of writing, strewn on her bed; she had sat up late last night researching topical issues to raise in the next weekly team meeting.

Despite the mess – Sylvie was not a neat-freak like her husband – she still loved her large airy bedroom. It was unusually spacious because Sylvie had had a builder in to remove the partition wall. John's two-bedroomed rental apartment was now a one-bed. And the changes hadn't stopped there. With her best friend's encouragement, Sylvie had spent her entire retirement lump sum on redecorating and refurnishing the apartment.

She hadn't started out with the intention of moving downstairs, but Sylvie was not prepared for the reality of life with John post-conversion. When Sylvie was living with John in the apartment upstairs, often she didn't feel welcome in her own home. It was as though she was invading his personal space like an unwanted house guest. Eventually, she got tired of John's incessant tidying up and living by his unspoken house rules.

The move downstairs was only meant to be temporary. Her best friend, Julia, bought a few little knick-knacks to make Sylvie feel more comfortable while she was staying in the rental apartment. However, it didn't stop there. Sylvie and Julia got carried away. The end result was that John's bland part-furnished rental, set up specifically for tenants, had been transformed into Sylvie's home. Sylvie didn't regret a bit of it.

She changed out of her expensive Ralph Lauren suit, tossed it on the bed, and quickly put on a comfortable pair of fawn chinos and a cream cashmere jumper. Sylvie returned to the lounge to find John hovering in the doorway to her apartment.

'You might as well come in,' said Sylvie irritably. 'Harriet said she wanted to see us both together.'

John gingerly stepped inside.

Sylvie rolled her eyes. 'Well, don't just stand there. Sit down for goodness sake. I'll go and put the kettle on.'

Sylvie was just heading for the stairs to the basement kitchen, when John said, 'She's been trying to see us for the past week, ever since she turned up last Tuesday. You'd already left for work.'

Sylvie turned around and stared at John. 'She came over last week?'

'Uh-huh.' John nodded. 'It was the morning after the party.'

'You could have told me!'

'Well . . . I thought Harriet was going to ring you herself. Besides, we haven't exactly been on speaking terms since . . .' he trailed off.

'And whose fault is that?'

'Now look here—'

'Mum . . . Dad.'

Sylvie and John turned in unison to find their daughter standing in the apartment doorway staring at them.

'Harriet – darling.' Sylvie walked towards her with open arms to give her a hug. Harriet looked all right; no tear-streaked face as though she'd been crying. That didn't really mean anything. Unlike her younger sister, Chloe, who was prone to theatrics, Harriet tended to put on a brave face and bottle things up. Sylvie wondered if this was one of those occasions because she didn't appear to be her usual chirpy self. She seemed very subdued.

It made Sylvie wonder if something had happened between Harriet and her husband, Dominic, although she very much doubted that. They had met at university where they both studied journalism. After nearly twenty years together – fifteen married – she assumed they were okay. She always thought their marriage was rock solid. However, that's what Sylvie's had always said about her and John and look where they were now – living apart. Sylvie brushed that thought aside and concentrated on her daughter. 'Come in, my sweet. I'll make a cup of tea.'

Harriet walked into the lounge and took a seat on the sofa next to John while Sylvie nipped downstairs to the basement kitchen. Kettle on, Sylvie quickly got the tea tray together with cups and saucers, a jug of milk and the sugar bowl. If there was something important Harriet had to say, Sylvie felt in need of a cup of sweet hot tea to digest the news.

Sylvie walked back upstairs with the tea tray and sat down in a single rattan chair opposite them. She took a sip of sweet tea and set the teacup down on the saucer. Sylvie studied her daughter intently. Was she pregnant with her second child? That would be wonderful news. Or was she upping sticks and taking her husband, Dominic, and their daughter, Gertie, with her to America to work for the magazine at their New York office? There had been talk of that in the past. Although it would amount to a promotion for Harriet, as far as Sylvie was concerned that would be terrible news; she already had one daughter, her middle daughter Jess, living abroad in Australia. She couldn't bear the thought of another one of her girls moving so far away.

By the look on her face, Sylvie was guessing that Harriet wasn't pregnant, and she wasn't moving to New York, because both those scenarios should have put a smile on her face.

Harriet wasn't smiling as she announced, 'I'm returning to work full time.'

John and Sylvie exchanged glances and breathed a collective sigh of relief. They thought *is that all* and then both looked at Harriet wondering why she had to call a family meeting just to tell them that. Neither made a comment. Instead, they sat patiently waiting to hear if there was anything further she had to say to them.

There was more. John was about to discover he wasn't the only one in the family with financial problems. Both Sylvie and John knew Harriet was a part-time magazine editor, working mostly from home so that she could spend as much time as possible with Gertie. The few hours she spent at the office, she took Gertie with her and left her in the company crèche for a morning or an afternoon twice a week.

Harriet had also been in the fortunate position of supplementing her part-time income by writing freelance articles for another magazine, for which she was paid a good second income. The magazine she worked for as an editor had no problem with Harriet moonlighting in a freelance capacity. However, without warning, the other magazine had pulled the plug on her lucrative freelance work. They had taken on a new weekly columnist. To Harriet's chagrin, it had ousted her column. Harriet and Dominic could not afford to lose her second income. That had forced Harriet to return to work full time a lot sooner than anticipated.

'I couldn't believe it,' moaned Harriet. 'They dropped me like a stone and replaced me with an anonymous blogger who writes some stupid blog with a ridiculous name. I still can't get over the fact that I've lost my freelance work.'

'Oh dear, that is not good news,' said Sylvie, commiserating as she poured herself another cup of tea. On the other hand, thought Sylvie, no one was ill. No one had died. And no one was moving to New York. 'Well, it's not the end of the world,' added Sylvie.

Harriet rolled her eyes. 'You might look at it that way, but you and Dad haven't got a hefty mortgage and huge bills and credit cards that need paying at the end of this month!'

Sylvie pursed her lips and bit her tongue as she glanced at John across the room.

John smiled weakly. 'Harriet, what was the ridiculous name?'

'Pardon me?'

'The name of the blog. You said it had a ridiculous name.'

Sylvie stared at John. She narrowed her eyes as he stole a glance in her direction. She knew what he was up to, swiftly changing the subject in case she spilled the beans about their dire financial situation. Sylvie picked up her cup of tea.

'It has got a ridiculous name, Daddy. It's some anonymous blogger called Love on the Rooftop!'

Sylvie nearly dropped her teacup. *Goodness me!* She knew Harriet supplemented her income with some freelance work, but Sylvie had no idea she wrote a column for *that* magazine. Harriet never mentioned them by name and Sylvie never thought to ask. It didn't occur to her that by accepting the job as a columnist for the magazine, another writer – namely her daughter Harriet – would be losing theirs as a result.

Sylvie glanced nervously at the bookshelves, adjacent to the fireplace, where she was building up a nice collection of the weekly magazine she was now writing for. She bought a copy every week, without fail, so she could have the satisfaction of seeing her own column in print.

Harriet continued with her diatribe about the blogger. 'I bet it's only because the editor discovered the popularity of their blog that they've even been offered a weekly column. Everyone knows that magazine has been eclipsed by their rivals for years. They're grasping at anything they can think of that might turn their fortunes around. I bet this anonymous blogger isn't even a proper writer. I bet they've had no training or experience whatsoever in journalism. I bet—'

Sylvie had had enough. 'So, tell me Harriet,' she interrupted, 'what, in your humble opinion, makes a *proper* writer?'

This was precisely what Sylvie was afraid of. She wouldn't be taken seriously as a columnist if Harriet found out what she was doing, especially now that she had ousted her own daughter, the professional journalist, from her freelance work.

Sylvie continued, 'How do you know this blogger hasn't had any training or experience in journalism? How do you know it isn't one of your fellow journalists? Have you thought about that?' Sylvie said crossly.

John said, 'Your mother has got a point, Harriet.'

Sylvie looked at John in surprise. Why was he defending this anonymous blogger? Sylvie ignored John. She was more concerned about Harriet's professional opinion of her writing.

Perhaps Harriet's rant wasn't altogether unreasonable. Maybe Harriet thought this blogger, Sylvie, wasn't a serious writer for a good reason. It made her wonder if, after reading the articles, she felt they were not up to the standard she expected. Harriet was an editor. It was her job to weed out the dross; Sylvie had seen that first hand when she visited her office.

Perhaps Harriet was right. The magazine had only taken her on because of the sudden interest and popularity of her blog, and they didn't see her as a professional writer at all. Maybe her column, *Love on the Rooftop*, was just a means to boost the popularity of their magazine – nothing more.

Even if that were true, Sylvie still wanted to know Harriet's professional opinion of the articles she had written. The problem was she didn't see how she could expect an objective answer from Harriet who was still upset about losing her freelance work. Sylvie didn't bother asking the question.

But John did. 'What did you think of the articles?'

'What do you mean?' said Harriet defensively, clearly not interested in having this discussion.

'Did you like them? Did you think they were well written, interesting and informative?' John paused. 'You have read them – haven't you?'

'Of course I have,' said Harriet glumly.

'All of them?' blurted Sylvie, trying to keep herself in check but failing miserably.

'Yes,' said Harriet curtly, 'I have read all of them.' She was well aware that this new columnist was some blogger who had made a success of living apart together. They were writing a weekly column all about how their new living arrangements had brought romance back into their marriage. It was an interesting topic, and Harriet knew it was very popular with readers who were lapping it up.

Sales of their rival magazine, which had sat in the doldrums for years, had all of a sudden gone stratospheric. But what aggrieved Harriet the most was not losing her freelance work or even the thought that this anonymous blogger had no qualifications or experience and no business writing. What Harriet didn't agree with was that the articles were too one-sided. Harriet glanced at her Mum and Dad. Perhaps their readers should know what happens when things go wrong and living apart doesn't work out quite so rosy.

In truth, the articles had upset Harriet over what, in contrast, had been going on at home with her parents.

'Well?' John asked Harriet.

'Well, what?'

'What did you think of them?'

Sylvie leaned forward in her chair. She felt as though she was sitting in front of Marcia, her editor, all over again waiting to hear the verdict on her first submission.

'They were very good,' mumbled Harriet.

Despite the subject matter, Harriet had to concede that they were most likely written by a fellow journalist with years of writing credentials behind them.

John put his hand to his ear. 'Pardon?'

A smile played on Sylvie's lips as she watched this exchange. That's what John used to do years ago when the girls were naughty and had to own up to something they would much rather not.

'I said the articles were really good.'

'In your professional opinion as an editor of a magazine?' John prompted.

Harriet rolled her eyes at Dad. 'Yes, in my professional opinion the column is well-written, informative and entertaining.'

John nodded.

'And if you must know, I really look forward to reading the next instalment each week.'

'You do?' said Sylvie, quite shocked by this revelation.

'Yes,' Harriet whispered as though it was a cardinal sin to admit she was enjoying this blogger's column.

John smiled. 'There, that wasn't too hard, now was it?'

Sylvie looked from John to Harriet, and the penny dropped; John suspected that Harriet was upset not only because she had lost her freelance work, but this anonymous blogger, who had appeared out of nowhere, had knocked her confidence.

Harriet turned to Sylvie. 'I think you're probably right, Mum. On the evidence of the column, I can honestly say they are most likely a fellow journalist. You know how I've always said journalism is a small world? Well, I wouldn't be at all surprised if I have probably bumped into them on occasion too.'

Sylvie felt her face flush bright crimson at that last comment. Harriet only ought to know.

John said, 'I'll bet what cheeses you off more than being ousted from your freelance work, is the fact that you didn't discover this blogger first and they're now working for your rival magazine, not for you.'

Sylvie stared at John.

'How very astute of you, Daddy,' said Harriet miserably.

Sylvie smiled at John across the room. She knew she had the tendency to jump to conclusions and get over-emotional when it came to their children, whereas John always managed to get to the bottom of what was really going on.

'We organised this competition to find new writing talent,' explained Harriet. 'I just wished that writer had entered the competition and submitted their article to us. I would have snapped them up.'

Oh really. Sylvie folded her arms and looked at Harriet askance. She was thinking about her last visit to see Harriet at work. Sylvie had been ready to hand over her article for the competition when she witnessed Harriet tossing all those entries on her slush pile simply because they didn't fit neatly into a particular demographic. Harriet hadn't even bothered to read them first. She just made a snap decision that they were too old to write for her magazine or any magazine. It was as if what they had to say didn't matter, dismissing an entire generation as irrelevant. They were a generation of baby boomers, reaching their twilight years, with plenty to say but nobody to listen.

It made Sylvie think about getting older; it seemed that as we get older, with each passing year, we disappear a little more. Disappear from society as we lose our jobs and retire. Disappear from roles that have defined us at each stage of our lives. Until there is nothing left but old age and obscurity. Sylvie decided this baby boomer wasn't disappearing any time soon because this baby boomer had something to say on the matter. Thinking back to that episode, Sylvie was livid that Harriet could dismiss an entire generation of potential writers, among them perhaps the voice of her generation. She was about to give Harriet a piece of her mind when Harriet stopped her in her tracks.

'I have a confession to make,' admitted Harriet. 'I made a mistake . . . at work.'

Sylvie shut her mouth and listened. She never thought she would see the day that Harriet, always extremely confident and self-assured, would admit that she was not infallible and could make a mistake just like the rest of us.

Harriet continued, 'When we received the entries for the competition to find new writing talent, I was hasty dismissing anyone over the age of fifty. It was very wrong of me. I can see that now.'

I bet you can, thought Sylvie. Because of Harriet's mistake, she would never know whether that blogger had approached their magazine first. Harriet only ought to know that the blogger in question had been sitting right in front of her, ready to hand in her submission, when Harriet was making her rash judgement to consign all entries over a certain age to the rubbish bin.

'We had a meeting about it just the other day,' continued Harriet. 'It was all about how the writer, Love on the Rooftop, has turned our rival magazine's fortunes around.'

Sylvie listened with interest. She had no idea what effect her column was having on the magazine she was writing for. She knew what effect it was having on her blog; the magazine editor, Marcia Hunt, had been right about the fact that her column had brought her to the attention of a much wider audience who were now reading her online blog too. *Love on the Rooftop* was more popular than ever.

'Don't get me wrong,' said Harriet, 'I don't begrudge them their success. However, because of my poor judgement, our readership has plummeted. I think our readers are leaving us in droves for our rival all because of their new column.' Harriet took a deep breath. 'There has been talk of job cuts.'

Oh no. Sylvie looked at Harriet aghast. On top of losing her freelance work, Sylvie wouldn't want Harriet to lose her job as an editor too. She held her breath almost afraid what Harriet was going to say next. Was this it? Was this the news she had come over to tell them; that she had lost her job, the position she had aspired to and worked so hard to achieve, and now she had to accept a demotion and return to work full time in another position? Sylvie wouldn't want that to be the price of her own success.

'I found out yesterday my boss is letting go of some staff at the magazine.'

'Oh Harriet,' said Sylvie, wringing her hands. 'I'm so sorry, this is all my—'

'It means I can no longer work part-time if I want to keep my job.'

'You mean you haven't lost your job?' said Sylvie, still unsure she had heard her correctly.

'No, Mum, I haven't lost my job. However, they are expecting me to show them that I am fully committed to the magazine.'

John asked, 'What does that mean?'

'It means I have to return to work full time with immediate effect.'

Sylvie exhaled. 'I'm so relieved.'

'So am I, Mum. It was a close call. But I've got an excellent track record. That's what swung it in my favour. It's up to me now. I've got to prove to my boss that I can turn things around.'

'How are you going to do that?' asked John, sounding like a concerned parent.

'Well, here's the thing . . .' She paused. 'This is just between you and me, so word mustn't get out.' Harriet lowered her voice as though she was about to tell them a big secret.

Sylvie and John moved forward in their seats to listen as Harriet said in a hushed voice, 'I've had my researchers trawling the internet – and you'll never guess what?'

Sylvie and John exchanged glances.

'Don't keep us in suspense,' said John eagerly. 'What is it?'

Harriet announced, 'We've found another blogger.'

'What do you mean *another blogger*?' said Sylvie in surprise.

'Talk about a coincidence and a stroke of good luck,' Harriet continued. 'The reason I want it kept quiet at the moment is we haven't approached them yet to write a column for our magazine. It has to be passed up the chain first to be approved by the management.' Harriet smiled. 'We're confident that decision won't be long now. I'm crossing my fingers hoping they'll say yes. I really need this writer on board.'

Sylvie sat back in her chair feeling a bit deflated at this news. *Another blogger.* 'But won't the articles by this other blogger be a bit . . . samey?' asked Sylvie. 'Why would people read the same thing from somebody else?'

'That's a valid point, Mum. But here's the thing,' said Harriet excitedly, 'this is going to be different. You see, it's all about someone in the same situation – living apart together – for whom things didn't work out. We think the readers would be interested to hear the other side of the story.'

'Hmm.' Sylvie slowly nodded her head. She could see the reasoning. It made her feel better about the fact that, whoever this other blogger was, they wouldn't be in direct competition with her column.

Sylvie looked at her watch. She was glad that Harriet had come over and told them the news. However, it had taken far longer than expected and Sylvie had things to do and places to be. She had to get back to work. Sylvie stood up.

Harriet remained seated on the sofa next to John. She looked up at her Mum. 'There's one more thing . . .'

3

Sylvie was thinking about her busy schedule at work when she thought she heard Harriet mention she had one more thing to tell them. Sylvie was already on her feet intending to walk them to the door and see them out. She eyed her daughter who was still seated on the sofa. Sylvie was starting to worry how long this family meeting would go on. She had promised Marcia she'd make it into work by ten o'clock.

'Can't it wait until another time, my sweet?' Sylvie glanced at her watch. As much as she wanted to stay and chat, she wasn't retired any longer and didn't have all the time in the world to hang around and entertain her daughter – unlike John. Sylvie frowned at her husband across the room, comfortably ensconced on her sofa.

'No, it can't wait. The reason I'm here,' began Harriet, 'was to tell you that I've got to return to work full time with immediate effect.'

'Yes, yes,' said Sylvie impatiently. The clock was ticking, and she had an article to write, her blog to update, and a million and one other things outstanding. And that was just for today.

Sylvie wasn't prepared for what was coming next.

'I need someone to look after Gertie.'

Sylvie sat down.

'I can't leave her in the company crèche all week. I need you to look after Gertie full time. You and Dad. Together.' Harriet looked at Sylvie a long moment. 'Dad told me all about your seventies-themed party and generally being irresponsible.'

'Ex-cuse me?' Sylvie glared at John. She bet he hadn't told her about his antics upstairs over the past few weeks.

'I get it. I do,' said Harriet, in a patronizing tone of voice. 'I get that you are trying to recapture some of your youth, but now it has got to stop.'

John was sitting on the sofa, very still, very quiet, letting Harriet take charge. He didn't expect this. He had no idea Harriet was going to ask them to look after Gertie. And he had no idea Harriet was about to give Sylvie a lecture. He stole a glance at his wife. Maybe this was just what Sylvie needed, one of her daughters talking some sense into her.

Harriet continued, directing all her attention at Sylvie. 'This separate living nonsense has got to stop for Gertie's sake. I don't want Gertie to go to a childminder. I want Gertie to come to you. But not like this.' Harriet cast her eye around Sylvie's apartment. 'I want things to get back to normal – with you and Dad.'

John smiled despite himself. This was manna from heaven. There was no way Sylvie could refuse a request like that.

Sylvie took a moment to consider her response. Was this a family conspiracy to get her to move back in with Dad? She glanced at John across the room and caught him grinning. Sylvie scowled at him before she turned her attention back to Harriet. What right did her daughter have to judge what was normal, or to dictate the way she chose to live her life?

Family conspiracy or no, Sylvie decided she wasn't giving in. She stood up. 'We don't always get what we want in life, Harriet.'

Harriet's mouth dropped open in surprise.

It clearly wasn't the response she was expecting, and Sylvie knew why. In the past, Sylvie always gave in. As Julia so aptly put it, the old Sylvie wouldn't say boo to a goose, let alone utter the word *no* to her family. But this wasn't the old Sylvie anymore; that person had long gone. Sylvie was more confident, more assertive and she wasn't standing for any nonsense. Certainly not from her daughter telling her how she should live her life.

'Does that mean you won't look after . . . ?'

'Of course, I will look after my grandchild.' Sylvie glanced across the room at John. 'And so will Dad.'

Harriet tentatively smiled at her mother, still unsure what that meant.

John wasn't sure what that meant either. Sylvie hadn't come right out and said they were moving back in together. He wasn't surprised. They had been growing apart for some considerable time *before* Sylvie moved downstairs. Unfortunately, Harriet didn't fully grasp the situation; they weren't just living in separate apartments, they were leading separate lives. Perhaps looking after their grandchild would change that. John raised an interested eyebrow. It had potential. It wasn't something John would have considered, but he wasn't about to look a gift horse in the mouth. They had a responsibility now. A commitment they had to fulfil looking after their grandchild together.

Together. John mulled this over. That could work. In fact, that could work very well indeed. They would have no choice but to spend time together. It was what Harriet wanted and what Sylvie had just agreed to. John smiled. He could see another plan in the making, and this time it had all the hallmarks of a winner. What could be sweeter than little Gertie, their two-year-old grand-daughter, bringing them back together? When all hope seemed lost, and he had completely given up, Harriet, like an angel, had brought him a little miracle called Gertie.

John was so overcome with emotion he thought he might weep. He turned to Harriet and enveloped his eldest daughter in a bear hug. 'I can't wait to look after Gertie. When do we start?'

'I'm glad someone sounds pleased to look after their grand-child,' said Harriet sarcastically, hugging her father and throwing Sylvie a disapproving look.

Sylvie caught that look of disapproval. She had no intention of moving out of her apartment just because that's what Harriet wanted. She couldn't possibly move back in with John now. Sylvie knew what would happen if she did; it wouldn't take long before she slipped back into her old routines living with John. On top of that, with the rental income coming in her work would take a back seat, *she* would take a back seat, and that would be the end of her new career. Sylvie couldn't let that happen. But she wasn't about to tell Harriet all that. Harriet either had to accept the way things were and get on with it or hand Gertie over to a childminder.

Sylvie stood there staring at John. She narrowed her eyes. With the way John had been behaving upstairs of late, a fact that Sylvie had bitten her tongue and decided not to share with Harriet on this occasion, she doubted Harriet would be thanking her father for looking after Gertie. Sylvie shook her head. She wondered what her reaction would be if she found out that only last week her father hadn't been in any fit state to look after himself, let alone a two-year-old child. Sylvie decided not to put

Harriet in the picture. Her daughter had enough on her plate, returning to full-time work, without finding out what was really going on at home.

Sylvie wanted to help Harriet in whatever way she could. However, she knew how difficult it would be juggling looking after her grandchild with her work commitments. Sylvie shifted her attention to John. If she was going to do this, she would need John's help. He would have to grow up, take responsibility, and start acting like a mature adult rather than a spoilt child. She hoped he could do that for both their sakes. Fortunately, the parties upstairs had stopped but what about John's new lady friend?

That was something else Sylvie noticed John had failed to mention. He had a new acquaintance called Barbara. They had met over the park when John started walking Alfie. Sylvie recalled that day she returned home from work to find John standing on the doorstep waving goodbye to another woman.

Sylvie had sat in the taxi outside their house stunned to see that woman, with her two little dogs, leaving their home. It only confirmed her suspicions that the romantic interlude with John was just a ruse to get her to move back in with him before she found out about their dire financial situation. He needed her to move out of the garden apartment so he could start letting it out. When she dug her heels in and refused to play ball, the new romantic John dropped her like a stone and quickly found somebody else. That's when the parties started. Sylvie recalled storming up to John's flat the first night he had a party upstairs. When John answered the door – drunk or stoned or both – Sylvie didn't recognise any of the people there. She guessed they were Barbara's friends.

Sylvie gazed at Harriet sitting beside her father on the sofa. Harriet didn't appreciate that it wasn't as simple as asking her parents to move back in together; things were a lot more complicated than that. This was no longer a question of deciding to make up and go back to the way things were. Those days, that trial separation was long gone.

Sylvie looked at John. She knew they were both avoiding telling their daughter the honest truth. What Harriet failed to realise was that Mum and Dad were no longer together.

'You could at least pretend you want to help me out,' said Harriet, still throwing her a disapproving glare.

Sylvie sighed. How could she tell Harriet the real reason she wasn't exactly jumping up and down with joy at the prospect of looking after her only grandchild? It had nothing to do with Gertie and everything to do with the amount of work she was doing to keep the money rolling in, pay their debts, and prevent losing the roof over their head. Harriet had no idea how lucky she was that she still had a family home to visit to share her news. Things might have been very different. She could have turned up to find her parents' home up for sale in a desperate bid to clear all their debts. When Sylvie had finally worked out their finances, it really was that serious.

How could she tell Harriet that to keep the roof over their heads she now had a full-time writing career, and that it was she who had usurped her weekly column at the rival magazine? What would happen if Harriet found out her Mum was none other than the anonymous blogger and writer calling herself Love on the Rooftop? It didn't stop there. Sylvie's column was only one of many projects she now had on the go. The work just kept coming in.

Unbeknown to Harriet and John, Sylvie was making quite a success of herself and earning a considerable amount of money in the process. Their youngest daughter, Chloe, had shown her how to earn money from advertising on her blog, although she had no idea her mother was now writing for a magazine. Sylvie was being paid handsomely as a columnist and earning a good third income as a features writer for a Sunday newspaper. Sylvie was also making a regular appearance on a radio phone-in show. All this because people believed that her new living arrangements, living apart together, had made her relationship go from strength to strength when it was quite the opposite.

Marcia Hunt, her editor, had even talked about whisking her off to appear on a chat show in New York. Sylvie wouldn't dream of doing that. She wanted to protect her anonymity. Now more than ever. Sylvie had become too successful for her own good. What nobody else in that room realised was that they weren't just in the presence of a wife and mother. The woman standing before them was, in fact, almost famous.

Sylvie couldn't tell her family any of this because her success was built on a lie. If people found out the truth, it would all come crashing down like a deck of cards. She needed the work. She wanted to be in demand. But now the question of her real identity, the writer calling herself Love on the Rooftop, had finally raised its head. Interest was gathering pace in the person behind the blog. The pressure was mounting to reveal her true identity.

It was only last week that Marcia Hunt had called Sylvie into her office, and told her quite bluntly, 'You, my dear, are the celebrity writer everybody has heard of, but nobody knows. They are calling you *The Enigma on the Rooftop.*'

Marcia went on to say, 'In this day and age, when it appears that everybody wants to be a celebrity, people are beginning to question why you do not want to reveal your identity.'

Sylvie had read an article by some journalist suggesting that it was all a fiction; he believed the house in London, and the converted apartments presumably where the writer and her husband live, didn't exist. Marcia Hunt knew for a fact that this wasn't the case. She had visited Sylvie at home and seen her apartment first hand, along with a copy of the plans of the conversion that were lodged with the local council. Marcia had refuted the journalist's claims. But was it too late. The damage was done. People were beginning to question why she didn't want her fans to know who she was.

Sylvie remembered one appearance on a radio programme where she was put on the spot; for the first time, they raised the question of her anonymity.

In answer to their question, Sylvie claimed she wished to stay anonymous because her family were very private people and she didn't want the media camped outside their doorstep. She would rather just remain that ordinary couple, living in an extraordinary way, living apart together.

Of course it was all lies, lies, lies. Sylvie abhorred telling lies in order to hide up their real circumstances. The only shred of truth in that statement was that Sylvie really didn't want any media attention. She was quite happy for her fans to enjoy her writing and for that to be the end of it. However, Marcia Hunt had told her, in no uncertain terms, that things didn't work like that. The interest in her blog and her column was at a record high. Sooner or later she would have to come clean and tell her fans who Love on the Rooftop really was.

Right now, Sylvie was less concerned with her fans finding out who she was, than her daughter discovering it was because of her mother's success that she had lost her lucrative freelance work. Things had suddenly got a lot more complicated than Sylvie could ever have imagined. All Sylvie could do now was hope Harriet didn't find out the truth, and to keep calm and figure out how she was going to juggle her covert writing career with looking after her grandchild.

4

John sat at the kitchen table with his little black book and a pen to hand. He opened it and turned to a blank page. He wrote his name at the top of the page and underlined it twice. John paused for a moment and stared at his name. It wasn't that long ago he was writing Sylvie's name in his little black book.

Soon after the conversion was completed, John had bought the little black book. It was the builder's suggestion to write a snag list of anything untoward that may crop up in the apartment downstairs that might need sorting out before tenants arrived.

John absently flicked through page after page. There was plenty that needed sorting out downstairs, but it wasn't something the builder could do anything about. At the top of every page, John had written Sylvie's name. Since moving downstairs, John's little black book had turned into a detailed account of all the irritating, irksome little things that got on his nerves about his downstairs neighbour – Sylvie. What irked him the most was that it was his idea for Sylvie to move downstairs in the first place. She was only meant to be down there ironing out the wrinkles, so to speak, before the tenants arrived. When John handed over the keys to the garden apartment, he had no idea where it would lead.

John didn't want to think about Sylvie and her new life downstairs. He turned back to the blank page where he had written his name. Starting today, John was turning over a new leaf. He knew it was high time he cleaned up his act, especially now he had grandparent responsibilities. John stared at the blank page in front of him and smiled. He was going to start by making a new plan, courtesy of Harriet and Gertie.

John was already feeling back on track. He was a family man at heart. However, now his children had all flown the nest and without Sylvie around, or a job to occupy his time, John had lost his sense of purpose. That was most apparent when he woke up on the sofa to find Sylvie standing over him. The look on her face had left John in no doubt what she thought about the state of him and the state of his apartment. It was at that moment John realised he had hit rock bottom. But now, in the course of one eventful morning, things had changed.

Looking after his grandchild had given John a renewed sense of purpose. It wasn't just the thought of spending time with Gertie that had lifted his spirits. It was also the opportunity to spend time with Sylvie. He knew she wouldn't say no to taking care of their grandchild. However, he was surprised Sylvie didn't tell Harriet what had been going on in his apartment over the last few weeks. She only ought to know about the parties, the drinking and the spiral downwards to the slob Sylvie had discovered sleeping it off on the sofa. Fortunately, Sylvie didn't say a word. It had given John a chance to get his act together.

He knew it was about time. He had already put a stop to the house parties. The antics upstairs in his apartment were over. He was going to put all that behind him and make preparations to be a good grandfather to Gertie. That was his priority. He had no way of knowing whether spending time with Sylvie, looking after their grandchild together, would change things between them. Although being forced to pull together to help out Harriet was a start. At least it would open up the lines of communication between them.

John looked at the blank sheet of paper in front of him. Before he started his grandparent duties, he was going to make some long overdue changes. It started with this list. The first thing John intended to do was to pack up all the stuff his brother, Dave, had brought over and left around his apartment. He was sick and tired of lava-lamps and long-haired faux fur cushions, and all the other retro paraphernalia cluttering up his flat. It had been Dave's idea to dress John's apartment in a similar fashion to Sylvie's downstairs, in order to impress her and encourage her to move back in with him. It had impressed her back when they were still talking to each other. Not anymore.

It was all going back in the boxes. Sylvie and John's tastes were very different. John wanted his minimalist, contemporary, *boring* according to Dave, apartment back. John was looking forward to his place returning to normal, with its bare magnolia walls and uncluttered feel. When John had a spare moment, he'd put the boxes in the boot of his car and drive over to Dave's house. John wrote it down in his little black book: *Pack up all Dave's crap into boxes and dump it on Dave's doorstep.*

The next thing on his list was the new clothes he'd bought to impress Sylvie. John had grown accustomed to wearing the designer labels Chloe had helped him shop for. He decided the casual look suited him and made him look younger than his years. Furthermore, they would be far more comfortable to wear when he was looking after Gertie.

John wrote it down: *Keep casual clothes because I look darn good in them*. As an afterthought, John added: *Slight problem with the jeans. They no longer fit. Waistline too tight. Need to lose weight, but I haven't got a bloody clue how to go about it because I am not* – John underlined the word, *not,* several times – *going back to the gym*.

John still had to pay an entire year's subscription for gym membership he had no intention of using. It had been his brother's idea to join the gym. On his first visit, John had been trying to impress a young woman. Rather than watching what he was doing, he had picked up the wrong size weight and dropped it. A quick sidestep meant it narrowly missed his foot. However, that quick-footed sidestep resulted in a badly sprained ankle, a trip up A&E, and his foot in an orthopaedic boot. John had no intention of a repeat performance.

John re-read the last entry about losing weight. It got John thinking. Sylvie was right: he *had* turned into a slob. John needed to start taking better care of himself. He decided his first course of action was to start cooking proper meals. He might even invest in a cookbook because living on chicken pies was not going to help his expanding waistline. It was the only thing he had learnt to cook since Sylvie moved downstairs.

John wrote it down: *Stop being a slob. Stop eating fast food. Buy a cookbook. No more chicken pies.*

John quickly added: *No more booze.*

Then almost as an afterthought: *No more parties.*

John's pen hovered over the page as he tried to think of anything else he could add to the list. Nothing came to mind, so John put his pen down and glanced at his watch. He had been ready and waiting for them to arrive for over an hour. John had decided to do the list to pass the time. He thought it was well worth the effort. John closed his little black book and heard the doorbell chime downstairs. He looked up and smiled. Their first day of grandparent duty had arrived.

John made his way through the lounge into the small lobby, opened the door to his apartment and glanced down the stairs. He saw Harriet wheeling the buggy into the communal hallway. John was looking forward to spending his first day with Gertie and finding out what Sylvie had in store for their time together. He walked down the stairs and stood next to Sylvie in the hall outside her apartment.

Sylvie smiled at John.

John smiled back.

They were presenting a united front for their daughter on their first day of grandparent duty. It was what Harriet was expecting. John was pleased to see they were both making an effort, even though they had barely said a word to each other since Harriet's visit.

Harriet looked them over as though she were inspecting two small children before they started their first day of school.

John had the impulse to hold out his hands for her to check under his fingernails, but didn't think now was the time to joke around. He glanced at Sylvie. They both had to be on their best behaviour.

Harriet approved. 'Good,' she remarked.

John winked conspiratorially at Harriet. He knew she wasn't happy that she was dropping Gertie off to grandparents who weren't living together. It wasn't what Harriet wanted. It wasn't what John wanted. So, when John and Harriet left Sylvie's apartment together after her visit, John had taken his daughter to one side and told her that this was just what they both needed;

looking after their grandchild meant they would be spending more time together. He believed things had a way of working themselves out and, given time, they would get back together. John had every faith that this would work. It was, after all, an excellent plan. "Just you wait and see," were his parting words to Harriet. His knowing wink was a reminder of that conversation.

Harriet gave John a tentative smile as she handed him a large pink shoulder bag containing all Gertie's odds and ends. She had packed snacks, lunch, nappies, a change of clothes, and some books and toys.

'Right – you're all set.' Harriet looked down at Gertie who was fast asleep in her buggy. 'I'll be off then.'

Harriet lingered.

Sylvie and John exchanged a glance, and then both spoke at once, trying to reassure Harriet that everything will be fine as they edged her out the door.

When Harriet had finally departed, still appearing anxious, John shut the front door and turned to Sylvie. She looked very smart, very chic, and very attractive dressed in a blue trouser suit, cream blouse, and designer shoes. When John walked down the stairs and first saw her standing in the hall with Harriet, John's first thought was that he had dressed too casually, and he should have made more of an effort with his attire.

Now he was thought that although they had to make a good impression for Harriet, Sylvie's outfit was a bit impractical to wear to look after a two-year-old. John glanced at her four-inch heels. Perhaps she intended to change her clothes into something more comfortable as soon as Harriet left.

'John, I won't be a minute. I've just got to . . .' She pointed at her apartment door.

John looked down at Gertie, who was still fast asleep in her buggy, and said, 'Go right ahead.'

Sylvie emerged a few minutes later.

John frowned. She hadn't changed her clothes as he expected. Instead, she had a brown leather briefcase in her hand and a small note of paper which she handed to John.

'What's this?' John wasn't referring to the note she had just given him, but the fact that she had walked out of her apartment carrying a briefcase. Was she going to—?

'That's my new mobile number,' said Sylvie, pointing at the note in John's hand. 'In case you need to contact me in an emergency.' Sylvie opened the front door.

'But—?' John looked past Sylvie, through the open door, to a black taxi cab that had pulled up at the kerb outside their house. John stared at Sylvie. 'Is that taxi for you?' He didn't need her to answer that question. The united front was all an act. The clothes. The briefcase. The note. It was all planned. She had no intention of looking after Gertie today because, just like Harriet, Sylvie was leaving for work.

John looked down at Gertie. 'I thought we were going to do this together?'

Sylvie said, 'Think of it as a job share.' She looked at her watch. 'Goodness me, is that the time!'

'But what am I meant to do with Gertie all day?'

'I don't know. You'll figure it out.' Sylvie turned to go and then swiftly did an about-turn. 'Oh, there's just one more thing.'

John watched Sylvie dart from the front door back inside her apartment. She reappeared saying, 'Silly me, I nearly forgot—'

'Oh no,' said John, backing away from Sylvie as she approached. 'Not that too!'

Sylvie held out the lead.

Alfie yapped and woke up Gertie. She giggled in delight and held out her hand towards the little black spaniel.

Sylvie let go of his lead.

Alfie raced over and sniffed the soft little hand protruding from the buggy.

'Right – you're all set,' said Sylvie, sounding just like Harriet not less than five minutes ago.

John's shoulders sagged in defeat. He couldn't very well stand here and argue about it. Gertie had woken up. He had a dog running around in circles, yapping excitedly at his new playmate. And a taxi driver was hooting his horn impatiently outside in the street.

Sylvie turned in the direction of the door. 'Must dash. See you at five.'

'Don't be late,' warned John. After all the promises he had made to Harriet, he didn't want her to find out what was really going on. They both had to be home at five o'clock, so they could present a united front to hand Gertie back to Harriet.

'I won't be late. I promise,' said Sylvie. 'Oh, and one more thing . . .' Sylvie rushed back and gave John an unexpected kiss on the cheek before she left.

John tentatively touched his cheek as he watched her run out the door to the waiting taxi. 'Hmm, I think I'm back in Grandma's good books, don't you?' John smiled at his granddaughter.

Gertie was busy stroking Alfie.

The dog had stopped running around in circles and was sitting calmly beside the buggy enjoying the attention.

John walked over and shut the front door. He wished Sylvie had warned him he would be looking after Gertie on his own today. He would have had time to plan how he was going to spend the day with her.

John shrugged. 'I suppose we'll have to wing it.' He hoped this was just a one-off. Sylvie wouldn't be working every day, surely. He frowned when he recalled something she had said about treating it as a job share. John still wanted to stick to the plan and do this together. He was already looking forward to tomorrow when hopefully they would all be spending the day together – Sylvie included.

'Come on, you two,' said John, stepping forward and picking up Alfie's lead. 'Why don't we start the day with some breakfast?'

John was just kneeling down, intending to take Gertie out of the buggy and carry her upstairs to his apartment, when something caught his eye. In her haste to leave this morning, Sylvie had left her door ajar. John looked down at Alfie and imagined him jumping up on his sofa and spreading dog hairs all over the place. He glanced at Gertie. She was busy munching on half a Jammie Dodger biscuit she had found in her buggy. John thought of sticky fingers up his walls.

'Sod it,' said John, steering Gertie's bugging towards Sylvie's apartment.

'Sod it,' repeated Gertie as John shut the door behind them.

5

John's decision to wing it was working surprisingly well, along with making use of Sylvie's apartment for the day. It saved him carting everything up and down the stairs. Sylvie's kitchen was larger than his so there was plenty of space to feed the dog at one end of the kitchen, and feed Gertie her Weetabix at the kitchen table the other side of the room.

Feeding Alfie was simple enough. He slapped the bowl of dog food on the floor and Alfie dug in. Feeding Gertie wasn't working out quite so well; Weetabix was all around her face, the kitchen table and the floor. There was even a Weetabix hand-print on John's nice clean shirt. He wondered what proportion of the Weetabix in her bowl, she had actually eaten. John looked down at his shirt and sighed. Next time he might need to bring along a clean change of clothes for himself.

During breakfast, John tried to think up as many ideas as he could for how to spend the day with a toddler. It wasn't proving easy. He thought back to when his three girls were small and what they used to do with them. John frowned. The fact was they didn't do much of anything together. When John wasn't at work, he was busy renovating the house. For a person who prided himself on being a family man, the plain truth was John couldn't remember spending much time at all with Sylvie and the girls. Sylvie was the one who took care of the children, took them out, spent time with them. John, with regret, did not.

Sitting with Gertie, having breakfast together, John wished he could have those precious years back and do things differently. It wouldn't have changed the long hours from Monday to Friday he had to be at work, but in hindsight, he wished he had spent less time wrapped up in the house and more time with his family. Maybe then things would have turned out differently. Perhaps they would be together right now, looking after their grandchild, instead of leading separate lives.

John's reverie was rudely interrupted by Gertie hurling her plastic plate across the room. It landed next to Alfie's bowl making him yelp in surprise. He scooted across the room and disappeared up the stairs.

John looked at the two upturned bowls on the floor. There was dog food mixed in with the remains of Gertie's Weetabix. 'Well, I think that marks the end of breakfast,' observed John, feeling only too pleased that it wasn't *his* kitchen floor splattered with dog food and Weetabix.

John found some face wipes in Gertie's pink bag. After he had wiped her hands and face – and his own – John said, 'I have an idea. Why don't we go to the park?' He looked at Gertie hopefully.

Gertie smiled at Grandpa, and said, 'Swing-park.'

'Good. That's settled then,' said John in relief. He was taking things one step at a time. He was in uncharted territory. It was years since the girls were small and even then, he had rarely taken care of them all on his own. He didn't have a clue what to do with her after breakfast; the park was the only thing that came to mind. Alfie needed a walk and he could take Gertie into the swing-park.

John put on her coat and shoes, gathered up her bag, put Alfie on the lead, and finally set off. Within five minutes John returned home to collect the buggy. They had only made it to the front gate when Gertie decided she didn't want to walk anymore. She wanted Grandpa to carry her all the way to the park. John didn't realise two-year-olds couldn't walk very far. Grandpa's arms were aching just carrying her back up the path and into the house. He put her straight in the buggy and wheeled her out of the house.

A short time later he returned home, pushing a wailing Gertie in her buggy up the front path. She was crying for Alexander – whatever that was.

To John's utter relief he found the dog-eared teddy in the hall where Gertie must have dropped it on their way out.

On his third attempt, they made it all the way to the park, without having to turn back. John was already getting the impression that, contrary to his expectations, looking after his grandchild was *not* going to be a walk in the park.

As soon as they walked through the park gates, Gertie insisted on getting out of her buggy. John had to try and keep hold of her hand, push a buggy, and hold on to Alfie's lead all at the same time. John was feeling decidedly frazzled. By the time they reached the swing-park, Alfie's lead was entangled in the wheels of the buggy, and Gertie was on the verge of a temper-tantrum because Grandpa wouldn't open the gate and let her in the swing-park.

John was on his knees trying his best to untangle Alfie's lead from the buggy single-handedly while keeping hold of Gertie's hand, when a stranger came to his rescue.

'Here, let me help you with that.' A young man knelt down beside John to take a look at the lead entwined in the wheel of the buggy. He gave it a yank. It came free. He handed the end of the lead to John.

John breathed a sigh of relief. 'Thank you.'

'No problem,' said the young man as they both stood up. 'Glad to be of help. I know what it's like to have your hands full. He gestured at his three children standing beside him, all quite close in age, all pre-school.

John thought the youngest looked about the same age as Gertie. Thinking of Gertie, John looked down at his hand; the one now holding Alife's lead that was, just a moment ago, holding Gertie's hand.

Gertie!

The young man registered the look of panic on John's face. 'It's all right, mate. She's right there.' He pointed at the gate to the swing-park.

John felt overwhelming relief at the sight of Gertie, standing just a few feet away, in front of the small wrought iron gate that led into the swings.

'You have no idea how many times I've mislaid one of them,' said the father-of-three as he held open the gate for four children, two buggies, one dog and a grandpa. 'It's sheer panic-inducing terror worthy of any horror movie, is it not?'

'I'll say,' said John, his heart still pounding in his chest. Even though she was right there the whole time, he had an almost indescribable feeling of panic – the like of which he had never experienced before – at the thought that he had let go of her hand and she had wandered off. John needed to sit down. Fortunately, there were plenty of places to sit down inside the swing-park.

The helpful stranger sat down next to John on a park bench, both their buggies parked to one side. They sat watching the children play.

Alfie was also watching the children avidly.

John kept a firm hold of Alfie's lead; otherwise he knew the dog would be off like a shot to join in. John turned to the friendly stranger. 'I'm John, by the way.'

'Sayid. Pleased to meet you.' He gestured at Gertie playing with his little girl in the sandpit. They were building a sandcastle. 'Your grandchild?'

'Yes, her name is Gertie.'

'That's an unusual name. Is it short for Gertrude?'

'No, just Gertie,' said John, launching into the familiar story of how Gertie got her name, or rather kept her name. When Harriet was pregnant, for want of just referring to her unborn child as Bump, Harriet and Dominic had randomly chosen to call her Gertie. After many hours spent trawling the internet, looking for a suitable name for their baby, when she was born Harriet had looked down at her daughter, and said, 'Pleased to finally meet you, Gertie.' And that was it. The name had stuck. John smiled.

Sayid glanced at Gertie. 'Her name suits her.'

John thought so too. He shifted his attention to the little girl, about the same age, playing happily with Gertie. 'What's the name of your little one?'

'That's Jasminder, our youngest. We call her Mindy. My two boys . . .'

John looked over at the two boys chasing each other up the slide.

'That's Naveen and Arun. They're non-identical twins. I can't believe they'll be four this year.'

'You *have* got your hands full,' commented John. 'Day off work?' He imagined Sayid's wife appreciated her husband taking them out for a few hours.

Sayid, who had been chatty up until that point, suddenly looked at his shoes and fell silent.

John wished he hadn't been so forward. He didn't mean to pry. 'Sorry, I didn't mean to . . . '

'That's quite all right, John. Actually, it's not a day off work. You'll find me here most days, sitting on this bench. I take the kids to the swing-park every morning. You see, I lost my job. It's the second time I've been made redundant, and I'm only thirty-six. It makes me wonder if I'll ever find another job again.'

It turned out that Sayid had been made redundant from his job in I.T. Despite sending off dozens of job applications, Sayid wasn't having much luck getting an interview, let alone securing another position. That was two years ago.

John empathised. It made him feel guilty that he had kicked up such a fuss about losing his own job and being forced to take early retirement when it really wasn't that bad; at least he hadn't been put out to pasture at Sayid's age. He'd had a pretty good innings as far as his career was concerned. John had worked for the same company most of his working life. It had provided job security and a pension he could rely on, which was more than could be said for most jobs nowadays.

John glanced at Sayid. He had no doubt that their generation were having a tough time of it trying to keep hold of their jobs and homes and pensions, the basic necessities that John's generation probably took for granted. They were certainly not the things that John had to worry about during his working life. Job security seemed to be a birthright. Unfortunately, that was a thing of the past.

'I'm sorry to hear about your work situation, Sayid.'

'Don't be,' said Sayid emphatically. 'Before I was made redundant, I was working crazy hours in my job. When I wasn't in the office, I was on call to sort things out on my own time. I hardly saw my kids. I was scared that if I didn't work those ridiculous hours, I would lose my job. But I lost my job anyway. And you know what? I'm not sorry. Not in the least. Because the upside is that now I get to see my kids and spend time with them.'

John glanced at Gertie playing in the sandpit.

'I'll tell you something else. If I do get another job, I'm not making the same mistake. I'm going to make sure work fits around my family life and not the other way around. They're my priority now. Until the right opportunity comes along, I'm just happy to be a stay-at-home dad.'

The cost of childcare meant it made sense for Sayid to be a stay-at-home-dad so that his wife could return to work full time until things looked up in the I.T. sector. His wife didn't have a problem with that. It was an economic fact of life that traditional roles were being reversed and tough choices had to be made. Unfortunately for Sayid, a first generation British Asian, his parents were less understanding about this role reversal. They were appalled that their son was not at work supporting his family and that his wife was taking care of him instead. Those sentiments had rubbed off on Sayid.

'I'm okay with being a stay-at-home dad,' said Sayid, glancing at his children. 'What concerns me is when they get a bit older and start school. What will they think of their father if I am still out of work, sitting at home all day doing nothing? What sort of role model will I be for my kids?'

John scratched his chin. 'I.T, you say?'

Sayid absently nodded his head.

'My daughter, Chloe, is a computer software engineer.'

'Is she still in work?'

'Yes, as a matter of fact, she is.'

'She's lucky,' Sayid observed.

Talking of Chloe gave John an idea. He didn't want to say anything to Sayid just yet, but John intended to speak to Chloe and ask her if there was any way she could help Sayid. She was always saying how busy she was with work and how often she had to turn down new clients. John thought that perhaps if she could pass some contract work his way it would fit around caring for his children.

Apart from the occasional visit to a client, John was aware that Chloe did the majority of her work solo from home. John thought that this sort of contract work, while it might not be as secure as a permanent position, might suit Sayid's circumstances. It was well paid and flexible enough that Chloe seemed to manage to fit her work around her extra-curricular activities – namely clubbing.

In Sayid's case, the flexibility of working from home would neatly fit around his own circumstances, with his childcare commitments, and still allow his wife to remain in full-time work. He remembered Chloe once said that, in her line of work, it wasn't necessarily all about what you know but who you know. And Chloe knew a lot of people.

John smiled at Sayid. He was intended to phone Chloe and ask her if she could help out his new friend.

'That's enough about me,' said Sayid, changing the subject. 'I'm sure you came over the park to spend time with your granddaughter, not to listen to me bore you with my life story. Sorry about that. When you are around kids all day, you crave some adult interaction.'

'That's perfectly all right,' John assured him.

Listening to Sayid had put his own circumstances into perspective. It made John realise that he would rather be spending time with his grandchild today instead of being at work. If John had not been forced to take early retirement, then he would be missing out on this time with Gertie. He had already missed out on time he could have spent with his daughters growing up. John couldn't have the years back, but he could learn valuable lessons from the past. Sayid had taught him that.

'What about you, John. Are you still working, or are you retired?'

'I'm happily retired.' John knew that wasn't entirely true, but he didn't want to talk about his marital problems. Or his financial problems. However, at this moment he was more than happy to be sitting on a park bench watching his grandchild playing in the sandpit. 'My daughter has had to return to full-time work. The problem is I haven't got the first clue what to do with Gertie all day, apart from taking her to the park,' admitted John. 'I'm afraid I'm rather new to all of this.'

'Are you looking after her on your own?' ventured Sayid.

'I'm afraid so.' For today at least, thought John. 'You see, we have something in common. My wife is at work too.'

Sayid grinned. 'I'll tell you what, how about I show you the ropes? Meet me here in the swing-park, and I'll show you all the things I do with my kids. There's a visit to the library. That's always a favourite one. You can choose some books with Gertie. My kids love bedtime stories. I usually save that for when the weather is not that great . . . '

A sudden crack of thunder sent all four children running towards the park bench where John and Sayid were sitting.

Alfie whimpered and hid under the bench.

John looked up at the dark sky.

'Looks like rain,' said Sayid, gathering up three coats.

John stood up holding Gertie's coat as Gertie and Jasminder came running over together, holding hands.

'I'll tell you what,' said Sayid, 'how would you like to come along to the library with us now?'

John didn't hesitate. 'I think that is an excellent idea.' The wind was picking up. John could feel the first spots of rain.

Once all the children were wearing their raincoats, and the two girls were back in their buggies, John and Sayid walked out of the swing-park.

Alfie trotted alongside Gertie's buggy.

The two boys skipped along either side of Jasminder's buggy.

As Sayid and John pushed the buggies down the tree-lined avenue towards the park entrance that led into Kensington High Street, Sayid continued to give John some ideas for what other things he could do with Gertie. 'There's a music session at the library on Thursdays.'

John made a mental note.

'Parent-toddler sessions at the local community centre on Mondays.' Sayid glanced at John. 'I'm sure grandparents are welcome to come along.'

John made a mental note.

'You could visit a soft play centre on a rainy afternoon.'

John made a mental note, although he didn't know what a soft play centre was.

By the time they walked to the library, Sayid had given John enough ideas to fill a weekly calendar. With that thought in mind, John made another mental note to buy a calendar, so he could write down Gertie's weekly activities.

Thanks to Sayid, John had a plan for what he and Sylvie could do with Gertie tomorrow. This pleased him no end. He imagined Sylvie would be impressed that he had not only looked after their grandchild all by himself today but even planned what they could all do together the following day.

By half-past five Gertie was sitting in her buggy in the hall, with her coat on and bag packed, ready to be collected by Harriet. When the doorbell rang, they were all ready and waiting. John glanced to his left at the line-up. Sylvie was standing beside him presenting a united front. They were keeping up appearances for Harriet's benefit. Next in line was Gertie in her buggy. Last in line was Alfie.

John did a double-take when he saw the dog. He wasn't supposed to be there. John had left the dog inside Sylvie's apartment, but evidently, he hadn't closed her door properly. Not to be left out, Alfie had wormed his way around the apartment door and sat down next to Gertie's buggy when John wasn't looking. He eyed the dog. Alfie also appeared to be on his best behaviour.

As soon as Harriet stepped into the hall, she walked along the line like a sergeant major inspecting her troops. She gave them all the once over, even Alfie, who wagged his tail when she approached.

To John's relief, Alfie kept his bottom firmly on the parquet flooring and didn't utter a single yap.

'Good,' said Harriet. She gathered up Gertie's bag and pushed the buggy out the door.

John helped lift the buggy down the front steps.

'Same time tomorrow?' said Harriet.

'Absolutely,' replied John, nodding an affirmative.

'How did it go, with you and Mum?'

'Absolutely,' said John, avoiding eye contact. He didn't want to get into a conversation in case he said the wrong thing and accidentally let the cat out of the bag. He could not afford for Harriet to find out that they had not looked after Gertie together.

Harriet furrowed her brow. It had not gone unnoticed that John had failed to answer her question. In fact, his reply didn't make any sense. Harriet wasn't surprised. She could just imagine her parents had a rude awakening looking after a toddler all day, especially Dad. He was probably too exhausted to talk, let alone string a coherent sentence together.

'Do you want me to drive you home?' offered John.

'No thanks, I'll walk home. I think you've done more than enough today. Besides, I think the exercise will do me good.' Harriet waved from the front gate and took off down the street pushing Gertie's buggy in the direction of home, a thirty-minute walk away.

John walked back inside the house and closed the front door. To his surprise, the entrance hall was deserted. He turned towards her door. John thought she would invite him into her apartment to hear all about his day and discuss the arrangements for tomorrow. They didn't have a chance to talk about anything before Harriet turned up to collect Gertie.

Sylvie had arrived home just in the nick of time, her taxi pulling away from the kerb less than five minutes before another cab pulled up outside their house with Harriet inside. John had been frantically standing at the front door checking his watch and perspiring until Sylvie finally turned up, running up the front path and throwing her briefcase and coat inside her apartment.

'What time do you call this?' John had said angrily. Those were the only words that had passed between them before the doorbell rang and Harriet had arrived.

John looked at Sylvie's door and narrowed his eyes. Was she avoiding him? And to think he had gone to all that trouble of cleaning up the mess from breakfast time. He had even washed her kitchen floor. John knocked on her door. He wanted to know what the plan was for looking after Gertie tomorrow.

He waited and waited, but Sylvie didn't answer the door. John was getting the distinct impression that Sylvie would not be joining him for grandparent duty the following day.

6

John was staring at his little black book when he heard the doorbell chime downstairs. He looked up and frowned. He slowly rose from the table and tossed the little black book in a kitchen drawer. What a difference a day makes, thought John miserably.

He couldn't believe it was only yesterday that he was looking forward to their first day of grandparent duty, and gleefully writing in his little black book all about the unexpected visit from Harriet and his new plan to win Sylvie back.

This morning he had written down in his little black book that his brilliant plan, whereby Gertie brought them back together, was futile if they weren't going to share the responsibility of looking after their grandchild. He was bitterly disappointed. This was his last hope of a reconciliation with his wife. John had tried every which way to get her back. He thought Gertie would be the answer to his prayers. Now John wasn't so sure. So what to do? John had already made a new plan; he hoped that by taking care of Gertie on his own, without complaining, he could get into Sylvie's good books and then see where it led from there. John knew it was a long shot, but what had he got to lose?

He walked through the lounge and opened the door to his apartment. John paused in the doorway. Something had just occurred to him. There was an alternative. He could tell Harriet what was really going on. Better still, he could throw a tantrum and blackmail Sylvie into looking after their granddaughter together; otherwise, he would spill the beans and tell Harriet all about their little deception.

John shook his head. He suspected Sylvie wouldn't simply drop everything to look after Gertie even if he tried to coerce her into doing so. The way Sylvie dressed and carried herself, with an air of confidence and self-assurance which he had never seen before, gave John the impression she wasn't working as a part-time secretary anymore. He didn't know how she did it but, by the looks of things, Sylvie hadn't just landed herself a new job; she had a *career*. John raised an eyebrow. It was a complete mystery to him how his wife, approaching sixty, with few qualifications, had pulled that one off. But she had. However, regardless of her new career, John couldn't imagine that Sylvie would not want to spend some time with her grandchild.

John recalled that soon after Gertie was born, Sylvie had bemoaned the fact that while most of her friends were looking after their grandchildren, she didn't get a look-in. Harriet insisted she didn't need their help. Now things had changed. Sylvie finally had a chance to spend time with Gertie. It made John wonder if perhaps that's why she wouldn't speak to him yesterday evening after Harriet and Gertie had left. It wasn't the fact that she didn't want grandparent duty, it was the fact that she did. No matter how much she loved her new job, John suspected a part of her wished she had all the time in the world, like her husband, to devote to their only grandchild.

This new perspective lifted his spirits considerably. Things had been fragile between them at best. John didn't want to rock the boat and upset the status quo; she did her own thing, and he didn't ask any questions. It was clearly what Sylvie wanted. At least now with the advent of grandparent duty, they were communicating, in a manner of speaking, through presenting a united front for Harriet. It was a darn sight better than passing her in the hall and being ignored. He would still have preferred that she answered her door last night, but John reminded himself that Rome wasn't built in a day.

He walked down the stairs smiling. John was focusing on the positives. Looking after his grandchild gave him a renewed sense of optimism. It had thrown them back together in the most unexpected way, even if it hadn't quite worked out as he thought. However, it had opened the lines of communication, and that was better than nothing.

Sylvie was already standing in the hall waiting for Harriet's arrival. She turned at the sound of his footfalls on the stairs.

John smiled at her warmly.

She returned his smile.

John noted her crisp trouser suit, high heels, and makeup. She looked stunning. It was a wonder Harriet didn't comment on her appearance yesterday, thought John as he stood there staring at his wife. However, Harriet was in a rush to drop Gertie off and make it into work through the rush hour traffic.

John took his place beside Sylvie. They both exchanged a glance and then nervously stared at the front door, preparing for the once-over upon Harriet's arrival and possibly a few awkward questions about what they intended to do with Gertie today. John looked at Sylvie and decided he better do all the talking.

John stepped forward as soon as the doorbell rang and opened the front door.

Harriet immediately deposited a wailing Gertie into John's arms. 'Sorry, Dad, I think she needs a nappy change.' Harriet barely gave Sylvie a second glance before dashing off to the waiting taxi. She called out, 'Sorry I can't hang around, I've got an important meeting this morning.'

John glanced at the buggy left outside the door. He turned around with Gertie in his arms to find Sylvie racing into her apartment.

Seconds after Harriet had left, another taxi turned up outside the house. Sylvie rushed past John still standing in the doorway. She rushed back and gave John a peck on the cheek. 'Don't forget Alfie, will you.' She kissed Gertie, and added, 'I wish I was spending the day with you.'

John took that to mean Gertie and not himself.

John felt something brush his leg. He looked down to find Sylvie's dog had joined them. Alfie was sitting by John's feet looking out the front door.

Gertie stopped crying when she saw the dog. 'Alfie.'

John watched Sylvie get into the black taxi cab and wave as the taxi departed. He heaved a sigh and turned from the front door, kicking it closed with his foot. He carried Gertie inside Sylvie's apartment and headed downstairs to the basement kitchen for the first activity of the day – a nappy change. At least he wasn't taken by surprise when he was left holding the baby this morning. John smiled at Gertie. Today he had a plan.

John stood outside the jobcentre with Gertie in her buggy and

Alfie on the lead. It was almost eleven o'clock. After a bus ride which Gertie enjoyed, and Alfie didn't, and a long trek down the high street because John had got off at the wrong bus stop, Gertie had dozed off. It would have been far easier to make the journey by car. John knew this. That's why he had deposited Gertie in the back of the car and only then realised something was missing; he couldn't take the car because he didn't have a child car seat. That was something else he would have to put on his to-do list.

So, after the usual shenanigans at breakfast, which ended with John cleaning Sylvie's kitchen floor, they had set off on an adventure – so John called it – to get the bus. And here he was standing outside the jobcentre already feeling decidedly frazzled. At least all was quiet on the buggy front. John thanked his lucky stars Gertie was still asleep.

Talking to Sayid yesterday in the park had encouraged John to start thinking about resuming his job search. He didn't mention this to Sayid – how could he? John had qualified as an accountant and worked for the same company until he was sixty. And he had retired on a good pension. John wasn't about to tell Sayid the reason he still needed a job, because of his own stupidity underestimating the cost of the house conversion. Of course, the fact that his wife refused to get out of the apartment he was meant to be renting out hadn't helped matters. But that was beside the point. The fact was he needed to return to work.

John was acutely aware that he didn't have any luck when he was searching for a job before; that was straight after he was forced into early retirement. However, the difference then was that he was after a full-time position in accountancy. Looking after Gertie had changed his priorities and given him an idea.

Although John desperately needed as much income as he could lay his hands on, he believed the way back into work was to look for something part-time. And to set his sights on something other than what he was qualified to do.

He had read a promising article in the newspaper about the number of part-time jobs available. With his new responsibilities, looking after Gertie, he thought that working part-time would be ideal considering his sudden change of circumstances. Even though he hadn't consulted Sylvie about his idea, he thought they could work something out between them if he did get a part-time job. It wasn't exactly what he wanted. He'd rather spend all his time with Gertie. But he needed the money.

Watching Sylvie leave for work this morning, John had felt a little envious that she had managed to get herself a job in this economic climate. That, more than anything, had spurred John on to renew his job search. Surely, if she could find work, he could too. Perhaps they would be able to share the childcare of Gertie and both work part-time.

John was confident he had hit on the perfect plan. It still meant they wouldn't be looking after her together, although John had an idea Sylvie would appreciate seeing him do something about their financial situation. Perhaps if he were bringing in some money too, it would free her up to spend time with her grandchild. That would put him in her good books. All he had to do was get a job.

John glanced at Gertie still asleep in the buggy. He took a deep breath and walked up to the automatic doors, pushing the buggy forward with Alfie trotting alongside. Last time he visited the jobcentre, on a crusade to find work, it was demoralising, to say the least. He wasn't looking forward to repeating that experience. At least this time he was under no illusions; he wasn't going to waltz into another high-flying management accountancy position any time soon. This time around John was prepared to be a lot more open-minded.

He thought back to that one time he went shopping at the supermarket with Sylvie. John had noticed how many people his generation were sitting on the checkout or stacking shelves. He had no experience in customer service, but if there was a job going in retail, he was confident he could pick up the ropes. He was a quick learner, trustworthy, and sure he would have no trouble operating a till.

John recalled his brief experience volunteering in a local charity shop. He now regretted leaving at a drop of a hat when the conversion got under way. That would have been a good reference. However, at the time he had no idea what financial mess he was getting himself into and where it would lead. John shook his head as he looked around the jobcentre. This wasn't exactly what he had in mind when he was converting the house and making plans for their retirement.

John sighed heavily as he sat down on a plastic seat in the reception area. He wondered how long he would have to wait to see the job advisor. John glanced at Gertie; she was still sound asleep in her buggy. He didn't really want to bring her here, but John was eager to get back in the saddle and start applying for work. Besides, at the rate things were going he suspected he would be looking after Gertie all week. At least he would have time in the evenings to fill out application forms.

John looked about him. The seats in the waiting area were emptying quickly. He felt optimistic that he would be seen before Gertie woke up. Before long there was only one woman ahead of him. John saw her smiling at Gertie. He followed her gaze to find Gertie's large blue eyes staring up at him.

'Grandpa – naa-na!' demanded Gertie.

John rummaged in her pink bag and found what she wanted.

Gertie held out an insistent hand as John hastily peeled the banana.

A moment later she was happily eating her naa-na while Grandpa rummaged in her pink bag for a wet wipe. He glanced at Gertie. She would be happy enough for as long as the banana lasted. Then if he didn't let her out of the buggy everybody in the jobcentre would know about it.

John stood up. 'Well, I guess I won't be seeing an advisor today after all.' He pointed the buggy in the direction of the exit.

The woman ahead of him in the queue saw John get up. 'Please take my spot. I don't mind waiting.'

'Oh, I couldn't possibly jump the queue,' said John.

'I insist. It's not like I've got anywhere to be. Besides, I don't think you'll be that long. I'm guessing you might just get a minute or two to talk to the advisor while she finishes her banana. Then she's gonna want out of that buggy. Am I right?'

John nodded.

'She's such a cutie.'

John thought so too until he'd spent an entire day yesterday with Gertie and found out his grandchild could throw quite the tantrum when she had a mind to. Little wonder they called it the *terrible-twos*, thought John as he steered the buggy over to a small desk a few feet away.

'Ah, hello there.' The advisor seated at the desk greeted John like an old friend. 'I haven't seen you for quite some time.'

John tentatively smiled at the young advisor whom he recognised from his frantic job search a few months ago. 'I stopped looking for a job in the end. I came up with another idea, but um that didn't exactly work out.' That other idea was converting the house into two apartments. Once that was under way John realised he no longer needed a job to validate himself. He was quite happy to retire, become a landlord, and enjoy some quality time with his wife. And he would have additional income to boot.

Last time he visited the jobcentre it was all because of the five-year plan; to remain in work for another five years until he officially retired at the age of sixty-five. John wasn't ready to move into the next stage of his life – retirement. That's why he needed a job. What he didn't need back then was the money. Now things had changed.

'So, how can I help today?'

'I need money.'

'Ahem.' The advisor cleared his throat. 'Well, that's er getting straight to the point. So you're looking for a job?'

'Yes.'

The advisor looked down at some paperwork. 'I still have the original forms you filled in, so let's refresh my memory. It says here that you are a qualified accountant and you're looking for—'

'Anything,' John interrupted. 'Not fussy. I've heard there's loads of part-time work out there.'

The advisor looked up in surprise. 'But you're highly qualified, and you said here that you would only consider—'

'Yes, I know that,' John snapped. 'But that didn't exactly get me anywhere did it!'

'So, you want to broaden your search criteria?'

'Yes. It sounds so much better when you put it like that,' John said dryly.

'Alrighty then, let's see what we have for you.'

John smiled down at Gertie. He had every confidence that the advisor would come up with something; after all, he couldn't broaden his search criteria beyond *anything*.

The Advisor was taking his time. John hoped that was a good sign there would be rich pickings lower down the food chain. Thinking of food, John noted Gertie was getting towards the end of her naa-na. John rolled his eyes at the advisor, willing him to get a move on, and then glanced around the office. His eyes drifted to a sign displayed in the window – *no dogs except guide dogs* – just as Alfie let out a wide yawn culminating in a doggy whimper.

The advisor looked up.

John clapped his hand around Alfie's muzzle. Fortunately, he was only a small dog, so the advisor couldn't see the spaniel sitting on the floor beside John's chair. The dog had obviously gone unnoticed when John walked over to take a seat at the desk. John pretended to stifle a yawn.

The advisor resumed his job search.

John released his hand from Alfie's muzzle.

Alfie started play-biting John's hand.

John tapped him on the nose to put a stop to it and then placed both hands on his lap out of reach – or so he thought.

Alfie jumped up and nuzzled John's hand.

John kept his eye on the advisor, who was busy writing some notes, as he pushed the dog off his lap. John leant over and tapped his rump to make him sit down. Satisfied Alfie was behaving himself, John leaned back in his chair and sat there staring at the advisor. He glanced at his watch impatiently.

'NO!' shouted Gertie suddenly, making John jump.

He looked down to find Gertie holding an empty banana skin, and Alfie wolfing something down which John had no doubt was the last of Gertie's banana. He rolled his eyes and glanced at the advisor who was peering over his desk.

John was just about to apologise for the dog, when the advisor said, 'Is that your grandchild?'

'Oh er yes. This is Gertie.' John looked around for Alfie. His lead was still tied to the buggy which meant he couldn't have gone far. John spied a paw and guessed the dog had darted behind Gertie's buggy to finish the rest of her banana. John glanced at Gertie. Her face was like thunder.

She threw the banana skin on the floor. 'I want *naa-na*!'

'I don't think I've got another banana, sweetheart.' John grabbed the pink bag and had a look inside. He was pretty sure Harriet would not have packed two bananas for her snack. John didn't find a banana, but he did find the next best thing. 'How about some banana bites?' John held up the small bag of dried banana pieces to show Gertie.

Gertie eyed Grandpa.

John stood on tenterhooks staring at her little face. She seemed to be thinking it over. Finally, she held out her hand.

Mightily relieved that a disaster of epic proportions had been averted – John didn't fancy another one of those temper-tantrums he had witnessed yesterday – he undid the bag and handed them over. John noted it was a small bag. He turned back to the advisor. 'Look, I don't mean to sound rude, but do you mind hurrying it up a bit? Any minute now my granddaughter's patience is going to wear thin.' And come to think of it, so is mine thought John.

The young advisor looked at John apologetically. 'I'm afraid I haven't got anything for you, Mr Baxter.' His eyes flickered to Gertie in the buggy. 'However, I do have something for her.'

'That's hilarious,' said John, rolling his eyes and smiling at the joke. In all the time he had visited the jobcentre, regular as clockwork every week – sometimes two or three times a week out of desperation when he first lost his job – the advisor had never once cracked a joke. It did make him wonder if it was a job requirement to leave their good old British sense of humour at home. John got out of his seat. 'I'll see you next week.' John was still smiling.

The job advisor said, 'That was no joke.'

'Pardon me?' John stood there looking down at the advisor who was looking back at him with his usual deadpan expression. John's smile faltered. He really wasn't joking. John had enough insecurities over the possibility that his age was excluding him from the job market, without finding out a two-year-old could walk into the jobcentre and get a job over him.

'What on earth can a two-year-old do that I can't?' demanded John, glancing at Gertie.

'Look cute in front of the camera,' replied the advisor.

'Oh.'

'Take a seat and let me explain.' He motioned at the chair.

Despite his scepticism, John sat down.

'Talent scouts are looking for cute baby and toddler models. I think she fits the bill – don't you?'

They both peered at Gertie. She was sitting in her buggy munching on her banana bites and smiling contentedly. Alfie was busy mopping up the crumbs from the floor. John frowned at his granddaughter. She might look like butter wouldn't melt but the advisor had not seen Gertie, with Weetabix smeared all over her face, hurling her plate across the room in a temper because John couldn't get the straps in her highchair unbuckled quick enough when she said the word *out*, meaning *get me out of this chair right now!*

'Here's how it works,' the advisor continued. 'The modelling agency's clients are big high street names. They are running a campaign looking for new faces to launch their autumn and winter fashion ranges. I believe the agency normally ask you to send in a photograph first. Then they may contact you to invite your baby or toddler to attend a photoshoot. This time they are going straight for the photoshoot. The shortlist of candidates taken on by the agency is then forwarded to the PR departments of their clients. If they are interested, the agency will contact you for a casting or audition. 'Well?'

John looked back at the advisor. 'Well, what?'

'Do you want to take her along to the photoshoot? I presume it's like some sort of screen test to see how she gets on in front of the camera.'

John's immediate reaction was to say no, but when he opened his mouth what came out was, 'How much?' John inwardly cringed. He couldn't believe he said that.

'Let me see. Ah, here we are.' The advisor gave John a figure he wasn't expecting.

John scratched his chin and regarded Gertie thoughtfully. 'That much?'

'Uh-huh. There's the potential for advertising campaigns, television commercials – you name it. I'm afraid there will be some stiff competition though. I expect there will be a lot of toddlers at the photoshoot. You know how it is – pushy parents seeing a way to make easy money.'

John coloured at that comment wondering if that description extended to grandparents too.

'But then I suppose who can blame them? The sky's the limit – and so is the money. Are you interested?'

John looked at Gertie, thought of the money, and then imagined Harriet blowing a gasket if she found out he was signing her daughter up to a modelling agency without her permission.

John shrugged, looked across at the advisor, and 'Where do I take her for the screen test?'

It wasn't as though John really expected her to be one of the ones to make it on to the agency's books, out of the hundreds or even thousands of hopefuls. As the advisor put it, there would be lots of pushy parents with their little darlings. They would most likely be dressed up to the nines with all sorts of girly accessories. All John had was a toddler dressed in a pair of corduroy dungarees and a blue striped tee-shirt. She looked like a sailor with a fondness for crispy banana bites.

John watched as her podgy little hand searched the bottom of the packet of banana bites. It was empty. She turned the packet upside down and emptied all the crumbs over her trousers. She now had sticky hands. Grandad had run out of face wipes. John shook his head. What an unlikely pair they were going to make turning up to the screen test.

John smiled at Gertie and then looked across at the advisor. 'What the heck – let's do it.'

The advisor handed John the details of the photoshoot.

John gathered up Gertie's pink bag and pushed her buggy towards the exit.

'Oh and Mr Baxter,' the advisor called after him.

John paused at the door and turned around.

'In future, please don't bring your dog into the jobcentre.' He pointed at the sign and then at Alfie. 'Although it might be worth taking him along to the photoshoot. They also take on cute pets.'

'Are you saying the dog might get work too?'

'You never know.'

John frowned at Alfie, and muttered, 'I don't believe this, even the damn dog can walk in the jobcentre and get a job!'

7

He didn't really think they had a hope of getting on to the agency's books. Gertie might be photogenic, but John didn't have the first clue how to dress her appropriately for the photoshoot. Besides, he didn't have the time; the photoshoot was this afternoon. However, the timing had been quite fortuitous. At least it would make a change from visiting the swing-park.

As for the dog, Alfie might be cute, but his coat was matted, and he needed grooming. Shouldn't he have a ribbon in his hair or something? John cast an eye over Alfie. He wouldn't mind if the dog earned some money; however, Alfie looked decidedly scruffy for a photoshoot. John was just debating whether not to bother attending when he stepped outside and discovered it was raining. That made up his mind. They couldn't go to the swing-park in this weather.

John still couldn't believe he had walked into the jobcentre looking for a position for himself and walked out with a job interview for his two-year-old granddaughter. What a wacky world we live in, thought John. He already thought his age was against him. That he was passed it. Obsolete. On the scrapheap. But this was ridiculous. How could he compete with a two-year-old? At least he could console himself with the thought that there would be stiff competition. He could forget any ideas of a celebrity granddaughter and instant riches, along with the problem of how to tell Harriet that, in her absence, Granddad had gone and got his grandchild a job. All John was thinking right now was that he had somewhere to take Gertie on a rainy afternoon. What harm could it do?

John stood on the street corner and decided to forget the bus and hail a cab. He couldn't really afford it, but they were all getting soaking wet waiting for the bus. John had spent several minutes waiting at the bus stop trying unsuccessfully to fix the infernal plastic rain cover over Gertie's buggy. Eventually, John gave up and held up his hand for a passing taxi. Perhaps the people at the screen test would reimburse his travel costs? He didn't think to ask in the jobcentre. John hailed a taxi anyway.

John gave the directions and opened the cab door. There was no child car seat. He looked at Gertie.

The taxi driver said, 'You don't need a child seat in cabs. You can sit her on your lap. Most people just load their kid inside still in their buggy.' He helped John lift the buggy into the back of the cab and park her by the seat.

Next in was Alfie. He jumped straight up on to the back seat, leaving wet paw prints on the black upholstery as he darted from one end of the seat to the other.

John scooted him off and sat down next to the buggy. He had already decided that if Gertie wasn't enjoying herself, then that was the end of the photoshoot. He certainly wasn't going to push her into anything. She was only two for goodness sake. This was all just a bit of fun to while away a rainy afternoon. If they weren't having fun, then they were leaving. Besides, John couldn't imagine anything would come of it. And that assumed they managed to take a photograph of her – in focus. For starters, she would have to sit still for the camera. Gertie wasn't exactly a sit still kind of gal. John didn't think they would get through the first hurdle.

Within twenty minutes the taxi arrived outside the modelling agency in Hoxton, East London. Gertie was sitting on John's lap; she wanted out of the buggy almost as soon as the taxi set off. John wasn't surprised. It's not as though she could see anything sitting down there. So John had scooped her up and made sure he had fastened his seat belt around both of them.

The taxi driver lifted the buggy out of the back of his cab while John stood on the pavement holding Gertie. He held Alfie's lead as John deposited a none-too-happy Gertie back in the buggy.

John gave the taxi driver a large tip he could ill afford. This was turning out a rather expensive afternoon. He was beginning to wonder whether he would have been better off waiting for the rain to stop and just heading to the park to meet his friend Sayid. But it was too late for that now. They'd arrived at the modelling agency, so John thought they might as well make an appearance.

Two hours later, John was standing back outside the modelling agency feeling distinctly cheesed off. The moment they sat Gertie down in front of the camera, it was as though somebody had flicked a switch on his petulant granddaughter. He'd never seen anything like it. She smiled, she laughed, she giggled, she looked coy, she looked cute. The camera lapped it up.

Shame she wasn't always like that when the camera stopped rolling, thought John. He was kneeling on the damp pavement, trying to strap Gertie into her buggy. Clipping the straps together was tricky at the best of times, without Gertie being difficult and attempting to struggle free.

'NO!' Gertie screamed into John's ear.

'Now look here, young lady, you need to sit in your buggy until we get to the bus stop.'

Gertie blew Grandpa a big raspberry in response and continued to squirm in her seat, making it impossible for John to clip her in. Eventually, he gave up and she got her own way. John lifted her out of the buggy and somehow managed to walk to the bus stop carrying her in one arm, while pushing the buggy and holding on to Alfie's lead. He felt like hailing a taxi but with the amount of money he had got through in one afternoon John couldn't afford it.

He stood at the bus stop thinking about the photoshoot. John was as pleased as punch to discover Gertie was so well-behaved in front of the camera. She was so good the modelling agency signed her up on the spot. John was ecstatic for all of ten seconds until he found out how much it would cost him to get his granddaughter on to the agency's books. On top of that, he had to pay for the professional photographs that would be sent to the agency's clients.

He was beginning to wonder whether this was all just a giant rip-off for over-indulgent parents with more money than sense. Until they reminded John how much Gertie could earn – sixty pounds per hour or three hundred per day, and that was just for a photoshoot. If she was lucky enough to scoop television commercials, Gertie could earn several hundred quid for an afternoon's work, and John a hundred pounds just for being her chaperone.

Hoping he wasn't being duped, John had handed over his

credit card. If nothing came of it at least he walked away with a copy of the studio shots which, to John's knowledge, were the first professional photographs of Gertie that had ever been taken. They in themselves were worth the money he had just racked up on his credit card. It was nice to have something to show for the afternoon because John doubted anything much would come of Gertie being on the agency's books.

John had sat flicking through one of their brochures while they waited for Gertie to be called for the photoshoot. He looked at the professional photos of other little protégés on the agency's books and concluded that Gertie had some stiff competition. At least if she did get an audition, as they called it, John now had every confidence that his granddaughter could hold her own and behave herself in front of the camera. That didn't mean it would lead to any modelling contracts with the agency's clients, but John wasn't bothered about that. What mattered was that Gertie had had a good time, both on and off camera.

In between shoots Gertie had been happily occupied in the well-equipped play area, along with several other children, enjoying herself and making new friends.

John had also enjoyed the afternoon. He'd sat with a cup of coffee and a pastry – which he didn't have to pay for – watching her have a good time. Even the dog was occupied. Despite his scruffy appearance, he had joined Gertie on the photoshoot. They made a great double-act. Gertie and Alfie had the photographer and her assistant in fits of giggles at their antics, along with Grandpa. There were lots of oohing and aahing as Gertie put her chubby arms around Alfie and gave him a cuddle at the end of the shoot.

Grandpa had watched this display of affection and wondered why he had never bought the girls a pet when they were children. They would have loved an Alfie. John frowned. He knew why they never had a pet, despite Sylvie asking him time and time again to get the girls a puppy. He wouldn't allow an animal in the house with their fleas and hairs and smells. John never understood the whole pet thing, not until he sat in that photoshoot and saw the way his granddaughter interacted with Sylvie's dog. It almost brought a tear to his eye watching them both.

At the end of the photoshoot, after John had handed over his credit card, the agency needed to know Gertie's availability in case a client got in touch and, they wanted her to attend an audition. It might be at short notice. Although they didn't expect him to drop everything, they did want to know when they were free in case something came up.

As far as John was concerned, they were available every day, Monday to Friday, until further notice. Unless something suddenly changed like, for instance, Harriet finding out that her parents weren't being honest about the arrangements for looking after Gertie. Or Sylvie decided she was having Gertie for a day. John didn't think that would happen in a month of Sundays; she was too busy with her new job. He wished she wasn't. John would have liked to have shared these moments with Sylvie. He and Gertie had had fun together. And the best part was it wasn't planned. John had no idea his trip to the jobcentre would lead to an enjoyable afternoon. Plus, he had walked away with some lovely photographs of his grandchild.

They got off the bus at Holland Park Avenue, a local parade of shops near their home. John nipped into a picture framing shop before they made their way home.

By half-past five John, Gertie, Alfie and Sylvie – who had just arrived home in the nick of time – were all lined up awaiting Harriet's arrival.

As soon as Harriet arrived, John handed her a photo frame carefully wrapped in tissue paper.

'What's this?'

'Open it,' said John. He glanced at Sylvie and caught her looking his way with knitted eyebrows.

John watched Harriet intently as she carefully peeled away the tissue paper to reveal the professional shot of her daughter. In the photo, Gertie was sitting on a white faux fur rug. She was looking winsomely at the camera and smiling sweetly.

For a split second, John thought she would start questioning what he had been up to today. Instead, she rushed over to Sylvie and gave her a hug. 'Oh Mum, thank you *so* much. That is so sweet of you.'

John frowned.

'And you too, Daddy,' she said, almost as an afterthought. Harriet gave him a hug and then stepped back to study the photograph. 'I can't believe she sat still for a professional photographer.'

'Neither could I.' John hastily rephrased. 'Neither could *we*.' He caught Sylvie's look of disapproval. It wasn't as though it was planned. Besides, even if he had intended to take her along to have some professional photos taken today, he couldn't have told Sylvie his plans even if he wanted to. Apart from meeting up in the communal hall for the handover, barely a word passed between them. Which was just as well because he had no intention of telling Sylvie where he had those professional photos taken – and why.

John watched Harriet walk out the front door with Gertie. When he turned around, Sylvie and Alfie were gone. The entrance to her apartment clicked shut leaving John standing in the hall all alone.

He turned towards the stairs and briefly stopped outside her door. Sylvie's sour expression a moment ago told him he was in her bad books – again. John trudged back upstairs and closed his apartment door. He slipped off his shoes and wandered into the lounge to admire the framed photograph of Gertie taking pride of place in the centre of his mantel shelf. John smiled. Harriet wasn't the only one who now had a lovely framed professional photograph of Gertie.

Downstairs, Sylvie's door opened. 'John,' she called out, but he had already disappeared upstairs. She looked down at the framed photograph of Gertie she was holding in her hands. Sylvie found it sitting on the mantel shelf in her apartment.

'Thank you, John,' she whispered to the empty hall.

8

It was just as well he had a plan for the next day, and the day after that, because John found himself looking after Gertie for four days in a row, on his own. Not that he was complaining. By the end of the week, John was in a routine. He had bought a large colourful family calendar. Each evening John wrote down the activities he had planned for the following day.

However, it seemed that as soon as he had made plans, the modelling agency were on the phone again with another audition. The day after signing up with the agency John received no less than three phone calls, in quick succession, offering Gertie to come along for an audition. Although there was no guarantee that any of these would lead to work, John had accepted them on the spot. They were all being held in London. Since John had already paid the joining fee for the agency, and they had come this far, he couldn't see the harm in taking her along to the auditions. Besides, seeing Harriet's obvious delight when he handed her the professional photograph of Gertie, John could just imagine she would be over the moon if she found out Gertie had been chosen for an advertising campaign by a major high street chain.

John was dying to tell someone about the success of her last audition which led to her very first assignment. It had gone beyond well considering that sinking feeling John had when he found out what they wanted Gertie to do. He thought they would just be taking photographs, but what they wanted was for Gertie to come along to the studio first thing in the morning and film her having breakfast. That's when John realised this was no ordinary photoshoot; Gertie had gone straight to the big leagues and was filming a television commercial. Why oh why, John remembered thinking, did it have to be Weetabix?

When they handed Gertie a bowl of Weetabix John sighed so loudly that he could actually be heard on camera. They had to re-shoot. John apologised profusely, aware that time was money. Unfortunately, what they didn't realise, and John knew only too well, was that they wouldn't get through the shoot without Gertie hurling the dish across the room when she was finished. He tried to explain this to the producer, but all she said was that sometimes their behaviour in front of the camera might surprise you. John doubted that. He sat in the chaperone's chair, which looked like a director's chair with the word *Chaperone* written on the back and waited for Gertie's breakfast encore.

They filmed the commercials in a proper studio film set. With all the activity behind the scenes – cameras rolling, bright studio lights, and so many people all focused on his granddaughter – John really doubted Gertie would rise to the occasion. However, it turned out that Grandpa was more nervous than Gertie, who seemed to be taking it all in her stride.

John had sat in his chaperone's chair watching Gertie put on quite a show. She looked adorable even with a drippy Weetabix beard. Then she picked up the plate. John moved his hand over his eyes, waiting for the inevitable. He opened an eye when he didn't hear the sound of a plastic plate clattering on the floor, but rather the voice of an actress who was acting as her mother.

'Thank you, my sweet,' she said as Gertie handed her the empty plate.

'Well, I'll be darned!' exclaimed John.

The crew all turned in his direction. Even Gertie appeared to look at him in exasperation.

'Sorry, so sorry,' said John meekly.

The director shouted, 'CUT!'

John was afraid they would ask him to pay for the cost of re-shooting, but thankfully the sound engineer stepped in and said he could edit out John's interruption.

In the event, Gertie had fun. John had fun. The producer and all the crew on set said she was one of the best toddlers they had worked with.

After all the excitement, Gertie had a two-hour nap in the afternoon when they arrived home. He had put Gertie down to sleep in Sylvie's bedroom and then sat down in the lounge, bored. John was unaccustomed to having more than thirty minutes during the day with nothing to do while Gertie had her nap.

Two hours later John had cleaned Sylvie's apartment, washed up her breakfast dishes, put her laundry in the washing machine and then hung it out to dry on the washing line in the garden. He then stood and ironed a pile of ironing he'd found sitting on top of the washing machine, that Sylvie either didn't have the time or the inclination to do herself.

John listened to the radio while he ironed, keeping one ear out for the baby monitor that he'd placed in Sylvie's bedroom in case Gertie woke up. When he finished the ironing, John had taken Sylvie's neatly pressed clothes and left them on the bed in her bedroom. Gertie stirred and opened her eyes, so John had lifted her out of the travel cot and folded the cot away. He tucked it behind the door, so Sylvie wouldn't have to do it when she came in from work.

Then they had taken Alfie for afternoon walkies to Holland Park, where Gertie got it into her head to pick some flowers when John wasn't looking. It wouldn't have mattered if they were wild flowers, but they came from a neatly manicured border.

John was about to throw away the evidence of his grand-daughter's first foray into vandalism, when he looked at the flowers in her hand and thought they would make a rather nice display in Sylvie's vase on her kitchen table. He remembered she used to love having fresh flowers in the house. John thought she might like these especially if they were picked by Gertie.

When they arrived home, Gertie helped John arrange the flowers in Sylvie's vase before placing it on the table. John had found a small piece of coloured card and some crayons among Gertie's toys. Together they'd made a card for Sylvie telling her all about their day, leaving out the part about Gertie making a television commercial. He would have loved to have shared that part of their day too. However, John still had the cheque in his wallet reminding him of the reason he had taken her along in the first place. It wasn't just about having fun; Gertie was working ostensibly to pay John's bills.

As soon as that cheque landed in John's hand the guilt trip started. He knew he should cash it and at least pay the electricity bill before they were cut off but try as he might John found any excuse not to go to the bank that afternoon.

Little wonder he couldn't tell Sylvie what they had been up

to in the morning. That evening, after Harriet left with Gertie, Sylvie disappeared inside her apartment with barely a second glance. John didn't bother knocking on Sylvie's door to find out her plans for Friday. He assumed, as with the rest of the week, that Gertie would be spending the day with Grandpa.

John had just closed his apartment door upstairs when Sylvie's door opened.

'John,' she called out, but he was already gone. She looked down at the homemade card from Gertie she was holding in her hand. The vase of flowers in the kitchen had not gone unnoticed too, along with the freshly laundered clothes that had appeared in her bedroom. To Sylvie's surprise, John had left her apartment all spick and span.

Sylvie stared at Gertie's card. 'Thank you, John,' she whispered to the empty hall.

On Friday morning Harriet deposited Gertie in the hall and gave Sylvie and John the once over before leaving for work.

John noted Sylvie was wearing casual clothes. He assumed it was dress-down Friday at work, so it took him by surprise when she didn't disappear out the door to a waiting taxi.

'Day off?' said John fishing. He hadn't asked her outright about her job, but that didn't mean he wasn't interested.

'Something like that,' said Sylvie, surprising John again by reaching down and picking up Gertie's bag. She pointed the buggy in the direction of her apartment.

John followed Sylvie as she manoeuvred the buggy through the doorway into her apartment.

Sylvie glanced over her shoulder and came to an abrupt halt.

She turned around to face John. 'Where do you think you're going?' Her tone of voice told him, in no uncertain terms, that he still wasn't in her good books.

'I thought we might spend the day together,' said John hopefully, realising Sylvie was not going into work today. 'We could—'

'No thank you, John,' she said, cutting him off.

'Oh, I see.' John couldn't hide his disappointment. On the other hand, after four days on the trot looking after a two-year-old, John felt so exhausted he thought he might crawl back into bed and sleep for a week.

Sylvie looked him over. 'John, I really appreciate you looking after Gertie.' Sylvie didn't add that she appreciated the fact that he had looked after her without complaint and with no questions asked. And without telling Harriet what was going on. He had made her feel terribly guilty that she'd just left him to it all week. So guilty, in fact, that she had decided not to go into work today and look after her grandchild instead. John deserved a day off. Sylvie could see by the dark rings under his eyes that he looked exhausted.

'You've done more than your fair share this week, John. You deserve a break. Why don't you have a rest and I'll look after Gertie today on my own.'

John felt much better about it when she put it that way. He just assumed she didn't want to spend the day with him. 'Perhaps you're right. I am rather tired.' That was an understatement. John was shattered. On top of looking after his grandchild on his own, John had been ferrying Gertie around London to auditions. Considering that Sylvie had sprung this on him, it was fortunate that Gertie didn't have any further auditions arranged until next week.

'That's settled then.' Sylvie knelt down to lift Gertie out of the buggy.

Alfie padded over to say hello to Gertie. He lay down on the floor, with his paws in the air, letting Gertie tickle his tummy.

John looked at Alfie. 'Do you want me to walk the dog?'

'No thank you, John.' Sylvie edged John out of the door, trying to close it with John on the other side.

John hovered in the doorway. 'Gertie likes Weetabix for breakfast. You have to watch out because she has a tendency to throw her plate across the room when she's finished.'

John turned to go and then had another thought. 'She likes the swing-park, but she always wants to get out of the buggy as soon as you walk through the park gates. Trying to hold her hand and push a buggy is quite feat, I can tell you.'

'I know, John. I have had some experience of all that.'

'Oh, of course you have.' Sylvie didn't have just one, but three girls to look after when they were small. John never stopped to consider how she coped looking after them on her own.

John turned to go but not before adding, 'If it rains there's the library to take her to.'

'Yes, John.'

John nearly forgot. 'Today there's a grandparent and toddler session in the community centre. They hold it on a Monday and Friday. Grandparents are welcome too. I went along on Monday, and we really enjoyed it.'

John caught an expression on Sylvie's face he couldn't quite read. 'What?' he exclaimed, wondering what Sylvie was thinking?

'See you at five o'clock, John.' As she closed the door behind him, Sylvie was thinking how much he had surprised her in the past week. How much he had changed. The parties had stopped, and she had not seen his new lady-friend, Barbara, or any of his other so-called friends lately.

John had even owned up to the fact that he was using her apartment. Apparently, it had started on his first day of grand-parent duty. In her haste to leave for work that morning, Sylvie didn't realise she had left her door open. John asked if he could continue using her apartment when he was looking after Gertie. He told her he didn't fancy lugging Gertie, and all her stuff, up and down the stairs.

Sylvie imagined that wasn't the only reason he wanted to use her apartment. To John's credit, he admitted he didn't want sticky fingers and dog hairs messing up his place upstairs. So, they came to an arrangement of sorts; when Sylvie was out, he could use her apartment. It made sense because her flat had a garden. On sunny days, John could let the dog out, and Gertie could play in the garden. On occasion, when Sylvie was working from home, John would have to take Gertie upstairs.

John had agreed; no questions asked.

What surprised Sylvie the most was how much John clearly enjoyed the time he spent with his grandchild. She never remembered John having much time for the girls growing up. He was always too busy at work or too busy renovating this house. It had made Sylvie wonder how John would cope with Gertie. He had practically no experience of looking after small children on his own. That's why Sylvie had given him her new mobile number.

She doubted he would make it through the first day without getting an emergency phone call from John. But that didn't happen, not once the entire week. And not only that, he had risen to the occasion and was coping remarkably well in his new role as Grandpa.

Even though things had worked out surprisingly well with John looking after Gertie, this wasn't what Sylvie intended. She would have preferred not to work so many hours, so she could spend more time with her only grandchild. She thought she could find a way to do that but try as she might Sylvie just couldn't make the time. She couldn't just drop everything. It wasn't just the money. She had a responsibility to her readers, and she had a contract with the magazine to keep writing those LAT living articles. Sylvie also wrote a Sunday newspaper column. Unfortunately, she was unable to find a way to juggle all her commitments and take care of Gertie for part of the week too.

She really didn't have the time to take the day off work today. However, throughout the week, Sylvie had found it increasingly hard to concentrate at work. She had conflicting emotions over the fact that she was working in her successful career rather than spending time with Gertie. Each day Sylvie found it harder and harder to lie to Harriet and then walk out the door to a waiting taxi, to whisk her off to work. She felt terrible, as though she was turning her back on her family for the sake of her career.

How many times, in the past, had she envied her friends who were looking after their grandchildren when their sons and daughters returned to work? They said she was lucky. They said they envied her freedom for not being saddled with childcare at their time of life.

Sylvie disagreed. That's why she had made a decision to squeeze all her work commitments into four days, so she could set aside one day every week for Gertie. Today, Sylvie decided, she had more important things to do with her time than write.

Today, and every Friday from here on out, her column, *Love on the Rooftop*, would have to wait.

Her mind drifted to thoughts of John looking after Gertie. On the one hand, she was pleased with the way things had turned out. When Harriet first announced she wanted them both to look after Gertie all week, so she could return to work, Sylvie had no idea how she was going to manage. Harriet was adamant she wanted them both to look after Gertie together. Sylvie fully expected John to tell Harriet that wasn't the case. When he didn't, Sylvie suspected John was trying to get into her good books. In his misguided wisdom, he probably saw another opportunity to get her to move out of her apartment and move back in together. Perhaps that was the reason he didn't tell Harriet the truth. He couldn't very well carry out his plan if he told on Sylvie, and then Harriet put a stop to the childcare.

However, the events of the past few weeks proved that John wasn't after getting back with her. Quite the contrary. It was obvious why John didn't ask any questions about what she did all day because he simply didn't care. It was just another nail in the coffin of their relationship. He had moved on with his life. Sylvie knew that for a fact because she had seen a noticeable change in John; he seemed a lot happier, and he had lost weight making him look even more attractive in his new casual clothes.

With all these positive changes she fully expected that he would meet somebody new; maybe he already had. Perhaps he was still seeing Barbara, the woman John had met in the park when he first started walking Alfie. Sylvie knew what that meant. It was time she moved on with her life too.

In all outward appearances she *had* moved on; she had her own apartment, her independence, and interesting work where she was meeting lots of new people. Some acquaintances were men around her own age. She could tell one was interested in more than just her job. Up until now, Sylvie had held back from these well-intentioned romantic advances, unsure why. She agreed with Julia when she said, "Time is a-wasting." Julia was right: at their age opportunities for second chances dwindled with each passing year until you start to give up on finding love a second time around.

'How will I know he is the one?' Sylvie had asked Julia when she told her best friend about a work colleague who seemed to be taking a romantic interest in her.

'Because there will be a sign,' Julia had said.

At first, Sylvie didn't have a clue what Julia was on about. She always thought her best friend was a little bit dippy. Julia believed in astrology and avidly read her horoscope in the newspaper. She often had her palm read. It was only later that Sylvie realised Julia wasn't talking about that kind of sign. Julia was talking about her recent experience meeting a like-minded individual who had the same dream as Julia, to live on a houseboat when they retired. It was a sign that they were meant to be together. It was a sign he was the one.

Now Sylvie understood. When the right person walked into her life there would be a sign; that's when Sylvie would know she had found the one to spend the rest of her life with. Sylvie sighed. So far there was not even a sign of a sign. No indication that any of the men she had met so far were the one.

The sound of a plastic plate clattering on the kitchen floor, followed by Alfie letting out a surprised yelp, woke Sylvie from her reverie. She saw Alfie disappear up the kitchen stairs. Sylvie looked at the kitchen floor where the remnants of Gertie's

Weetabix, from her overturned plate, were now mixed in with Alfie's dog food. She turned to Gertie, sitting in her highchair, and smiled. 'So that's why Grandpa washes my kitchen floor every day.'

9

John didn't realise just how much his days revolved around looking after Gertie and Alfie until today, his first day all week without them. John was at a loss as to what to do with himself. He had an entire day stretched ahead of him with nothing planned. It brought back unhappy memories of when he lost his job and was forced into early retirement; he had nothing to do all day but hang around the house bored.

He glanced at the calendar stuck to his fridge. John had filled it in for the week ahead with all the activities he had planned to do with Gertie. He studied the entries in the calendar. Their free time was now squeezed in amongst Gertie's numerous auditions. She already had another television commercial lined up. Just as well it was next week, not today, thought John. The modelling agency had been correct when they said it was quite a commitment; more often than not, he seemed to get a phone call for an audition at short notice. This meant John was frequently crossing things out on the calendar and rearranging planned activities to fit around her new job. Which, incidentally, reminded John of the cheque burning a hole in his wallet. He almost felt like ripping it up, but he wouldn't do that; it was money Gertie had earned. John sighed heavily. He couldn't put it off any longer; the time had come to bank the cheque.

In the lobby John slipped on a pair of shoes, grabbed his coat, and opened the door to his apartment. He was about to head downstairs when he stopped abruptly. He stood there for several seconds with the strangest sensation that he had forgotten something, until he realised what it was: walkies. John was so used to his morning routine – taking Alfie out for a walk to the paper shop and then on to the park – that it was almost second nature. He had even visited the library and borrowed a book on dog training, so he could teach Alfie some new tricks.

For a split second, something crossed his mind that would have been unthinkable just a few weeks ago; John was considering getting a pet of his own. 'Well, that is a ridiculous thought,' said John out loud as he closed his apartment door. He couldn't abide animals in the house. 'Absolutely ridiculous.'

Is it? A little voice in his head said.

John walked to his local parade of shops in Holland Park Avenue and bought a newspaper, something he once had delivered to his house back when he could afford life's little luxuries. Way back when his wife used to make his morning cuppa and bring it up to him in bed with his newspaper. John shook his head. Funny how it was the little things in life, the things that seemed so inconsequential at the time, that he missed the most. They were the things she did that he took for granted, as though it was noted down in some unwritten rule book when they first got married and not something Sylvie had chosen to do for him because she loved him once upon a time.

John stepped out of the paper shop. Sad thoughts of things past were quickly replaced by guilt at the idea of banking his grandchild's first ever paycheck in order to cover his electricity bill. God, he couldn't believe how low he could go; after all these years of being careful with money and working hard in his job to support his family, it had come down to this. All because he had a bright idea one morning to convert the house into two flats – little realising where it would lead.

'I'm an idiot,' said John.

'If you say so,' said a smart-mouthed teenager standing beside him at the level crossing.

John glared at him before crossing the road. He was aiming in the direction of the bank on the other side.

John was home by elevenses. He sat down in the kitchen, with a cup of coffee, and idly flicked through the newspaper. John was already bored. During the past four days, he had literally been run off his feet with a two-year-old and a dog to look after. There were plenty of times he wished he could sit down with a cup of coffee in hand and peruse the newspaper at his leisure. The trouble was, he had forgotten how slowly the time ticked by when he didn't have a jam-packed day full of activities ahead of him.

Staring forlornly at the calendar stuck to the fridge door, he drummed his fingers on the kitchen table. John knew what he could do with his spare time. It was something he had been putting off because he was too busy throwing parties and looking after his grandchild. But the dreaded day had finally arrived. He didn't have any excuses and couldn't put it off any longer.

John reluctantly got up from the table and walked into his

study. He sat down, opened the desk drawer, or tried to; it was stuck. John yanked it hard. The drawer flew out of the desk and landed on the carpet, its contents spilling out over the floor.

'What a mess.' John wasn't just referring to the contents of the drawer littering the floor. He knew he had been burying his head in the sand, ignoring the bills mounting up. Rather than deal with them, John had stuffed them in the drawer. He had also stopped bothering to check his post box; he bet that was full-to-bursting too.

Over the past week, despite feeling exhausted at the end of a day looking after Gertie, John had cleaned his apartment from top to bottom, every nook and cranny – well almost. The one place he hadn't ventured to clean was the desk in his study; the stuff of nightmares and collywobbles at four in the morning. Now it was time to face the dreaded desk drawer.

John knelt down on the floor, gathered up all the bills and put them in a pile on his desk. He thought he'd start sorting through this lot before he ventured downstairs to yet more unopened bills waiting in his post box. John was already worried that one day soon the electricity would be cut off or the bailiffs might turn up at his door. But what bothered John the most was that, just recently, the letters and phone calls had stopped. All of a sudden things had gone quiet.

He had read the horror stories of how unpaid bills and late charges soon rack up, and that the worst thing you could do under the circumstances was to ignore them. John wished, with a vengeance, that he had not ignored all those letters in front of him.

His imagination started to run riot; what if they were repossessing the house? What if he had to declare himself bankrupt?

John was acutely aware that he had a grandchild to look after now and people who depended on him, like his daughter Harriet. What on earth would she think if he lost the roof over his head and Gertie couldn't come over to Grandpa's house anymore? This was the reason John had finally sat down to take responsibility for his situation and get to grips with the state of their finances.

John thought of Gertie's cheque he had cashed today. He had put all the money, including his chaperone's fee, into a bank account; it was Gertie's first savings account. Her brand-new red savings book was tucked away in a manila file on which John had written, *Gertie's nice little earner.* John had slipped the file on the bookshelf next to another one which held all the original plans for the house conversion. John thought of the apartment downstairs he was meant to be renting out. That should have been his nice little earner. Instead, it was quite the reverse. John sighed heavily. He felt like scribbling on the front of that file, *John's money pit.*

John couldn't help but laugh at the irony. His two-year-old granddaughter now had savings, which was more than could be said for her grandpa; when John's pension went into his bank account at the end of the month, it was immediately swallowed up by his mounting overdraft. Gertie had a healthier bank balance than he did. John wouldn't have it any other way. It was her money. She'd earned it.

John didn't know how long his bank would keep agreeing to extend his overdraft before they cottoned on to the fact that he didn't have a hope of paying it off. If they did suddenly withdraw it . . . John shuddered at the thought.

Although some might argue that it was all a bit of a grey area when it came down to kids earning money. If that money was the difference between a child losing the roof over their head, then dipping into that cash might be another story. But at the end of the day, Gertie still had a home to go back to. It wasn't up to her to pay for Grandpa's house.

John already felt bad enough knowing everybody else was out at work – Harriet, Sylvie, and now his own grandchild – without stealing her money into the bargain. It had been a very foolish idea to think he could use the situation, looking after Gertie, to pay off his debts. What sort of grandparent would that make me, thought John? By the time John had stepped into the bank, he knew what he had to do. Gertie's very own savings account was the end result.

John's next thought was to put an end to this silly modelling business and cancel all her future auditions. Since the original idea of earning some money to pay his bills was now redundant, it seemed pointless for Gertie to continue.

It was a young clerk at the bank who changed his mind. While John was in the process of opening the savings account for Gertie, the clerk explained that even a small monthly deposit, until she reached eighteen, could accrue into a sizeable amount of money towards the deposit for her first house or her college fees or a car. This had certainly given John pause to reconsider.

John got up from his desk and wandered into the kitchen, stopping in front of the calendar. He agreed wholeheartedly with the bank clerk's sentiments. That's why he had opened the savings account on Gertie's behalf instead of just cashing the cheque. Even so, he still intended to cross out all her up-and-coming auditions and cancel the television commercial next week.

His pen hovered in mid-air as he recalled the conversation

with the bank clerk when he was depositing two hundred and fifty pounds into his grandchild's account. Gertie's parents, Harriet and Dominic, were always strapped for cash despite being well-educated and working hard in professional jobs. They were both fast approaching forty with a huge mortgage on their London home and hefty outgoings. He couldn't imagine they had much in the way of savings. It made him wonder how they would have the luxury of giving Gertie a helping hand in the future, like John and Sylvie had managed to do for Harriet when she went to university. They had also helped her with a deposit when she wanted to get on the first rung of the property ladder.

Provided John sorted out his debts, so they didn't lose the house, Harriet – along with her two sisters – would also come into a sizeable inheritance from their home in Holland Park. It's what John had planned all along, to leave his children and grandchildren a legacy when he died. However, he didn't want to dwell on the girls coming into their inheritance because John rather hoped he and Sylvie would still be here, with all their faculties intact, to see their first grandchild reach adulthood.

John decided that he was not checking out any time soon, so he thought about Gertie's future and her nice little earner instead. There were no guarantees that Gertie's job would continue. It would be good if it did because John calculated that just one assignment a month, over the next sixteen years, could net her £50,000. That was without the interest on top that would accrue if she didn't touch the money until she was eighteen.

Of course, that was going on a lot of assumptions; that she still got the assignments and wanted to continue modelling as she got older. But such is life. There were no guarantees. However, he wasn't about to look a gift horse in the mouth and give up

Gertie's lucrative little sideline. It fleetingly crossed his mind that perhaps now would be the time to ask her parents' permission before Gertie continued attending auditions and taking up any further assignments. The first couple were just a bit of fun. Quite frankly, John had no idea Gertie would be such an angel in front of the cameras. He really didn't think it would lead anywhere at the time. That was something he could truthfully tell Harriet and Dominic before they made up their own minds whether they wanted their daughter to continue.

On the other hand, John had a better idea. Rather than tell them now, if Gertie secured a few more assignments over the coming weeks, then John could deposit more money into her bank account. He was sure they would approve when they found out that Grandpa had been quite the entrepreneur and put the time he spent with Gertie to good use – financially speaking. He smiled at the thought of the surprise they would get when they found out just what the two of them had been up to. He couldn't wait to see the look on their faces when he handed over Gertie's first savings book with a nice healthy balance.

John thought about the professional photograph of Gertie that he had given Harriet. She was overjoyed when she saw it, although for some reason she assumed it had been Sylvie's idea. This time John would have the satisfaction of telling them it was *his* idea. At least he could take all the credit.

He smiled to himself as he wandered back into his study. John was still smiling at the thought of all that potential money accruing in a bank account for Gertie's future, when his eyes inadvertently settled on the pile of unopened letters on his desk. John sighed. It was time to stop thinking about Gertie's financial future and start focusing on his own, which was going to be a hell of a lot less enticing. He still didn't have the first clue how he was going to pay all his debts.

John sat down at his desk and reached for one of the unopened bills. He thought he'd start by finding out just what he was up against. John took a deep breath and opened his first letter.

10

'I'm sorry we can't offer you that option now.'

'Pardon me?' John knew this wasn't going to be easy, suffering the embarrassment of talking to a stranger about his financial problems. He had never been in this position before. John stared at the pile of bills on his desk. He'd finally opened all those letters he'd been ignoring. The red reminder letters and final demands for payment made for depressing reading.

John had got on the phone immediately. He was planning to make an arrangement with each of his creditors, to pay a small amount towards his debts so at least the late payment and default charges would stop. That would be a start. However, when he asked for help, he didn't expect an outright *no*.

John hit the roof. 'How on earth am I supposed to get on top of all my debts if you don't help me out?'

'As I said, I'm afraid we can't offer you that option now.'

John frowned. They offered him an arrangement before. John thought he'd remind them of that fact. 'You offered me that option before. Perhaps I was a little bit hasty in declining it the first time around,' John said evenly, climbing off his high horse. He realised that having a go at the person on the end of the phone was not going to help his situation. 'After careful consideration,' continued John, keeping his voice steady, 'I've changed my mind. I need that arrangement.'

'No you don't.'

'But I do,' John insisted.

'No you don't.'

John was trying very hard to keep it together and not lose his temper with the faceless employee whose smooth, calm telephone manner, and a patronising tone was irritating beyond belief. 'Now look here . . .' John began, about to give them a piece of his mind. This had not started out at all how John had envisaged. There was still a stack of bills to work through and more phone calls to make. He didn't want this to take all day.

'Mr Baxter, let me make this quite plain for you to understand.'

John rolled his eyes at that patronising tone of voice.

'You do not need to make an arrangement with us because all your payments are now up to date.'

'Excuse me?'

'Would you like me to repeat that?'

Yes, I bloody well would, thought John. He said, 'Yes if you would be so kind, although I believe there has been some kind of mistake. I think you have my account confused with somebody else.'

'No. No mistake. The arrears have been paid by . . . let me see . . . ah yes, here we are. They were paid by Mrs Sylvia Baxter.'

'My wife?' John nearly fell off his chair.

Six phone calls later, John had exactly the same conversation and each time he was told the same thing, 'The bill has been paid by your wife.'

By lunchtime, John had worked his way through all the letters on his desk and found out Sylvie had paid every single bill and cleared any outstanding arrears. Not only had she paid them, but she had also set up direct debits, for the household bills, in her name. She had done the same for the mortgage.

John nipped downstairs to retrieve the letters from his post box and discovered it was empty. John stood on the doorstep scratching his head. He remembered there used to be so many letters in the post box that some were even poking out the slit at the top. John walked back into the communal hall and stared wide-eyed at Sylvie's door as he passed by. To say John was stunned would be an understatement; he had no idea his wife was earning that kind of money. To John's utter amazement, and relief, they were not only out of the red, but for the first time in their married lives Sylvie had taken charge of their finances and become the main breadwinner. She was paying all the household bills and the mortgage and the new loan payment on the house. This left John to cover the credit cards Sylvie didn't know about.

John's next thought was how long would it last? He didn't want to get complacent. They still had a mortgage, and he still had the loan to pay off. And it wasn't cheap running a house this size. In fact, it was more expensive now the house had been converted into two apartments. It made him wonder how long Sylvie could keep up with all the outgoings single-handedly. On the other hand, the fact that Sylvie *was* paying all the bills – at least for now – made John stop and consider his next course of action. Continuing to visit the jobcentre and look for work appeared a pointless waste of time. Last week had proved that. He had asked for anything. Absolutely anything. They still couldn't find him a position.

John decided to stop looking for non-existent jobs. His time was far better spent ferrying his granddaughter to her auditions and photoshoots, and working on the relationship with his wife. If there was anything left of their relationship to salvage. John was acutely aware that was a big *if*.

With their financial issues at bay, they had settled into a routine of sorts for the first time since they started living in separate apartments. John had effectively called a truce on trying to find every which way to get Sylvie to move out of the garden apartment; his focus of attention had shifted from the issue of their living arrangements to their new responsibilities as grand-parents looking after Gertie.

John had taken over the childcare of Gertie practically full time, apart from Fridays when Gertie spent the day with Grand-ma, and John had a much-needed day off. He could have complained. He could have argued. He could have at least asked Sylvie what she was doing all day to earn that kind of money while he was left at home to look after Gertie and Alfie. John didn't ask. Whatever it was she was doing, she was paying all the bills which had got them out of a big financial hole.

John was still coming to terms with how much things had changed; Sylvie was now their main breadwinner, and he was the stay-at-home grandpa. John wasn't exactly complaining. He wouldn't have it any other way. He loved looking after Gertie. Even Alfie was growing on him. They had given him a new purpose in life, a reason to get up in the morning. And that wasn't all. When they met up to greet Harriet every weekday morning and evening, Sylvie often gave him a smile and a peck on the cheek. Sometimes he got a hug. If he was really lucky, he got all three. They might not be back together as a result of his misguided belief that looking after their grandchild would bring them closer, but at least he was back in her good books. That was something.

They had stuck to their unspoken agreement to display a united front for Harriet's benefit. After Harriet dropped Gertie off, sometimes Sylvie left in a taxi soon after, other times she walked back into her apartment, closed the door, and didn't emerge until Harriet returned at five o'clock. But whatever Sylvie was doing during the day, she never let John down. They were always both ready to take their positions, standing together in the communal hall to hand Gertie over, as if they had spent the whole day together. Harriet was none the wiser.

John intended to carry on with this little charade and simply enjoy the time he had with Gertie. His plan to get Sylvie back, through sharing the childcare of their grandchild, was never going to work; he could see that now. If anything, it just made John realise it was time to face the painful truth that they were leading separate lives, living in different apartments, no longer together. Deep down John had known this all along. That's why he didn't bother asking Sylvie what she did for a living. And she didn't offer to enlighten him. It really wasn't any of his business. Sylvie now had a life of her own that didn't involve him.

Although she was only downstairs, she might as well be living on the moon for all the good it was doing their relationship. That's why he didn't complain, he didn't argue, and he never once asked Sylvie a damn thing about her new job. This was his life now. And that, whatever it was, was hers. He knew he had to accept and respect that.

The problem was he couldn't accept this was it. John still loved his wife. She had surprised him in the most unexpected way; she had changed, she was different, and John liked what he saw – very much. If she was a stranger and he bumped into her walking down the street, then he hoped they might go for a coffee, have a chat, and get to know one another. He hoped they might become friends. He hoped it might lead to something more.

John was sitting at the desk in his study, staring into space, with all this going through his mind. He sighed heavily. That was just a pipe dream. Or was it? John raised an eyebrow. Could it be that he already had the makings of another plan to get her back? John was thinking about the framed photograph of Gertie he had left on Sylvie's mantel shelf during his first week of grandpa duty. Then there were the flowers Gertie had hand-picked from the local park which John had arranged in a vase and left on her kitchen table. He recalled doing her laundry and tidying her apartment, that one time, when Gertie had a rare two-hour afternoon nap and John was bored.

John decided, one way or another, he would find the time to do something for Sylvie during his Grandpa days when she was busy at work. John wanted to prove to Sylvie, once and for all, that he had changed. He might not be out at work, sharing the financial commitments, but by god he was going to make up for it in other ways. Looking after Gertie was a start. He also intended to continue helping Sylvie out with some of her domestic chores. Gertie always had a mid-morning nap, and enjoyed watching her favourite television programme around teatime, so John was sure he would fit it in somehow.

He knew Sylvie didn't have much free time these days. John

remembered when he was still in full-time work and how much he appreciated coming home to the dinner ready and the house neat and tidy. He wished he'd told her that at the time. He wished he'd told her a lot of things. But he didn't. Now he was going to make amends.

'Do nothing,' was his brother's last piece of advice regarding John's hitherto unsuccessful attempts to get Sylvie back. What he really meant was do nothing overtly obvious to make it appear that he was up to his old tricks again, trying to persuade her to move back upstairs. She would see right through him. That wouldn't stop him from making small gestures to show her he still cared, like she used to do for him when they were together.

It was always the small things that mattered the most; the inconsequential things that seemed like nothing at the time but were sorely missed when someone was gone. At least that's what John believed when he thought of all the things Sylvie used to do for him. Would she appreciate those small things he continued to do for her, like loading her dishwasher in the morning when she didn't have the time, or hanging her washing out, or leaving a vase of fresh flowers in her kitchen? Would she even care? Or would she just take it for granted? John couldn't be sure. That wouldn't stop him carrying out his new plan to win her back.

It wouldn't stop him baking Sylvie a chicken pie and leaving it downstairs one evening, for when she got in from work, in the hope she might invite him downstairs to join her. Thinking of baking, John had an idea. He picked up a pen from the stationery organiser on his desk and walked out of the study. In the kitchen, he noted down another activity on the calendar that he could do with Gertie; together they could bake some biscuits or little cupcakes as a surprise for Sylvie.

John noted down the cake ingredients he had to buy along with a car seat he needed to purchase so he could chauffeur around his little star by car instead of public transport. John added a pair of shoes to that list. He noticed he had to squeeze Gertie's feet into her shoes, so he decided to take her along to the shoe shop next week to get fitted for some new ones. Perhaps some boots too. Oh, and a new winter coat.

John was getting carried away. With Sylvie paying all the household bills and the mortgage and the new loan on the house, it wouldn't be long before John's overdraft and credit cards were paid off by his monthly pension. Soon he would have some money over to spend on his grandchild. He never thought that sitting down to look at the contents of the dreaded desk drawer would make him so happy.

John took a black sack out of the kitchen cupboard and returned to the study with a spring in his step. He deposited all the letters littering his desk into the rubbish. Afterwards, he sat down at his empty desk and thought about all the outstanding bills that were outstanding no longer. He hadn't exactly totted them all up, but John could hazard a guess that it was thousands of pounds.

'What in god's name is Sylvie doing to earn that kind of money?' said John out loud, trying not to feel envious. Not to mention peeved that she had managed to land herself a well-paid number when he couldn't even get a job stacking shelves at the local supermarket. John wasn't about to dwell on that. John was going to appreciate how lucky he was to be able to concentrate his efforts on the two people who meant the world to him – his granddaughter and his wife. A wife incidentally who must be earning more money than John had been making at the latter end of his forty-year career as an accountant.

John leaned back in his chair, with his hands behind his head, deep in thought. This was the first time he had really stopped to think about Sylvie in a career. The sort of money she was earning meant she wasn't a secretary any longer – that's for sure. And her new image, the like of which he had never seen in all the years they had been married, suggested some sort of professional job – but what? John shook his head. He had no idea. John frowned. This train of thought was making him feel uncomfortable. He was beginning to wonder how it came to be that after nearly forty years of marriage it felt as though he was living with a stranger under the same roof.

11

Sylvie arrived first and was shown to her table. She sat down, picked up a menu, and glanced at the empty chair opposite. Her best friend, Julia, was always fashionably late. Sylvie checked the time. It was a weekday and she was on her lunch break from work. Although she could take as long as she wanted for lunch, when she was in the office as opposed to working from home Sylvie liked to take the same breaks as everybody else. This was in part because it made her feel one of the team. She was also still sensitive about starting a new career at her age and being taken seriously as a professional writer.

Sylvie didn't want to be seen to be taking two-hour lunch breaks even though, on paper, she was free to do so. Besides, she counted the small team of journalists she worked with as friends, as well as colleagues, and didn't want to give them the impression that she was wafting in and out when she fancied. Which in fact she was. However, she did work just as many hours as everybody else, sometimes more when she worked from home. Sylvie was their most popular columnist.

She checked her watch for the third time. Sylvie was aware that her lunch hour whizzed by once they started chatting. This was now their regular lunch date and the only way Sylvie could fit in seeing Julia around her busy schedule. That wasn't the only reason Sylvie preferred to meet Julia at a café; she was avoiding another visit to Julia's houseboat in Little Venice where her best friend had chosen to retire. Unfortunately, Sylvie didn't like boats even if they were sturdy, stationary houseboats, as Julia constantly reminded her.

However, the arrangement suited both of them. Julia wasn't exactly complaining about the fact that she didn't have to visit Sylvie at her apartment; something she avoided wherever possible because Julia didn't want to bump into Sylvie's upstairs neighbour. Julia and John had never exactly got along.

It had always been a simple clash of personalities. Carefree, adventurous Julia, a retired primary school teacher whom Sylvie had known since childhood, had always been a bit bohemian. She was so unlike John. They had nothing in common. Consequently, the two of them never hit it off. More recently made worse by the fact that it was Julia who had encouraged Sylvie to stay in the garden apartment. She had even helped her redecorate; together they turned John's rental apartment into Sylvie's new home.

A waiter appeared at her table. Sylvie ordered a pot of tea. She watched the waiter weave his way between the tables towards the kitchen. Sylvie glanced around their regular haunt – The Rooftop Café.

It had been Julia's idea to meet somewhere a bit avant-garde. Trust Julia to be different. Not a new concept in London – there were plenty of rooftop restaurants – but what they both liked about The Rooftop Café was that you could dine inside or out, and you didn't have to make a reservation. It was also quite informal so you could have a simple lunch or just afternoon tea, or a slap-up three-course meal; whatever took your fancy. For Sylvie, it wasn't the food or the views – although they were marvellous – but what did it for her was the rooftop terrace garden. She had always loved the idea of a rooftop garden. The moment she stepped foot in The Rooftop Café Sylvie adored the place. Meeting up with Julia here was something Sylvie looked forward to every week.

The waiter reappeared with a pot of tea and another menu for Sylvie's fashionably late dining companion.

Sylvie poured her tea and glanced over to the entrance to see if she had arrived yet; there was still no sign of her. Sylvie sipped her tea and thought back to the first time they'd had lunch here. Although Sylvie later found out there were many rooftop restaurants and cafés in London, at the time she had no idea of their existence. It had taken Sylvie by complete surprise when she stepped out of the lift into a lush beautifully maintained rooftop terrace garden.

It still brought a smile to her lips when she thought back to the surprise Julia had promised her on their first lunch date here. She would never have guessed there was a garden on the roof. Her smile faded as she recalled the first time she had sat at this table and looked around the garden. Sylvie had felt an over-whelming sadness. Julia noticed the instant her best friend's happy disposition gave way to a bout of melancholy. She had asked Sylvie what the matter was. It wasn't that Sylvie didn't like The Rooftop Café, quite the contrary. Therein lay the problem. It brought back unhappy memories of what John had done to her garden during the house conversion. It was during their first lunch date at The Rooftop Café that Sylvie had finally opened up to Julia about what had happened to her garden at home.

Julia had already seen what had become of Sylvie's garden. She couldn't exactly miss it. Julia had been in and out of the garden apartment enough times, helping her redecorate. However, in all that time, Julia had never once brought up the subject of the dramatic change in her back garden.

Sylvie was immensely grateful that Julia sensed it was something she did not want to talk about. It was still so very raw what John had done behind her back. The garden that she had cultivated and worked so hard to develop, which gave her and her mother so much joy, had been torn up and destroyed in the space of one day. Sylvie was busy working in the charity shop at the time. She had no clue what was going on at home; her garden was being replaced by a bland square lawn and pathetic borders.

Her garden used to be so full of flowers that anyone would be forgiven for thinking it was a wild garden. A cobbled pathway used to zig-zag through the flowers to the old elm tree at the bottom of the garden. Sylvie and her mother used to sit on a bench that was positioned on a small patio under the tree. Her mother once told Sylvie it reminded her of the garden belonging to the cottage in Cornwall where she used to take her as a child. It was only then that Sylvie realised she had created their own little piece of Cornwall right in the heart of London.

Sylvie assumed John knew how much that garden meant to her; she had spent enough time out there, over the years, lovingly tending the flowers. She missed her garden, but what hurt the most was the realisation that it didn't matter to John. Following through on his plan to rent out the garden apartment was more important to him – that much was obvious. John had bulldozed right over her feelings the way he had bulldozed her garden.

Incidentally, that garden was the only thing she had put her own stamp on, in all the years they had lived in the house. It was meant to be her home too, but the garden was the only part of the house that Sylvie felt she could call her own. Then, in the space of a single day, it was gone.

His explanation for what he had done was that he needed a rental apartment he could easily maintain – and that extended to the outside space. Sylvie knew it was more than that. John had never liked her garden. He had expressed his distaste enough times over the years. Sylvie realised that the conversion just gave him an excuse to turn it into the garden he had always wanted for the house. He knew she would never agree to it. That's why he completely disregarded her wishes and went ahead with his plans anyway. For Sylvie, that more than anything spoke volumes about the state of their relationship, their marriage.

As the conversion neared completion, Sylvie had been contemplating moving downstairs, for a short time, to sort herself out. There had been so many fundamental changes in her life, what with her mother passing away and John losing his job. Then there was his sudden plan to convert the marital home into two flats and rent one out. At the time, Sylvie just needed some space away from it all to process everything and put things into perspective.

Moving into the flat downstairs was only meant to be temporary. She didn't move in there with the intention of turning John's rental apartment into her new home. But it was the constant reminder of John's garden, right outside her back door, which had spurred her on. She couldn't resurrect the garden that had taken years to cultivate. Sylvie didn't have the time left to recapture what once was, but she did have the keys to the garden apartment. With a lot of encouragement from Julia, she had put her own stamp on the apartment instead. And she hadn't stopped there. For the first time in her life, Sylvie was selfishly doing things for herself. She didn't give a jot what John thought or the rest of her family, for that matter.

Sylvie had finally confided in Julia that she was afraid what John had done to her beloved garden spelled the end of their marriage. If he had just talked to her about it first, then he would have understood the importance of the garden, especially in light of her mother's passing. Sylvie intended to scatter her ashes in their little corner of Cornwall in the heart of London. That was her back-up plan if she was unable to find the cottage in Cornwall where her mother requested her ashes be scattered in the garden overlooking the sea. But John didn't know that because John didn't ask, because John didn't care.

Although Sylvie had found the cottage, she was still waiting to hear back from the absent owner, an American by the name of Mr Morelli, seeking his permission to scatter her mother's ashes in the garden of his holiday home. For now, her mother's ashes were still sitting in an urn on the mantel shelf, still waiting for Sylvie to take her to her final resting place.

Sylvie poured herself another cup of tea and looked around the rooftop terrace garden. Her eyes settled on the café sign: *The Rooftop Café*. It reminded Sylvie of the other thing she had confided in Julia during one of their lunches together. Sylvie told Julia all about her recurring dream in which, quite bizarrely, she falls in love on a rooftop; where that rooftop is or who she falls in love with is a mystery – it is never revealed in her dream. Sylvie's dream had inspired her to call her blog, and magazine column, *Love on the Rooftop*. Julia was the only person she would ever tell this to because she knew that, with all her talk of *signs*

118

and *the one*, Julia would never ridicule her or think her dream was stupid.

As Sylvie predicted, Julia did no such thing. In fact, she was very interested to hear about Sylvie's recurring dream. Julia asked her if she could remember when it first began. Sylvie knew what she was getting at; Julia was trying to discover what it might mean. Sylvie had no problem answering Julia question. She distinctly remembered the first time because it coincided with the start of the conversion on the house.

Sylvie had never stopped to consider the significance. Perhaps it meant she was destined to meet somebody else. Maybe it was her subconscious telling her that the conversion marked the beginning of the end of her marriage. It sure felt like that now. They were living in different apartments, leading separate lives, no longer together. For the first time Sylvie felt truly alone.

When John was playing up and being a pain, trying to get her out of her apartment so he could rent it out, at least he was showing her some attention. Even if it was for all the wrong reasons. Now it appeared he couldn't care less. He hadn't taken the slightest bit of interest in her life since Sylvie adamantly refused to move back in with him or let John move in with her.

Sylvie finished her second cup of tea and thought about that brief romantic interlude with John. She was enjoying herself immensely until she discovered the truth; it had all been a ruse to get her to move back in with him before she found out about their dire financial situation. That's when she realised it was all about saving the house and not saving their marriage.

It was an episode she thought about often – the evening meals out together and the flowers he bought her and the romantic walks along Regent's Canal. The sheer pleasure of sharing those good times with someone who made her feel special; something she hadn't experienced in a very long time, perhaps decades.

It made her realise that although she was enjoying her new-found freedom. She was working in a new career she loved and living in her own apartment in which she could come and go, and misbehave, and stay up late, and do exactly as she pleased. However, there was still something missing from her life. Perhaps that's what her dream was trying to tell her. Her subconscious alerting her to the fact that she had yet to find the missing piece of the puzzle – the one who would make her life complete.

Despite this, Sylvie counted herself lucky that she still had her childhood best friend. At least she could confide in Julia, and no matter what was going on in Sylvie's life, Julia always had a knack of cheering her up.

After spending the last fifteen minutes dwelling on what John had done to her garden, then her recurring dream and feelings of loneliness, Sylvie was decidedly down in the dumps. It didn't help that she was in a crowded café, full of people sitting together enjoying their lunch, while Sylvie was sitting at her table alone. She could do with cheering up. Sylvie wondered what was keeping Julia.

Sylvie glanced at her watch and frowned. Julia had never been this late before. At this rate, they would barely have enough time to eat their lunch. Perhaps, just this once, she wouldn't hurry back to the office. With her busy work schedule, Sylvie barely found the time to see her best friend. Whatever Julia's excuse was for being this late, Sylvie decided she would stop for lunch and not worry about what time she got back to work. She was sure her editor, Marcia Hunt, wouldn't mind.

As the waiter approached Sylvie's table, her mobile phone rang. Sylvie breathed a sigh of relief when she saw it was Julia's phone number. She wasn't pleased when she realised it was her *home* number; Julia hadn't even left yet. Sylvie sighed heavily. The way things were going, the lunch menu would be over, and they would have to make do with afternoon tea and cake.

Sylvie answered the phone as the waiter collected her empty teacup and teapot. He placed them on a round plastic tray.

'Hello, Julia. Did you forget about our lunch date?' Sylvie said playfully. They met for lunch on the same day each week so it would be hard to forget; it made Sylvie wonder if something was up.

'Sylvie darling, I'm afraid I've got to cancel.'

'Why on earth didn't you let me know sooner?' Sylvie had wasted the last half an hour sitting there with only an empty stomach for company, growling for some lunch. She sighed down the phone. That's not what was really bothering her; Sylvie was disappointed she wouldn't be seeing Julia today.

'I'm sorry, Sylvie. I was on my way out when Holly started being sick. In between clearing up the mess, and phoning the vets, I forgot all about—'

Sylvie cut her off immediately, 'Julia, please don't worry.'

She could tell by the sound of Julia's voice that she was worried. Very worried. Poor Julia. Her dog, Holly, had been her faithful companion for the last ten years. Sylvie knew she would be devastated if she lost her.

'Just get her to the vets, Julia. Don't worry about me. Please get in touch, when you can, and let me know how she is. Okay?'

'Yes, all right Sylvie.'

Sylvie put her phone away.

The waiter was hovering by the table. He'd overheard Sylvie's brief conversation. 'Will madam be dining alone?'

'No. I'm leaving.' Sylvie handed the waiter her menu. She couldn't possibly sit here and dine alone. Sylvie recalled the number of times Julia had pestered her to come to dinner on the houseboat to meet Julia's new partner, Tom. Sylvie had refused. Not because they would be dining on a boat – although the thought of having dinner on the canal did turn her stomach – but it was more to do with the fact that she would be turning up without a date.

Sylvie had successfully sidestepped that invitation by saying that when she chose to dine with Julia and Tom, it would be because she could bring along the one. That way, she wouldn't feel awkward. Sylvie glanced at the other diners in the café. This was worse. She couldn't possibly sit at a table alone, surrounded by all these people. Sylvie spotted a young couple standing in the entrance, keenly looking around. They were waiting for a table to come available. That made up her mind. Sylvie stood up and gathered up her coat and bag.

She was just telling the waiter that she was leaving when the maître d' spotted one of his regular customers about to depart without ordering a meal. He rushed over to see what the matter was.

'It's nothing, honestly,' Sylvie reassured him. 'My friend can't make it for lunch, so I've decided to return to work – that's all. I thought the young couple over there might want my table.'

'That's very gracious of you,' said the maître d', 'but you haven't eaten,' he said, looking concerned.

'I know.'

'Aren't you still hungry?'

'Well yes, but—' I'd much rather go hungry that sit here eating alone.

'Would you care to join me?'

Sylvie and the maître d' both turned to look at the gentleman seated alone at another table.

'I hope you don't mind me butting in, but I overheard your conversation.' He was seated directly behind Sylvie and had turned in his chair to look up at her. 'I'm afraid we find ourselves in the same predicament. My dining partner stood me up too.' He nodded at the empty chair opposite. 'Would you care to join me?' he asked again.

Keen not to lose a regular customer, the maître d' was quick to pull out the chair opposite the gentleman. He stood there smiling at Sylvie and motioning for her to take a seat.

Sylvie glanced at the empty chair, looked at the stranger who seemed a pleasant sort around her own age, and recalled Julia's sage words about seizing opportunities.

Since Julia met her new partner, Tom, she had been optimistic that Sylvie would find the one. From her own experience, Julia's new mantra was that you never know when that special someone might walk into your life or, in this case, offer you a seat at their table.

Sylvie wasn't in the habit of talking to strangers, but with the maître d' keenly beckoning her to sit down, and Sylvie's stomach growling loudly, Sylvie walked over to the gentleman's table.

The gentleman stood up.

For a split second, Sylvie thought he was leaving, until she remembered it was old-fashioned dining etiquette for the man to remain standing until the lady was seated. Once upon a time, men always pulled out a lady's chair and waited for them to sit down. John never once did that. Sylvie gave him a tentative smile as they both took their seats. She glanced at the young couple sitting down at her table and noted no such dining etiquette there. The young man had already sat down and picked up the menu before his date was even seated. Nobody had pulled out a chair for her.

Sylvie returned her attention to the gentleman opposite her and smiled shyly. Now she was sitting down, and the maître d' had left them alone, she didn't know what to say. Sylvie was starting to feel awkward. She thought, perhaps it would have been better to dine alone after all.

'I didn't want to dine alone,' he said. 'I'd much rather dine with a beautiful lady than stare at a wooden chair.'

Sylvie was fast changing her view on dining alone. She'd much rather dine with a handsome man who gave her compliments like that than stare at an empty chair.

Sylvie kept that thought to herself. Instead, she said, 'You're just being kind. I'm sure you are disappointed that your dining companion couldn't make it.' Sylvie wasn't exactly feeling the same way about Julia. Although she missed seeing her best friend and was sorry to hear that Holly was unwell, she wasn't disappointed with her new dining companion – not at all.

'Can I tell you a secret?' He leaned forward in his chair, and whispered, 'I'm relieved she didn't turn up.'

'How come?' Sylvie blurted before she could stop herself, curiosity getting the better of her.

'I got talked into going on a blind date.'

His expression said he was embarrassed to admit it. Sylvie found that rather endearing. However, she was surprised to learn he was on a blind date. Sylvie imagined he was waiting for his wife or a lady friend. She didn't think for one minute that he might be single and available. This was interesting, thought Sylvie eyeing him across the table.

'You see, I have this friend who seems to think that just because I'm single . . .' he trailed off.

Sylvie caught his drift. 'I've got a friend just like that. She likes to play cupid, given half a chance.'

'Really?' He chuckled. 'How come when you find yourself single, your friends suddenly feel duty bound to find you someone else?'

Sylvie shook her head in absolute agreement, relaxing into the conversation now she discovered they had something in common.

'I'm so relieved my blind date didn't turn up because it means I got the opportunity to have lunch with you.'

'You're too kind,' said Sylvie blushing.

He looked down at his jacket and hastily removed the flower in his lapel. 'I better remove this just in case she turns up late.' He held up the pale cream carnation. 'This was going to be how we identified each other. It was my friend's idea. Apparently, my blind date would be wearing one too.'

'I see.'

He quickly glanced around the café and then his eyes settled on Sylvie. 'I have to admit that when I was shown to my table, I took a look around. I spotted you sitting alone and was kind of hoping it was you.'

'Really?' said Sylvie, amazed that a man had noticed her. Sylvie could feel her cheeks growing hot under his gaze. She used to turn heads a long time ago, before marriage, before children. She thought those days were behind her – obviously not.

'As the maître d' led me towards your table, disappointingly I could see you weren't wearing a carnation.' He looked down at the flower in his hand and then back at Sylvie. 'Will you do me the honour of being my blind lunch date?' He held up the flower. 'Actually, that didn't sound quite right – did it?'

Sylvie giggled.

'What I meant to say was . . .'

Before he had a chance to continue, Sylvie leaned forward and took the carnation. 'Of course, I will.' She put the cream carnation in the buttonhole of her trouser suit jacket. When she looked up, he was smiling at her.

'Now that's settled shall we have lunch?' He picked up a menu.

'I think that's a marvellous idea,' said Sylvie, smiling back at him. 'I'm Sylvie, by the way.' She held out her hand, realising that she hadn't introduced herself.

He leaned forward and took her hand. 'I'm Bertram. Please don't laugh. I don't know where my parents thought up that moniker, but there you have it.'

'I think it's—' Sylvie hesitated. 'Different?'

'Yes – that it is. Shame they didn't give me a middle name, so at least I had something to choose from when I grew up.'

Sylvie thought of her grandchild's name, Gertie. It was unusual, and it suited a cute two-year-old. Family and friends agreed. But when she went out into the big wide world – at school, at work – people might be a lot less forgiving of her parents' choice of the Christian name. That's why, unlike Bertram's parents, Gertie's parents had the foresight to christen her Gertie Isobel so that in the future, if she wanted to, Gertie had the choice to go by her beautiful middle name.

'Some of my friends call me Bertie, but that just sounds old.'
Sylvie didn't think he looked old.

'I'm only a year shy of sixty!'

The same age as me thought Sylvie. Perhaps that was a sign.

'It sounds like something my father's generation would be called, and he is in his eighties!' He paused and frowned. 'Hold on a minute, my father *is* called Bertram.'

Sylvie fell about laughing at that one. 'Really? You were named after your father?'

'I'm afraid so. Bertram Wyndom-Price – the second. Sounds rather pompous doesn't it.'

'No . . . er . . . not at all.'

'You are a terrible liar, Sylvie.'

'I know,' admitted Sylvie, trying to stifle a grin.

'I dropped the double-barrelled surname and *the second*. Now I just go by the name, Bertram Price.' He passed her a menu. 'I don't know about you, but I'm famished. Let's order some food otherwise I suspect we'll be sitting here chatting all afternoon and forget to have lunch.'

Sylvie was inclined to agree. Her stomach growled loudly. She blushed in embarrassment and quickly opened the menu.

As Sylvie perused the menu, she kept glancing over the top, taking a peek at Bertram Wyndom-Price – the second. He looked very business-like in his smart blue trouser suit, crisp white shirt and, blue tie. He wore cufflinks which suggested his suit was not off the peg but made to measure at a tailor.

Apart from a more portly physique, he could have made a passable lookalike for an actor who starred in one of her favourite movies years ago – *An Officer and a Gentleman*. However, what was attracting Sylvie to Bertram was not his expensive suit or his generous head of snow-white hair, or even those dark, penetrating eyes, but his self-deprecating sense of humour. She got a distinct impression that Bertram was a successful man. He exuded self-confidence. That didn't stop him poking fun at himself and making jokes at his own expense. She liked that.

They ordered their meal. The maître d' was aware that they had both been waiting for their respective dining partners for some considerable time before they chose to dine together. He had obviously prioritised their order for it seemed that no sooner had they ordered than their food arrived.

Although Sylvie was dying to know more about her dining companion – what he did for a living, whether he had children or grandchildren, was he divorced or widowed – they both ate their meals in silence, neither minding the temporary halt to the flow of conversation.

Sylvie declined pudding as she was watching her waistline.

Bertram was about to order coffee when Sylvie's mobile phone rang.

'I'm sorry,' said Sylvie, apologising as she picked up her phone. 'I better take this – it's work.'

'Of course – by all means.'

Sylvie answered the phone. Marcia Hunt and the team had been growing increasingly concerned when Sylvie didn't return from lunch. When she didn't turn up for the afternoon, they were worried something had happened.

'Goodness me. Is that the time?' exclaimed Sylvie, glancing at her watch and only then realising she'd taken a two-hour lunch break; something she swore she would never do.

'No, I'm fine Marcia, really. I'm at The Rooftop Café just around the corner. I was supposed to meet a friend here for lunch. I waited an absolute age for her to turn up, and then she phoned me to say she couldn't make it, by which time I was starving. A very nice gentleman invited me to have lunch with him.' Sylvie glanced at Bertram and coloured at Marcia Hunt's naughty remark. 'Of course I'm not picking up men in my lunch hour,' said Sylvie haughtily, although she guessed Marcia was just having fun with her. Sylvie ended the calling saying she would be back at work as soon as she could.

Marcia told Sylvie she didn't have to hurry back. She was just relieved her star writer was all right.

When Sylvie put her phone away and looked up, Bertram was smiling at her across the table.

He wasn't the only one who had overheard her conversation. People on the surrounding tables were looking their way.

Sylvie leaned forward, and whispered, 'Why are people staring at us?'

He whispered back, 'You do realise that you don't have to shout into your mobile phone?'

Sylvie coloured again. For some reason, she had never got out of the habit of doing that.

He added flirtatiously, raising his voice so the surrounding tables could hear, 'You can pick me up any time.'

'Honestly!' Sylvie looked at him aghast and then burst out laughing at the joke. As much as she would've liked to have spent the rest of the afternoon enjoying her new friend's company, she needed to get back to work. Sylvie looked at her watch. It wouldn't be long, and she would have to head off home. 'Look, I really should go.'

'Would you like to meet me after work for a drink?'

'I'd really like that,' said Sylvie genuinely, 'but unfortunately I can't. You see, I—' Sylvie halted abruptly. She was wondering how to explain to Bertram that she had to get home to meet her husband by no later than five o'clock every evening.

She could come up with some other excuse, but as Bertram had playfully observed earlier, Sylvie wasn't a very good liar. At least not to people's faces; on paper was another story, thought Sylvie. She frowned. Sylvie didn't want to think about the lies she had been writing in her blog and magazine column.

Sylvie didn't bother coming up with a lame excuse. All she said was, 'It's complicated.' Quickly adding, 'I'd love to meet you for a drink after work, truly I would.' Sylvie didn't want to give him the wrong impression, and he walked away thinking that she wasn't interested.

Bertram looked at her thoughtfully. 'Do you come to The Rooftop Café often?'

Sylvie nodded. 'I meet my friend here every week for lunch. I work just around the corner.' She pointed in the vague direction of the magazine office.

'Would you like to meet another friend for lunch – that friend being me?'

'Yes, I'd like that very much. But about this evening, meeting up for a drink after work—'

Bertram held up his hands in a placating gesture. 'Honestly, you don't have to explain. Besides, no one gets to our age without their fair share of baggage – good *and* bad.'

Sylvie thought of John.

'I've got an idea, Sylvie. Why don't we leave our baggage at the door? We don't have to talk about past history. Why can't we be just two individuals, in the here and now, meeting up and getting to know one another? How does that sound?'

Sylvie thought that was an excellent idea until Bertram reminded her why she had accepted his invitation to join him for lunch today – she was all alone.

'We're obviously both unattached, Sylvie, so it's not as though we have to worry about breaking up a marriage or anything like that.'

My marriage is already broken, thought Sylvie. That was the reason she was sitting here having lunch with another man. And the reason she would entertain the idea of meeting Bertram next week up, on The Rooftop Café, for a proper date.

'I'm sorry if I'm being a bit presumptuous, Sylvie, but if we like one another, isn't that all we need to know about each other?'

'But—' It's complicated, thought Sylvie.

He put his hand on his heart. 'I'm not married, I promise you. So what do you say?'

Sylvie looked across the table at her new friend. Now would have been the time to tell Bertram that it wasn't as simple as all that; she was married, even though they were no longer together. Things at home were . . . complicated.

Sylvie looked into his mesmerising dark eyes, opened her mouth, and all that came out was, 'Okay.'

'Excellent. It's a date. Same time next week?'

Sylvie bit her lip. That was the day she normally had lunch with Julia. Sylvie didn't want to appear that she was putting him off, so once again all she uttered was, 'Okay.' She would just have to phone Julia and rearrange next week. Besides, she couldn't wait to tell her all about the new friend she had met at The Rooftop Café, one Bertram Wyndom-Price – the second. Perhaps he was the one?

12

On the way back to work, all Sylvie could think about was Bertram. She wondered what he did for a living and where he grew up and whether he had any family. These were the sort of questions she wanted to ask Bertram. She didn't get a chance over lunch because they were too busy joking around and enjoying their meal. Next time she hoped to delve deeper into the mystery that was Bertram Price. In the meantime, she couldn't stop thinking about him. When she arrived back at work, she found herself sitting at her desk staring into space, until Marcia Hunt called Sylvie into her office.

Sylvie stepped into her office and watched Marcia with growing unease as she closed the door. In all the time Sylvie had worked there, she had never known her boss to ever close the door to her office.

Marcia turned around and pointed to one of the chairs in her office. She told Sylvie to sit down. 'I want to hear all about your lunch date with a mysterious stranger.' Marcia perched on the edge of her desk in front of Sylvie and grinned at her star writer.

'Oh please,' said Sylvie, trying to keep up the façade, praying her face didn't colour crimson and give away the next little white lie she was about to utter. 'It's not like that, and you know it. Have you read my column recently?' Sylvie said jokingly, keeping up the act. 'I'm happily married.'

'Of course you are, and I'm a monkey's uncle.'

Sylvie's face dropped.

They stared at each other in silence until Sylvie said, 'How long have you known?' And more to the point, how did she find out things weren't exactly hunky-dory at home? 'Have you been spying on me?' And then Sylvie's final thought on the matter. 'Am I fired?' Sylvie stood up with the expectation that Marcia would personally show her to the door.

'Sit,' commanded Marcia. 'Now, let's answer those questions one at a time, not necessarily in the order they were fired at me.'

'Sorry.'

'Firstly, no I have not been spying on you, Sylvie. I'm a busy working mum, and I haven't got time to spy on my colleagues. Besides, what you do outside of work is your own affair.'

Sylvie was pleased to hear it.

'Unless you are the writer, Love on the Rooftop.'

Oh dear. Sylvie shifted nervously in her seat.

'To answer your next question . . . '

Sylvie wasn't sure she had answered the first question, but she sat and listened nonetheless wondering where she was going with this, and whether was she still fired?

'It wasn't long after you came on board with your column about how living apart together had put a new spark in your relationship that I noticed the spark had gone out of the writer.'

Sylvie opened her mouth to say something, but Marcia held up her hand. 'Let me finish. I'm not talking about *Love on the*

Rooftop, the column. Your writing remained as excellent as ever. I'm talking about you, the writer behind the column. Something was bothering me that I couldn't quite put my finger on. You see, I couldn't marry up the person you were depicting in your blog and your column, who was meant to be head over heels in love with her husband, with the person I see practically every day in my office. Correct me if I'm wrong here, but your husband *is* retired – isn't he?'

Sylvie nodded.

'If you and your husband are so in love, and enjoy doing things together now he is retired, then why do you find every excuse to come into the office? Surely, you could work from home and fit your writing commitments around spending time with him?' Marcia stared at Sylvie. 'Something didn't add up.'

Sylvie studied her fingernails.

'Until it dawned on me that, despite putting on a brave face, the writer Love on the Rooftop isn't happy because she isn't really in a romantic relationship with her husband – or perhaps *any* kind of relationship.'

'We're separated,' admitted Sylvie, avoiding her gaze.

Marcia didn't seem surprised. 'Which leads me to my conclusion that you, my dear, have created an alter ego.'

Sylvie looked up. 'I don't understand . . . '

'Love on the Rooftop is your alter ego. It's all the things you'd like to experience in your life that just ain't happening for you, honey.'

Sylvie stared at Marcia. She had never thought about it that way before. Not only had she created a fantasy for her readers, but she had unwittingly created a fantasy life for Sylvie Baxter too, by way of her very own alter ego.

'And so, to your last question.'

'Am I fired?'

'You must be joking. Love on the Rooftop is our most valuable writer, and we can't afford to lose her. I can't afford to lose her. Our sales have rocketed since you came on board.'

'But it's all built on a lie.'

'I know. Truthfully, I think I've known for some time. Surely it's a misnomer, you can't be living apart *and* be in a committed relationship. I mean, come on, who in their right mind would really believe living apart together can actually work?'

'All my readers do.'

'Do you think they've actually tried it?'

Sylvie shrugged. 'I don't know . . . I'm guessing perhaps the majority haven't.'

'Quite right. It's a fairy-tale. That's what you've given them. A panacea where they can have all the good bits of a relationship and cut out the crap. Unfortunately, that's not real life.'

Sylvie wished it was. Sylvie loved living in her own apartment, and she wanted romance and a relationship too. Why couldn't she have it all? She knew why it was unrealistic; she would have to meet somebody who felt the same way.

Julia had. She'd met Tom. The reason things were working out so well between the two of them was all because, like Julia, he wasn't prepared to give up his own place. But how many Toms were out there who were ready for living apart together? Marcia was right. It was unrealistic. If she didn't want to end up alone, then she couldn't live the life of her alter ego – not permanently anyway.

Sylvie glanced at Marcia. 'So, what do you want me to do?'

'I want you to be happy, Sylvie. Meet this new friend of

yours, by all means. Have an affair. Take two-hour lunch breaks. Hell, have the afternoon off. But don't, for goodness sake, write about it in your column.'

Sylvie stared at Marcia.

'You must, above all else, keep your identity as the writer of *Love on the Rooftop* a secret. That's all I ask. We have to give our readers what they want. Don't forget, many of our readers have been married for years like yourself or are just starting down the path of a new relationship later in life.'

Sylvie nodded in agreement.

'What they want is to believe there's an alternative way to be together. You've given them that dream, Sylvie, through LAT living. I'll tell you this, if I thought it could work I'd be the first in line to move out and get my own place.'

'Really?'

Marcia smiled warmly at her star writer. 'Everyone deserves happiness, Sylvie, even writers and their alter egos – go find yours.'

Sylvie sat there.

'Go on. Out!' Marcia winked at her.

Sylvie slowly rose from her chair. It was five o'clock. She would love to meet Bertram after work for that drink instead of hailing a taxi and rushing home for half past five.

Bertram had written down his mobile number on a napkin and stowed it in Sylvie's handbag when she wasn't looking. She had found it on her way out of the office when she was searching for a tissue, and nearly blew her nose on it before she saw the black ink.

Sylvie stood on the pavement, outside the office building, and debated whether to phone John and let him know she couldn't make it home by five-thirty this evening. She could easily come up with a plausible excuse like she had to go to the dentist or something.

Sylvie found herself in a taxi, making her way home, on the phone to Julia instead. It just seemed simpler to stick to the ruse for everybody's sake. Sylvie didn't want to risk the fallout if John spilled the beans about what they had really been up to, or Harriet found out her mum had lied about the dentist. Sylvie knew lies had a way of catching up with you – sitting in Marcia's office today proved that. Sylvie stared out of the taxi window. It made her wonder when the real truth about her alter ego, Love on the Rooftop, would catch up with her.

Julia answered on the second ring. Although Sylvie couldn't wait to tell her about Bertram, the first thing she said was, 'How is Holly?'

'Holly? Whatever do you mean?'

'Remember at lunchtime you phoned me to say you couldn't make it because Holly was unwell . . . '

There was a pause on the end of the line. 'Oh yeah – that. How silly of me to forget. It was just a stomach upset. She's all right now.'

'Thank goodness,' said Sylvie, delighted to hear it. In the past, Sylvie could never understand people getting all soppy when their pets got ill or died. Now she had a pet of her own she understood. Alfie was just like a member of the family. If anything happened to him, Sylvie would be devastated.

'Julia, you'll never guess what . . .' Sylvie paused for effect. 'I've met someone.'

Sylvie lowered her voice when she caught the taxi driver glancing at her in the rear-view mirror. She made a mental note to speak quietly on her mobile phone for the duration of the taxi ride home. Sylvie continued her phone conversation in muted tones. 'It must be serendipity that the day you couldn't make it for lunch, a gentleman at the next table was stood up by his blind date. He invited me to join him. I don't remember seeing him before. I have a feeling it was his first visit to The Rooftop Café.'

'Gosh, Sylvie, how exciting. Don't you think it's a sign that he's the one?'

Sylvie didn't know whether she would go so far as to say that. It was early days. They'd only just met. All Sylvie managed was, 'Maybe.'

'What do you mean – *maybe*?'

'Well . . . I don't know much about him.' Sylvie narrowed her eyes as a thought occurred to her. 'Julia, if by any chance you are thinking about my dream – love on the rooftop . . .'

'It had crossed my mind, Sylvie.'

'The thing is, Julia, I kind of thought the rooftop in my dream was more like a garden, not a café.'

'But The Rooftop Café has gardens.'

'Yes, I know.'

Sylvie heard her best friend sigh heavily down the phone. 'Dreams are not a perfect science, Sylvie. By the sound of it, you assumed that your dream is set on the rooftop garden of a house. There's no reason it couldn't be in the gardens of a rooftop café,' Julia pointed out.

'Perhaps,' said Sylvie, thinking that she did have a point. Meeting Bertram on The Rooftop Café was pretty darn close. 'Let me find out more about him, and I'll get back to you on that one.'

'So, you're meeting him again?'

'Yes. Look, I'm afraid I'm meeting him on the same day next week when I usually meet you for lunch.'

'Well, it's nice to know where I come in the pecking order. You meet a man you hardly know, and I've already been ousted.'

'Oh Julia, I'm sorry. That was really insensitive of me.'

Julia laughed. 'I'm just pulling your leg, Sylvie. I'll tell you what, why don't we leave meeting up until the week after next? That will give you a chance to get to know him better and report back to me with all the details – and I do mean *all*.'

Sylvie raised her eyebrows. She knew what Julia was getting at. Sylvie didn't bother reminding her that she was still married. Julia wouldn't see that as an obstacle to starting a relationship with another man, especially as Sylvie was still married to her least favourite person – John.

Julia couldn't care less about Sylvie's marital status, but Sylvie did. In hindsight, Sylvie wished she'd told Bertram that she was, in fact, still married. Sylvie had no intention of jumping into bed with somebody else just like that. Unlike Julia, who'd had several relationships over the years, Sylvie had been married to the same person for the last forty years. It was going to be a big deal to give herself over completely to somebody else. If this was the start of a new relationship, Sylvie intended to take things slow. If Bertram didn't like that, then he wasn't the one.

Sylvie said goodbye to Julia and slipped her mobile phone in her coat pocket. She glanced out the taxi window as she opened her briefcase. Sylvie found her diary. She pencilled in her lunch date with Julia which they had arranged for two weeks' time. Sylvie stared at the diary entry and wondered what life had in store over the next couple of weeks. Meeting Bertram, quite by chance, just goes to show that you never knew what lay around the next corner, thought Sylvie. She sighed as they drew up to the house. Sylvie was still thinking of that offer to have a drink with him after work which she had to decline.

She paid the taxi driver and turned around to check there was no sign of Harriet pulling up in a taxi behind her before she alighted. Sylvie quickly made her way up the garden path towards the house. As soon as she reached the front door, John opened it and smiled at her even though she had left it tight – it was twenty-five minutes past five. She ran into her apartment and threw off her coat and shoes; thought she smelled baking wafting from her kitchen and resumed her position next to John. She bent down and gave Alfie a pat on the head.

John was holding Gertie in his arms. 'Gertie, would you like to give Grandma a big hug?' He passed her over to Sylvie.

Gertie put her arms around Grandma's neck and blew her a raspberry.

When the doorbell rang, John answered the front door.

Harriet stepped inside the house looking drawn and tired after a trying day at work. It made Sylvie feel guilty for even considering being in a bar with a man instead of being here for her daughter and granddaughter.

She recalled what Bertram said about meeting up and leaving their baggage at the door. That was easier said than done when your baggage, your past, consisted of a marriage that spanned four decades, three children, and one grandchild. She smiled at Gertie. Life, Sylvie realised, couldn't be so easily compartmentalised. Maybe his could. Perhaps Bertram had never been married and didn't have children, let alone grandchildren. As she handed Gertie over to Harriet, it made her even more curious about Bertram's past.

13

'Hello, Julia,' said Sylvie, answering her phone the evening before they were due to meet up for their lunch date at The Rooftop Café. A smile played on Sylvie's lips. She was guessing Julia couldn't wait until tomorrow to hear all the gossip. Before Julia had a chance to say anything more, she added, 'Julia, you are incorrigible. Couldn't it wait until tomorrow to hear all about it?'

'Oh, I see,' said Sylvie, when she found out the reason for her call. Julia had to cancel lunch because she was going away on holiday with Tom. It was something Tom had arranged for Julia as a surprise. She only found out about it this morning. Although Sylvie was disappointed that she wouldn't be seeing Julia for another week, Sylvie brightened when Julia said the word *holiday*. Sylvie couldn't remember the last time she'd been on holiday with John, but she was pleased for Julia. Her new relationship was obviously working out if they were going away together.

'Do you need me to look after Holly?' Sylvie offered, knowing full well she was out of the house most of the time, so she would probably have to ask John to look after her dog. He already looked after Alfie all day. He wouldn't mind. It's not as though he had anything better to do. Besides, Holly was older and would spend a good proportion of the day asleep on the rug in front of the fire. Of course Sylvie wouldn't dream of telling Julia that she was thinking of handing her dog over to John.

'Sylvie, that's kind of you to offer, but you don't have to look after Holly.'

'You're taking her with you?' Sylvie guessed they must be holidaying in this country. 'Are you sure they allow pets?' said Sylvie offhand.

'I'm quite positive.'

Sylvie heard Julia laughing down the phone. She narrowed her eyes. 'What are you not telling me?'

'Sylvie, this is going to sound strange. We're going away however; I'm not leaving home.'

Sylvie scratched her head. 'You're talking in riddles, Julia.' she was just about to ask her to explain when the timer on the oven pinged signalling that her evening meal was ready. 'Ah, I must turn the oven down.'

'Are you expecting company?' Julia asked. She was aware that since Sylvie moved downstairs, and started living on her own, she rarely cooked a full-blown evening meal. Without John around, Sylvie prepared simple suppers of salad, fish, pasta, rice dishes or perhaps a sandwich. They were the sort of dishes that Julia knew would have been unheard of in the Baxter household when Sylvie still lived with John. 'Is Bertram coming to dinner?'

'No. I haven't invited him over to my place – yet. But there is something I want to ask you. Hang on a moment, Julia, I'll be back in a jiffy.' Sylvie put the phone down and walked over to the oven, followed swiftly by Alfie.

'Oh no you don't,' said Sylvie to her dog. 'Bed!'

Alfie immediately turned around and trotted over to a wicker basket in the corner of the kitchen. He sat down on the dog blanket in the basket and watched Sylvie from afar.

Sylvie smiled at him. She had noticed a distinct improvement in Alfie's behaviour since he started spending all day with John. Sylvie double-checked Alfie was still in his basket before she put on some oven gloves and opened the oven door.

Sylvie reached inside and took out the homemade chicken pie that John had left baking in her oven. It smelled delicious. She set it down on the oven top and wondered where John found the time to bake in between looking after Gertie. Sylvie recalled that she used to prepare an evening meal for John, even when the girls were small, and she didn't just have one little girl to look after but three. Even so, it wasn't just the *how*, it was the *why*. Why had John gone to all this trouble?

And it wasn't the first time. A fortnight ago, on the day that she first met Bertram on The Rooftop Café, Sylvie had returned home after work to find a chicken pie baking in her oven. Although John hadn't said a word about it when they were handing over Gertie that evening, she knew it was one of John's homemade pies that he had left baking in her oven – just like this evening. It was very thoughtful of him, especially as she didn't have the time or the inclination to cook these days, or clean her apartment, or do her laundry. Although she was very appreciative of all the things he had been doing for her, on top of looking after Gertie, what bothered her was what it was all in aid of.

Sylvie placed the pie on a metal rack to cool. Her thoughts turned to Bertram; these days he was never far from her mind. They had met on The Rooftop Café several times since their first lunch together. The second time was pre-arranged. Then they had both turned up at The Rooftop Café around noon each day, in the hope that the other would be there. It had got to the point where they were meeting each other every day. Sylvie wasn't taking two-hour lunch breaks, or the afternoon off as Marcia suggested. She had returned to having her normal lunch hour.

The chat with Marcia Hunt had made her realise that although her boss was quite happy for her to do whatever she pleased, as far as her other colleagues were concerned Sylvie was happily married. Sylvie decided it was better to keep a low profile, take a normal break just like everybody else and avoid creating any office gossip. It meant luncheon with Bertram was a rushed affair. During one such lunch he asked her out on a proper date, inviting her to a restaurant for an evening meal.

'Do you think I should go?' asked Sylvie, when she returned to the phone and told Julia all about how she was meeting Bertram every day at The Rooftop Café for lunch.

'Why ever not? When has he asked you to go out on a date?'

Sylvie looked at the chicken pie that John had left baking in her oven. 'Actually, it's this evening.'

'This evening! And you are *still* undecided whether to go?' Julia paused. 'Come on, out with it, what's going on?'

'It's John.'

'Well, there's a surprise.' There was no mistaking the sarcasm in Julia's voice. 'And you are having second thoughts because . . .?'

Sylvie sighed. Although she had her own apartment, she didn't realise how awkward she would feel going out on a date when she was still living under the same roof as John. Sylvie explained all this, adding, 'It just doesn't feel right somehow.'

'To be honest, Sylvie, I don't see what the problem is. Remember you had Nigel round and you even had dinner together in your apartment?'

'Nigel was in my apartment ostensibly to train the dog, so it didn't really feel like a date. But this is different. That's why I have asked Bertram to meet me at the restaurant.'

'So, what's the problem?'

'Well . . . after the meal, what if he wants to see me home? I might want to invite him in for coffee. Then it got me thinking that I still don't know the first thing about Bertram, apart from the fact that he must work close by because he meets me almost every day for lunch.'

Sylvie confided in Julia, 'We've got this agreement. He doesn't want to talk about the people we used to be or past relationships. We're nearly sixty. There's a lot of years behind us, a lot of baggage. Bertram doesn't want that to taint what we have. He doesn't want us to look in the rear-view mirror.'

'Maybe he's got a point, Sylvie.'

'Maybe so. Then again, maybe he's got something to hide. What if he's like some axe-wielding psycho?'

Julia burst out laughing.

'I'm being serious, Julia.'

'Yes, I know. That's what's so funny. What on earth have you been staying up late watching on television?' Julia was well aware that Sylvie liked nothing more than to stay up late and catch a good old-fashioned black-and-white movie; the ones they probably show as fillers until the early hours. Since starting her new job, Sylvie now only did this of a weekend.

'Have you been watching *Psycho* by any chance?'

'Close, actually it's a new series called *The Bates Motel*. It's quite good.'

'I'll take your word for it. I never knew you were into that sort of thing.'

'Neither did I. There are lots of things I've discovered about myself since moving into my own place. I quite like a good Hitchcock film, it's just John would never stay up and watch one.' Sylvie wondered if Bertram liked Hitchcock.

'Talking of John and thinking of psychos,' said Julia, clearly enjoying putting *John* and *psycho* in the same sentence, 'have you considered that it might be of benefit having John just upstairs?'

'What do you mean?'

'If you're that worried, at least you know there will be somebody else in the house if you do fancy inviting him back for—'

'A cup of coffee, Julia.' Sylvie rolled her eyes. 'I was only inviting him back for *coffee*.' In this instance, Sylvie thought of the benefits of having John around upstairs.

'That's assuming John is in this evening,' added Julia.

'John is always in.' Sylvie hadn't seen Barbara or any of John's new friends around since he stopped the parties on Monday nights. Sylvie could pretty much guarantee he would be home. But it still felt a bit weird knowing she might bring back a date when her husband was still living under the same roof. It didn't seem to bother John when he was bringing Barbara home, but it bothered Sylvie.

'At least you can call for help if you do invite Bertram in for coffee and he turns into Norman Bates.'

'Now you're being silly.'

'*I'm* silly? Look, if you want my advice, Sylvie, go out and enjoy your evening meal at the restaurant. It will give you a chance to spend more time getting to know Bertram.'

Sylvie hadn't thought about it that way. Perhaps Julia was right.

'You don't have to invite him back for coffee. You don't have to share a taxi home. You don't have to do anything you're not comfortable with. You can keep meeting on neutral ground until you are ready to explain your interesting living arrangements.'

'You're a fine one to talk,' said Sylvie, referring to Tom and Julia's interesting living arrangements. They both had the same dream to retire on a houseboat in Little Venice. That's where they met. When Julia announced she was in a new relationship, Sylvie expected them to move in together. She couldn't foresee a problem because they both enjoyed living on a houseboat. All they had to decide was which houseboat – his place or hers. However, what they did next had surprised her. Tom moved his houseboat. They were now moored next door to each other, living apart together, on Regent's Canal. Sylvie smiled. It just proved that Julia had finally found the one.

In all her previous relationships, things went wrong when Julia refused to take the final step and give up her own place to permanently move in with someone. Now she didn't have to. Their relationship seemed to be going from strength to strength. And soon they were going on holiday together.

Thinking of their impending holiday, Sylvie was very interested to hear what they had booked. Presumably, they were renting a cottage or something as Julia was taking her dog. If that was the case, then it would mean they would be living under the same roof for an entire week. Sylvie wondered how that was going to work out. She knew how much Julia liked her own space.

Sylvie asked her how she felt about letting go of her private space for a week and whether she was worried it would affect her new relationship.

'I'm not in the least bit worried, Sylvie. You see, we're going on a cruise.'

'And you're taking your dog?' Sylvie had never heard of a cruise line that allowed you to take your pets.

'Of course I'm taking Holly. There's no reason for her to stay behind as we're not leaving home.'

'Pardon me?'

'We're having a relaxing canal holiday.'

'Ah, I see.' Sylvie finally understood. 'You're taking your houseboats with you – *both* of them.'

'Absolutely. It was Tom who suggested it. I think it's a marvellous idea – don't you?'

'It's fantastic. Good for you.' Sylvie smiled. Who would have thought that after all these years, Julia would finally meet someone who was just as barmy as she was.

'Tom has been showing me how to manoeuvre the boat through the locks. You'll be really impressed the next time I take you out for a spin on Regent's Canal.'

Sylvie grimaced. That wasn't going to happen in a month of Sundays. Sylvie held her tongue.

'You know what your problem is, Sylvie?'

She didn't, but she was sure her best friend was about to enlighten her.

'You over-egg the situation. Too much thinking, too much worrying. Now, about your dinner date. Just go with it and see what happens. I'm sure everything will work out, you'll see. Promise me you will go out this evening.'

'I promise.'

'Are you absolutely sure because I will want a full report on how your evening went when I return.'

'I might be able to do one better than that, Julia. You know how you keep on at me about coming over to yours to meet Tom, but I keep putting it off because I would feel a bit of a heel if I couldn't bring along a date.'

'Yes.'

'If this evening goes well, I could bring Bertram along and we could all meet up for lunch tomorrow before you set off on holiday. How about that?' Sylvie paused. 'Julia, are you still there?'

'Yes. I . . . er you've taken me by surprise. I'll need more time to arrange it.'

Sylvie furrowed her brow. Since when did Julia need time to make arrangements? She wasn't that type of person. Julia didn't plan much of anything; she was much more likely to drop everything and just do things on a whim.

'Gosh, Julia, anyone would think you don't want to meet him,' chided Sylvie.

'Don't be daft. Of course I want to meet Bertram. I've just got a million and one things to do before we go on holiday. We'll catch up when I get back. Promise. Now for goodness sake get off the phone and get ready for your hot date.'

Sylvie smiled and put the phone down. She picked it up again to order a taxi. When that was done, she put the phone back in its cradle and glanced at the chicken pie. Sylvie felt a pang of guilt that John had gone to all that trouble to cook her an evening meal, little realising that she was going out tonight. She debated whether to call in upstairs with the pie to see if he fancied it, but then swiftly cast that idea aside. Sylvie didn't relish the thought of having to explain that she was going out tonight on a date. Sylvie covered the pie and slipped it into the fridge.

Alfie whined as he watched the chicken pie disappear.

Sylvie shut the fridge door and turned to look at Alfie. 'You'll be all right for a couple of hours on your own, won't you?'

She could ask John to dog-sit, but once again the thought of telling John about her date was not very appealing. Sylvie frowned. They were separated. She was living in her own place. There really was no reason for her to sneak around behind his back. After all, he had been dating Barbara in the not-too-distant past, hadn't he?

Sylvie looked down at the wedding ring on her finger. If Bertram noticed it, he hadn't said anything. Sylvie had told him she was unattached, which was true – kind of. The wedding ring was reminding her of the *kind of,* bit. It was different meeting Bertram on The Rooftop Café. It didn't really feel like a date. Just two friends meeting up for lunch. Nothing to be guilty about. But Sylvie knew this was different. This was a proper date with another man. Although she was separated, and John seemed to have no qualms carrying on with Barbara, Sylvie had plenty of doubts about starting a relationship when she was still married.

Sylvie knew deep down that she had been holding out on meeting someone else, in the misguided belief that there might still be a remote possibility they could salvage their marriage. Sylvie always believed marriage was for better or worse, and marriage was for life. However, since moving downstairs, she had changed that view; marriage shouldn't be a life sentence if it wasn't working. Even so, Sylvie decided that until she was absolutely sure, until in fact she was divorced, she would just concentrate on her career and reject any romantic advances.

So why was she taking Julia's advice and still getting prepared to go out on a date? What made Bertram so special? Sylvie knew the answer to that question. She wouldn't be going out with him tonight if it wasn't for one thing; her recurring dream about finding love on a rooftop.

14

John was sitting in the lounge wondering if Sylvie was enjoying the homemade chicken pie he had baked for her today. He was disappointed that she hadn't called upstairs to invite him to join her. Not that he expected Sylvie to do so, but it would have been nice if she'd at least popped up to thank him. John was just contemplating whether he should use it as an excuse to call on Sylvie, when he thought he heard the sound of the front door in the entrance hall downstairs bang shut.

John leapt from his chair and raced to the lounge window to see if Sylvie was having visitors this evening. He hoped she hadn't asked Julia to share the pie or worse invited that dog trainer, Nigel, over for dinner. John didn't think it was Nigel. He hadn't seen him since he came over for that one-to-one dog training session with Sylvie.

John stared out of the window. There was a black cab parked outside their house. He was about to close the curtains when he was surprised to see Sylvie walking down the garden path towards the taxi. In the hue of the street lamp, John saw Sylvie was wearing a black dress under a three-quarter length winter coat. She was also wearing heels. John recognised the outfit;

that's what she had worn when he had taken her out for a restaurant meal one evening. John looked at his watch and frowned. Was she going out for a restaurant meal this evening?

When Sylvie opened the door to the taxi, the interior light blinked on. John couldn't see anybody else in the cab except the driver. That was a relief. But that didn't mean she wasn't meeting somebody. John's shoulders sagged. The way she was dressed suggested only one thing – Sylvie had a date.

'Dammit!'

Before Sylvie got into the taxi, she suddenly turned to look up at the house.

John darted from the window hoping she hadn't seen him spying on her. It was dark outside, his light was on, and the curtains were wide open. John waited until he heard the sound of the taxi take off down the street before returning to the window.

He considered racing downstairs with the car keys and jumping in his car to follow her, but if she was out on a date what did he expect he could do about it, apart from embarrass her and show himself up? Besides, the fact that she had paused before climbing in the taxi suggested she was having second thoughts. Perhaps she was feeling guilty that he had gone to all the trouble to cook her a chicken pie on the day she was going out. John smiled. It then occurred to him that she might not be going out on a date at all. Perhaps it was a work thing.

'In a dress like that?' said John out loud to the empty room. 'Who's kidding who,' he said glumly. John closed the curtains. He wondered who she was going out with tonight. At least when Nigel, the dog trainer, stayed for dinner he knew where she was and who she was with. She was only downstairs, and he could keep an eye on things – on her, on him, on them.

John glanced at the clock on the mantel shelf. It was seven o'clock. He couldn't imagine with work tomorrow that Sylvie would be out too late. John decided to stay up until she returned, partly because he wanted to make sure she didn't bring anyone back with her, but mostly to check she arrived home safely.

John made a cup of coffee and sat down on the sofa in the lounge. He read the newspaper from cover to cover and then turned to the page with the television listings. He wanted to see what might be on this evening after the nine o'clock watershed when John was normally tucked up in bed with his novel. Nothing much. However, there was a Hitchcock film. 'Hmm, sounds interesting.'

John was quite partial to a Hitchcock film, although he had never stayed up late to catch one on terrestrial television. John made a mental note to watch the movie. If it turned out that he had to stay up late, it would probably be interesting enough to keep him awake.

John tossed the newspaper to one side and sat there in silence. Although he was now living alone, he never felt lonely knowing Sylvie was around in the apartment below him. He had grown accustomed to the familiar background noise of his neighbour living downstairs. Even the sound of her television late at night, which used to be a bloody nuisance, now didn't bother John in the slightest. What bothered John more was the thought that one day she might walk out that door and never come back.

'I'm losing her,' said John to the empty room.

A howl suddenly pierced the silence.

He sat up with a start until he realised where that almighty racket was coming from. John slumped back in his chair and stared at the floor. He wasn't the only one feeling sorry for himself. Welcome to my world, thought John as he listened to a howl of loneliness coming from the apartment downstairs.

John wished Sylvie had called upstairs to ask him if he could look after Alfie this evening while she went out. He knew why she hadn't; he was pretty sure she wasn't interested in telling him where she was going or what she was doing, or who she was with. Consequently, poor Alfie had to sit on his own all evening howling for her to come home – or did he?

John had a key to Sylvie's apartment. She had relented and given him one when he started looking after Gertie so he could use her apartment when she was at work. Sylvie had given him the key on the proviso that it was for grandpa duty only. He couldn't just nip in and out when he felt like it. But Alfie wasn't happy down there on his own. John wasn't happy up here on his own. They both needed some company.

He would have preferred some human company – Sylvie's company, in particular – but Alfie was better than nothing. Besides, Sylvie would understand that he couldn't just leave him down there howling; what would the neighbours think? John wasn't really thinking about the neighbours. John was thinking about himself – and Alfie.

John found the key that he kept in the desk drawer in his study. He walked out of his apartment leaving his door wide open. When he put the key in the lock downstairs, he could hear Alfie sniffing at the door. Sylvie hadn't shut him in the basement kitchen. That explained why he could hear Alfie howling so loudly from upstairs in his apartment.

As soon as John opened the door, he was met with an over-excited cocker spaniel jumping up at him, forgetting his manners.

John had taught Alfie not to jump up at people. However, rather than scold the dog and give the command *down,* John let it go this one time.

John knelt down and gave him lots of attention until Alfie, who John had discovered was one bright little fella beneath all that cute spaniel playfulness, wriggled free and darted up the stairs. He watched the dog disappear inside his apartment. John wasn't surprised. Alfie didn't want to be shut inside Sylvie's apartment all alone again.

He was about to close her door when his eyes settled on the picture frame he had given Sylvie, with Gertie's first ever professional photograph. It was sitting in pride of place on her mantel shelf, just like John's identical one upstairs. Next to the framed photo of Gertie was another picture frame. John walked over to take a closer look and was surprised to discover it was a photograph of Grandpa holding Gertie. John remembered the photograph; it was taken in the hospital when their grandchild was just one day old. He had no idea Sylvie had had it framed. There was a little caption on the picture frame –*Grandpa and Gertie.*

John stood there staring at the picture. Sylvie had plenty of family photographs dotted around her apartment, but there were only two on her mantel shelf. John was thinking that he must be doing something right for a photo of Grandpa to be sitting on her mantel shelf. His plan to get into Sylvie's good books must be working. Thinking of which, John wondered what had become of his chicken pie. If Sylvie had been in a rush to go out, she might have left it in the oven by mistake. John thought it would be prudent to check. He just hoped she hadn't given it to the dog. She wouldn't do that – would she? If she had, John wouldn't have felt that inclined to make a special trip downstairs to say hello to Alfie. And he certainly wouldn't have made such a fuss of the mutt.

John walked down the stairs to Sylvie's kitchen to find out what had become of his chicken pie. He glanced at the kitchen table as he strode by and saw the flowers that Gertie had picked in the park. John had helped Gertie arrange them in Sylvie's favourite vase. He knew Sylvie loved fresh flowers. John bent down to check the oven to make sure Sylvie had remembered to switch it off before she left. The oven was off, but it was warm to the touch. The kitchen was still full of the mouth-watering aroma of John's homemade shortcrust pastry that had been baking in Sylvie's oven.

He looked around the room and spotted Alfie's dog bowl on the floor by the french doors. John walked over to take a closer look. There was no sign of the remnants of his pie in Alfie's dinner bowl, only some unappetizing dried dog food. John turned around and crossed the room to Sylvie's larder fridge. He opened the fridge door and looked inside. There on a dish, wrapped neatly in cellophane, was John's chicken pie. A small pink post-it note was stuck to the bowl on which Sylvie had written the words, *John's scrumptious chicken pie*.

John smiled at the post-it note and then shut the fridge door. He shook his head and tutted at the plethora of post-it notes and scraps of paper stuck to her fridge door. He was just thinking that Sylvie really ought to get more organised, and consider investing in a calendar, when something caught his eye; stuck to the door with a fridge magnet was a paper napkin with a mobile phone number written on it. Printed on the napkin were the words, *The Rooftop Café*. Next to the phone number was a name.

John didn't have his reading glasses, so he stepped forward to take a closer look. 'Bertram Wyndom-Price – the second.' John arched an eyebrow. 'What a pompous-sounding git.'

John was guessing that Bertram Wyndom-Price – the second was having dinner with his wife at this very moment. He sounded ancient. With a name like that he also sounded rich. Perhaps Sylvie was after his money, thought John jokingly. He didn't really think it was a laughing matter. But honestly, what sort of name is Bertram? He's got to be eighty if he's a day, thought John rather pleased with this development.

John had half-a-mind to ring the mobile phone number on the napkin and find out if this Bertram what's-his-face did sound like someone in their eighties. John shook his head. With that name he didn't have to. Besides, if this was the person Sylvie was meeting this evening perhaps it wasn't a date, as he feared, but some kind of work do. That didn't explain why he had written his name and number on a napkin from The Rooftop Café.

'Maybe they had a working lunch at this café.' John was thinking aloud. He stood there staring at the napkin. Writing your phone number down on a napkin was something an old person would do. Even John knew how to enter his mobile number into someone else's phone.

'Old,' concluded John. 'Nothing to worry about.' But he still intended to stay up just to make sure Sylvie arrived home safely. And make sure she didn't bring anyone home with her.

John was standing there staring at the fridge door, scratching his chin, when he was startled by the sound of a dog yapping behind him. He turned around to find Alfie sitting on the bottom stair wagging his tail.

'Come on,' said John, heading back up the kitchen stairs with

Alfie scurrying up ahead of him.

Alfie scampered across the lounge and out the door. He disappeared upstairs into John's apartment before John had even stepped foot in the communal hall.

John shut Sylvie's door and glanced up the stairs. What Alfie didn't know was that he was going to be deposited back in Sylvie's apartment, on his own, before she returned home. John had to make an educated guess when that might be, but he would rather Sylvie didn't discover he had been snooping around her apartment, even if that wasn't really his intention.

Alfie was sitting in the lounge making himself comfortable on John's sofa. His head popped up to look over the back of the sofa at John as he walked into the room.

John frowned at Alfie. He was no stranger to the problem of black dog hairs on his white sofa. John walked over and sat down next to him on the throw which now permanently covered his sofa cushions.

Alfie tried making himself comfortable on John's lap, but he didn't seem to understand that he wasn't a puppy anymore and his adult-sized self could no longer fit snugly on John's lap. He made do with his muzzle and two paws on John's lap, the rest of him spread-eagled along the sofa.

John looked down at Alfie. Sylvie's tiny puppy had turned into quite a sizeable dog for a cocker spaniel. John patted his head and reached for the television controls, then the newspaper to check what time the movie was on. He glanced at his watch and wondered how long she would be out. John sighed. The peculiar thing was this reminded him of when the girls were teenagers and going out with boyfriends on the weekend. He used to wait up until they were safely home. Who knew that all these years later he would be waiting up for his wife to return home from a date.

'She is *not* on a date,' John told Alfie.

15

Before their date Sylvie googled where they were having dinner, although it wasn't really necessary; everybody has heard of The Savoy. Sylvie was a bit taken aback when she found out where he had booked them a table. She wasn't very pleased. Sylvie was intending to go Dutch and split the bill between them. When she discovered they were dining at The Savoy, she didn't want to think about what the meal may cost, never mind paying her share. Sylvie was still getting on top of the bills at home, so could ill-afford such a lavish evening out.

When she arrived by taxi at the hotel and met Bertram standing outside, she immediately suggested they find somewhere smaller, more intimate. Sylvie didn't want to sound ungrateful, but she wanted him to know that he didn't need to take her to expensive restaurants just to impress her.

To her embarrassment, he guessed she meant somewhere cheaper. Of course, he was too polite and gentlemanly to come right out and say it, although he did reassure her that it was his treat. Next time they could have takeaway fish and chips on her.

Bertram swiftly backtracked on that comment. He wasn't implying she was poor, or a fish and chips kind of gal. 'Not that there's anything wrong with people who like fish and chips.' Bertram was getting himself in knots. He frowned. 'Oh darn, I think I'm making a mess of things.'

Sylvie linked her arm in his and turned in the direction of the elegant double doors leading into The Savoy Hotel. 'Come on. Let's have dinner.' She smiled at him warmly.

'That's an excellent idea.' Bertram breathed a sigh of relief.

'Bertram, I hope you've also booked us a room here for the night,' she quipped jokingly.

Bertram thought she was being serious and came over all shy. 'Oh er I didn't think you'd want . . . well I wouldn't on a first date. Not that I wouldn't want to . . . with you. Oh darn, here I go again putting my foot in it.'

Sylvie nudged his arm. 'I was only pulling his leg.' She was relieved by his reaction because, as Sylvie had pointed out to Julia, she really didn't know him all that well. When she found out they were having a meal in the restaurant of a hotel – and an expensive hotel at that – she began to wonder what he was expecting in return.

'Thank goodness you're joking about the hotel room, Sylvie. I was hoping to take things slow. Meeting up at The Rooftop Café was one thing, but this feels like a proper date. Despite outward appearances, I must confess that underneath I'm really rather nervous.'

'You are?' said Sylvie, surprised that someone who appeared so self-assured was just as nervous as she was.

Sylvie spent the meal looking at her dining partner anew. Julia was right when she said that if they spent an evening out together, it would give Sylvie a chance to get to know him better. The meal had certainly given her the opportunity to find out more about the man she now met on The Rooftop Café most days. Just like Sylvie, he hadn't dated in years. Over dinner, she found out why. He had been deeply in love but had sadly lost his wife.

Bertram wouldn't go into the details. All Sylvie knew was that he had thrown himself into his career to get over her loss. It had worked, to a degree, but over the years he regretted not coming to terms with her loss sooner and moving on with his life. Perhaps he might have found someone else. It was only recently, approaching the age of sixty, that he had begun to wonder why he had wasted the last two decades missing out on sharing his life with somebody. The wasted years, the loss of what might have been, weighed heavy on his heart.

Sylvie finished her coffee while Bertram waited for the bill. She smiled at him across the table. Now Sylvie understood why he wanted to shut the door on his past and start over. Loss haunts you. As Bertram pointedly remarked, it keeps you anchored in the past at the expense of living your life to the full. He obviously loved his wife dearly, but Sylvie firmly believed, now more than ever, that life is short, and you must open your heart and seize opportunities before they pass you by. Here was a case in point. Sylvie was sitting in The Savoy Hotel, enjoying a meal with a charming man, all because she had agreed to join a stranger for lunch one day.

Bertram wasn't keen to talk about his work, where he had channelled his energy, over the last twenty years, and made a success of himself at the expense of personal happiness. Sylvie didn't really know what he did for a living apart from the information he volunteered. Apparently, he worked in the hotel industry.

Sylvie put her empty cup down on the saucer and watched Bertram get out his wallet. He handed over a card to the waiter.

The waiter's eyes went wide. 'The Black Card.' He looked at Bertram a moment before taking it for payment.

Sylvie watched the waiter walk over to the maître d' and show him the card. They both turned to look at Bertram across the room.

Sylvie glanced at Bertram and bit her lower lip hoping there wasn't a problem.

The maître d' returned with Bertram's card and receipt on a silver tray.

Bertram quickly put the card back in his wallet, not before Sylvie saw the words *American Express* in grey lettering on the black card.

When the maître d' left, Sylvie turned to Bertram and smiled in relief. 'For a minute there, I thought they weren't going to accept your card.'

Bertram looked at Sylvie in surprise.

Sylvie caught him staring at her with an expression she couldn't quite fathom. 'Did I say something wrong?'

'No, no – not at all.'

In the corner of the room, a lady started to play the piano. Sylvie was gathering up her coat to leave when she noticed a couple get up from the table. She watched the gentleman take her hand and walk her to the small dance floor in front of the piano. To Sylvie's surprise, they started to dance a slow waltz in front of all the diners seated at their tables. She stared at them in fascination as they glided across the dance floor. Sylvie glanced at Bertram who had noticed them too. He was also watching them transfixed.

'Aren't they amazing,' gushed Sylvie.

'Do you like dancing, Sylvie?'

'Do I? Oh yes, but I haven't danced since . . . well let's just say it was a very long time ago and we can consign that to the baggage cupboard,' said Sylvie, trying to make light of a touchy subject. Sylvie used to love going to dances when she was a teenager; it was always the highlight of her weekend. And then she met John. That's precisely when she stopped going dancing. It wasn't John's thing which meant it stopped being Sylvie's.

She recalled when John lost his job and was forced to retire. He had been bored stuck at home at a loss as to how to spend his time. So Sylvie had made a list of all the things they could do together. At the top of the list she had written down dancing, in the hope that John would take a chance and try something new. She remembered his reaction; hobbies were a waste of time. Over the course of forty years, John hadn't changed one bit.

Sylvie was lost in thought. She didn't notice Bertram get up out of his seat. Suddenly he was standing there beside her chair, holding out his hand.

Sylvie reached for her coat. 'Sorry, I forgot we were leaving.'

'We're not.' He was still holding out his hand.

Sylvie looked up at him curiously.

'Would you do me the honour of this dance?'

'Oh. I haven't danced in years. I couldn't possibly—'

Before she could protest any further, in one deft movement Bertram had hold of her hand and had gently pulled her out of her seat. He led a reluctant Sylvie to the dance floor. She could already feel her face growing hot with embarrassment at the thought of the other diners watching them.

Bertram came to a halt and whirled Sylvie around to face

him. They were standing practically nose to nose. He said in a husky voice, 'Look into my eyes.'

Sylvie stifled a giggle. This was all so ridiculous. She glanced at the couple already dancing. Sylvie looked into Bertram's chocolate brown eyes, and whispered, 'They're sooo good. Do you think they're professional dancers?'

'No, they're just like us – here to dine. Anybody can take to the floor if they wish.'

'I think you'll find they're not like us at all. You see, I haven't danced in years.' Sylvie frowned. She was feeling terribly self-conscious.

'What's wrong?'

'I'm about to make a fool of myself in front of all these people.'

'Look around you, Sylvie. Nobody is watching. They're all too busy eating their meals and chatting with their partners.'

Sylvie cast a glance around the room. Bertram was right. Nobody seemed bothered by the two couples who had taken to the dance floor.

'Does that make you feel better?'

'Not in the least,' said Sylvie. 'They'll soon be looking when I trip over my own feet.'

'Well, if you do trip over your own feet, I'll be here to save you.' He put an arm around Sylvie and rested his hand on the small of her back. 'The trick is don't think, just follow . . .'

Sylvie rested her free hand on his shoulder, relieved that at least Bertram knew what he was doing.

'And if you can do that,' he said, taking his first step forward, 'then I'll tell you a little secret.' He leaned forward to whisper in her ear, 'I haven't danced in years either.'

'Now you tell me!' exclaimed Sylvie but they were already gliding around the room as though they did this sort of thing together all the time.

'It's just like riding a bike – no?' said Bertram, smiling from ear to ear. 'You never forget.'

'Isn't that what they say about sex?' commented Sylvie. The words were already out there before she had a chance to censor what came out of her mouth.

Bertram chuckled and whirled her around the room even more vigorously, his expression leaving Sylvie in no doubt that he was enjoying himself immensely.

He wasn't the only one enjoying the moment. Sylvie closed her eyes and imagined she was seventeen again, dancing in the local community hall with a date whose name she couldn't even remember. What she did remember, vividly, was the rush, the euphoria, the feeling that anything in life was possible.

Sylvie tilted her head back and everything melted away until it was just her, her dance partner, and the music. It was bliss. Two people in perfect harmony dancing to the same tune; it was the perfect metaphor for a relationship. Two people who together were stronger than the sum of their individual parts. That's what dancing was all about – synergy. Sylvie decided that if she had her way, before a couple made a long-term commitment, they should see how well they danced together.

Sylvie opened her eyes to discover they were the only couple on the dance floor. When the piano stopped playing, the music didn't end; Bertram and Sylvie were still dancing. When they did finally come to a stop they stood for a moment, staring at each other, until Sylvie surprised herself and her dance partner by leaning forward and giving him a kiss full on the lips. She didn't linger, afraid she had made a mistake and he might not want to kiss her back. Or was it that she was afraid he would?

He looked as surprised as she was at that sudden display of affection. Before either of them had a chance to say anything, they were suddenly reminded that they weren't the only people in the room when a round of applause went up from the other diners. Sylvie and Bertram had obviously put on quite a show.

Bertram took a deep bow and then motioned at his dance partner – Sylvie.

Sylvie went all shades of red and scuttled back to her table. She was dying to sit down and melt into the background.

The maître d' was standing nearby also clapping. He pulled out her chair as Sylvie rounded the table.

'You dance very well together,' he remarked.

'Thank you,' Sylvie managed, feeling her face burning up. She didn't know what had embarrassed her the most: dancing for the first time in years, in front of all those people, or the fact that she had kissed Bertram.

As Bertram approached their table, she wondered what he was thinking. Sylvie thought that for someone who was determined to take things slow, she hadn't got off to a good start. Bertram said he wanted to take things slow too. She hoped he didn't think she had come on too strong and put him off. After they danced so well together, she wouldn't want that.

The maître d' hovered by their table.

As Sylvie took her seat, she was looking anywhere but at Bertram. She was thinking about that kiss. Sylvie didn't know what had come over her.

Bertram said, 'I had such a good time. Weren't we amazing out there?'

'Simply magnificent,' said the maître d', reminding Sylvie this wasn't a private conversation. 'And the kiss afterwards . . . simply exquisite.'

Sylvie wished he hadn't brought *that* up especially as she was the one doing the kissing. Sylvie ignored the maître d' and leaned forward to whisper, 'Look, about that—'

'Would sir like me to order a taxi?' The maître d' cut straight across Sylvie.

'Ah, yes of course,' replied Bertram, staring at his dance partner. He asked her, 'Would you like to share a taxi home?'

The maître d' didn't bat an eyelid.

'I live in Holland Park. Are you sure we won't be going out of your—' Sylvie stopped abruptly.

'Sylvie – what's the matter?'

'Oh, nothing.' Sylvie avoided his gaze. The conversation had suddenly reminded her of the restaurant meals out with John and the taxi shenanigans on the way home. She missed that. Did it mean she missed John? As always, it seemed that whenever she thought of John, it only muddied the waters.

'Bertram, I think I would prefer to take a taxi home on my own. You don't mind – do you?'

'Of course not.' Bertram glanced up at the maître d' who nodded and left to order two taxis, one for the lady and one for the gentleman.

There followed an awkward silence.

'Are you up for another evening out together, Sylvie, or has Bertram Wyndom-Price – the second bored you to death already, and you would prefer to call it a day?'

Sylvie smiled at him. She still found it endearing the way he sometimes referred to himself in the third person. She was also smiling because it was a question Sylvie thought she would be asking Bertram, not the other way around.

Bertram's face lit up when he saw Sylvie smile. 'Do I take it that you enjoyed my company this evening?'

'Very much so. It's just . . .' Sylvie trailed off.

Bertram leaned across the table and tentatively put his hand on hers. 'Sylvie?'

'About that kiss . . . I don't want you to think—'

'Ah, I can assure you that when I offered to share a taxi home, I didn't think you wanted . . . we would . . . not that I wouldn't want to er stay the night . . .' Bertram was getting himself in knots again.

Sylvie smiled. 'I would love to go out with you again.'

'Wonderful, wonderful.' Bertram exhaled in relief. 'Would it be too soon to meet up for lunch tomorrow?'

Sylvie nodded an affirmative.

'Our usual place?'

'Our usual place,' repeated Sylvie, breaking into a wide grin.

'The Rooftop Café,' confirmed Bertram.

John had fallen asleep on the sofa. The late-night movie on the television was still playing in the background. John's newspaper was on the floor by the sofa where he had tossed it earlier. He was awoken by the sound of newspaper pages rustling.

'Alfie,' moaned John as he rolled over on the sofa, 'do be quiet.' With a start, John realised he must have fallen asleep. 'Good heavens, what's the time?' John rubbed his eyes and tried to focus on his watch. It was probably about time he deposited Alfie back downstairs before Sylvie arrived home; otherwise he'd be in trouble. 'Come on Alfie, time to go back downstairs,' said John yawning. He looked up and was startled to find Sylvie's face peering down at him.

She bent down and picked up the newspaper under her foot.

John stared up at her with a strong sensation of *déjà vu*. She was standing over him, hands on hips, looking very smart in her little black number. John hastily tucked his shirt in his trousers, trying to make himself look more presentable as he pulled himself up to a seated position. He wondered how long she had been standing there. Her eyes shifted to the empty bottle of wine on the coffee table. John glanced sheepishly at his wife. The look on her face said he wasn't in her good books.

With the shock of finding Sylvie standing over him, John had momentarily forgotten about the fact that he had been in her apartment while she was out. Then he remembered.

'Sylvie, it's not what you think. Alfie was howling and—'

'And you thought it would be okay to waltz into my apartment without asking?'

'No, no it's not like that at all . . .' John noticed she still had her coat on which meant she'd just arrived home. She must have marched straight upstairs when she discovered her door was unlocked. Through the alcoholic haze, John remembered why he had waited up; partly to make sure Sylvie arrived home safely and mostly to check she didn't bring anyone home with her.

He suddenly darted from the sofa, clambering past a bemused Sylvie, and made it to the window just in time to see a black London taxi cab moving away from the curb. There was nobody inside the taxi apart from the driver. John turned to look at Sylvie and nearly lost his balance when a wave of dizziness caught him unawares. 'Is someone downstairs?'

'Someone? Who?'

That pompous-sounding git, thought John, Bertram whatever, whoever, the third - or was it the second?

'Of course not – why?'

'Oh, nothing.' John reminded himself that Bertram whatever, whoever, the third – or was it the second – must be in his eighties and was probably somehow connected to Sylvie's job. Although he sounded too old to be at work. Perhaps he was some sort of partner in a firm who just liked to laud over the little people.

Sylvie gave John an exasperated look as he made his way back to the sofa. He was forced to lie down to stop the room spinning around. It wasn't his intention to drink a whole bottle of wine, but one glass led to another and before he knew it the bottle was empty. John had underestimated the effect of several glasses too many when he had abstained from alcohol for so long. The last party he'd held in his apartment was some weeks ago.

'I see you're back to your old tricks again,' said Sylvie, glancing at the empty bottle of wine on the coffee table. 'Have you had a party while I was out?'

'Of course not,' said John indignantly, if he didn't count the party-of-one he'd had with the bottle of wine. Or would that be a party-of-two? Perhaps I should include the dog, and then it would be a party-of-three?

'What on earth are you on about?'

'Did I just say that out loud?'

'You're drunk.'

He noticed Alfie was no longer sprawled along the sofa next to him, but sitting obediently by Sylvie's feet as though John's current predicament had nothing to do with him.

John pointed at the dog, and said, 'You little turncoat.'

Alfie crept behind Sylvie.

'Oh god, you *are* drunk,' moaned Sylvie. 'You do realise it's only Wednesday. How are you going to be in any fit state to look after Gertie tomorrow?'

'Oh god!' repeated John. He had forgotten all about grandpa duty tomorrow.

'You idiot!' Sylvie swept out of the room with Alfie hot on her heels.

'What are we going to do about tomorrow?' John called after her. A wave of nausea hit him as he caught sight of the large box of takeaway pizza that he had ordered and sat and eaten all to himself, bar the one slice Alfie had scoffed.

Sylvie slammed his door shut and marched downstairs. In the kitchen, she walked up to the fridge to fetch the paper napkin with Bertram's phone number. Sylvie put the fridge magnet back on the fridge door. She paused to look at the napkin and noticed something else scrawled beside Bertram's name.

"Sounds like a pompous git, if you ask me," Sylvie read out loud. It was John's handwriting. She narrowed her eyes and cast them heavenward. If it wasn't so late, and she didn't unexpectedly have her grandchild to look after tomorrow, Sylvie would march back upstairs and give John a piece of her mind. As it was, it was the wrong side of midnight, and she had a full-on day tomorrow looking after a two-year-old.

Sylvie rang Bertram's number and left a message explaining that she wouldn't be meeting him for lunch tomorrow because something had come up. Sylvie didn't want to elaborate; however, she didn't want him to think she was blowing him off either. He might get the wrong impression, considering she had refused to share a taxi home. So Sylvie said how much she had enjoyed their evening out together, and ended the call by asking him out on another date on Saturday night. She would let him know when and where. Sylvie smiled. She rather fancied dancing again.

16

John was asleep on the sofa when the sound of a car drawing up outside woke him up. He roused feeling shattered. John checked the time. For a split second, he couldn't understand why he wasn't tucked up in bed at this hour. Then he remembered. It was Friday night and Sylvie had gone out for the evening. He refused to think of it as a date.

Once again, John decided to wait up until Sylvie returned home. This time it wasn't consuming a bottle of wine that had sent him to the land of nod – John wouldn't make the same mistake twice. He hadn't touched a drop of alcohol or ordered a pizza this evening, but he *had* looked after Gertie all day today. That's why he was dog-tired.

Friday was usually his day off from grandpa duty. However, Sylvie had insisted on looking after Gertie all day on Thursday after discovering John in a drunken stupor on Wednesday night; John's mistake was feeling sorry for himself and opening a bottle of wine to drown his sorrows. If he hadn't forgotten to return the dog, she would have been none the wiser.

John sighed heavily. She didn't think he would be in any fit state to face a two-year-old the following morning – and quite frankly neither did he. John was very grateful that Sylvie had stepped in like that, especially as she didn't mention it to Harriet when she arrived to hand over Gertie that morning. John recalled trying his level best not to sway in front of Harriet; the effects of the bottle of wine he had consumed the night before were still very much in evidence. He had gargled mouthwash just to make sure she didn't smell alcohol on his breath.

As soon as Harriet was gone, John took himself back to bed. When they met up again at five-thirty in the communal hall, waiting for Harriet to arrive for the handover, John decided to treat it as though they had swapped days. He insisted on doing Sylvie's Friday. He wanted to make amends. Also, Gertie had passed another audition with flying colours. John had received a phone call with a last-minute booking for the following day – Friday.

He wasn't sure whether Sylvie would agree to swap days, or whether she was still cheesed off with him and would insist on sticking to her regular day just to make a point. John hoped she understood that he had slipped up this one time and it would never happen again. He had missed Gertie on Thursday.

John expected some resistance to his suggestion. What he didn't expect was for Sylvie to be surprised by his offer and to thank him for swapping days. What John didn't realise at the time was that she had plans for this evening; it suited Sylvie not to spend an exhausting day looking after Gertie.

Sylvie stepped out of the taxi and glanced up at the house. She'd had another lovely evening with Bertram. Sylvie would have preferred to go out with Bertram on Saturday evening, but he was tied up at the office. He mentioned some conference call he had to take at the weekend. Sylvie guessed that with Bertram employed in the hotel industry he would have to work unsocial hours on occasion. That left Friday evening. The problem with Friday was that Sylvie wanted to go dancing. She didn't know where she would find the energy after a whole day spent with Gertie. Although she enjoyed looking after her grandchild immensely, Sylvie knew she would be too tired on Friday evening for anything other than collapsing on the sofa, with a cup of hot Cocoa, before getting an early night. It was probably one of the rare occasions when Sylvie actually felt her age.

Looking after grandchildren was no small thing at their age. Things were so different in her parents' day. Back then it was just about visits at the weekend when Sylvie used to take the girls to see Nanny and Grandpop. At their grandparents' house, they were fed too many sweeties, bought presents when it wasn't their birthday, and generally spoiled rotten. However, what their grandparents didn't do in those days, was provide childcare. Back then, that wasn't their role.

Things had certainly changed in a generation. Sylvie used to take her hat off to her friends who looked after their grandchildren, especially those who did it full time. She took her hat off to John because, as much as she loved Gertie, she couldn't imagine going back to being at home all day looking after small children. At her age, now more than ever, Sylvie needed outlets, and adult company. She didn't know how John was managing it all day, every day, for practically the whole week.

Although she was mightily ticked off about what happened on Wednesday night. It wasn't the fact that he'd been in her apartment; she appreciated that he couldn't sit upstairs all evening listening to Alfie howling. What she didn't understand was John getting plastered in the middle of the week when he had responsibilities the following morning. Sylvie depended on John to keep it together so that she could work, plus she could do without Harriet finding out about their arrangement. It wasn't easy having the sole responsibility of a toddler to look after for most of the week – Sylvie understood that. He had to let off steam sometime. But what she saw on Wednesday night worried her.

Sylvie thought about all the things John had been doing around her flat while she was out at work. It was as though she had a house husband at home. Sylvie couldn't remember the last time she cleared her own breakfast dishes away or hung out her washing or did the ironing. Apart from wondering where John found the time, she was getting rather used to it. But that episode on Wednesday night left Sylvie feeling concerned about whether John had taken it upon himself to try and do too much. It was enough taking care of Gertie.

Sylvie could excuse one slip up if he wasn't slipping back into bad habits. It was that, more than anything, that bothered her. He'd been an absolute angel up until now. Sylvie couldn't help thinking that perhaps it had all been too good to be true. So imagine her surprise and delight when John offered to make amends by looking after Gertie on Friday. Sylvie accepted without hesitation and even gave John a hug and a kiss on the cheek. She wondered what he would have thought if he'd known the reason she was so happy. Sylvie was going dancing again.

John stood at the window frowning at Sylvie as she alighted from the taxi in the street below. When he offered to look after Gertie, at the time John thought her reaction was a bit over the top. Then he discovered why she appeared so ecstatic about getting out of Grandma Duty today. Sylvie had a date. He couldn't imagine she would have been quite so fresh-faced and eager to go out this evening if she had looked after a two-year-old all day. John knew, only too well, how he felt after a day with Gertie. He was fit for nothing. Tonight was a case in point. John was already nodding off on the sofa during the seven o'clock news.

John was still frowning as he watched Sylvie walk up the garden path, laughing and joking, hanging on to some stranger's arm. 'Damn!' John realised too late his mistake, offering to look after Gertie today.

The curtains were drawn closed. John was peeking through one side until his nose was practically touching the pane of glass. He watched them disappear up the steps to the house. John could no longer see them but could hear the faint sound of two people having a conversation on the front porch outside. Frustratingly, he couldn't make out what they were saying.

John reached for the catch on the window. He debated whether to open it and lean his head outside, to try and get the gist of the conversation. He had just released the catch when things went quiet. John wondered what they were doing. An unwanted image came to mind of a long, drawn-out goodnight kiss. John shook his head trying to rid himself of that ghastly image of Sylvie kissing some strange man in an expensive suit.

John thought the stranger in the expensive suit looked about his own age – or younger. It was hard to tell in the dull light of the street lamps outside. What John did note was his wavy snow-white hair. John recognised an expensive salon cut when he saw one. He also had a tanned complexion, even though it was the middle of an English winter, suggesting he had recently spent time abroad in warmer climes.

'Damn!' John muttered again. Then he heard the sound of the front door downstairs. John waited at the window to get a better look at the stranger when he returned to the taxi.

John waited for several seconds and watched in horror as the taxi driver set off without a passenger.

Alfie let out a low growl.

John glanced at Sylvie's dog. He was standing upright, with his front paws on the window sill and his nose up against the window pane, which reminded John that Sylvie hadn't exactly rushed upstairs to collect her dog. However, this time Sylvie didn't return home to find her dog missing. Sylvie had asked John, very nicely if you please, if he would keep an eye on Alfie for the evening.

John had just shrugged his shoulders and agreed. He wasn't that bothered if she was going out again with what's-his-face – the second. He sounded ancient. But the man John spied walking arm-in-arm with Sylvie to the door clearly wasn't him.

John could hear the low murmur of voices downstairs; one of those voices distinctly male.

Alfie heard them too. He shifted his two front paws from the window sill and paced the floor, following the sound of voices beneath him. He stopped and cocked his head to one side listening. Alfie started growling again.

John looked at the dog and felt like growling too. He was feeling *uber* upset right now. After everything he'd done for her, leaving her flowers and cakes, and his homemade chicken pies for supper. Not to mention going along with looking after Gertie on his own – no questions asked. He thought they were building bridges. He thought, mistakenly as it turned out, that it might lead to something more. But it had all been for nothing.

John felt incredibly stupid and incredibly hurt. When he was a slob, partying at all hours, it wouldn't have surprised him in the least if she had met somebody. Now he had got his act together, and relations between them were better than ever, he assumed he was in for a chance. But no, while he was at home taking care of their grandchild, cleaning her apartment, doing her washing and ironing, and feeling like some sort of house husband. While he was doing all this for Sylvie, and even cooking her dinner and leaving it in the oven for when she returned home from work, she was seeing somebody else. John felt such a fool.

John wasn't just going to sit upstairs and take it on the chin. He looked at Alfie. 'I think it's about time I took you home.'

John was looking for an excuse to knock downstairs and disturb their little tête-à-tête. On top of which, he rather fancied introducing himself to Sylvie's new friend. John had a feeling that she probably hadn't told her date about their interesting living arrangements; namely, that her husband was right upstairs. If he had been aware of that, he probably wouldn't have been all that eager to come inside. They were still married, for goodness sake. It wasn't over until the fat lady sings, or they got a divorce.

He thought, stupidly, that they had an understanding. He thought Sylvie would at least wait until the ink was dry on the divorce papers before she . . . before she . . . John couldn't even bring himself to think it.

'Well, I'll tell you one thing,' said John, raising a finger in the air, 'they are *not* doing it under my roof.' With that, John marched up to his door, opened it, and walked out. He stopped halfway down the stairs when he discovered his furry friend was not following. John glanced upstairs to find Alfie sitting in the doorway, head poking around the door frame watching him. John sighed. This wasn't going to work if he didn't have the dog.

John walked back upstairs. 'Look, I don't fancy meeting him either, but I want to put a stop to whatever is going on behind that door – don't you?'

Alfie yapped once, which John took as a yes, and got off his behind to follow him downstairs.

17

'What was that noise?' Bertram was sitting on the sofa, his cup of coffee suspended in mid-air. He turned to Sylvie. 'I thought I heard a . . . dog?'

'No . . . no dog,' said Sylvie, shaking her head and casting a nervous glance heavenward. John should be tucked up in bed fast asleep by now. Sylvie had asked John to look after the dog because she didn't fancy Alfie exuberantly introducing himself to her date when they arrived home. That's why Sylvie had whispered in Bertram's ear when they entered her apartment, asking him to try and keep it down so they didn't wake her neighbour. She didn't feel inclined to elaborate on who was living upstairs. If anything could kill off a romantic nightcap, before Bertram's taxi arrived to take him home, finding out her husband was still living under the same roof would do it.

Sylvie's frown turned to a smile. She was still on a high over the evening they had spent dancing. When they arrived at her apartment for a nightcap, they were both a little tipsy. So, when Sylvie told Bertram they had to keep it down, talking in hushed voices sent them into a fit of giggles. It made Sylvie feel for all the world like a teenager again, sneaking home to her parents' house in the dead of night when she had missed her curfew. She remembered when the girls started dating. They thought they had snuck in unnoticed until Mum and Dad appeared in their dressing gowns.

Sylvie recalled many a time her and John had stood at the kitchen door watching with folded arms and unamused expressions as one or other of the girls, with their respective boyfriends, were raiding the fridge for toast and Marmite at some unearthly hour on a Sunday morning. Now it was Sylvie's turn. Except, unlike the girls who just had their parents to contend with, Sylvie had a husband upstairs. On no account did she want to wake him up and complicate things.

'Sylvie, I could have sworn I heard—'

A loud knock on Sylvie's door made her jump and nearly spill her coffee. Sylvie's eyes darted to the door. What in heaven's name was *he* doing up at this hour? Sylvie could hear Alfie whining behind the door. *Oh no, he's brought the dog back.* Sylvie didn't even know if Bertram liked dogs.

'Is that your neighbour upstairs?'

'Uh . . . yes. Look, stay right there and I'll see what he wants.'

'He?'

Sylvie offered Bertram a weak smile and went to answer the door. When Sylvie explained on the way home in the taxi that she was living in the ground-floor apartment of a house divided into two flats, for some reason Bertram assumed it was another woman living in the apartment upstairs.

Sylvie failed to correct him on that assumption, along with some other details she had neglected to fill in about her neighbour upstairs. Sylvie opened the door a crack, and hissed, 'What do *you* want?'

'I've just popped downstairs to hand Alfie back.' John glanced at the dog sitting by his feet.' You didn't want Alfie to sleepover, did you?' said John innocently, knowing full well Sylvie didn't expect him to call downstairs at this hour. John looked her up and down. Sylvie was not in a state of undress which was a good sign. She hadn't even taken her shoes off.

John was bobbing his head this way and that trying to get a look at what was going on inside her apartment. Specifically, whether her new friend was behaving himself and not in a state of undress either. The problem was he couldn't see a thing. Sylvie only had the door open a matter of inches. However, it was enough for Alfie to squirm his way around the door and passed Sylvie's feet unnoticed.

Sylvie was still standing behind the door staring angrily at John. She knew what he was doing here. He was spying on her. She was about to give him a piece of her mind when she heard a commotion behind her. The sound of china shattering on her wooden floor was swiftly followed by a low guttural growl and Bertram shouting out, 'Help! Help! Get this thing *off* me!'

Sylvie turned around and sprung across the room. In her haste, she forgot to shut her door. And lock it.

John pushed the door wide open and leaned casually against the door frame, enjoying the show from his vantage point in the doorway. Her new friend with the snow-white hair and expensive suit now had a huge coffee stain down the front of said suit.

Alfie was on the sofa, two front paws on Mr Snow-White's lap, standing almost nose to nose with Sylvie's new friend.

Alfie let out another low guttural growl.

Good dog, thought John.

'Bad dog,' said Sylvie, grabbing Alfie's collar. 'You are a *very* bad dog.' Sylvie turned to Bertram.' Oh, my goodness. I am *so* sorry, Bertram. He has never behaved this way before.'

Bertram? John did a double take. Surely not Bertram what's-his-face – the second?

'Just get that thing *off* me!'

'Of course, of course.' Sylvie managed to pick Alfie up and deposit him in the inner hallway that led to her bedroom. Sylvie made sure the door was firmly shut.

John smiled. *Perfect.* With Alfie behind that door, guarding the only way through to Sylvie's bedroom, there was no way Bertram what's-his-face – the second was getting any tonight.

Sylvie turned around and caught John standing in the doorway grinning. She marched over and slammed the door shut in his face. Sylvie took a deep breath and returned to her guest. 'Bertram, I'm really, really sorr—'

'Please, Sylvie, there's no need to apologise.' Bertram was still seated on the sofa. He was busy wiping the front of his shirt with a white handkerchief that was turning a distinct shade of brown with every wipe. 'No harm done.'

'But—'

'No *buts*, Sylvie. It's just one of those things. I'm more concerned about your bone china cup I dropped on the floor.'

They both looked down at the shattered teacup in pieces on Sylvie's wooden floor.

'It wasn't your fault. I should have told you about the dog. I didn't expect my . . . neighbour, who was looking after him this evening, to bring him back at this hour.' Sylvie knelt down to pick up the pieces of her broken cup.

Bertram knelt beside Sylvie to help clear up the mess. 'I didn't take you for a dog kind of person.'

Sylvie looked up sharply wondering what he meant by a *dog kind of person;* it almost sounded derogatory. 'What do you mean by that?'

'I guess because we seem to have so much in common, I just assumed you didn't have pets.' He cast a hand around her apartment. 'Your place is so clean and tidy and organised.'

Sylvie frowned at him. She wasn't sure why he assumed people who had pets lived in a pigsty. Sylvie put the broken pieces of china on the coffee table in front of her and glanced around her lounge. Apart from the broken china cup, it was spotless. Sylvie's lounge didn't normally look like this. Bertram wasn't exactly seeing her apartment at its normal worst; it was never this tidy. Sylvie shook her head. She knew who she had to thank for that.

Since John started using her apartment most weekdays, while taking care of Gertie, he somehow found the time to leave it looking like a show home. She didn't mind him doing her washing and ironing, or stacking the dishwasher, but Sylvie didn't appreciate John tidying away her stuff. It reminded her of a time in the not-too-distant past when she was living with him in the apartment upstairs. She'd return home to find her magazines, books, and personal things she left lying around had disappeared, tidied away by her infuriately fussy husband.

Sylvie didn't want her things put in drawers and cupboards out of sight. She liked to see magazines on the coffee table, and her favourite dog-eared paperbacks crammed all higgledy-piggledy on the bookcase. She liked clutter. She liked stuff. For Sylvie, it made her home feel lived in. It made her home feel her own; it was something she'd never felt she had in all the years living with John – a home she could truly call her own.

Sylvie got off her knees and watched Bertram pick up the

last piece of broken china. She studied him intently wondering if she'd met another John. 'So I take it that pets are not really your thing, Bertram?'

Bertram put the last piece of broken china on the coffee table and sat down on the sofa. 'I don't really know, to be honest.' He raised an eyebrow. 'Perhaps I should give it a try.'

'Give it a try?' Sylvie frowned. 'Having a pet is quite a responsibility, you know. You can't just give one a home then decide it's not working and get rid of them. It's a long-term commitment.'

'Well said, Sylvie. You sound like one of those adverts on television.' He pointed at Sylvie, and joked, 'Remember, a dog is for life not just for Christmas.'

'It's not a joking matter!'

'Of course not,' he said apologetically, realising Sylvie was dead serious. 'Sorry.'

Sylvie wrapped the broken china in a newspaper.

Sensing he had said the wrong thing, Bertram rose from the sofa intending to leave.

'Why don't I make a fresh pot of coffee? We can start over.'

Bertram looked at her in surprise. He was expecting Sylvie to ask him to go. 'I'd love another cup of coffee.' He sat down on the sofa once more. 'I'll try not to drop it this time.'

'Oh don't be silly. That wasn't your fault, and you know it.'

Sylvie could hear Alfie whining behind the door. She still felt terrible about Alfie's behaviour. He had never behaved like that with anyone before. It was almost as though John had put him up to it, which was a ridiculous thought; he might be good with dogs, but he wasn't *that* good.

Sylvie took what was left of her broken china cup downstairs and put it in the rubbish bin. She switched the kettle on and got two bland white mugs out of the kitchen cupboard. Sylvie wished she hadn't used the fine china displayed in the Welsh dresser. In all the years she'd had that china set – it was a wedding gift from her parents – she had not broken or chipped a single piece, until today.

Sylvie sighed as she stood staring at the kettle waiting for it to boil. It wasn't Bertram's fault that Alfie had acted so out of character. However, the more she thought about it, the more she came to the realisation that her dog wasn't acting out of character. Alfie wasn't a pup anymore. There was a good explanation for her dog's behaviour. Alfie was used to the comings and goings of familiar faces, made up of immediate friends and family. Bertram wasn't one of their circle. Since Nigel, the dog trainer, came around when Alfie was still a puppy, Bertram was the first stranger she had brought home.

Sylvie bit her lower lip thinking that perhaps it had been a mistake to offer Bertram home this evening for coffee.

The kettle started to boil. Sylvie didn't hear the knock on her door upstairs.

18

Bertram rose from the sofa at the sound of a knock at the door. He was getting an idea why Sylvie appeared reticent to invite him back to her place. By the looks of things her neighbour upstairs could be a bloody nuisance.

Bertram walked over to the door wondering what her neighbour wanted this time. He opened the door. 'Sylvie is downstairs in the kitchen making a pot of coffee. Shall I fetch her?'

'No. That won't be necessary. I must apologise. With all that commotion over Sylvie's dog, I didn't get a chance to properly introduce myself.'

'Oh, why yes of course.' Bertram held out his hand and offered Sylvie's neighbour a warm smile. 'I'm Bertram Price.'

'Really,' said John flatly, noticing that he had left out the *Wyndom* and *the second*. 'Bertram sounds kind of . . . old.'

Bertram's smile faltered. 'I'm named after my father.'

That explained a lot, thought John taking his hand.

'And you are?'

'I'm John . . . '

Bertram was still smiling, still shaking his hand.

'John Baxter – Sylvie's husband.'

'Husband?' Bertram's smile vanished. 'I . . . I knew she had a neighbour but . . . but I had no idea—' He cast a nervous glance heavenward.

John grinned. He didn't think so. He remembered Sylvie didn't put Nigel in the picture either. John thought he'd put Bertram in the picture and see whether he was as open-minded as Barbara when it came to their rather unconventional living arrangements.

'She said you were separated.'

'I see. I take it that she didn't tell you I live upstairs?' John feigned surprise.

'Er no. It must have slipped her mind.'

I bet it did, John thought sarcastically. It wasn't something you'd really want to share when you brought a date home. Of course, that depended on the date. John recalled Barbara's reaction, the woman he had met in the park when he started walking Alfie. Her car had broken down, so he had invited her home for a cup of tea while she waited for the AA to arrive. He hardly expected her to jump at the chance to go home with a virtual stranger; he had offered out of politeness more than anything. But she had accepted and didn't bat an eyelid when John told her he was separated and lived in his own apartment, and his wife lived just downstairs.

Barbara had been quite open-minded when it came to their unconventional living arrangements. John peered at Sylvie's date. The look on Bertram's face gave John the impression that he wasn't quite so liberal. Oh dear, it looked like Sylvie had some explaining to do.

'Well, I'll be off then. Goodbye, Bertram.'

'Uh. Goodbye, John.' Bertram lingered at the door watching

John walk back upstairs to his apartment. He knitted his brow surprised that Sylvie's husband seemed okay with all this because he certainly wasn't.

Sylvie walked upstairs carrying a tea tray containing a fresh pot of coffee, two plain white china mugs, a small jug of cream and a dish of brown sugar cubes. She set the tea tray down on the coffee table. 'Sorry it took so long. One of these days I'll have to buy a rapid-boil kettle,' joked Sylvie as she poured the coffee. 'Cream and sugar?'

When Bertram didn't answer, Sylvie looked up to find him perched on the edge of the sofa looking uncomfortable. 'Is something the matter?'

'Perhaps I should go.'

'Don't be silly.' She handed Bertram a mug of coffee.

He took it reluctantly.

She smiled at Bertram. Sylvie had an idea what was up. 'Don't worry. The dog can't get out, so we can have our coffee in peace this time without any interrup—'

There was a loud knock on the door.

Bertram nearly dropped his mug. He managed not to drop Sylvie's china on the floor this time, but he did spill some of the hot coffee over his hand. '*Yeow!*'

'Oh dear. Are you all right, Bertram?'

'It's nothing.' Bertram used his damp coffee-stained handkerchief to wipe his hand and the coffee stain on his trousers.

There was another loud knock on her door.

Bertram looked up. 'Shouldn't you answer that?'

Sylvie gave him a wane smile and apologised yet again for the interruption.

'Don't apologise. I think I'm getting used to it.'

Sylvie caught a note of irritation in his voice. 'I'll just be two ticks,' she said and slunk off the sofa. Sylvie turned towards the door, her face like thunder.

John was standing outside Sylvie's door grinning. He knew he was being a bloody nuisance, but he had every intention of disrupting their evening. While he stood there waiting for her to answer the door, he counted how many times he had made the trip downstairs . . .

He had knocked on Sylvie's door to hand over Alfie.

He had knocked on Sylvie's door the second time and was delighted when Bertram answered the door. John relished introducing Sylvie's date to her unusual living arrangements.

He knocked on Sylvie's door about the arrangements for Monday morning, even though it was completely unnecessary; it was Grandpa Day, and he knew it.

He knocked on Sylvie's door about Alfie, just to let her know that he was a trifle concerned she had shut him out of the lounge without any company and he might be lonely.

As if on cue Alfie had started to howl which elicited a grin from John, and a slammed door from Sylvie.

He knocked on Sylvie's door just because he could.

It had been his idea to have a communal entrance hall for the two apartments so that he could keep an eye on the comings and goings of the tenants downstairs. John was unaware at the time that it would come in handy for keeping an eye on his wife.

Sylvie was sitting in the lounge, drinking luke-warm coffee, when

John knocked on her door for the umpteenth time. Sylvie was seething. '*What now!*?' She didn't make a move to answer the door.

Bertram put his empty mug down on the tea tray. He glanced at Sylvie and sighed. So much for a cup of coffee together. Sylvie had spent more time this evening talking to her husband.

During one of their countless conversations about the dog or their grandchild, or god-knows-what, Bertram had phoned the taxi company. He was going to do that anyway. It was never his intention to stay the night. He was just stopping by for a nightcap to round off their pleasant evening together. Perhaps if her husband knew that he wouldn't have been so intent on disrupting their evening. If John hadn't intruded, he would probably have left a lot sooner because he wouldn't have spilled a cup of coffee all down himself.

Sylvie still hadn't made a move to answer the door, despite the insistent knocking.

Then all of a sudden, the knocking ceased.

They both turned to look at the door wondering what John would get up to next. Then they heard footfalls on the stairs and the sound of the apartment door closing upstairs. John had finally got the message.

Sylvie heaved a sigh of relief.

Bertram turned back to Sylvie. 'Why didn't you tell me your husband lives upstairs?'

Sylvie looked at him in surprise. 'How on earth did you know my husband lives upstairs?'

'He introduced himself while you were making coffee.'

Sylvie narrowed her eyes and glanced at the door. She knew it was a bad idea to invite Bertram back here. There was a reason she didn't want to tell him about her unconventional living arrangements; she had a feeling Bertram would not be so enamoured when he discovered that, although she was separated from her husband, they were living apart under the same roof. So, in the spirit of keeping their baggage in the closet, or upstairs as was the case, Sylvie hadn't told him.

She was sure there was plenty Bertram had not told her about his life. She still didn't know an awful lot about him apart from the fact that they enjoyed each other's company and danced well together. What's more, considering John had been a royal pain in the behind this evening, Bertram had acted like a perfect gentleman under the circumstances.

Sylvie was aware she had probably spent more time with John, up and down answering the door, than paying attention to her guest. It made Sylvie wonder whether Bertram thought this was more trouble than it was worth.

'I must say, Sylvie, your living arrangements are a bit . . . strange.' He glanced up at the ceiling. 'Have you considered moving out and living somewhere else?'

No Sylvie hadn't. She liked her flat. The anomaly was that since moving downstairs, Sylvie had felt more at home than in all the years she had lived in this house. She couldn't explain it.

Sylvie didn't answer Bertram's question. Instead, she asked, 'What did John say *exactly*?'

'Nothing much, really. He just introduced himself. I have to say he was quite pleasant, all things considered.'

'Pleasant? You call the constant interruptions *pleasant*?'

'What I meant Sylvie, was that he could have made things very awkward indeed.'

'Why would he do that?'

Bertram looked at her in surprise. 'You have no idea do you.'

Sylvie shook her head wondering what he was on about.

'Are you quite sure things are over between you two?'

'What makes you say that?'

'I don't know.' Bertram shrugged. 'Perhaps if I was still in love with my wife, and she brought a date home, I'd do my bloody best to disrupt it too.'

Sylvie stared at Bertram and then averted her gaze. She sat on the sofa lost in thought.

Bertram stood up. 'I think I'd better go.'

Sylvie looked up. 'Oh . . . er yes, I suppose so.' Something told her this was the last she was going to see of Bertram. 'I'm really sorry about—'

'Please, there's no need to apologise.'

Sylvie rolled her eyes. Poor Bertram, how many times had he said that this evening? Sylvie got up and walked him to the door.

He said, 'Don't you think it would be better if—'

'—We called it a day?' said Sylvie, finishing his sentence for him as she opened the door.

'Is that what you want, Sylvie?'

'I thought, after this, it's what *you* want.'

Bertram stepped out of Sylvie's apartment into the communal hall. He gazed upstairs. 'Things are a bit complicated in your neck of the woods.' He turned to Sylvie. 'But what I was going to say was don't you think it would be better if next time you came round mine for coffee?'

Did he just say, 'Next time?'

'Yes – next time. I was rather hoping we could go dancing again.'

Sylvie smiled at Bertram. She stood in the doorway watching him walk across the hall before she closed her apartment door.

Sylvie was doing a little foxtrot in the lounge, humming to herself as she imagined Bertram in her arms twirling her around the dance floor, when there was a knock on her door. She danced over to the door, with a smile, wondering if Bertram had forgotten something – like their goodnight kiss? Sylvie opened the door to find John standing there. The imaginary dance music vanished along with her smile.

John's head was bobbing this way and that as he tried to get a good look inside her apartment.

Sylvie sighed heavily and swung the door wide open. 'He's gone – see!' Sylvie assumed that's what he was here to find out. 'What is wrong with you?' She'd lost count of the number of times John had interrupted their evening. She couldn't exactly get a restraining order to stop him knocking on her door, but next time she could have coffee with Bertram elsewhere. That's what she intended to do. Lucky for her there was going to be a next time – no thanks to John. She scowled at him.

'What is wrong with *me*?' John said sarcastically. 'I'm not the one bringing home a date when we're still married.'

Sylvie looked at him curiously. 'You are joking. You call this a marriage?' She stopped abruptly. 'Why am I defending myself? You're a fine one to talk.'

'What are you on about?'

'Barbara – who do you think?'

'Barbara?' John thought back to the parties he used to hold upstairs, on Monday nights, for Barbara and her friends. Every Tuesday morning, he would find an assortment of her friends sleeping it off in his lounge. Barbara would be in the kitchen, cooking breakfast, wearing his dressing gown.

He raised an eyebrow at Sylvie. 'But nothing happened.'

'Oh really. So how come I saw her walking past your window, one Tuesday morning, wearing your dressing gown?' Sylvie had been waiting outside for the taxi to take her to work, when she happened to glance up at the house and spot Barbara.

'I don't know why she was wearing my dressing gown. I can't remember.'

'How do you know that nothing happened if you can't remember?'

'Well . . . if something *did* happen, it couldn't have been that memorable.'

Sylvie threw her arms in the air.

'What?'

'If you don't get it, I'm not explaining it to you.' Sylvie slammed her door shut. A few moments later she opened the door again expecting John to be standing the other side.

He was.

Sylvie thrust Alfie into John's arms. 'Here, take your partner in crime. I've had enough of the pair of you.' Sylvie slammed the door shut.

John looked down at Alfie cradled in his arms. 'Guess we're both in the doghouse.'

Alfie yapped in agreement and licked John's face.

John glanced at Sylvie's door. 'Does that mean you want him to sleep over after all?'

Sylvie heard that comment. She swiftly opened the door to get the last word in. 'If you pull a stunt like that again, I'm moving out.'

That wiped the smile off John's face. He didn't want her to move out. What's more, the last thing he wanted was for Sylvie to move in with that pompous git. Perhaps that's what she was considering. It made him wonder how long this had been going on. John wanted to know more about her new friend. 'How long have you been seeing Bertram what's-his-face?'

'Two weeks,' said Sylvie automatically, before trying to back-track with, 'it's none of your business.' She wasn't getting into a conversation with John about Bertram. Sylvie slammed her door shut for the final time.

John turned toward the stairs. In two weeks, she had only been out on a date with him twice, mused John as he carried Alfie upstairs to his apartment. The relationship was in its infancy; fertile ground for him to dish the dirt on Bertram – if he could find any – and end this relationship before it got serious. First, he had to do some detective work. John raised an eyebrow. Just who was Bertram Wyndom-Price – the second?

19

John was standing outside Sylvie's apartment on Monday morning waiting for Harriet to arrive with Gertie. He was early. He couldn't wait for Sylvie to emerge, so he could question her further about Bertram. John smiled. This time she couldn't exactly slam the door shut in his face.

The moment Sylvie stepped out of her apartment she knew what she was in for.

'Tell me about Bertram.'

'No. It's none of your business.' Sylvie stared at the front door willing Harriet to arrive early.

John persisted. 'But what do you know about him?'

'Enough,' said Sylvie, between gritted teeth.

'And what is that exactly?' What John really wanted to know was what Bertram had that he didn't – apart from the tan and the pompous double-barrelled surname.

Sylvie turned to John. 'If you must know, he loves dancing.'

'Dancing?' John looked at her askance. 'What do you mean – *dancing*?' said John disdainfully

'Years ago, I used to go to dances. That all stopped when I met you,' said Sylvie, in an accusatory tone.

John shook his head. Why couldn't Sylvie see right through him? Bertram sounded like an old lothario who was using some dance moves to seduce gullible, lonely women. What a tosser, thought John. It just made him determined to find out more about Sylvie's dance partner.

The doorbell rang.

Sylvie breathed a sigh of relief.

'Dancing,' mused John as he walked over to answer the door.

Harriet stepped into the hall. She checked everybody was present and accounted for – meaning both grandparents – and plonked Gertie in John's arms. 'I must dash.' She gave Gertie a kiss goodbye. 'Now you be a good girl for Grandma and Grandpa.'

Gertie blew Mummy a raspberry and smiled at Grandpa.

John waved Harriet goodbye and closed the front door. He turned to Sylvie. 'So, what does he do for a living?'

Sylvie grimaced. She didn't have time for this. Her taxi would be here any minute. Sylvie didn't have to go into work this morning. She could have worked from home. But there was no way she was going to stay indoors knowing John could call on her at any time and start on about Bertram.

After John's antics on Friday evening, she had managed to avoid him for the rest of the weekend. However, she knew as soon as Monday arrived, he would have his opportunity. Sylvie wished she'd never brought Bertram home for coffee. It was making her seriously doubt how she thought she could stay in her apartment and have a personal life. It wasn't going to work with John living upstairs.

In hindsight, Sylvie was really surprised by John's behaviour towards Bertram. She remembered how she felt when she first saw Barbara leaving John's apartment. It was like a physical blow when she discovered there was someone else.

Even though they were separated, the fact was forty years of marriage – and all the emotional baggage that went with it – could not be unravelled overnight. She didn't know what Bertram's history was, but he was right when he said hers was complicated. A long marriage will do that. Being with the same person for all those years was not something she could easily put behind her.

After John's behaviour on Friday evening, it was apparent he felt the same way. However, Bertram was wrong when he said John must still be in love with her. Sylvie believed you couldn't just click your fingers and erase the person you had shared the past forty years of your life with. Sylvie couldn't and evidently, neither could John. It would take time. But it didn't mean they were still in love.

'Is he divorced? Does he have children?'

John's questions cut across her thoughts. Sylvie was in her bedroom, trying to get ready for work.

John had followed Sylvie inside her apartment and was standing in her bedroom doorway. He looked at Gertie in his arms. 'Does he have grandchildren?'

Sylvie paused to look at their grandchild. Gertie was concentrating hard as she tried to do up Grandpa's top shirt button. Sylvie sighed. She couldn't very well tell him to get out of her apartment. Sylvie turned around, opened her wardrobe, and chose a pair of shoes. She glanced at John. The problem was she didn't know if Bertram had children or grandchildren. All she knew was that he worked in hotel management and loved to dance.

Sylvie closed the wardrobe door, sat down on the bed to put her shoes on, and then walked out of her bedroom carrying her briefcase. She glanced over her shoulder as she made her way down the stairs to the basement kitchen. John was following behind with Gertie.

Sylvie walked over to the kitchen table to pick up her new notebook. She'd bought it recently for work because it was a lot slimmer and lighter to carry around than her bulky laptop.

'Well?' said John as he lifted Gertie into the highchair.

Sylvie rolled her eyes. John wasn't going to give up. If she didn't put a stop to his incessant questions now, he would be pestering her this evening after work when they met up again to hand over Gertie.

Sylvie slipped the notebook into her briefcase and turned to look at John. He was putting a Weetabix into Gertie's cereal bowl. Sylvie walked over to the fridge, got out a pint of milk, and heated a small jug of milk in the microwave. She handed it to John. She watched him pour warm milk over Gertie's Weetabix.

John sat down at the kitchen table next to Gertie's highchair and put the bowl in front of her. 'Here's your Weetabix, Gertie.' John handed her a spoon.

'Bix-bix,' said Gertie, taking the spoon and waving it in the air.

'He doesn't want to talk about the people we used to be or the relationships we once had,' began Sylvie.

John looked up.

'We're both nearly sixty. There's a lot of years behind us, a lot of baggage, but he doesn't want to look in the rear-view mirror. He wants us to think about the future not dwell on the past. I'm inclined to agree.' Sylvie eyed John. 'He just wants us to be two people meeting up, with no talk of past relationships or family ties.' She hoped that would shut him up.

John narrowed his eyes. 'Doesn't that sound a bit suspicious to you?' It did to John. 'It all sounds rather convenient – if you ask me.'

'What do you mean?'

'Hasn't it occurred to you that he might be hiding something?'

'He's not married if that's what you're suggesting.'

'Then perhaps there's something else.'

'Like what?'

'I don't know. Maybe there's something in his past he doesn't want you to find out.' John lowered his voice and whispered, 'Perhaps he's really dirt poor, and he's after your money.'

'Don't be so stupid.'

'Stoo-pid Grandpa,' said Gertie with a mouthful of cereal.

John didn't think Grandpa was stupid for not trusting someone who wanted to keep their past a secret. Sylvie may not want to find out what he was hiding, but John did.

Sylvie dismissed stupid Grandpa with a shake of her head and smiled at Gertie. She walked over to the table and bent down to give her a kiss goodbye, trying to find a spot on her cheek that wasn't smeared with Weetabix. Sylvie stood up and glanced in John's direction.

John grinned at her and pointed at his cheek, indicating that he wanted a kiss goodbye too.

She glared at him. 'You must be joking.' Sylvie turned towards the door and caught sight of Alfie.

He was lying in his basket, head on his front paws, looking up at Sylvie with doleful eyes.

'Oh, Alfie.' Sylvie knelt down and made a big fuss of him, apologising for kicking him out on Friday night and leaving him with John all weekend. It wouldn't happen again.

John glared at the dog, getting such a fuss, and then frowned at the thought of Bertram not giving anything away about his past. Something didn't smell right. Who didn't bring up their history in conversation – it was second nature. Besides, surely it was better to know as much as you could about someone before you got too involved? And it cut both ways. Bertram certainly had a surprise on Friday night when he discovered Sylvie's husband was living under the same roof.

John watched Sylvie disappear up the kitchen stairs, off to work. It made John wonder what surprise was in store for her when she eventually found out what he was hiding. And she would find out because John had every intention of getting to the bottom of why Bertram was keeping his past so close to his chest. The problem was John didn't have a clue where to start.

Gertie had finished her Weetabix. She waved her spoon at Grandpa. 'Booberries.'

Grandpa wasn't listening. Grandpa was lost in thought trying to figure out how he was going to find out about Bertram's past.

John was snapped back to grandpa duty with a start by the sound of Gertie's empty cereal bowl landing, with a loud clatter, across the other side of the room.

'Booberries!' shouted Gertie indignantly.

John wiped Gertie's face with a wet wipe and went over to the fridge to fetch some blueberries. When John closed the fridge door, he saw the paper napkin stuck to it with Bertram's phone number scrawled across it.

'The Rooftop Café,' said John, reading the embossed black

lettering running up the side of the napkin. He turned around and smiled at Gertie. 'I think we have our first lead.'

John walked back to the table and sat there watching Gertie scoffing fistfuls of blueberries. She dropped several on the floor which were instantly hoovered up by Alfie, reminding John that he hadn't fed the dog.

He got up and poured some dried dog food into Alfie's bowl, which reminded John that he hadn't eaten breakfast either. He put a slice of bread in the toaster and stood there watching Gertie. John thought about the calendar upstairs. Gertie didn't have any auditions or photoshoots today. He'd also checked his mobile phone first thing this morning. The model agency hadn't been in touch, so nothing had come up last minute. That meant they had a free day. John thought of all the activities written down on the calendar that he had planned for today and suddenly decided to ditch the plan.

John took his toast back to the table and sat down opposite Gertie. He spread his toast with butter and a big dollop of jam.

Gertie took one look at Grandpa's toast, threw the rest of her blueberries on the floor, and held out a plump hand.

John cut his toast into quarters and gave her a triangle.

They sat eating John's toast together while he explained to Gertie his plan for today. 'Gertie, today we are going to play detectives.'

'Tectives,' repeated Gertie, licking the jam from her fingers.

'That's right. You can be Dr Watson and I'm Sherlock Holmes. What do you say? Does that sound fun?'

Gertie nodded her head up and down as she reached for another piece of Grandpa's toast.

Thinking of the famous detective, after they had followed up their first lead John intended to take his granddaughter to the little café opposite 221B Baker Street – the famous detective's house – to have a hot chocolate and a bun after their busy morning sleuthing. He couldn't wait to show Sylvie that behind that perma-tan, and suave, sophisticated exterior, Bertram was hiding something. John had every intention of finding out what that *something* was. He smiled confidently. 'The game is afoot.'

20

After John had done a preliminary bit of detective work and discovered the location of The Rooftop Café – fortunately, there was a phone number printed on the back of the napkin – John ordered a taxi. He did consider going in the car. John now had a brand-new child car seat fitted for ferrying Gertie around London to her auditions and photoshoots. Although it would be cheaper to take the car on this occasion, it would be one hell of an inconvenience to try and park the car in central London.

The tube and buses were out of the question; John wasn't in the mood to struggle with a two-year-old, her buggy, and an excitable cocker spaniel on public transport. Once was enough when he'd taken them on his last visit to the jobcentre. Besides, since Sylvie started paying all the bills, John now had some disposable income. He could afford to splash out on some of life's little luxuries – London taxis being one of them.

John was not ready when the taxi arrived. He was looking forward to following up his first lead at The Rooftop Café. Unfortunately, they would be setting off much later than he had anticipated. John had to phone the taxi company and let them know that he'd been delayed and would call them back. He had been dying to go out all morning, but Gertie had chosen today, of all days, to have a nap halfway through the morning instead of mid-afternoon.

Harriet had warned him that she'd been up in the night teething. Gertie did look very tired when she first arrived. By the time she'd had a play, and John was getting things ready to take Alfie for his morning walk, Gertie was lying on the sofa asking to watch Peppa Pig.

John raised an eyebrow. He knew what would happen; one episode of Peppa Pig would lead to another and, before he knew it, it would be lunchtime. He was about to say *no* when John took one look at her grumpy face and decided he better switch on the television.

He was on all fours, fiddling with the DVD, when she shouted out, 'Gertie!'

John looked up. She was sitting on the sofa, sucking her thumb, and pointing at the television.

John glanced at the television and dropped the DVD. He fumbled for the remote control and turned up the sound. 'You're on telly!'

John sat down on the sofa next to Gertie. He picked her up and put her on his lap for a cuddle. Together they watched Gertie on the TV commercial having her breakfast cereal and smiling sweetly for the camera.

John smiled knowingly. He'd been there when they filmed that commercial. Gertie was quite the little actress. She didn't wave her spoon in the air, splattering Weetabix on the walls like she did at home. She didn't toss her dish across the room afterwards. And she didn't shout for *booberries* when she'd finished her cereal.

208

John was still smiling until her screen mum came on and he was reminded of Harriet. At least she was at work and not at home watching daytime programmes. It's not that John didn't think she would be chuffed to discover her daughter was on television. It's just that John wanted to be there to see Harriet's face when she found out.

He lowered the volume when the commercial ended and discovered Gertie had fallen asleep in his arms. John carried her through the lounge and put her down in the cot in Sylvie's bedroom. He pulled down the blinds. John looked at his watch expecting her to have a quick half-hour nap.

Two hours later, John was climbing up the walls itching to go out. So was Alfie. John eventually let Alfie out in the garden while he made up some lunch.

Under normal circumstances, John would have cleaned Sylvie's apartment from top to bottom, put some washing on and done her ironing. Instead, he slumped on the sofa, waiting impatiently for Gertie to wake up.

John was sitting there, drumming his fingers on the arm of the sofa, when a strong odour wafted up his nostrils. He sniffed the air and grimaced. 'What's that smell?' John gazed around the room until his eyes settled on Alfie, curled up content as could be, having a snooze on the sofa next to him. He stared at the dog, taking in his muddy paws and matted coat.

John whipped out of the lounge, down the hall into Sylvie's bathroom. A few minutes later he reappeared.

Alfie was still asleep on the sofa.

John called out, 'Alfie!'

Alfie opened his eyes, yawned and looked at John.

'Here boy!' John patted his trouser leg.

Alfie bounced off the sofa and bounded after John, wagging his tail as he followed him down the hall.

John walked into the bathroom.

Alfie stopped in the doorway and cocked his head to one side at the sound of running water.

John turned off the bath tap, rolled up his sleeves and checked the water temperature. He turned around and looked at Alfie. 'Have I got a surprise for you!' John grinned.

Bath time with Alfie was not an experience John was going to repeat in a hurry.

Standing in the bath, sopping wet, bedraggled and miserable, it was the first time Alfie had ever growled at John.

John guessed Alfie's morning hadn't gone quite as planned either.

As the taxi pulled into Hanover Square, John asked the taxi driver if he had heard of The Rooftop Café.

The taxi driver helpfully pointed to a building across the street.

John saw a sign outside: *Upstairs to The Rooftop Café.*

'Sorry, mate, but there's nowhere to park otherwise I'd drop you right outside.'

'That's quite all right,' replied John as the taxi driver pulled the car to a stop around the corner. John paid his fare and arranged for the taxi to come back and pick them up in an hour.

With Gertie back in her buggy, and Alfie obediently walking along beside him, they all set off in the direction of The Rooftop Café. John was familiar with this part of London. Mayfair was where Harriet worked. The magazine's head office was based in

Hanover Square. John stopped and looked up at the building. He knelt down beside Gertie's buggy. 'Look, Gertie, that's where Mummy works.' John pointed at the old Georgian building in front of them.

'Snack,' said Gertie.

John fumbled in her pink bag and found a packet of Jammie Dodgers he had bought the other day. He gave her one. John was about to put the packet of biscuits back in the bag when Alfie whined loudly.

'Oh all right, you can have one too.' John looked at the biscuits and decided he also fancied a Jammie Dodger – or two.

When they'd all had a snack, John thought of calling in to see Harriet as he was in the neighbourhood, but then thought the better of it. John imagined it wouldn't go down well if he dropped in unannounced. Less so, when she found out Grandma wasn't with them. Besides, she was now the editor of the magazine and would be too busy with work to take a social call.

He remembered when she started out in journalism. Her first job was right here in Hanover Square. He glanced across the square at the modern office building, on the corner, where she once worked. The magazine where Harriet began her career was still located in that building. She now called that magazine her arch rival. According to Harriet, that's where the writer by the name of Love on the Rooftop worked.

John suspected Harriet's antipathy towards that writer had less to do with the fact that Love on the Rooftop had dramatically increased the sales of their rival magazine and more to do with Harriet losing her freelance work. He wondered how she felt, looking out of her window every day, knowing that just across the square was the columnist who had stolen her lucrative freelance work. John raised an eyebrow. If it weren't for that anonymous writer, probably sitting in that building at this moment, Harriet would not have had to return to full-time work. Which meant John would not be spending this precious time with his grandchild. Looking after Gertie was often stressful and exhausting, but he wouldn't give it up for the world.

For a split second, John debated whether to call in on Love on the Rooftop unannounced instead. He rather fancied meeting this writer. He was staring at the office building, pondering whether to do just that, when Gertie suddenly shouted, *'Bad dog!'*

John shifted his attention to find Alfie standing there with his head down, guilty eyes looking up at him. He was licking his chops. John glanced at Gertie. She was pointing at the dog, her face like thunder. John sighed as he reached in the bag for another biscuit.

Alfie crept up to the buggy.

'Oh no you don't. I think you've had quite enough biscuits for one day.' John unwound Alfie's lead from the buggy handle and pulled him out of reach of Gertie and her Jammie Dodgers.

As Gertie was munching her biscuit, John heard Alfie whining. He sighed. Any thoughts of paying a visit to the celebrity writer, with a two-year-old and a spaniel in tow, swiftly vanished.

John turned the buggy in the direction of The Rooftop Café. He could see the sign for the café, with an arrow pointing upstairs. John stopped on the other side of the street and gazed up at the elegant Georgian building. There were people seated at tables in what appeared to be a garden on the roof. John had no idea there were rooftop garden restaurants in London.

John's shoulders sagged. Now he was here, he didn't have the first notion what to do next. 'Some detective you are,' said John under his breath as he waited to cross the road. If he were the real Sherlock Holmes, now that would be a different story; some clue or suspect, or body would present itself just at the right moment. 'Elementary, my dear Watson,' said John, imagining the scene. He furrowed his brow pretty sure Holmes never once uttered those immortal words in any of Sir Arthur Conan Doyle's books.

John was still waiting to cross the road. He was beginning to think this was a giant waste of time when he spotted them; Sylvie and Bertram had emerged on the street from The Rooftop Café. They were standing together, on the pavement outside, talking.

John watched them avidly from across the street. He glanced at his watch; they must have met up for lunch. John remembered the paper napkin he found in Sylvie's kitchen, with Bertram's phone number scrawled across it. It made him wonder how long this had been going on – meeting up for lunch at The Rooftop Café. He assumed Sylvie had only been on two dates with Bertram. Now John was beginning to suspect things were more serious than he first thought. He frowned at Bertram. It made John all the more determined to find out who he was and what he was up to.

Gertie pointed, and said, 'Grandma.'

John glanced down at Gertie in her buggy. Fortunately, there was no way Sylvie would hear Gertie's little voice from across the other side of the busy street. John could barely hear Gertie himself over the noise of the traffic. Sylvie didn't see them because she was too engrossed in conversation with Bertram.

John stood transfixed watching them. He wondered if this was how they had first met, having lunch on The Rooftop Café. If that was the case, thought John putting his detective hat on, it meant Sylvie must work in the local vicinity. John was just wondering in which direction they were headed, when they parted – Bertram heading in one direction, Sylvie the other.

John hesitated. He was here to find out about Bertram and yet a part of him wanted to follow Sylvie. He hadn't asked her where she worked, or what she did for a living, but that didn't mean he wasn't curious. For an instant, John thought his curiosity would get the better of him as he watched Sylvie walking down the street. He turned Gertie's buggy in her direction and glanced over his shoulder at Bertram.

'Damn.' John was rather hoping that Bertram would change his mind and accompany Sylvie back to work. Clearly, that wasn't happening. John's head swivelled from side to side, suffering from indecision until he remembered the plan. He always stuck to a plan, and the plan was to find out about Bertram.

John watched Sylvie striding purposefully down the road before he reluctantly turned Gertie's buggy in the other direction. John started walking. He followed Bertram, albeit at a safe distance, keeping a close eye on him from across the street.

Across the road, Bertram arrived at a junction. Instead of crossing the road and continuing forward, as John anticipated, Bertram rounded the corner.

John stopped at the kerb, looked left and right, and crossed to the other side of the road. Quickening his pace, John followed in Bertram's wake and arrived at the same junction. He rounded the corner, into the side street, only to discover Bertram nowhere to be seen. John came to an abrupt halt. He couldn't just disappear into thin air. John stood there scratching his head. He hadn't been that far behind Bertram. He must have entered one of the buildings in the street. But which one?

John's eyes settled on a row of majestic five-storey Victorian townhouses that turned out, on closer inspection, to be a hotel. John stopped outside the canopied entrance and stared at the doorman dressed in a black and gold uniform. *Now what?*

'Wee wee,' said Gertie.

'Oh no!' John slapped the front of his forehead. Gertie was in the process of being potty trained, so Harriet had asked them to refrain from putting her in nappies. John was fine with that. The trouble was when she needed to go, she needed to go. That's why he always brought several changes of clothes in case they got caught out without a public loo. John frantically looked up and down the street. This was clearly one such occasion.

Unless . . .

John pushed Gertie's buggy forward.

The doorman spotted them and reached for the door.

John smiled at the doorman as he pushed Gertie's buggy through the open doorway into the hotel lobby. He hoped the hotel staff inside were just as amenable and would let Gertie use their facilities. John was also praying he didn't bump into Bertram.

He quickly scanned the spacious foyer for any sign of a tanned man in a fancy suit. There was no sign of him. John could only draw one of two conclusions; he worked here – which was the most likely scenario – or he had a hotel room here. John didn't like the thought of the latter, especially as Bertram had been meeting Sylvie just around the corner. John thanked God that they went their separate ways after lunch.

John approached the young woman at the reception desk who was impeccably dressed. He thought she looked like one of those fashion models on the cover of a women's magazine, with her slicked back blonde hair and bright red lipstick.

Behind the stern, business-like veneer was a warm smile for Gertie. The receptionist was only too pleased to let John use the facilities. She even showed him the way to the toilets.

John was extremely grateful because by now Gertie was clutching her trousers. He could tell an accident was imminent.

After Gertie had used the toilet and stood unravelling great swathes of loo roll from the holder when John was busy doing up her trousers, John washed Gertie's hands in the plush marble sink. As he did so, he glanced about him. The gold-coloured deep pile carpet matched the gold wallpaper. There was a green chaise longue chair in a soft velour material. Two watercolour paintings adorned the wall behind the sofa. By the door was a large vase containing an indoor house plant. John wasn't very au fait with plants, but it looked like a fern. In terms of public facilities, John had never seen anything like it. The hotel loo was expensively furnished and more spacious than his lounge at home.

John was drying Gertie's hands on a fluffy white hand towel when he thought he heard a commotion outside in the hotel foyer. John walked Gertie over to the door and opened it a crack to see what was going on. A young woman was standing in front of the reception desk. She was arguing with the receptionist. John wondered what was going on.

He looked her up and down. Not to be unkind, but she didn't look like one of the hotel guests. She seemed very young, perhaps in her early twenties, and she was wearing faded, ripped jeans, a black tee-shirt, and a worn leather jacket. John cast his eyes down at the little boy, around Gertie's age, sitting in a buggy. Perhaps they walked into the hotel hoping to use the facilities too. John frowned. Why was she being treated differently?

He was about to step outside and give the receptionist a piece of his mind for not letting her child use the facilities too, when the receptionist picked up the phone.

'Mr Price, it's the front desk. I'm sorry to bother you.'

John opened the door wider, straining to hear.

'She's here again asking to see you.'

'I'm not leaving until I see him. I mean it this time.'

The receptionist gave the young woman a look of disdain before she continued on the phone. 'I'm afraid she says she's not leaving until you come down here.'

Blimey. John's eyebrows shot up. If the receptionist on the phone was talking to Bertram Price, then John's detective work was paying off – big time.

The young woman suddenly reached across the desk and grabbed the phone. She shouted, 'I don't want your money, Bertram. I just want you to be in his life.'

John looked at the little boy in the buggy. *Blimey*. This was a cook up for the books. He didn't expect this.

'I'm not leaving,' she barked down the phone before the receptionist managed to wrestle the phone out of her hand.

John stared at the young woman. She might not be leaving but he better had, just in case Bertram changed his mind and decided to make an appearance. Besides, John was worried about Alfie; he had tied his lead securely to a lamppost outside the hotel, but that wouldn't stop a dognapper spotting a cute spaniel and making off with him.

John picked Gertie up and felt something tickle his nostril. 'What's this?' John looked at his granddaughter. She was holding a long green stem in her hand, with a fern leaf on the end.

Gertie held it out of John's reach. The look on her face said:

It's mine, Grandpa. John glanced at the potted house plant by the door and sighed. One of the stems had been broken off. John was learning the hard way that he couldn't turn his back on her for a minute without Gertie getting up to something.

Although Gertie was Harriet's child, she reminded him an awful lot of Auntie Jess. He smiled as a memory resurfaced of the first time they had taken all three girls to the Natural History Museum in South Kensington. Whilst their eldest and youngest – Harriet and Chloe – held hands and stayed close to Mummy and Daddy, Jess did no such thing. He could smile about it now, but he'd never forget that gut-wrenching moment when their attention was diverted for a milli-second and she vanished. John recalled leaving Sylvie with the other two girls while he took off on a frantic search for Jess . . .

He tried to keep calm. He tried to think, think, think what might have caught her attention and caused her to wander off, but his heart ruled his head, and he couldn't for the life of him think straight. Eventually, he found himself back in the central hall where a large crowd had gathered. John had his back to them. He was looking up and down the cathedral-like Hintze Hall for any sign of her when three security guards raced past John.

'Who's that child?' someone exclaimed.

He turned in their direction and watched the crowd part as the security guards made their way towards the main exhibit – a massive replica skeleton of a dinosaur, affectionately known as Dippy the Diplodocus. John had seen it a zillion times before. He would have hardly given it a second glance if it wasn't for the new edition to the exhibit. John's eyes went wide in disbelief. 'Oh

God!' Sitting atop Dippy's bony back was a small child grinning at the crowd. *Jess!*

Someone started to clap. A round of applause went up from the crowd. John didn't know whether to laugh, cry in relief, or join in the applause – god only knows how she got up there. John soon found out when she came down the same way she climbed up – along Dippy's tail.

'At least if I take you to the Natural History Museum, you won't climb on Dippy,' said John, cradling Gertie in his arms.

Not that he wouldn't put it past her to try. However, Gertie couldn't get up there even if she wanted to because Dippy's tail no longer trailed along the floor. John recalled reading about some new scientific research that apparently proved their tails didn't drag along the floor after all. That was the official reason why the tail was repositioned high above the floor, suspended over people's heads. John often wondered if it had anything to do with the day a child got it into her head to ride a dinosaur.

John smiled at Gertie and made a mental note to take her to see the famous diplodocus before the dinosaur cast was moved to make way for a skeleton of a blue whale. Although John was saddened when he read about it in the newspaper – he was rather fond of Dippy who had lived in the museum's Hintze Hall since the 1970s – there was talk of him going on tour. John smiled at the thought that other children, from around the country, would get to meet Dippy.

Gertie was starting to fidget in John's arms.

'Come on. It's time to go and fetch Alfie.'

John stepped outside the toilets and grabbed the buggy. With

Gertie still in his arms, he walked briskly past the reception desk where the young woman was still arguing with the receptionist. John gave the young woman a sideways glance as he walked by. On closer inspection, with her short spiky black hair and slight frame, she looked barely out of her teens. John shook his head. No wonder Bertram was keeping his past indiscretions close to his chest; what would Sylvie think of him if she saw all this? A smile played on John's lips as he imagined the look on her face when she found out the truth about Bertram Wyndom Price – the second. He might have a fancy name, thought John, but he was no gentleman.

John was just walking by, trying to keep a low profile, when Gertie pointed at the other buggy, and shouted, '*Boy!*'

John closed his hand around Gertie's finger as both women stopped arguing and turned to look at them.

He smiled weakly. Avoiding eye contact with the young woman, John thanked the receptionist for the use of the facilities and made a swift exit through the double doors out on to the street. Alfie, thank goodness, was still where he had left him.

Alfie started to bark as soon as he spotted John.

'Shhh!' John turned to look up at the hotel, afraid that Bertram was in one of the hotel rooms overlooking the street and had heard a dog barking. The last thing he wanted was Bertram glancing out the window and catching him outside.

John quickly untied Alfie's lead, thanked the doorman for keeping an eye on him, and then deposited Gertie in the buggy. 'I think it's time for tea and a bun,' said John. They'd earned it. He smiled at his granddaughter as he strapped her into the buggy. 'We make quite a detective duo – you and me.'

Alfie yapped.

'And you too, Alfie,' added John, reaching out to stroke the dog. Although he was well aware it was less about detective work and more about being in the right place at the right time, John could congratulate himself on the fact that he had followed up a lead. And like all good detective yarns, the pieces of the puzzle just seemed to fall into place.

In hindsight, when his sidekick, Gertie, pointed and shouted out *boy,* John knew he could have struck up a conversation with the young woman in the hope of finding out more. But it was totally unnecessary; he had dug up all the dirt he needed on Bertram. You didn't need to be Sherlock Holmes to figure out what was going on. However, as much as John wanted to discover what Bertram was hiding, what he hadn't expected to find was a young woman, with a small child, who was clearly distressed and in need of help.

John was whizzing Gertie up the street, to get as far away from the hotel as quickly as possible, when he passed a cash machine. John stopped abruptly and backtracked. Five minutes later, John was whizzing Gertie back in the opposite direction, taking a huge risk that he might bump into Bertram when he returned to the hotel.

John quickly got Gertie out of her buggy, left Alfie with the doorman, and peered through the double doors. The young woman with the child was gone. *Damn.* Luckily there was still no sign of Bertram. John carried Gertie back into the hotel lobby.

The receptionist spotted him, and said, 'Ah, she needs the toilet again?'

'Nope.' John sat Gertie on the reception desk in front of him. 'Have you got an envelope?'

'An envelope?'

221

'Yes. Something small. Nothing fancy.' John didn't know why he added that last comment. Probably because the hotel was quite fancy.

'Here.' She passed him a small white envelope.

John opened his wallet and got out all the cash he had just withdrawn from his bank account, which was pretty much his entire month's pension. He looked at the wad of notes. This was the first time his pension had not immediately been swallowed up by a hefty overdraft. Sylvie's money was paying all the bills. He didn't have to worry about the roof over his head. It didn't matter if he had to dip into his overdraft this month as a consequence of withdrawing all this money. Thanks to Sylvie, come next month, his pension was free and clear.

He didn't know whether the young woman with the little boy was in some financial straits. Although he had overheard her say she wasn't after Bertram's money, that didn't mean she wasn't here to ask for his help. She could be behind with her rent or have a mortgage and not know how to meet next month's payment.

Perhaps she had debts and loans she was drowning in. John could imagine all sorts of desperate scenarios because, just recently, he had been there himself. He wouldn't wish financial worries on anybody, not least somebody with the responsibility of a child to support.

On the other hand, perhaps she was truthful when she said she didn't need Bertram's money. Whatever the case, John saw a desperately unhappy young woman. Even though he didn't know her, John wanted to help in any way he could.

John stuffed the cash in the envelope. He was about to seal it shut when Gertie shouted, 'No, Grandpa.' John paused to look at his granddaughter, with a bemused expression. 'What's the matter?'

'Gertie lick it.'

'Oh.' John rolled his eyes and nervously cast a glance around the foyer while Gertie took her time licking her way along the edge of the envelope.

When she had finished, John went to take the envelope.

'Noooo.'

'What now?' John said in exasperation.

'Isn't she adorable?' said the receptionist, gazing at Gertie.

John frowned at Gertie, looked at his watch, cast another glance over his shoulder and tapped his foot impatiently. He watched the receptionist hold the envelope flat on the desk while Gertie rolled her fingers into a little podgy fist. She stamped her fist along the edge of the flap, sealing the envelope closed.

'Right, that's it. All done.' John breathed a sigh of relief. 'Now let's give the envelope to the nice lady—'

Gertie grabbed the envelope and tucked it tightly under her armpit. She looked at Grandpa crossly.

'Gertie. That's not yours. Now give it to—'

'NO!'

John was reaching for the envelope, resigned to the fact that he was going to cause a scene, when he heard the receptionist exclaim, 'Wow, what have I got here?'

A pink envelope appeared on the desk in front of Gertie.

'I wonder what's inside.' The receptionist smiled at Gertie. 'Shall we open it and find out?'

John watched his grandchild take a moment to consider. Gertie wasn't stupid. She looked at the receptionist suspiciously before setting her sights on the pink envelope.

A moment later, Gertie was happily eating one of the sweeties inside the envelope. She even offered Grandpa one, although she wouldn't let him near her pink envelope. John didn't mind. He had his envelope back.

John turned to the receptionist. 'Thank you.'

'You're welcome.'

He was about to hand the receptionist the sealed envelope, to give to the young woman, when he realised he hadn't addressed the envelope. 'The young woman who was here earlier . . .' John hoped the receptionist would tell him her name. 'She had short dark hair and a child about Gertie's age, a boy?'

Gertie turned around and gave the receptionist her sweetest smile. 'Boy,' she said.

The receptionist smiled at Gertie, mesmerised by her big blue eyes. 'You must be talking about Amy,' she said, in answer to John's question.

John picked up a pen from the desk and wrote the name *Amy* on the front of the envelope. 'Sorry, I don't mean to be nosey, but I couldn't help overhearing raised voices when I left.'

She sighed. 'It's always the same. She comes, she brings the kid and demands to see him, he refuses, and eventually she leaves.' The receptionist rolled her eyes in exasperation. 'I don't know when she'll get the message.'

'Do you think you can give her this, the next time you see her?' John held up the envelope.

'Of course.' She took the envelope. 'What is it?'

'It's . . . it's a gesture. Tell her . . . just say that it's from a good samaritan. I wanted to help – that's all.'

'I will put it in a safe place and make sure she gets it.'

To John's surprise, she walked out from behind the reception desk and gave him a hug, whispering out of ear-shot of Gertie, 'You've given me hope that not all men are complete losers.'

'I don't know what to say.'

She smiled at John and resumed her place behind the reception desk as two hotel guests walked into the lobby. They were talking in loud voices about a cruise they had just returned from.

John turned around and watched the couple, around his own age, debating whether they were off to the Caribbean or Africa on their next cruise as they headed across the expansive foyer towards the reception desk.

John picked Gertie up, whispering, 'Who cares about seeing the Caribbean or Africa when I get to see you every day.' He smiled at his grandchild as he crossed the foyer. On his way out, John overheard the woman say, 'If you give us a room near that child I'm taking my business elsewhere. I need my beauty sleep.'

John glanced at them and pitied any grandchild of theirs.

'Of course, Madam. I can assure you that won't be a problem. This chain of hotels caters exclusively for adults, and those of a more . . . discerning persuasion.'

'Yeah – right,' scoffed John under his breath, wondering what Bertram was doing here then.

John took Gertie back outside and thanked the doorman once more for keeping an eye on Alfie. He put Gertie in the buggy and headed back to the spot where he had arranged for the taxi to pick them up. Next stop was the little café in Baker Street for a drink and a teacake. John was looking forward to it. What he wasn't looking forward to was returning home this afternoon and telling Sylvie the unsavoury truth about Bertram. She deserved better. And so did Amy – whoever she was.

21

Sylvie frantically checked her watch. She had arrived home from work and legged it up the garden path, expecting John to throw open the front door like he usually did. Imagine her surprise when this didn't happen. Sylvie had nearly run right into the front door. She rang the doorbell and knocked but to no avail. Luckily, she had her door key. Sylvie had unlocked the door and stepped into a deserted hallway. John, Gertie, and Alfie were nowhere to be found.

That was ten minutes ago. Sylvie checked the time; it was now almost half past five. Harriet would be arriving any minute to collect Gertie. 'Good grief! Where are they?' She looked out the lounge window, up and down the street. There was still no sign of them. Sylvie threw her arms in the air. This had never happened to her before. But it had happened to John – plenty of times – when she got held up in traffic or lost track of time. Although she always managed to make it home just in time, Sylvie had no idea how stressful it must have been for John until she was on the receiving end.

Sylvie frowned as an unpleasant thought occurred to her. Things had been going swimmingly until she invited Bertram back for coffee and John discovered she was seeing someone. Then it all changed. It was the Monday after that disastrous weekend. Sylvie didn't come home to find John had cleared away her breakfast dishes or hung her washing out, or done any ironing, or hoovered and tidied up. She cast her eye around her apartment; it was exactly as she had left it when she walked out this morning. In fact, it was worse because for some reason, hitherto unexplained, there was a pile of damp towels on her bathroom floor.

Sylvie wasn't really bothered about a bit of tidying up. She wasn't a neat freak like her husband. But she had missed returning home, after a long day at work, to the smell of something baking in her oven. Today there was no chicken pie with the heavenly shortcrust pastry. No home-baked cookies or cakes. Not even a vase of fresh flowers on the kitchen table.

And there was no sign of Gertie and John.

Sylvie was standing there bemoaning the fact that John hadn't done all those things he usually did, and perhaps this was his way of getting back at her over Bertram when a ghastly thought occurred to her; what if he had been unable to do any chores because something untoward had happened today? What if he wasn't here because something had happened to Gertie and he had to take her to A&E?

Only then did it occur to Sylvie to ring his mobile phone. She had been in such a panic when she arrived home and discovered they weren't in, that she didn't know what to do. Sylvie was just reaching for her bag to find her phone in case John had left her a message, when she glanced out the window and spotted John pushing the buggy along the street.

'Oh, thank heavens!' Sylvie raced out of the house to meet

them. She forgot to prop the front door open on her way out. It drifted shut behind her. She opened the gate for them and peered at her granddaughter in the buggy. Gertie looked fine and dandy. Sylvie smiled at her in relief. She turned to John. 'Where on earth have you been? Do you know what the time is?'

'Of course I know what time it is!' John barked in frustration. He was struggling to get Gertie's buggy through the garden gate.

Sylvie relieved him of Gertie's pink bag and slung it over her shoulder. She then took Alfie's lead.

Alfie jumped up at Sylvie, excited to see her, and left black muddy paw prints on her new cashmere coat.

John caught Alfie misbehaving. 'Down!'

Alfie immediately stopped jumping up at Sylvie and walked obediently by the side of the buggy.

Sylvie and John were making their way up the garden path together when the taxi ferrying Harriet to her parents' house pulled up outside.

Harriet glanced out of the taxi window and saw them. Typically, when she arrived from work, they were already home. It was a pleasant surprise to catch her parents bringing their grandchild home after a day out together. Harriet sat in the back of the taxi savouring the moment. At first, she wasn't sure how things would work out when they both started looking after Gertie. Quite frankly, with all that had been going on at home, she wasn't convinced they could set aside their differences and be civil to one another. Let alone spend every day together looking after Gertie.

Harriet opened her purse to pay the cab driver, smiling at the thought that perhaps spending more time together would put an end to this living apart nonsense.

'Where in heaven's name were you?' asked Sylvie as they approached the front door. 'I was going out of my mind with worry. What on earth were you thinking?'

John glared at her. He had half a mind to tell her exactly what he was thinking – for once she had a taste of what he went through most evenings when he was forced to wait on tenterhooks for her to arrive, praying Harriet didn't turn up first. Thanks to Sylvie, that was a regular occurrence.

Instead, John held his tongue and told her the reason they had been delayed. 'I took Gertie to the little café in Baker Street, opposite the Sherlock Holmes museum, but I didn't account for how long it would take to get home.'

He looked sheepishly at Sylvie. What John didn't account for was how long it would take to get home on the bus. He had deposited all the money he'd withdrawn from the bank into the envelope for the young woman called Amy. The problem was, after tea and a bun in Baker Street, John didn't leave himself with enough money for the taxi home. That was a stupid oversight on his part. John had enough loose change for a bus ride home; however, the journey took twice as long.

'Sorry,' said John as he unlocked the front door.

'You took Gertie to the little café in Baker Street where we used to take the girls?'

'Uh-huh.' John pushed Gertie's buggy into the hall, resisting the urge to tell Sylvie what else they had been up to today. It was bad enough that he had arrived home in the nick of time, without causing a scene by raising the subject of Bertram just before Harriet turned up. He doubted Harriet would be pleased if she arrived to find them having an almighty row in front of Gertie.

'I haven't been to that café since the girls were small,' mused Sylvie as she looped Gertie's pink bag over the handle of the buggy.

'It hasn't changed a bit, Sylvie. I must confess it was strange sitting there with Gertie. Looking at her across the table, it's as though someone had turned back the clock. I could have been sitting there with Harriet.' John smiled at his grandchild and then looked over at Sylvie. 'I wish you could have been there,' John blurted.

'So do I.'

John raised an eyebrow, surprised by that remark.

They both fell silent.

Sylvie smiled at Gertie, dozing in her buggy. She glanced at Alfie sitting obediently beside the buggy. Finally, Sylvie raised her eyes to look at John. He was standing to attention, at the end of the line-up, ready for Harriet's arrival. But he wasn't watching the door.

John was staring at his wife. 'Sylvie, do you remember the first time we took all three girls to the Natural History Museum?'

Sylvie furrowed her brow. 'The first time?'

'Yes – you remember. It was when Jess scared the living daylights out of us by disappearing. I left you with the girls while I went to find her.'

'Oh goodness, yes. How could I forget?' Sylvie cupped her hand to her mouth stifling a laugh. 'Sorry, I know it wasn't funny at the time, but I really didn't expect you to find her having a ride on Dippy the Diplodocus.'

'Me neither.' John started to laugh.

As Harriet approached the house, she heard laughter coming from inside. She stopped on the doorstep and looked at the front door in surprise. After all these months of uncertainty over where her parents' marriage was leading, Harriet could hardly believe what she was hearing. Perhaps Dad had been right after all and that spending more time together, through sharing the responsibility of looking after their grandchild, would bring them closer together. It certainly sounded like it from where she was standing.

Harriet stood there thinking that at least her parents weren't stressed out over their change in circumstances, taking over the childcare of Gertie. Unfortunately, Harriet didn't feel the same way about her change in circumstances, returning to full-time work. She hated every minute of it. She missed Gertie and desperately wanted to return to her part-time job. However, financially it just wasn't possible.

Harriet raised her hand to knock on the door. She paused a moment longer to listen to their laughter. There wasn't much laughter at her house these days. Harriet had been away from the rigours of a full-time work commitment for nearly two and a half years. Before she became a mother, Harriet was a career woman through and through. She thought nothing of working long hours at the office and bringing work home with her. Her career was her life.

When she returned to work full time, she assumed she could easily find that career woman she once was. She thought she'd enjoy returning to the cut and thrust of a high-flying career. Harriet soon discovered she was kidding herself. She had no idea how much having her first child would change her priorities.

Harriet didn't mind when she was working as an editor part-time and doing freelance work. She was working practically the same hours as before. The difference was she had more freedom.

There was more flexibility to fit her work around her home life, and not the other way around. She had got used to that.

Returning to work full time had been a mistake, not financially; they needed the money. After losing her freelance work, she had no choice. Professionally speaking, she was back on track. But on a personal level, being away from her child all week was taking its toll. Harriet's heart wasn't in it. This was causing tensions and rows at home because Harriet wanted a way out and there wasn't one. She was stuck, and she knew it.

She couldn't see what good had come out of her current predicament until she arrived in the taxi this evening and saw her parents together. From what she had seen, it was just possible that the change in her circumstances had inadvertently saved their marriage. She didn't expect that to happen. In fact, every time Harriet had handed Gertie over in the morning, she sensed something she couldn't put her finger on, like there was tension in the air even though her parents were always smiling. Everything was perfect – too perfect.

Harriet had started to get paranoid that her parents weren't being straight with her and something was going on. However, this evening, catching them both together looking after Gertie, had put a stop to her feelings of paranoia, which she suspected in part wasn't really helping her cope in her job.

It dawned on her that while she was at work, she had been inexplicably worried about Gertie. Now she knew why. Harriet didn't believe they were taking care of Gertie together until she had seen it with her own eyes. Perhaps now she could finally put her head in her job and stop taking it out on Dominic. She breathed a sigh of relief and knocked on the door.

John answered with a smile.

Sylvie was sitting on the bottom stair bouncing Gertie up and down on her knee.

Alfie padded over to greet Harriet. He sat down in front of her and raised a front paw in the air.

John said, 'I've been teaching him some new tricks – that's hello.'

Harriet laughed and knelt down to shake his paw. She gave her dad a sideways glance. She was never allowed to have a pet as a child because Daddy didn't want animals in the house. Daddy didn't like pets. Harriet looked at Alfie and still found it strange that, after all these years, they finally succumbed to getting a pet – and a dog at that. The funny thing was Harriet always imagined her dad with a cat, probably because cats were so clean.

Harriet found a tissue in her bag and wiped her hands after shaking Alfie's muddy paw. She put the tissue in her pocket and made a big fuss of the cute spaniel. Harriet wished she could take Alfie home with her. She'd always dreamed of getting a dog. As soon as she bought her first house with Dominic, that's what she intended to do, but he said it was impractical because they were both working full time. Then she was going to get a puppy when Gertie was born. She wanted their child to have the experience of growing up with a pet; something Harriet had never had the opportunity to do. Dominic wavered but talked her out of it by going on and on about how she wouldn't have the time to look after a baby *and* a pet.

Harriet sighed as she watched Gertie get down from Grandma's knee and sit on the floor by Grandma's feet.

Alfie came bounding over and skidded to a halt in front of Gertie. He licked her face.

Gertie said, 'No, Alfie,' and wiped her face with the sleeve of her jumper. She then put her little arms around his neck and gave him a cuddle.

Harriet walked over and gave Gertie a kiss before sitting down on the bottom stair next to her mum. She watched Alfie raise his paw for Gertie.

'Good dog,' said Gertie, shaking his paw.

Harriet couldn't help but smile. She guessed Gertie would grow up with a pet after all – thanks to her grandparents.

John stood at the door looking around the hall at this happy familial scene. Sylvie and Harriet were sitting together on the bottom stair chatting about her day at work. Alfie was doing tricks for Gertie, rolling over and making her fall about in fits of giggles. It brought back happy memories of a time before the conversion when the house used to be a home and they were still together.

In the heat of the moment, John asked, 'Harriet, would you like to stay for supper? Your mother and I are quite partial to my homemade chicken pies.'

Harriet looked at him curiously. '*Your* homemade chicken pies? Since when did you start baking?'

Since I started living on my own upstairs, thought John frowning. He brightened. 'Actually, I rather enjoy it. It's nice to have some hobbies.'

Now it was Sylvie's turn to look at John curiously. Since when did he like hobbies?

'I made one earlier and left it in Sylvie's fridge. My shortcrust pastry is to die for. All we need to do is heat it up.' John didn't add that he left it in Sylvie's fridge this time, rather than her oven, because he wasn't sure whether she might have arranged to go out with Bertram tonight.

'You made a chicken pie today?' said Sylvie in surprise. She only had a cursory glance around her apartment when she returned home but didn't think to look in her fridge.

'Yep, I made the pie when Gertie had a nap this morning – remember?' John cast a nervous glance in Harriet's direction.

'Oh . . . yes of course. I forgot. How silly of me,' said Sylvie, quickly trying to cover up her gaffe. She stole a glance at Harriet. Thankfully, Harriet didn't notice.

'That's really kind of you to offer, Dad, but Dominic is cooking tonight, and I promised him I'd be home by six.'

Sylvie studied her daughter's profile. Harriet had deep dark rings under her eyes, a sure sign she wasn't sleeping properly. Sylvie knew her daughter; if something was on her mind, then her sleep was the first thing affected. Sylvie put an arm around Harriet's shoulders. 'You seem a little tired. Is everything all right at work?'

'Nothing I can't handle,' replied Harriet, not really handling her job anymore but not wanting to worry her parents; there was nothing they could do about it. At least she knew Gertie was in good hands – *two* pairs of good hands. If it wasn't for that, she really thought it would all implode. At least she knew she could rely on them.

As Harriet gathered up Gertie's bag, preparing to leave, John opened the front door and caught sight of a bus going by with Gertie's sweet face plastered on a huge poster advertisement along the side.

'Crickey!' exclaimed John, and slammed the door shut.

Harriet, Sylvie, Gertie, and even the dog, all stopped what they were doing and stared at John.

'What's wrong?' Sylvie and Harriet spoke in unison.

John smiled nervously. 'Oh . . . er . . . nothing.'

'It couldn't have been *nothing*,' persisted Sylvie, folding her arms.

John looked at Gertie. He was trying to think on his feet, which wasn't easy with all of them staring fixedly at him.

Alfie saved the day by doing his new trick again. He held up his paw to Sylvie this time.

'That is the cutest trick,' marvelled Harriet as Sylvie took his paw. 'I wish I could have a pet.'

Sylvie frowned. 'Just go and get one – what's stopping you?'

'Dominic.'

Sylvie glanced John's way. 'I see.'

'He said that now I've returned to work full time it would be impossible to get a pet.' Harriet didn't mention that it was just the latest in a long line of excuses. When she was only in her job part-time, and doing freelance work from home, she would have had time for a puppy. She wished she hadn't listened to her husband. Perhaps she'd have one now and it wouldn't be a puppy anymore, but all grown up like Alfie.

Harriet sighed. 'Well, I'd best be off.' She rose from the stair and scooped Gertie up into her arms.

'Nooo.' Gertie tried to wriggle free. 'Alfie.'

'You'll see him tomorrow, darling, with Grandma and Grandpa.'

Sylvie pursed her lips. She was feeling terribly guilty at the thought that, unbeknown to Harriet, she wouldn't be spending the day with Gertie. It was on her mind what would happen if Harriet discovered their little charade. It was up to both of them to make sure that didn't happen. She looked across the hall at John and watched him open the front door a crack. He appeared to be hiding behind the door. Sylvie rolled her eyes. What in heavens name had got into him?

John was standing at the front door peeking outside, checking the coast was clear. *Crickey*, how many London buses were driving around with Gertie's face plastered on the side? John had no idea. He had taken Gertie to so many auditions and photoshoots that he had lost track of the specific details of each advertising campaign. It made him wonder where she might pop up next.

Sometime soon John would have to spill the beans and tell Harriet all about Gertie's extra-curricular activities. Otherwise, it was highly likely she was going to find out what they had been up to. Gertie had proved quite a hit with the model agency and their clients. She was earning so much money that John could, if he wanted to, skim of his chaperone's fee and she would still be left with a sizeable lump to add to her savings pot. He didn't do that because, thanks to Sylvie, he no longer needed the money.

Sylvie walked over to stand by John at the front door while Harriet put Gertie in the buggy. He was still hiding behind the door. She looked at him askance. 'Is there a problem, John?'

John jumped at the sound of Sylvie's voice right behind him. He turned around. 'Nope. Everything is tickety-boo.'

'I see.' Sylvie stared at him. 'Do you mind opening the door, so Harriet and Gertie can leave?'

John looked past Sylvie at Harriet standing behind her with the buggy. 'Yes, of course.' John took one more peek outside before he threw the door wide open. 'The coast is clear.'

'Pardon me?'

John smiled nervously. 'Er . . . what I meant to say was it's a clear night.'

Sylvie narrowed her eyes. John was up to something – she could tell.

She was about to ask him what was going on when Harriet stopped in front of her on the way out.

Harriet gave her mum a hug. 'You know how much this means to me, both of you looking after Gertie.'

Sylvie caught John throwing her an apologetic look. They'd had a near-miss this evening when he turned up with Gertie at the last minute. Any later and Harriet would have arrived first. Then their little charade would have been over. Sylvie made a silent promise that from now on she would always make it home from work in good time.

Harriet was just pushing Gertie's buggy out of the house, when John said, 'Would you like a lift home in the car?' He gestured at his car parked on the driveway. 'I've had a car seat fitted for Gertie.'

'You have?' said Sylvie in surprise.

John turned to Sylvie and raised his eyebrows.

'Oh yes, silly me, I forgot,' Sylvie lied. She stared at the car. What on earth did he need a car seat for? The park was just around the corner and the public library was one stop on the bus. Sylvie couldn't imagine where John was taking her in the car.

Harriet paused. It was dark already and the wind was picking up. She looked at Dad's car and was tempted. However, this evening she rather fancied walking. Besides, she was chained to a desk all day at work so walking home from her parents' house was the only exercise she had during the week.

Harriet glanced up at the cloudless night sky. 'Maybe next time, Dad. If it's raining, we will definitely need a lift home.'

'Right you are.'

Sylvie looked at John. Perhaps the car seat wasn't a bad idea after all.

Harriet walked down the garden path and turned Gertie's buggy in the direction of home, a twenty-minute walk away. She paused at the garden gate and waved at her parents standing together on the front porch. Today, Harriet was going to enjoy the walk home because today she was quite certain that her parents weren't getting a divorce.

Setting off down the street, pushing the buggy, Harriet glanced over her shoulder at the house she grew up in. She was nearly forty, she had a family of her own, and her parents had their own lives to lead now. Whatever they did, however they chose to lead their lives, really was none of her concern. It was entirely out of her hands.

The problem was it did concern her – very much. Harriet knew, deep down, that her world would never be the same again if her parents weren't together. Since her mum moved into the apartment downstairs, it was a reality she had been trying to prepare herself for, but one she didn't really want to face. And now, by the looks of things, she didn't have to. Harriet smiled as she walked Gertie home, feeling far happier than she had felt in ages.

Harriet was already well out of ear-shot and did not hear the almighty row that erupted when John told Sylvie what he had been up to with the rest of his day.

'I don't believe it!' Sylvie pointed at John. 'You were at The Rooftop Café today. Were you spying on me? When you saw me outside, did you follow me?'

John peered at Sylvie and knitted his brows. He was pretty sure he'd just told her that Bertram had a hotel room around the corner from the café. He hadn't got so far as to tell her about a certain young lady he had seen in the hotel demanding to see Bertram. He didn't get a chance before Sylvie lifted off.

'Well?' Sylvie put her hands on her hips. 'Did you follow me?'

'No, I did not follow you.'

Sylvie inwardly breathed a sigh of relief.

John frowned. She didn't seem that concerned about the hotel around the corner. It made John wonder if she already knew about the hotel room. It made John wonder if, on occasion, they did more with their lunch breaks than just have lunch.

'Did you know about the hotel room?' demanded John.

'Hotel room?' Sylvie didn't give a fig about a hotel room. What she was more concerned about was that John might have discovered where she worked. She had promised Marcia Hunt that nobody would find out she was writing under the pseudonym, Love on the Rooftop. And Marcia meant *nobody* – not even her husband. Sylvie intended to keep that promise. To that end, she could well do without John snooping around. He hadn't followed her this time, but what if he got curious? What if turned up at the café again and decided to follow her instead of Bertram?

'Well, what about that room in the hotel around the corner?' John was convinced she was hiding something.

Sylvie glared at him. 'In answer to your question, John, I did not know about the hotel room. However, I wouldn't be at all surprised if he is staying in a hotel.'

'Oh.' John realised he had been too quick to jump to conclusions and hadn't thought of the most obvious explanation: Bertram didn't live in London. He was probably just here on business – whatever that was. It was good news if he was because there was no way Sylvie would up sticks and move out of London.

'Is he in London on business?' John blurted. 'Wait a minute. It's pointless asking you because you don't know the first thing about him,' John said sarcastically. He didn't add that he was intent on finding out for himself.

'Actually, John, after you kindly pointed that out this morning,' said Sylvie, returning the sarcasm, 'I decided to find out more about him.' Sylvie smiled. 'Which I did over lunch today.'

John gaped at her. 'And?' He expected her to tell him to mind his own business. She didn't.

'The reason I'm not surprised he has a hotel room in The Grand Hotel,' continued Sylvie evenly, 'is that he owns the hotel. In fact, he owns the whole chain. He's got hotels in London, Paris, New York, Dubai . . .' Sylvie ticked them off her fingers like some sort of grocery list. 'Gosh, there's so many I can't recall them all. You see, it turns out he's a very wealthy, successful businessman, John.'

John took that as it was intended – a personal dig.

Sylvie continued enjoying putting John in the picture. 'The reason he was reticent about telling me all this was that he wanted something real. He had to be sure that he was starting a relationship with somebody who genuinely wanted to be with him and was not just after his money. Apparently, he's had some bad experiences in the past.'

'Really?' John saw his opening. 'Has he told you about those bad experiences, by any chance?' asked John, gearing up to tell Sylvie all about one called Amy.

'Well – no. I think they are too painful and he would rather not.'

I'll bet, thought John. 'Look, Sylvie, there's something you should know . . .'

Sylvie walked over to her apartment and opened the door. She stepped inside and turned around to look at John. 'Whatever it is you think you're going to tell me to make me change my mind about Bertram – save it.'

John opened his mouth to say it anyway, before Sylvie added, 'Whatever you think you've got on Bertram, I wouldn't believe it coming from *you*.' She glared at John across the hall.

John shut his mouth.

Sylvie slammed her door shut.

'Damn and blast!' John stood in the empty hall staring at her door. She didn't understand that he only had her best interests at heart. As much as he didn't want to see her in a relationship with another man, more importantly, he didn't want her to get hurt. Bertram wasn't the man she thought he was. But she was right: no matter what he said, she wouldn't believe a word that came out of his mouth. John shook his head. Unfortunately, Sylvie would have to find out the truth for herself.

22

Despite keeping up appearances for Harriet's sake, barely a word had passed between them the rest of the week. Sylvie made sure of it. What he had done was totally unacceptable. When she invited Bertram in for coffee, it was one thing John knocking on her door and being a general nuisance. It was another thing spying on them at The Rooftop Café. It was still playing on her mind, the thought that John could easily have followed her back to work. What if there was a next time? For the rest of the week, Sylvie found herself continually looking over her shoulder when she met up with Bertram for lunch.

Sylvie walked over to the fridge and looked at the paper napkin, stuck to the fridge door, with Bertram's phone number scrawled across it. Her eyes drifted to the name of the café printed in large black lettering along the edge of the napkin. If only she hadn't kept it, then John would have had no idea where they met for lunch.

Sylvie sighed and took it down from the fridge. She had already written down Bertram's number in her diary but kept the napkin for sentimental reasons; it was a reminder of when and where they first met. Now, every time she looked at it, it was a reminder of how stupid she'd been leaving it around for John to find. She scrunched it into a ball and threw it in the bin. Still, it could have been worse, thought Sylvie. John could have followed her back to work and discovered her secret.

Sylvie was under no illusions that everything she had – this apartment, her financial independence, even Bertram – was all built on a lie. John could so easily have discovered the truth and outed her as the writer by the name of Love on the Rooftop. Then where would she be? She risked losing her flat, her career and her new friend.

Bertram knew she was a writer and worked as a columnist for a magazine in London. But he wasn't aware of the lies she was spinning every week for her readers. If he found out, would he believe her when she told him that it was all just a fiction? Or would he think that she hadn't been honest with him and she was still with her husband albeit living apart together?

Perhaps he'd start to wonder if they were in some kind of open relationship. She was aware he had been hurt before although she didn't know the details. The last thing Sylvie wanted to become was just another part of his baggage that he would rather forget. Bertram came across as such a nice, kind, decent person that whatever John thought he had on Bertram, whatever John was so eager to tell her, nothing was going to change Sylvie's opinion of him. *Nothing*.

Sylvie's mobile phone bleeped with a text message. Bertram had arrived in the taxi to pick her up for dinner. He was waiting outside. Bertram had no desire to set foot inside her apartment after the last time. Sylvie had a sneaking suspicion he was more afraid of the dog than John.

Sylvie glanced at Alfie lying in his basket. He was looking up at her with those sad brown eyes, doing his best to make her feel guilty that she was going out and leaving him home alone. She bent over, gave him an affectionate pat on the head, and promised that she wouldn't be gone long. Just dinner and coffee afterwards at Bertram's place.

Unfortunately for Alfie, Sylvie had no intention of asking John to look after him this time. Sylvie wouldn't make the same mistake twice. However, as it turned out Alfie didn't have the option of spending the evening in the apartment upstairs because John had gone out.

Ten minutes ago, Sylvie had been standing by the window waiting for Bertram to turn up when a taxi drew up outside. Sylvie had grabbed her coat and rushed to the door. She was wondering why Bertram hadn't texted to let her know he'd arrived, when she heard the sound of heavy footfalls racing down the stairs. Then the front door in the communal hall banged shut. From the window, Sylvie saw John striding down the garden path. He was looking very dapper in a smart black suit. How odd. John never went out on a Saturday night, or any night for that matter.

Sylvie had strained to see if somebody else was in the back of the taxi, like Barbara for instance. John opened the car door. The light in the cab illuminated the inside. He was alone. She wondered who John was spending the evening with. Sylvie had wondered about that as they made their way to the restaurant, then all through dinner, while they danced afterwards, and even during the taxi ride over to Bertram's place.

Finally, Bertram turned to Sylvie, and said, 'You've seemed preoccupied this evening.'

'Have I? Sorry.'

'Don't apologise, Sylvie. Look, I know what it's about.'

'You do?' Sylvie hoped not. She wouldn't want him to know that although she had spent the evening with him, she had spent the entire time thinking about John.

As they arrived at the apartment building where Bertram lived, he said, 'You hardly know me, and you are coming back to my place for coffee – alone.'

Sylvie looked at him in surprise. What a peculiar thing to say. Suddenly she wasn't preoccupied with John anymore but the thought that she hadn't told John – or anybody else for that matter – where she was going this evening after the restaurant meal. If Bertram was trying to get out of having coffee at his place, then it was working.

'That's why you've been preoccupied all evening.'

'Oh . . . I see.' Sylvie stared at Bertram and decided not to tell him the truth. In fact, Sylvie hadn't given it a second thought until he brought it up. Now, after what he said, Sylvie was thinking that going to Bertram's place for coffee was a bad idea. Sylvie looked out of the car window at the apartment building. She turned to Bertram. 'John has gone out this evening so why don't we go back to my place for coffee instead?'

'But we're here now.' Bertram leaned forward and handed the cab driver the fare. 'The lady is just popping up to my place for coffee. Will you wait here for say half an hour, to take her home?' Bertram handed over two more twenty-pound notes.

The taxi driver looked at the cash. 'You want me to sit here doing nothing for half an hour?'

Bertram nodded.

'Well, it's your money, mate.' The taxi driver shrugged as he pocketed the cash from the well-dressed dude in the back.

Sylvie stepped out of the taxi and glanced at the driver. He had leaned his head on the headrest, closed his eyes and dozed off. She lowered her voice. 'Bertram, that really wasn't necessary.'

'I know, but I just wanted to put you at ease that I'm not some psycho.'

Sylvie's face coloured. 'Oh, I didn't think that.'

Bertram smiled at Sylvie. 'All writers have quite an active imagination, and I'm sure you're no different.'

Sylvie's face went a deeper shade of purple. She wished he hadn't said that, considering the basis of her work at the moment.

'Besides, I really didn't fancy having another run-in with your dog. I don't think he likes me.'

'He'll come around once he gets to know you.' He better do, thought Sylvie, because she had a feeling this friendship might, just might, be going somewhere.

'Let me introduce you to Maurice and Alfred.'

'Who?'

At the door to the apartment building, Maurice, the doorman, was impeccably dressed in a grey pinstripe suit. He was also wearing a dark wool coat to keep out the winter chill in the air. There was a single cream carnation in the top left buttonhole of his coat. His dapper outfit was topped off by a bowler hat. He looked like he had just stepped out of another era – or a film set. If Bertram hadn't pointed him out first, Sylvie would have mistaken him for another resident who lived in the building.

Maurice opened the door and tipped his hat. 'Good evening, Mr Wyndom-Price.'

'It's Bertram – remember?'

'Of course, Mr Wyndom-Price.'

'Can I introduce you to Sylvie?'

'Good evening, madam.'

Sylvie smiled. 'Hello.'

'She's popping up to have a cup of coffee with me. When she leaves, would you be so kind as to show her to the taxi waiting outside?'

'Of course, Mr Wyndom-Price.'

'It's Bertram.'

'Yes, sir.'

On the way through the lobby, Bertram whispered to Sylvie that he had been trying to get on a first name basis with Maurice for years.

'Have you lived here long, Bertram?'

'I've owned the apartment building since it was first built. I kept one of the apartments to use when I'm in London.'

Sylvie's eyes went wide. She had no idea he owned the whole building. Sylvie was getting the impression that she may have underestimated just how wealthy her friend, Bertram, was.

'The trouble is, Sylvie, I hardly ever use the apartment. I much prefer to stay in one of my hotels. In fact, that's the reason we first met. I often stop by The Rooftop Café for lunch because I have a suite at The Grand Hotel just around the corner.'

'You do?' said Sylvie, feigning surprise. She was trying not to think about that conversation with John yesterday evening, when he told her he'd followed Bertram to The Grand Hotel. She was still seething over the fact that John was spying on them.

'Yes, you see I find it rather lonely when I'm in my apartment all by myself. A hotel has more going on. I can go to the bar, the restaurant, and . . . well it beats sitting on my own all evening.

'You should get a pet.'

Bertram smiled. 'That is a consideration, Sylvie. But as you know, I travel extensively with work and, to be honest, pets don't make the best conversation. And you can't take them dancing.'

Sylvie laughed. 'That's true.' She was relieved Bertram had brought up the hotel room because she had a feeling John was building up to say something. She didn't know what it was. However, Sylvie was convinced it was nothing of consequence, especially now Bertram had told her about his reasons for keeping a room in a hotel. It made perfect sense.

'I wouldn't dream of inviting you back to my hotel room for coffee,' said Bertram as they walked into the lobby of the apartment building.

'Why ever not?'

'Well, er wouldn't it smack of impropriety, inviting a lady up to one's bedroom on the second date?'

'Oh – I see.' Sylvie hadn't thought of that. She gave him a sideways glance. Whatever John thought he had on Bertram, there was no denying he was a gentleman through and through.

They approached the front desk where a young security guard, by the name of Alfred, greeted them. 'Hey Bertram, how goes things?' He glanced at Sylvie and grinned. 'Is this your hot date?'

Bertram introduced Sylvie.

'Pleased to meet you,' said Alfred.

'Likewise,' responded Sylvie, smiling at the friendly young man.

As they rode up in the lift, Bertram explained that Alfred was new and that he and Maurice didn't exactly get along like a house on fire. 'Maurice is kind of old school. You can see how they rub each other up the wrong way.'

Sylvie smiled. She was feeling very foolish that it had even crossed her mind Bertram might not be all that he appeared.

The lift travelled to the top floor. When the lift doors opened, Sylvie was surprised to find they didn't step out into a hallway as she had expected. The lift doors opened directly into his apartment.

'It's the penthouse suite,' explained Bertram, noting her surprise.

Sylvie knitted her brow. 'But what if a stranger walked into this lift, couldn't they get into your apartment from the lobby downstairs?'

'Not unless they have the key to this lift, Sylvie. It's a private lift to the penthouse apartment only.'

When they stepped out of the lift, the doors remained open ready for her to leave after coffee. 'If you are trying to impress me, you're succeeding,' joked Sylvie.

'Oh, I didn't bring you up here to show off.'

'I bet you say that to all the girls.'

Bertram's smile faltered.

She touched his arm. 'I'm only joking, Bertram.'

Joking aside, Sylvie couldn't fail to be impressed as he led the way across the expansive reception room towards a set of double doors at the far end. The sound of Sylvie's heels echoed on the marble floor as she followed Bertram. When he stopped at the double doors and flung them wide open, Sylvie gasped.

It wasn't the room that had taken her by surprise. Although the enormous sitting room, with its vaulted ceiling, did take her aback. But what really caught Sylvie's attention was the view of the London skyline from the floor-to-ceiling windows that ran the length of the room. Even though it was dark outside, the views of the city were spectacular. Sylvie walked up to the window. 'This certainly beats the views from The Rooftop Café.'

The Rooftop Café was only six floors up, whereas Bertram's apartment was on the top floor of a twenty storey high-rise. Sylvie didn't think she had ever been this high up before.

Bertram walked over and stood beside her. 'I wish I could show you the magnificent views from my hotels in Paris, New York, Dubai, Budapest . . .'

'Now you *are* showing off.'

'Pick a city, and we'll go tonight.'

Sylvie gave Bertram a sideways glance. 'That's crazy.'

'Is it?'

Sylvie regarded her wealthy friend. A weekend break in Paris or New York sounded out of this world. 'Would we be back by Monday?' Sylvie said half in jest, not really believing she would jet off with him at the drop of a hat.

'Can't you take your work with you?'

Sylvie wasn't thinking about work. What was on her mind was John, and the silent promise she had made never to be late for Gertie's handover. Sylvie inwardly sighed. It was a nice dream while it lasted, but she wasn't jetting off anywhere. Sylvie turned around and stared at the London skyline once more. She smiled. Who needed Paris or New York when you lived in the best city in the world?

Sylvie was drinking in the view when she noticed a glass door that led outside. She walked over and peered through the door; it was pitch black out. She turned around. 'Bertram, does your penthouse apartment have a rooftop garden?'

'A rooftop garden? That's a strange question.'

Sylvie pointed at the door that led outside.

'Ah, I see why you might think that. I'm afraid not, Sylvie. But I do have a rather nice balcony.' He flicked on a switch illuminating a small rectangular shaped balcony. There were a couple of topiary plants, in one corner, looking a bit sad and neglected.

'Oh.' Sylvie couldn't hide her disappointment. She stared at the bland patio guessing that Bertram didn't venture out there much – if at all. Perhaps the balcony would be more appealing in daylight, thought Sylvie.

'If it means that much to you, I can buy you one.'

'I'm sorry – what?'

'A penthouse apartment with a rooftop garden.'

Sylvie started to laugh. She stopped abruptly when she caught the look on Bertram's face and realised he was serious.

'Actually, it's not a bad idea if I do say so myself,' continued Bertram. 'It would kill two birds with one stone. You would have your rooftop garden, and I could get you out from under John – pardon the expression.' Bertram guffawed. 'That way, I could come over to your place for coffee without the constant inter-ruptions from your neighbour upstairs.' The look on Bertram's face said he thought it was a done deal.

Sylvie frowned at Bertram. She didn't need somebody else telling her how she should lead her life or where she could live. She already had a husband who had proved quite adept at doing that.

Sensing Sylvie wasn't that enamoured by his suggestion, he swiftly changed the subject. 'Please sit down, Sylvie, and I'll go and make some coffee.' Bertram indicated the L-shaped cream leather sofa that faced a huge wall-mounted plasma television.

Reluctantly, Sylvie sat down. She perched on the end of the

sofa and nearly slid off the smooth leather upholstery. Sylvie caught herself just in time.

Bertram had left by way of the double doors into the lobby. She heard his footsteps on the marble floor as he headed to the kitchen somewhere deep inside the mammoth apartment.

Sylvie glanced up at the giant plasma television mounted on the wall in front of her. Although she already knew he owned a string of hotels around the world, she didn't appreciate how wealthy he was until the moment he had, in all seriousness, offered to buy her an apartment with a rooftop garden right here in London. Something like that, in a building like this, would cost several million pounds. Sylvie looked around his penthouse apartment and got the impression that it was just small change to someone as wealthy as Bertram.

Sylvie felt out of her depth and out of her comfort zone. She wanted to go home to her cosy little flat and her old tube television and her scruffy dog. This was a mistake. Besides, with all his money doubtless women would be falling at his feet. Bertram could date virtually any woman he wanted. It made Sylvie wonder *why her*? Why not someone half her age? With that thought, Sylvie got up to leave. She scooped up her black clutch bag and walked through the double doors into the lobby.

She was about to step into the lift when the sound of a phone ringing startled her. Sylvie stopped beside an expensive oak sideboard and looked at the phone. She didn't know whether to answer the phone, call out for Bertram, or just get in the lift.

Sylvie sighed, and called out, 'Bertram!' She looked to her left, down a long hallway, and then to her right which was a mirror image. By the time she had called out his name once more and dithered which way might be the kitchen, the phone had stopped ringing and the answerphone had clicked in. Sylvie remained rooted to the spot on hearing a young woman's voice.

Bertram? Please answer your phone. I only want to talk to you. Look, I'm sorry about the way I behaved at The Grand Hotel on Monday.

'Monday?' said Sylvie out loud. Wasn't that the day John was there spying on Bertram? Was this what he was trying to tell her?

I just wanted to say, thanks for leaving me the money in the envelope. I know it was you. I really appreciate it – for Rory's sake. I don't care if you turn your back on me, but Rory needs you.

Sylvie could hear the unmistakable sound of a young child, a toddler, in the background. She shook her head in dismay; so this was what Bertram didn't want to talk about. This was his baggage. Little wonder he started dating older women, thought Sylvie bitterly. At least he was safe in the knowledge that women her age had put their child-rearing days behind them.

The lift doors were just closing when Bertram walked into the lobby carrying a silver tray, with a napkin draped over his arm.

'Sylvie?' He blinked in surprise when he caught a glimpse of her before the lift doors closed. Unsure whether his eyes were playing tricks on him, he glanced through the double doors into the empty lounge. Then Bertram caught sight of the red light blinking on his answerphone.

Bertram put the silver tray down on the sideboard and played the message. He pressed the *stop* button as soon as he heard her voice. Bertram rolled his eyes in the direction of the lift. He didn't have to listen to the entire message to guess what had just happened.

'Oh hells bells!'

23

In the evenings, after a day spent with Gertie, John cleared up his apartment as best he could. Despite using Sylvie's flat most of the time, Gertie also enjoyed visiting Grandpa's place upstairs. Consequently, Grandpa's apartment no longer looked pristine and clutter-free. Gertie's toys took up so much space that his lounge was beginning to look like a toy shop. There were finger marks up the walls and dog's hairs on the sofa. Alfie appeared to be malting.

Not that long ago John would have been fuming over all this. Now he thought a bit of mess was a small price to pay for the company of his grandchild. Even Alfie was growing on him. John had learnt that life was too short to have a paddy over a few dog hairs or a bit of clutter. Thinking of which, John's thoughts drifted to Sylvie downstairs.

He still wondered what it was she did for a living, but John was too busy with Gertie's modelling assignments to return to The Rooftop Café to find out. Besides, it was too much of an effort to make a special trip to Hanover Square just on the off chance he might spot Sylvie leaving The Rooftop Café. He would then have to follow her back to work.

The other reason John was not too enamoured at the prospect of returning to that neck of the woods, was the thought of seeing Sylvie with that Bertram fellow again. It would be far simpler if he just asked Sylvie about her new job – not that she would tell him. That's why John didn't bother asking. At least whatever it was she was doing had put paid to his financial worries. That was fine with John providing she kept it up. The house conversion had come in way over budget, so they weren't entirely out of the woods yet.

John sighed. Looking after their grandchild was the least he could do under the circumstances. On top of which, John was done with all these games to get his wife back. Apart from anything else, looking after Gertie practically full time on his own meant he didn't have the time or the inclination to even think about another plan to get her to move back upstairs, let alone have the energy to carry it out.

If Sylvie thought that's what he was up to when he went to The Rooftop Café to spy on Bertram, then she was mistaken. Of course he wanted to find out more about him and dish the dirt if he could. However, it was less about getting Sylvie back – although that would have been a nice bonus – and more about protecting her from the real Bertram Wyndom-Price. John had tried every which way to get his wife to move back upstairs. Now he conceded that it was out of his hands. If she didn't want her husband back – if she wanted Bertram instead – then so be it; such is life. It wasn't what John wanted, but perhaps it was time to acknowledge he was on a losing streak.

John tried not to dwell on that. He was still worried about Sylvie and what would happen when she found out Bertram wasn't all he appeared to be. He wished she'd at least given him a chance to say his piece. He knew why she hadn't. His behaviour the other day, constantly knocking on her door for no reason other than to sabotage her evening was deplorable. He could see that now. But at the time, all that was on his mind was the thought that if he didn't do something, he would lose her for good. In hindsight, he couldn't believe how stupid he'd been. After all he had done over the last few weeks, looking after their grandchild and getting into her good books, he'd blown it in one idiotic evening.

John cringed. Perhaps he should have thought of that before he rushed headlong into destroying Sylvie's already fragile opinion of him. He really didn't want to dwell on that either. John had more important things to do with his free time than beat himself up over past mistakes. He turned his attention to the laptop in front of him. John was sitting at the desk in his study. The evenings and weekends were the only free time he had to work on his blog.

John leaned back in his office chair and re-read what he had just typed. It had taken a bit of time, and a suggestion from Chloe, but he had finally found a use for his new laptop; John had been writing in a blog about everything that had been taking place in the Baxter household since Sylvie moved downstairs, making his little black book redundant weeks ago.

John recalled when he first got the idea to write a blog. He had been alone in Sylvie's kitchen during one of his missions, waiting for Danger Mouse to reappear. It had been his brother Dave's idea to plant his grandson's pet mouse in Sylvie's kitchen while she was out. She thought there was a rat infestation in the garden apartment. It was another ploy to encourage Sylvie to move out of the garden apartment and back in with him. John had come to the rescue and got rid of the infestation, meaning he had put some cheese inside the mouse cage to entice him back; Theo's pet mouse was very partial to English Cheddar.

While John had sat idly waiting for the mouse to reappear, he happened to glance at Sylvie's laptop sitting on the kitchen table. The laptop was switched on. That's when John noticed the icon, *Sylvie's Blog*, on the homepage. Unfortunately, he didn't have a chance to click on the image before Danger Mouse reappeared. John had to take the mouse back to his apartment, ready for Dave to collect.

John had trawled the internet in search of *Sylvie's Blog*, very interested to know what she had been writing about. John never found anything by that name on the net. He was disappointed but not surprised. Sylvie must have had reservations about her personal life being out there and decided not to go ahead with the blog Chloe had set up for her.

John, on the other hand, would have no qualms about telling the world all about his wife's behaviour. That's what he thought until he started writing a blog of his own. In the beginning, John worried about his personal life being out there for all and sundry to see, especially all his private thoughts about his wife living downstairs. He wasn't from Chloe's generation who were used to social networking sites. John was a baby boomer. It all felt very unnatural, peculiar even, to think people you didn't even know could read all about your life on the internet.

He could well imagine that for Sylvie, writing a blog about her personal life would be a step too far. That's how it felt for John until Chloe reassured him that lots of people write blogs; nobody takes a blind bit of notice. That's when John thought, what the heck; he had to find some use for his new laptop.

John started his blog and never looked back. It had become an integral part of his life, almost as much as looking after his grandchild and walking Sylvie's dog. However, his blog would never have got off the ground if he hadn't thought of a way around his main reservation – namely, putting his personal life in the public arena. John had the presence of mind to protect his identity. He had no intention of simply calling it *John's Blog*.

His personal life might be out there, but it didn't mean anybody had to know who was writing that blog. Or whom he was writing about. From the get-go, John decided he wanted to assume a new identity, create a new persona, have some fun with an alter ego. That's what you could do on the net – reinvent yourself and be whoever you chose to be. And remain anonymous into the bargain.

John spent many hours coming up with a whole variety of personas, and fictional names to go with them. They all sounded good but, for some reason, John wasn't entirely happy with any of them. In fact, the whole exercise – which had started off as a bit of fun – ended up getting royally on his nerves to the point where he was on the verge of giving up on the whole blog idea. John didn't understand why he couldn't just pick one of them and be done with it. Nobody but himself was going to read the damn thing anyway.

Then Chloe had made a suggestion. 'You don't have to use a fictitious name, just go with something that sums up what your blog is all about.'

With that sage piece of advice *Dear John*, the blog was born. John was well aware that he had made a complete U-turn with his intention not to use his own name. But that common phrase summed up what it was all about. His blog was one long Dear

John letter about his wife leaving him. It was a harbinger for what was to come.

One day, John fully expected he would get a Dear John letter from the occupant of the apartment downstairs, telling him she had found somebody else. As far as John was concerned, it was inevitable. This was where their relationship was leading. It was all about how their separate living arrangements, living apart together, spelled the end of their relationship – the end of their marriage.

John had no qualms writing all about living apart together under the pseudonym Dear John. He could rant and rave to his heart's content, about his neighbour downstairs. Nobody would know it was John Baxter living at number 67b Penfold Street, Holland Park W11. Besides, he didn't need to substantiate his story; it wasn't as though he was making it up. Unfortunately, it was all true. The one issue John had of late was that he was only able to work in the evenings and weekends; this wasn't leaving him enough time to update his blog *and* answer all the comments and questions posted on his site.

This had been a recent phenomenon – the sudden and un-expected interest in his blog. It had caught John unawares and taken him completely by surprise. *Dear John* had finally been discovered. John had an idea how this came about. With the success of the anonymous blogger, Love on the Rooftop, it wasn't long before people, men in particular, wanted to hear the other side of the story. John would be the first to admit he was riding on the back of the success of the other blogger, but there was a market for this kind of thing and, right now, he happened to be it.

Suddenly he was on the media's radar. It wasn't long before

he had several offers from magazines, all vying for an article from the mystery writer and blogger calling himself Dear John. What John didn't realise, or Sylvie either, was that the conflicts and in-fighting that had been going on between them, in private, at home, had now resumed online through their blogs. Although things seemed to have settled down into an accepting truce at home, leaving each other alone to get on with their separate lives and the day-to-day practicalities of looking after Gertie, they didn't realise it was now all being played out online in the public arena.

Bloggers at War, one newspaper had called it. When John saw that headline on the front page of a national newspaper, he suddenly realised just what level of media attention Dear John and his arch-rival, the writer Love on the Rooftop, were attracting. No wonder these magazines were falling over themselves to ask him to write an article for them. They were offering good money too. John was thinking about what the other writer may be earning as a result of their blog, and how much he could earn out of his little hobby too.

It wasn't as though he needed the extra cash. He could survive well enough now that Sylvie was paying all the bills. However, John's ego was severely dented when he discovered Sylvie had sorted out their financial situation. He had always taken care of his wife and his family; that was meant to be *his* job – the breadwinner. It made John feel ashamed and inadequate that he wasn't even capable of doing that. Little wonder she didn't want him back. He was useless.

John looked at his blog. Perhaps this offered a way to redeem himself. If he could bring in some extra money, then he could start paying off the massive loan he had taken out for the conversion and thereby show Sylvie that he was doing something about their financial situation. With this in mind, John had emailed all the magazines giving them the same spiel that he would go with the highest bidder.

John was just browsing his emails, to see who had responded, when a new email popped into his inbox. Another magazine was offering John the opportunity to write an article for them. Just like the others, there was also the possibility that he might be offered a position as a columnist. John recognised the name of the magazine instantly. It was the same magazine Harriet worked for. The email had been sent from the editor herself – Harriet. She had no idea that the email recipient, Dear John, was none other than her very own dear father, John Baxter.

John sat there staring at the email recalling that day, several weeks ago, when Harriet had turned up at their house to tell them the news – she was returning to work full time. It was during that conversation that she also told them how her researchers had trawled the internet and found a mystery blogger to rival Love on the Rooftop.

When Harriet mentioned she was going to contact them to write an article for her magazine, John had to bite his tongue to stop himself asking the name of this blog. It couldn't be *Dear John,* could it? That was before all the sudden interest in his blog. But as the weeks rolled by, and nobody got in touch, John realised he had been premature. It couldn't have been his blog that Harriet was talking about. At the time, John wasn't all that surprised; why would anybody be the least bit interested in hearing about John Baxter's life? Surely they had better things to do with their time than read his blog? Apparently not.

John re-read Harriet's cloying email. She sounded desperate

to get him on board. The number of people buying their magazine was dwindling because of the popularity of the column, *Love on the Rooftop*, in their rival magazine. He distinctly remembered Harriet saying that if she was given the go-ahead by her boss to approach this other mystery blogger, she had no doubt in her mind that their popularity would turn her fortunes around. Harriet had made it quite clear that her job, her career, depended on getting them on board.

John typed a response. He sent her the same email he had sent the other magazines, informing her that he was going with the highest bidder. He didn't want to do that. John wanted to ring her up right now and surprise her by telling her Dear John was him. But he couldn't do that. This wasn't a game. These were serious offers of employment.

Although John had no intention of working for the magazine who offered him the most money, now that Harriet had been in touch, he still felt it was the right thing to do – for professional reasons – to respond in exactly the same way as all the others. He didn't want Dear John, the writer, to lose his credibility. Nobody would be aware of each other's offers; they were all private and sent in confidence. Consequently, whichever magazine he chose to work for would assume they had the most money on the table, even if in actual fact it wasn't true.

John couldn't deny it would be difficult if there were a huge disparity, but of the few that did respond to his email – and there were some who didn't appreciate his tactics and bowed out – they all pretty much offered the same standard fee, give or take. It was good money for a freelance article. John raised an eyebrow. Little wonder Harriet had been so peeved at losing her lucrative freelance work to that other blogger, Love on the Rooftop.

He sat tapping his fingers impatiently on the desk, waiting for a response from Harriet. He knew she wasn't at work. At this time in the evening, she would be sitting at home working on her laptop. John didn't have to wait long for a response. Just as he anticipated, all Harriet offered was the standard fee. Although she did mention that it was at the top end of the scale, generally reserved for their more experienced freelancers. The reason for this was that they had decided to match what they believed their rival was paying Love on the Rooftop.

It wasn't significantly more than what the other magazines' were offering to pay John. However, Harriet was the only one who had thought to entice him by introducing a little competitive edge to the proceedings. As an added carrot they would consider offering him a bonus if he increased their readership.

Never mind the bonus, John was very receptive to the thought of knocking Love on the Rooftop off her pedestal. He leaned back in his chair and puffed out his chest. That writer was about to find out there was a new blogger on the block. He grinned.

John emailed Harriet back via the new email address he had set up to keep his identity a secret. Using his professional blogging name, Dear John, he agreed to her terms.

Harriet responded promptly, requesting an article sharing his experiences of the phenomenon living apart together; Harriet called it LAT living.

John didn't realise someone had coined a phrase, let alone an acronym. He typed the phrase into the search engine and was taken aback by the results. He had no idea it was so common-place that some couples considered doing it on purpose. LAT living wasn't something John would recommend to save a relationship – far from it. His attitude was that if your relation-ship wasn't working living together, how on earth did people think they would stay together, living apart? It was absurd.

This viewpoint was exactly what Harriet and the editorial team wanted him to write about. They wanted Dear John to share his experiences as a man in a similar situation to the blogger, Love on the Rooftop, but for whom the experience of living apart together had not gone well.

John couldn't help thinking about that other blogger out there whose experience of LAT living was so different to his own. It had turned out to be the making of their relationship. John had read her blog. He had been following it for some time. John wished that had been him and Sylvie.

He was just preparing to write his first article for the maga-zine, when he received a response to his acceptance. John nearly fell off his chair when he read what Harriet had proposed next. 'She wants to meet me for an informal chat?' John stared at the email in dismay. He knew what an informal chat was; it was a bloody job interview. John hadn't been to a job interview in decades. His shoulders sagged. 'Damn!'

John was less concerned about the informal chat and more concerned about what would happen when he stepped into her office, and Harriet discovered the real identity of the blogger, Dear John. Would she still take her new columnist seriously when she found out it was only her dad? John recalled her attitude towards the anonymous blogger, Love on the Rooftop. John rolled his eyes. Harriet knew he didn't have any professional training or experience as a journalist. She knew he wasn't a *real* writer – whatever that was supposed to mean. But the one thing John did have in his favour was that his blog was popular. And right now, by the sound of things, he was all that stood between the success or failure of the magazine. If the magazine went down the toilet so would Harriet's job. What choice did she have?

With that thought in mind, John shot off another email agreeing to come along to the informal chat. He wanted to help Harriet out in any way he could. His only qualm was how Sylvie would react when she found out their dysfunctional relationship was appearing in a magazine article for all and sundry to read.

John decided his best course of action was to follow the lead of the writer, Love on the Rooftop, and remain anonymous; if the other blogger could do it, then so could he. It would be his only stipulation before he wrote a single word for the magazine. John was confident that once Harriet discovered it was her dad writing that blog, she would understand the need for anonymity. That assumed she still wanted Dear John after he walked into her office and she found out the truth. He hoped she really had learnt from her past mistakes and did not dismiss him out of hand. John shrugged. He'd just have to turn up to the interview and find out.

John walked out of his study with a pen to hand. He was going to make a note on the calendar, so he wouldn't forget. In the kitchen, John stopped in front of the calendar stuck to the fridge door. His pen hovered over the date. He didn't realise the interview was on a Thursday.

'Oh fiddlesticks!'

When he had shot off that email to Harriet, confirming he would be attending the interview, it had slipped his mind that he could only come on a Friday. John frowned. He couldn't very well email Harriet back and ask, *By the by, can we change that to a Friday because that's the only day your mother looks after Gertie?*

John stood there staring at the calendar. There was only one thing for it: he would have to ask Sylvie to swap days and look after Gertie next Thursday instead of Friday. John thought that was a reasonable request. He wrote it down on his calendar. John just hoped that when the boot was on the other foot Sylvie would say yes to his request – no questions asked.

24

Sylvie decided to leave work early. She had spotted snow flurries outside the office window. As the afternoon went on, Sylvie grew increasingly concerned that she might get held up on the way home from work. She knew she was probably worrying out of hand; although it was settling, it was only a light dusting. All the same, Sylvie didn't want to take any chances that she wouldn't make it home in time when Harriet arrived to collect Gertie.

It would make a pleasant change not to have that mad dash across London after work, leaving John waiting anxiously for her to turn up. She'd had a taste of that just recently when John took Gertie to the café in Baker Street and got held up on the way home. Her stomach had been in knots until they arrived.

Sylvie hadn't really thought about what she was putting John through each evening when she got home just in the nick of time. Today, Sylvie wanted to come home early and surprise him. She settled herself into the back of a black taxi cab for the journey home.

'I guess the weather forecasters got it wrong,' said the cab driver conversationally. 'We might be in for a white Christmas after all. What do ya think?'

'I don't know – maybe.' Sylvie wasn't feeling very talkative.

The taxi driver turned on his windscreen wipers. 'The snow's really settling. Mind you, it could just be a cold snap. It *is* only the first of December. Might be all gone by tomorrow.'

As she gazed out the window at the thick snow flurries, and the people rushing along the pavement wrapped up in coats, hats, and scarves, her thoughts turned to John. Sylvie had been giving him the cold shoulder for the past couple of weeks.

She thought back to that evening, two weeks ago, when she had accompanied Bertram back to his place for coffee and made a surprising discovery about a past relationship, courtesy of a telephone message. The woman Sylvie overheard leaving a message on Bertram's answerphone sounded so young. And to make matters worse, she had a child whom Bertram wanted nothing to do with.

Sylvie was cross with John because he had been right about Bertram all along. He must have seen the young woman when he followed Bertram to the hotel – that's what he was trying to tell her. So why didn't he? Sylvie knew why he hadn't said anything. She didn't give him a chance. She was adamant that nothing he said would change her mind about Bertram. How wrong she had been. And how foolish. She should have listened. It wasn't John's fault he had been right, and Bertram was hiding something. Even so, Sylvie didn't want to give John the satisfaction of telling him he'd been right all along, especially now the tables had been reversed and John was seeing someone.

Every Saturday night, since that disastrous evening with Bertram, Sylvie had watched from her lounge window as John climbed into a waiting taxi and went out for the evening. Sylvie guessed he must be out on a date because he was always dressed in one of his smart suits. Sylvie had waited up to see if he brought someone back with him. Both times John arrived home without his date. Sylvie wasn't surprised. After his behaviour, when she brought Bertram home that one time, John was probably wondering if his neighbour downstairs would take the opportunity to get her own back and disrupt his evening. He obviously wasn't taking any chances.

However, just because he didn't bring anyone home didn't change the fact that whoever she was – Barbara or somebody else – he was out on a Saturday night. He was seeing someone. It came as a surprise to Sylvie that after all this time living apart, leading separate lives, it should bother her that John had a life too. But it did bother her. It bothered her a great deal.

Sylvie glanced at the briefcase on her lap and sighed. She thought she'd better jot down some ideas for her next article to keep her mind off thoughts of John going out on a date, not to mention her unexpected reaction to this new development.

She was just reaching into her briefcase for a notepad when her mobile phone rang. Sylvie rummaged in her handbag and found her phone. She checked the number first, in case it was Bertram. He kept ringing her mobile phone and leaving her messages. Every message began with the words, *I can explain . . .* Sylvie didn't bother listening to the rest of those messages before deleting them. She wasn't taking the bait. Whatever he thought he was going to explain didn't change the facts.

Sylvie sighed in relief when she read the phone number. Thank goodness it wasn't him. 'Oh Julia, it's so good to hear from you. When are you coming home? I've missed you.'

Julia's week away had turned into a month. It sounded silly, but Sylvie was despairing of her ever coming back. Julia had phoned Sylvie at the end of the first week and told her they were having such a blast that they were just going where the mood took them. Julia said she had finally discovered what retirement was really about – the freedom of the open road. Or in Julia's case the open water. However, it sounded as though they were finally heading home. They had turned their houseboats around and were drifting along the canals, making their leisurely way back to London and their permanent mooring in Little Venice.

Sylvie was going to make sure Julia didn't change her mind. She balanced the phone in the crook of her neck and got out her diary. 'As soon as you get home, I want to see you,' said Sylvie, hoping she didn't sound too desperate to see her best friend.

On the end of the line, Julia smiled. It was good to hear her friend's voice. 'Rest assured, darling, I *am* homeward bound, and I *won't* change my mind.'

'Do I sound that desperate to see you?'

'Just as desperate as I am to catch up with you.' Julia couldn't wait to see Sylvie and tell her all about her fantastic holiday with Tom. It was the first of many. They were already planning their next adventure together. She wouldn't be home long before they were off again. Julia thought it best not to mention that to Sylvie just yet.

'When do you expect to arrive home?' asked Sylvie.

'What day is it today?'

'Pardon?'

'I know it must sound silly, darling, but with nothing on the horizon – no alarm clock to set, or appointments to keep, or work to do – we tend to lose track of time. Sometimes, I even forget what day of the week it is – do you know what I mean?'

Unfortunately, Sylvie didn't. Quite the reverse. Sylvie's life revolved around her alarm clock and appointments and work. Sylvie thought it must be wonderful to feel so carefree. Once upon a time, that's just what she imagined her retirement with John would be like. God knows they had worked hard enough all their lives, to arrive at a point where they should be able to relax and smell the roses. If only John hadn't lost his job. If only John hadn't converted the house. If only—

'Sylvie, are you still there?'

'Oh yes, of course. Sorry. Today is Tuesday.'

'Tuesday,' mused Julia. 'Just a minute, can you hold the line while I ask Tom when he thinks we will arrive back in Little Venice?'

'No problem.' Sylvie sat in the back of the taxi tapping her pen against a random page in her diary. The page was no different to every other page, crammed full of editorial meetings and time she'd scheduled in for researching and writing her weekly column, *Love on the Rooftop*. Then there was the agony aunt column, answering fan mail, and all the other myriad things she was involved in as the magazine's star writer.

She was always on a tight schedule to get everything done. That's why she had to see where she could fit in Julia on her return. The weekend would be ideal. But now she was looking after Gertie one day a week, socialising at the weekend was out of the question. The evenings and weekends were the only free time she had to work on her blog.

Sylvie flicked through the pages of the week ahead to see where she might be able to squeeze Julia into her busy schedule. Sylvie didn't begrudge the time she spent at work. She loved her new career. What she resented was spinning a web of lies for her readers all because she needed the money to pay off John's debts.

If only John hadn't miscalculated the final cost of the house conversion. It was still a mystery to Sylvie how he could have got it so wrong. He'd been an accountant all his working life, how on earth did he manage to make such a mista—

'Tomorrow!'

Sylvie nearly dropped her phone at the sound of Julia's loud, excitable voice on the end of the line.

'We arrive home tomorrow evening, Sylvie. I can't wait to see you. Why don't we meet up for a spot of lunch one day this week?'

Sylvie smiled. 'Perfect.' Since she stopped seeing Bertram, her lunch hour was completely free. Sylvie looked at her diary, chose a day, and pencilled their lunch date into her diary.

'Where shall we meet up, Julia?'

Julia suggested the usual place.

'Oh.'

Hearing the disappointment in Sylvie's voice, Julia thought she knew what the problem was. 'Let me guess. You forgot you'd already arranged a lunch date with Bertram that day.'

'Not exactly.' Sylvie didn't particularly want to get into this over the phone, although she would have to tell Julia why she wasn't that keen to return to The Rooftop Café. 'Look, about that, I'm afraid things didn't work out with Bertram.'

'Why – what happened?'

Sylvie glanced at the taxi driver. 'I'd rather not talk about it on the phone.'

'Oh, come on Sylvie, don't keep me in suspense. It can't be as bad as all that.'

'It is – believe me.' Sylvie lowered her voice when she saw the taxi driver looking at her in the rear-view mirror. She cupped her hand over the phone, and whispered, 'I found out about a past relationship with a young woman, and worst of all I think he's got a child that he's refusing to acknowledge. I overheard a phone message from the young woman when I went for coffee at his apartment. I could hear the child in the background – a boy. She called him Rory.'

Julia, who was not normally lost for words, was so quiet on the end of the phone that Sylvie thought they'd been cut off. 'Julia – are you still there?'

'What did Bertram have to say on the matter?'

Sylvie stalled. 'Well, he didn't say anything. I just overheard the phone message and left.'

'You haven't spoken to him since?' said Julia in surprise.

'No.'

'Sylvie are you sure you're not jumping to conclusions. How do you know the child is even his?'

'Because she told him she doesn't want his money and said she didn't care about herself as long as he stayed in Rory's life.'

'Oh.'

'Yes – *oh*.'

'Don't you think you should at least speak to Bertram and give him a chance to explain?'

'No, why should I? I'm not interested in hearing about his sordid past. I've found out quite enough already to know he's not the person I thought he was.' Sylvie sighed. 'Now perhaps you can appreciate why I'm not exactly eager to meet you at The Rooftop Café.'

'Bad memories?'

'You could say that, plus he keeps leaving me these phone messages.'

'What sort of messages?'

'Oh, you know. "I need to see you. I can explain . . ." Well, I don't want any chance that I might bump into him at the café. We used to meet there every lunchtime.'

'I see.'

Sylvie was pleased she understood. 'So, where shall we meet up instead?'

Sylvie put her mobile phone back in her handbag and frowned at the entry in her diary. Julia always had a way of twisting her arm and getting what she wanted. And what Julia wanted was to have lunch at The Rooftop Café, just like they used to. She said she'd found it first, so why should a man put a stop to them meeting up at her favourite place? Julia had a point. She did promise Sylvie that if Bertram happened to be there, she would make sure he got the message that her friend did not want to talk to him ever again.

Sylvie glanced out of the car window as the taxi pulled up outside the house a full hour earlier than usual. Sylvie paid her fare before she got out of the cab. It was still snowing outside; the snow flurry was so heavy that she could do with putting up her brolly. Sylvie didn't bother. Instead, she held her briefcase over her head and made a mad dash along the garden path, up the steps to the porch. She unlocked the front door and stepped into the communal hall.

Sylvie was standing in the hall, brushing the snow from her coat, when she noticed the door to her apartment was ajar. Sylvie walked through the door expecting to find John and Gertie in her lounge. She had given John the key to her apartment this morning before she left for work. Since that episode, when Sylvie returned home from an evening out with Bertram to discover

John had been in her apartment, she insisted John relinquish her spare door key at the end of each Grandpa Day.

'I'm home,' Sylvie called out.

There was no reply.

She walked downstairs to the basement kitchen. They weren't in the kitchen either. However, the french doors were wide open and Sylvie could hear voices coming from the garden. She walked up to the french doors, glad that she hadn't taken her coat off as soon as she arrived home; it was decidedly chilly in the kitchen. Sylvie stood at the open door, buttoning up her coat. She glanced outside. The snow had settled like a powdery white blanket covering the grass. She spotted John in the garden gathering up snow. He was making a small snowman with his little helper – Gertie. She was dressed in an all-in-one snowsuit and bright red wellies.

Alfie was close by, jumping up and down trying to catch snowflakes before they landed on his nose.

Sylvie stood watching John and Gertie building their snowman. In his haste to gather up some more snow, John slipped on the wet grass.

'Oh no,' said Sylvie, her voice drowned out by Gertie shouting, 'Silly Grandpa.' She started giggling.

John joined in the laughter and then proceeded to slip on the snow a few more times, making Gertie giggle even more.

Alfie forgot about the snowflakes and belted over to join in the fun. He jumped on top of Grandpa lying on the wet grass and licked his face.

'All right, Alfie.' John gently pushed Alfie away to stop any more doggy kisses. 'That's quite enough of that.' John got up and pointed at Alfie. 'Sit!'

Sylvie watched her dog obediently sit.

John then walked over to Gertie and knelt down to whisper something in her ear.

Gertie looked at Grandpa, nodded her head, and turned her attention to Alfie. She said, 'Alfie, roll over.'

Sylvie watched in amazement as Alfie rolled over.

Gertie started to giggle again.

John laughed and pulled a funny face.

Sylvie watched all this in amazement. This was a side of John she had never seen before. The old John, the uptight John, would never have rolled around in the grass, or pulled funny faces at the girls, or had the time or the inclination to build a snowman. Or, heaven forbid, look after a pet.

Sylvie glanced at her dog. That was another thing that had not gone unnoticed. Alfie was a reformed character. He sat when Sylvie asked him to. He stayed when she asked him to. He didn't pull on the lead. And he didn't beg at the table or whine outside the local shop. Her dog had turned into a little angel who was a pleasure to live with.

Sylvie had a good idea how this came about. She'd found a library book that John had left behind, on her kitchen table, after one of his Grandpa days; it was all about training your puppy. Sylvie couldn't believe it. John had not only looked after Alfie but taught him to be an exceptionally good dog. John clearly had hidden talents. Furthermore, it was evident from the antics in the garden that John, who didn't *do* pets, had grown quite fond of Alfie.

Standing at the door in the freezing cold, watching John, Sylvie was thinking how much he had surprised her in the most unexpected way. He had changed, he was different, and Sylvie liked what she saw – very much. She thought, if he was a stranger and she had bumped into him walking down the street, then she hoped they might go for a coffee, have a chat, and get to know one another. She hoped they would become friends, and it might lead to something more.

Sylvie sighed. That was just a pipe dream. It was all in the past, their past *not* their future. Surely, they had grown too far apart to find a way back to each other. At that moment, Sylvie knew it was time to stop dreaming and move on.

'Grandma!' Gertie spotted Sylvie standing at the door.

All three of them raced across the lawn in her direction.

'Sylvie!' exclaimed John, catching his breath as he came to a halt in front of her. 'I didn't expect you back so soon.'

Sylvie smiled at the look of surprise on John's face.

'Is everything all right?'

'Of course. I just fancied coming home early for a change – that's all.'

'Grandma, Grandma.' Gertie pointed at the miniature snowman they had made in the back garden.

'It's wonderful, my sweet,' said Sylvie as she picked Gertie up in her arms. She stepped back into the kitchen as John closed the french doors.

Alfie jumped up at Sylvie. He wanted some attention too.

'Down!' John commanded, swiftly followed by, 'Bed!'

Alfie turned around and slowly padded over to his dog basket in the corner of the kitchen. He slumped down on his blanket and gave them all the sad brown eyes – *nobody loves me* – routine.

Sylvie glanced at her dog and fell for it. 'Oh, Alfie.' She put Gertie down and rushed over to give him a fuss.

John groaned loudly.

Sylvie turned around and gave him a look.

'What?'

Sylvie heard that groan of disapproval. One thing she didn't miss, living downstairs on her own, was her husband following her every move. Sylvie was starting to wonder why she bothered coming home early.

She took off her coat and left Gertie sitting beside the dog basket stroking Alfie. Sylvie checked the time. Harriet wouldn't be calling around for another half an hour. Time enough for a nice cup of tea. 'I'll put the kettle on.' She got out two mugs and glanced at John hovering by the french doors. He had something on his mind – she could tell.

Sylvie put the mugs down on the worktop and folded her arms. 'Well, what is it?'

'Excuse me?'

Sylvie sighed heavily. 'I haven't got time for games, John. If there's something you want to tell me . . .'

John offered Sylvie a nervous smile. 'The thing is, Sylvie, I was er wondering if you wouldn't mind swapping days with me next week?'

Sylvie raised a questioning eyebrow.

'I was rather hoping you could look after Gertie next Thursday.'

'Thursday?'

John nodded his head vigorously. 'I can look after Gertie on Friday. I only need Thursday off from grandpa duty. . .' John trailed off. He eyed Sylvie keenly.

Sylvie was about to ask John what was so important that he couldn't look after Gertie on Thursday when she remembered he was now going out every Saturday night. He must be meeting this special someone on Thursday too. Sylvie knew she could just say no. She could make it difficult. But who was she to stand in the way of John's new life? It didn't mean she wasn't curious to know where he was going, what he was doing, whom he was seeing. Sylvie didn't ask because she was convinced he was meeting a woman. Besides, it really was none of her business. She reminded herself that John had his life now and she had hers.

'Of course I can swap days,' said Sylvie. She knew she'd just have to juggle things around. 'I will write it down in my diary.'

Sylvie forgot to write it down in her diary.

25

John checked his watch for the third time in as many minutes. He looked out of the window for any sign of a black taxi cab turning up outside the house.

Where was she?

John glanced at Gertie sitting on the rug in front of Sylvie's fireplace. She was busy playing with her HappyLand zoo, oblivious to Grandpa ringing his hands in desperation. If Sylvie didn't turn up pronto, he was going to be late for his interview. What on earth was keeping her? Had something cropped up at work? Perhaps the taxi was delayed in traffic on the way home? John couldn't see why that would be the case. It wasn't as though she was travelling home in the rush hour; it was only one o'clock in the afternoon. What if she had been in an accident on the way home? John's anxiety levels rocketed at the thought.

John was still ringing his hands, and pacing frantically back and forth in front of the window, when all of a sudden he thought of a much more plausible explanation. He stopped abruptly. What if she had simply forgotten? Of all the scenarios John could think of, he knew that was probably it. She was busy at work and it had slipped her mind.

Drat! John wished he'd thought of that a lot sooner. Instead of standing by the window, wasting valuable time watching the minutes count down to his interview, he could have been on the phone to Sylvie chivvying her up. She could be well on her way by now if he'd just had the presence of mind to contact her the minute she didn't show up at the agreed time. John started searching his pockets for the mobile phone number Sylvie had given him, some weeks ago, when he first started grandpa duty. He recalled that she made it abundantly clear the phone number was strictly for emergencies.

Drat! This was an emergency and he could not find the note of paper with the phone number. Why oh why hadn't he written it down in his diary? And why oh why did he expect to find it still in his trouser pocket all these weeks later? Hell, he couldn't even remember what he was wearing on that day. Perhaps, thought John hopefully, he had put it somewhere safe. But where? He would have to search his apartment from top to bottom to try and find it.

Drat! That was going to waste valuable time. But he didn't have a choice. It was the only contact number he had for Sylvie. He *had* to find it. In hindsight, John regretted not asking Sylvie where she worked although he got the impression she would not have volunteered that information. It was ridiculous that he had no idea what she did for a living. What was the big secret? John narrowed his eyes. It was the first time it had crossed his mind that perhaps Bertram wasn't the only one who had something to hide.

John brushed that thought aside for the time being. Right now he had bigger fish to fry, like how he was going to get in touch with Sylvie if he couldn't find that phone number.

John was still hoping that she hadn't forgotten, and she was just late. After all, she did say she would write it down in her diary . . .

Sylvie was sitting at a table, in The Rooftop Café, staring at the diary open in front of her. She frowned. Julia had promised she would be here when Sylvie arrived. When Sylvie discovered she wasn't, the first thing Sylvie did was open her diary to check she hadn't made a mistake and turned up on the wrong day.

Sure enough there was Julia's name pencilled in for lunch on Thursday. Now Sylvie was sitting there, staring at that diary entry, unable to shake the most peculiar feeling that she had forgotten something.

The sound of Sylvie's mobile phone interrupted her reverie. Sylvie answered it without checking the number first; she expected it was Julia phoning to say she was late.

It *was* Julia, and she was late. Too late to make their lunch date. It turned out they had got waylaid on their way home. A barge ahead of them had broken down blocking their route. Although repairs were underway, it sounded as though she wouldn't be home until this evening.

Trust Julia to leave it to the last minute to let me know, thought Sylvie miserably. Since Sylvie arrived, she had been anxiously peering around the crowded room, looking for any sign of Bertram. Fortunately, he wasn't here. That didn't mean he wouldn't turn up. Sylvie wasn't going to hang around to find out.

She was just putting her phone and diary back in her bag, getting ready to leave, when she heard someone say, 'Sylvie, do you mind if I join you?'

She looked up to find Bertram standing by her table. There was an awkward silence when Sylvie didn't answer his question.

The maître d' intervened. 'Mr Price comes here every day for lunch, but today we're so busy I'm afraid I was about to turn him away. Then I saw you sitting alone, and I thought as you know each other . . .' he trailed off expecting Sylvie to ask Bertram to join her.

Sylvie shook her head. 'We don't know each other at all.' She stood up and turned to the maître d'. 'The table is free. I was just leaving.'

'Please, Sylvie, at least give me a chance to explain?'

Sylvie walked straight past Bertram. She wasn't even going to dignify that with a response. She headed towards the exit.

'She's my daughter!' Bertram shouted at Sylvie across the crowded café.

Sylvie stopped abruptly.

'The young woman you heard on the phone,' continued Bertram, raising his voice to be heard above the other diners, 'she's my daughter, and Rory is my grandson.'

Suddenly there was a hushed silence as people waited to find out what would happen next.

Sylvie slowly turned around. She stared at Bertram across the room. 'Why didn't you tell me about them in the beginning?' Sylvie fired back angrily. If she had known, then she wouldn't have jumped to conclusions when she heard that phone message.

She waited for him to answer, along with the rest of the café. Everyone was staring at Bertram waiting for his response.

Finally, he said, 'It's complicated.'

Sylvie thought about the occasions he had asked her to meet him after work for a drink. How many times had she fobbed him off, saying she couldn't – it was complicated? She hadn't explained about Harriet and Gertie either.

'Please, Sylvie, have lunch with me and let me explain.'

The maître d' pulled out a chair at the table and waited to see if his other regular customer would stay for lunch.

The other diners turned to look at Sylvie.

Sylvie looked around the crowded café. People seated at their tables were staring avidly at her. She suddenly felt like bolting out the door. As soon as she made a move towards Bertram's table, the maître d' started to clap enthusiastically, precipitating a round of applause from the rest of the café.

Feeling extremely embarrassed that they had caused a scene in the middle of The Rooftop Café, and very much doubted she would ever set foot in the place again, Sylvie made her way as quickly as possible to the table. Her curiosity had got the better of her. She wanted to hear all about the daughter and grandson she never knew he had.

She took her seat opposite Bertram. Perhaps it was about time she told him all about Gertie and Harriet, and the reason she couldn't have a drink with Bertram after work. Or disappear to New York or Paris, or some other far-flung place at the drop of a hat, no matter how tempting it might be. She had a life here. A family. She had a daughter and a grandchild who needed her, and she wouldn't let them down. Sitting there, opposite Bertram, finding out belatedly that he too had those sorts of responsibilities – people who needed him, a history that wasn't so easy to leave out of the equation – it made her finally able to share her own complicated circumstances.

They ordered lunch. Sylvie noticed that once she was seated, he seemed reluctant to talk. Sylvie thought it might help if she opened up first and told him about the little complication in her life. She told him all about the charade her and John had been keeping up for Harriet's sake, pretending that they were both looking after Gertie when Sylvie was really at work. It wasn't something Sylvie was proud of. She constantly worried that one day soon the truth will out, even if she couldn't see how that might happen. As far as she was concerned, providing she was home by half past five, nothing could go wrong.

Bertram listened in silence. When Sylvie finished, he smiled. 'When you said you couldn't meet me after work, I thought that perhaps you weren't being completely honest with me. In the beginning, I did wonder if you weren't really separated from your husband. That would explain why you always had to be home by teatime.'

'It had crossed my mind you might think that,' Sylvie revealed. She leaned forward in her chair and broached the subject Bertram was avoiding. 'When I heard that message on your answerphone, you can imagine what I thought.'

Bertram took a deep breath and proceeded to explain why he found it immensely difficult to talk about his daughter. 'The trouble began in her early teens when she started playing truant from school . . .'

Bertram was beside himself with worry because the long hours in his job meant he wasn't there for her. He suspected that was part of the problem. She needed a mother and all she had was an absent father too busy with work. As his business empire grew, his trips abroad became more frequent.

'Left to her own devices, with no boundaries and plentiful access to cash, she fell in with the wrong crowd.'

He should have seen it coming.

'That's when I made the decision to send her to boarding school. She saw it as the ultimate betrayal.' During their last shouting match, before he sent her away, she had screamed at him that he was abandoning her.

'I had to, don't you see? I had to send her away for her own good.'

Sylvie nodded her head.

'She didn't speak to me. She refused to come home during the holidays. She didn't want to see me. Four long years she kept that up, with just fleeting appearances when the school closed for Christmas and New Year.'

Sylvie shook her head. 'How awful, Bertram.'

'Then one day she arrived home, after sitting her 'A' levels, a changed person. She had achieved excellent grades and was off to university in the autumn. I couldn't be happier. Sending her to boarding school had paid off. My daughter was off to university.' He smiled at the memory. 'She had a bright future ahead of her. She was on the cusp of starting her journey towards a happy, successful life and I was looking forward to moving on, free of the responsibilities of raising a child. I thought we'd turned a corner.' His smiled vanished.

Sylvie stared at him across the table. 'Bertram, tell me what happened?' she asked softly.

Bertram looked at Sylvie and sighed. 'It wasn't long after she left boarding school that her groupies found out she had returned to London. She soon fell back in with the wrong crowd, and then . . .' he trailed off, staring into space. 'I blame myself. If I had been around more, and not spent so much bloody time consumed with building my hotel empire, then perhaps things might have turned out differently.'

Sylvie reached across the table and gave his hand an affectionate squeeze. 'You mustn't blame yourself.' Sylvie had brought up three daughters. Although she hadn't had to raise them on her own, and didn't have to deal with the sort of issues Bertram had to face, she was a parent. She could empathise. However, Sylvie knew there came a time when you had to let your children go to make their own way in the world – mistakes and all.

Bertram continued, 'She had her whole life ahead of her. All I could think was that I gave her everything and this was how she repaid me?' He shook his head. 'Maybe I was the problem. Everything came too easy. When I found out she was pregnant by a boyfriend who didn't even stick around, I decided, there and then, enough was enough. She'd made her bed, and I wasn't bailing her out – this time she was on her own. I wanted my life back.'

Bertram gazed across the table at Sylvie. 'I know it sounds harsh, but I worked hard for her. She will inherit my fortune. She's going to be a wealthy lady someday, but in the meantime, I want her to learn to stand on her own two feet. I've had no serious relationships, no personal life of my own to speak of. I was too busy working to provide for my daughter. Now I would like someone to share my life with. What I don't want is the responsibility of an errant child anymore.'

'Surely, there's been someone between then and now?' Sylvie found it hard to believe he had been alone all these years. 'I bet women have been throwing themselves at your feet – a successful gentleman like you?'

'You mean a *wealthy* gentleman like me,' corrected Bertram. 'I have been out on some dates,' he said half-heartedly. 'All of them were women half my age or even younger.'

Sylvie's face dropped at that comment until he explained the reason things never worked out with these younger women.

'We had nothing in common. Although one worked in the hotel industry and another loved to travel, as do I, they were looking for different things in life. I wanted intelligent conversation. Someone my equal. Somebody to share the rest of my life with. They were looking for someone to take care of them.'

Sylvie listened in silence.

'To be honest, Sylvie, I have been taking care of a young lady for years – my own daughter. I didn't want to look after somebody else. Or have more children. I wanted to meet an independent, career-minded individual – someone not unlike you – who would enjoy my company and see me for who I am, see the man behind the money.'

Raising the subject of money reminded Sylvie of what she was sitting here to discuss. She steered the conversation back to his daughter – or tried to.

Bertram wasn't having any of it. 'Let me remind you that my daughter and I are estranged.'

She was the most important thing in his life, but she was also his biggest failure. He didn't want to see her because every time he did, he was reminded of that fact. Bertram realised too late the irony that if he had concentrated less on his career, less on building an empire, perhaps he would have been able to give her the one thing she really craved – a father. Maybe then things would have turned out differently. But it was too late for that now.

'Is it too late?' Sylvie ventured.

'She just wants money.'

'That's not what I heard on the answerphone,' Sylvie reminded him gently.

'I don't know what she was on about, but since she got pregnant, I haven't given her a penny. I don't intend to start now.'

'Don't you think that's a bit harsh? She wants you in her life. She wants you in your grandchild's life.'

Bertram shook his head. 'It's no good. She's made her bed. Now she's got to get on with her life – without me.'

Sylvie noticed one area he hadn't touched upon. 'What about her mother?' she probed.

'What mother? I told you – she's dead.'

Sylvie sat back in her chair and folded her arms. Something didn't quite ring true. Sylvie asked bluntly, 'How did she die?'

Bertram didn't seem hurt or offended by such a direct question. 'She didn't exactly die,' he said cryptically. 'But she's dead to me,' he added with a note of finality in his voice.

Sylvie sat there staring at him across the table. She was still waiting for an explanation.

Bertram stirred uneasily in his chair under Sylvie's penetrating gaze. Finally, he said, 'I don't think she ever really wanted children.' He paused, breathing deeply as though it was an effort to force the words out into the open. 'I think she was relieved when they didn't come along. She was happy. We were happy, just the two of us until the baby arrived.'

They had her late in life when he had given up on having children. He was in his early forties and did not anticipate he would find himself in the position of raising a child on his own. 'I woke up one morning to find a note; she was gone. She abandoned her when she was three months old.'

Sylvie studied his pained expression. 'You mean she abandoned *you*.' She could tell by the look on his face that she had touched a nerve. Sylvie had an idea what this was really all about.

'Do you blame her? Do you blame your daughter for losing the woman you loved?'

Bertram turned around in his chair and motioned for the maître d' to bring the bill. He turned back to Sylvie with a stony face. 'I think lunch is over.'

'Fine. Be like that.' Sylvie gathered her bag and stood up. 'But know this, Bertram Price, one of these days your daughter is going to stop knocking on your door, and if you lose them, you are going to live to regret it.'

Sylvie stormed off in the direction of the exit not caring if people were staring at her. She wasn't really angry with Bertram. She was worried about him. She had no idea what it was like to be estranged from your own daughter and not see your grand-child – she hoped she never found out. Sylvie only wished there was some way she could make Bertram reconcile with his daughter before it was too late, and he lost them for good.

Sylvie had just stepped on to the street outside the café when her mobile phone rang. She already knew who it was before she answered it. Sylvie sighed as she stood there on the phone listening to Bertram. He didn't want her to leave without apologising. He also wanted to see her again and resume their lunch dates. Sylvie smiled. She wanted that too. Sylvie slipped her phone into her handbag and headed back to work.

John had looked in on Gertie from time to time, over the past twenty minutes, but she didn't seem to mind the change of scenery. She had settled down quite contently to play with her HappyLand zoo in John's lounge after he had taken Gertie, her zoo, and Alfie up to his apartment while he conducted his search

291

for Sylvie's elusive mobile phone number. He was still praying she would just turn up, although that was becoming increasingly less likely as the minutes ticked by. John was resigned to the fact that it was more likely he wouldn't make it to the interview.

John had checked his coat pocket, all his trouser pockets, even the ones in the laundry, and the wet ones that had come out of the wash. Then he had rifled through all the desk drawers in his study until he eventually found a phone number. But it wasn't the one he was looking for, it was Barbara's.

John gave up. He had two choices if he still wanted to make it to the interview with Harriet. Plan A. Take Gertie with him and start the meeting by explaining to Harriet why Sylvie was not around today to look after Gertie or most of the week as it happened. Furthermore, they had both been complicit in lying through their teeth about what was really going on during the week, when Gertie was presumably being looked after by *both* grandparents. John cringed at the thought.

Or Plan B. Phone Barbara and ask her if she wouldn't mind awfully doing him a huge favour and popping round to his house to look after his grandchild; it would only be for a couple of hours at most, and nobody would be any the wiser.

John had already made up his mind what he was going to do before he even finished that thought. He had the phone number in his hand. Plan B was a go. He just hoped Barbara was at home and she wouldn't mind doing him a favour. She had children and grandchildren of her own, so she wasn't a stranger to looking after small children. But she *had* been a stranger lately; John made sure of it by calling a halt to the parties and not returning her calls. He wondered what the reception would be when he made that call.

He rang the number and nervously chewed a fingernail. To his surprise, not only was she at home, but she sounded happy to hear from him even though he was being a cheeky chappy, phoning her on the off-chance she could do him a huge favour at incredibly short notice.

He didn't have to ask twice. Within ten minutes John spotted Barbara's car pulling up at the kerb outside the house. He watched her get out of the car. John noticed, thankfully, she was not one of those people who had to take her toy dogs with her everywhere she went. There wasn't a bichon-frise in sight.

John picked up Gertie and carried her down the stairs. He opened the front door and introduced her to Barbara, the lady who would be looking after her and Alfie while Grandpa nipped out for a little while. John explained to Gertie that Grandpa would bring her back a present if she was a good girl for Barbara. John tried to dismiss the feeling of guilt using the bribery ploy.

Barbara had been very thoughtful and brought over some toys that her grandchildren used to play with. She thought Gertie might like them. She was right. The HappyLand zoo got relegated to the toy box in the corner of John's lounge, in favour of her new toys, courtesy of Barbara. She got a tentative smile and a little hug from Gertie in return.

John was as pleased as punch. This was going to work. Even so, he hovered by the door staring at Gertie playing happily with her new toys.

Barbara walked over and handed John his coat. 'It wasn't that long ago I was looking after my own grandchildren. Everything will be fine, I promise you.'

John put his coat on. 'You've got my mobile phone number in case?'

'For the third time, John, yes I have your number right here.' Barbara held up her phone and showed John his mobile phone number saved in her contacts list.

'Sorry.'

'There's no need to apologise. Now, do I get a goodbye kiss?'

'Oh er yes, I suppose so.' John bent down and gave her a quick peck on the cheek.

Barbara smiled up at John. She hadn't seen him in quite some time. He appeared to have lost some weight. The parties and the late nights obviously didn't agree with him because, despite looking after a toddler, John looked better than ever. Barbara watched John walk down the stairs. She still liked what she saw.

Back when the parties were in full swing, she had hoped to move their friendship up to the next level. However, by the time Barbara plucked up the courage to ask John if he would like to get romantically involved, he had been landed with the care of his grandchild, and he was either too busy or too tired to entertain Barbara's suggestion.

Barbara didn't know whether that was just a polite brush-of,f or he genuinely was too tired and too busy to start a new relationship. Barbara was hoping it was the latter. That's what she was here to find out. She was hopeful that when the dust settled on John's marriage, and the divorce papers finally come through, there might be a chance for them to resume their friendship and it might lead to something more.

In the meantime, she was more than happy to help him out of a tight fix this afternoon. She saw it as a good sign that John had approached her for help. Even better when she found out the reason: his wife had reneged on her promise to look after

Gertie. Barbara could tell he was exceptionally pleased that she had stepped in to help. Barbara made it quite clear to John that he could call on her any time because she was reliable. Barbara, unlike some people she could mention, did not renege on her promises.

John climbed into the back of the waiting taxi. He was thinking about how he could repay Barbara for being such a good samaritan and stepping into the breach like that, especially when he had made a point of not contacting her in all these weeks since the parties stopped. John thought that perhaps he would take her out one evening for a meal.

As the cab took off down the street, he glanced back at the house and smiled. John had every confidence that Plan B was the right decision. What could possibly go wrong?

26

John was already fifteen minutes late by the time he climbed out of the taxi and hot-footed it across the central plaza into the building. He thought he would have no problems finding her office. He was wrong. And he was a further ten minutes late because he had exited the lift twice on the wrong floor. Then he was completely flummoxed when he finally exited on the right floor, only to find a sea of desks in an open-plan office where several different companies shared one huge space.

By the time he found Harriet's office, he overheard her on the phone to her secretary asking if she had seen the Dear John blogger because she was not impressed by his tardiness; he was twenty-five minutes late.

Harriet put the phone down and looked up to find her dad standing in her office. 'Where's Gertie?'

John had prepared himself for various questions she might ask, but he had forgotten the most obvious one: where's Gertie? John stood there staring at Harriet feeling uncomfortable at the thought of telling her a fib.

'*Oh. My. God.*' Harriet suddenly gripped the armrests of her chair. Her face went sheet white. 'What's happened?'

John quickly and calmly reassured Harriet that nothing had happened to Gertie, that everything was tickety-boo, and she had absolutely nothing to worry about.

'So, what are you doing here?' asked Harriet, the colour returning to her cheeks as she remembered to breathe in and out. She looked past John into the office beyond. 'Is Mum here with Gertie?'

'Er . . . no. Gertie is at home,' said John, taking a seat. So far Harriet had not forced him into a corner with a question that called for an outright lie.

Harriet furrowed her brow. 'Dad, I'm at work.'

'Yes, I can see that,' said John, a little irritated by that remark.

'Look, I'm really busy. Can't this wait until later?' Harriet looked across the desk at her dad and suddenly had a strong sensation of déjà vu. Harriet seemed to recall her mum had stopped by her office one day, just to say *hello*. Harriet rolled her eyes. This was ridiculous. What had got into them lately?

Harriet blamed it on living apart together. What was that all about? Why didn't they just get on with it and either get back together or split up for good? This dance they were doing couldn't go on forever, and neither could this strange behaviour just turning up at her work like this. Didn't they understand she had a job to do? Harriet tried to be diplomatic. 'Look, Dad, you can't be here. I'm expecting someone to turn up for an interview at any minute . . .'

'But—' John tried to get a word in.

'So as much as I'd love to stop and have a chat,' Harriet made it quite clear that, 'I. Am. At. Work!'

'Fine!' John stood up. 'If you don't want to interview Dear John, that's your prerogative.' John headed to the door.

'Wait!'

He turned around.

'How do you know about Dear John?'

'Because,' said John, walking back to her desk and smiling sheepishly at his daughter, 'you are looking at him.' He couldn't wait to see her reaction.

'Right – that's it!' Harriet finally lost patience. 'I can't take much more of this!' She flew out of her chair, rounded the desk and glared at John. 'I'm not retired with a nice fat pension. I've got a job to do and a career to salvage, and you are not helping.'

John stared at Harriet in surprise. 'But—'

'I don't know what your game is, but I've had it up to here.' Harriet patted the underside of her chin with her hand. 'I want you and Mum to get back together, properly, in one apartment.'

'Pardon me?'

'Or better still, forget the apartments and turn the house back to the way it was. I wish to god you'd never converted it in the first place. That was our family home, you know. That was the house we grew up in. *My* childhood home. You had no right. You had no right to tear it to pieces on a whim!'

John's mouth dropped open at Harriet's sudden outburst. Since when did this conversation stop being about work and turn into something personal?

Harriet looked as though she was about to burst into tears.

John took in his daughter's pained expression. He had no idea how much she had been affected by what he had done to the family home and how upset she was over Mum and Dad splitting up. God knows John was upset enough himself over the way things had panned out. But shit happens. Marriages fail, people lose their homes or move house, or convert their houses;

in short, life moves on. People move on. And sometimes there's not a damn thing we can do about it.

He wanted to tell Harriet all that, but this was neither the time nor the place to have a serious heart to heart with his daughter. She was at work, and it was time to get down to business.

'Just go home, Dad. Please. Whatever it is, we can talk about it later.' Harriet returned to her chair, and sat down behind her desk, looking deflated.

John would much rather go home after that outburst. It made him feel terribly guilty that it was his idea to convert the house, and he was responsible for where that had led – to the breakdown of his marriage. It was all his fault. However, as much as he wanted to, he couldn't leave. Unbeknown to Harriet, he was here in the capacity of the blogger, Dear John, and he had every intention of working as hard as he could to get her career back on track and the magazine out of a funk.

'I can't leave, Harriet.' John sat down. 'You have to believe me when I tell you that I have an informal chat arranged, right here with you, at one o'clock. You have to excuse my tardiness for being late. Something cropped up.' John took a deep breath, and announced, 'I am the blogger who goes by the name Dear John.'

Harriet gaped at her father.

'And before you ask, no you did not make the best offer. It was the middle of the road. What I did like, however, was your suggestion that if I increased your readership, I might knock that other blogger, Love on the Rooftop, off their pedestal.' John leaned forward in his chair. 'Now I'd like to see that – wouldn't you?'

Harriet slowly nodded her head.

'I'm not doing it for the money, or to see Love on the Rooftop come down a peg or two. I'm here to help my daughter—'

John was interrupted by the sound of the office door opening. Harriet's secretary poked her head around the door.

'What is it?' hissed Harriet.

'Sorry to interrupt, Harriet, but your one o'clock appointment is still a no-show.'

Harriet looked at her father, and said, 'My one o'clock is sitting right here.'

'But that's your father.'

'Thank you for that astute observation,' said Harriet sarcastically. 'Now please shut the door. We are in a meeting.'

When the door was firmly closed, John opened the new leather briefcase that Gertie had helped him pick out when they went shopping the other day. He put several sheets of typed A4 paper on Harriet's desk; it was the article he had prepared in advance to bring along to the interview as requested. He sat back in his chair and anxiously watched Harriet pick it up and leaf through the pages.

She looked up. 'You know, the funny thing is I always thought that one day Mum would walk through my office door with something she had written, hoping that I might publish it in the magazine. I knew she always wanted to write.'

John raised an eyebrow. That was news to him.

'I think that's why she encouraged me to become a journalist. I just never expected it would be *you* walking through my office door – with *this*.' Harriet held up the article.

John fidgeted in his chair wondering what she meant by *with this?*

'It's good,' said Harriet, shaking her head in disbelief. 'It's *bloody* good. I think we are going to give that rival magazine a run for their money.'

John's face broke out into a wide grin. He knew it was good. 'Well, what can I say? I'm obviously a man of hidden talents.'

'I'll say,' said Harriet, staring at her father. 'I never knew you could write.'

'Neither did I,' admitted John, feeling extremely chuffed that, in her professional opinion as an editor and a writer, she thought his article was not just good but *bloody* good. That was something, coming from Harriet.

John had never considered writing as a proper career. That's why although Sylvie had encouraged Harriet to be a journalist, John had not. He wanted her to be a lawyer or a doctor or an accountant; something that offered job security and a defined career path. However, over the years Harriet had proved him wrong and made quite a success of herself in her career in journalism, despite John's initial reservations.

In fact, all three of his daughters had proved John wrong and settled into work lives that were very different from the choices John had made at their age. Chloe, with her contract work in I.T, had no job security and no career path, but plenty of money and plenty of flexibility. It was just the life that suited Chloe and made her happy. Jess, living on the other side of the world, eventually settled down and became a naturalist and Australian wildlife expert working for Melbourne zoo, just the life that suited Jess and made her happy. He admired all three of his daughter's achievements. They hadn't compromised for the sake of a monthly paycheck. They had taken care of their dreams, nurtured them, and eventually found their calling in life.

It made John think about his own career. He had been an accountant for years. However, just like his brother, Dave, with his interest in all things military, John had another interest and a little secret he had kept all to himself. John's favourite movie was *All The President's Men*. The film was about two reporters working for the Washington Post on the Watergate scandal. John loved that movie because he had always rather fancied himself as a hack working in Fleet Street for a national newspaper. But that was only a dream he hadn't taken care of or nurtured, until he eventually found himself in another life altogether because he thought his dream was stupid and unrealistic.

It was something he never shared with Sylvie when they first met. He had just started sitting his accountancy exams, and he was afraid that if he told her the truth, that he felt like jacking it all in to become a journalist, she might change her mind about him. She might think he was not a good prospect as a husband if he didn't have a reliable job that could support a family.

John wasn't blaming Sylvie for the choices he had made; it was his own fault for not having the gumption to take a chance and have faith that things would work out. Unfortunately, all those years ago that wasn't who he was. He wasn't a risk-taker. He would never take a chance on a dream. Everything had to be planned to distraction. John now realised his life had been a little poorer as a consequence.

He had made a plan in life, followed it through, and sure enough, it had led to a career, a house, a car, a retirement income. The problem with the plan, John realised belatedly, was that it was predictable, dull, boring. There was no wriggle room for the unexpected. There was no possibility of rounding a corner, metaphorically speaking, and bumping into something that he didn't know was missing from his life. This was a case in point. John sat there staring at the article he had written.

Harriet was taking her time reading it through once more. The expression on her face said she was enjoying it immensely.

John's whole life had been on one long ramrod-straight trajectory. It was a ridiculous notion, at his age, to think he could change direction and resurrect a once-cherished dream. When it came to work, John assumed that he was a one-trick pony. Soon after he was forced to take early retirement, John had tried to find other work. But he found himself inevitably drawn back to the same profession he had worked in all his life, in the safe, familiar world of accountancy; the same pattern repeating itself from years ago, for fear of taking a chance, for fear of trying something new. For fear of failing.

He didn't think he would have the opportunity to do anything else. He never, for one moment, thought he had it in him to start a new career as a writer, and as a consequence, he would find himself in the most unexpected place: sitting in an editor's office, writing articles for a magazine, fulfilling his dream of becoming a journalist – for real. John smiled. Who would have thought that one day something quite extraordinary would happen – he would outgrow *the plan*.

John was almost startled by this revelation. But it was true. For John, this was a brave new world. No plans, no destination in mind. For the very first time in his adult life, John felt truly free. This wasn't about choosing a career, for financial security, that could support a family in the long haul. And this wasn't just about helping out Harriet, or paying off his loan, or finding a second career to subsidise his retirement income. It wasn't about the money. John would have accepted the job as a columnist whatever they paid him; you couldn't put a price on a dream. This was about doing something for himself purely for the pleasure of it. This was about finding the real John buried beneath the layers of breadwinner and husband and father and grandparent. It was something few people in adulthood had the luxury of ever discovering – their true selves.

This made him stop and think about Sylvie living downstairs. When she found out about the financial mess they were in, John had given her an ultimatum: if she didn't move out of the garden apartment, they would lose the house. It was no idle threat. A short time ago, before Sylvie got a job and took it upon herself to sort out their finances, things really were looking that bleak. The only way out was to rent the garden apartment for a sizeable rental income. What John couldn't understand at the time was why Sylvie *still* wouldn't compromise. Now he had an idea why. John raised his eyebrows. Sylvie had finally found herself – something she had been talking about doing since she left her secretarial job. Perhaps part of that journey of self-discovery had something to do with living independently.

Maybe she was afraid that if she went back to the way things were, living together in the apartment upstairs, she would lose her new identity; the career woman he saw leaving for work each morning, carrying a briefcase, who was slim and attractively dressed in designer outfits. It wasn't just her appearance. She exuded self-confidence, something John had never seen in all the years he had known her. It made him wonder, not for the first time, what it was she did all day. Had she also taken a chance and found her true calling in life?

As for John, in the process of finding himself he had made an interesting discovery: he was a closet writer. He'd never had the time to figure that out until he retired. He had always liked the *idea* of being a writer, but never once tried to do anything about it until he started his blog. Once he started writing, John discovered he couldn't stop. He loved to write. Sometimes he would lose track of time and work long into the night.

Sitting there in front of Harriet, watching her reading his article, John realised this was what he wanted to do with the rest of his life. John had found his true calling. This suited him down to the ground. He wasn't ready to retire and sit at home and vegetate. It might suit some people. Not John. He wasn't the retiring type. Besides, he couldn't retire now. Dear John was about to take off. His life's work was just beginning.

This was very different to the job he had worked in over the last forty years. John never felt particularly proud of his achievements in accountancy, or particularly inclined to let people know what he did for a living; he only did it for a monthly paycheck. This was different. This was something he wanted to tell everyone about because John was proud to call himself a writer. It's just, for the moment, John couldn't mention it to a soul, apart from Harriet.

He was aware that once the article was published in the magazine, their personal life would be well and truly out there; a fact he was pretty sure Sylvie would not be pleased about – at all. So, for the time being, it was Harriet and John's little secret. John was also aware that if his popularity soared. And he reached anywhere near the dizzy heights of the famous anonymous writer, Love on the Rooftop. Sooner or later he might find himself in exactly the same position as that writer, with people clamouring to find out the identity of the writer, Dear John.

At least he could console himself with the thought that if

Sylvie found out, and confronted him over writing about their personal lives, he could tell her that it was for a good cause. He did it for Harriet, for her career. They both knew they would do almost anything for their children. The fact that John had secured a new job as a journalist into the bargain was just incidental, which it wasn't, not really; he would have gone with one of the other magazines in a heartbeat. But Sylvie wasn't to know that. Besides, this way he helped Harriet, and he helped himself by having something to say to Sylvie to sweeten the pill if she found out what he had been up to; John was building a new career on the back of their personal situation at home, and the demise of their marriage.

John signed on the dotted line, sealing his contract with the magazine. *Dear John*, the new weekly column, was born. John felt quite overcome. Harriet even offered him a desk, not his own office with a large desk and a nameplate like Harriet of course, but a small cubbyhole somewhere out there in the vast open office. This was all on the proviso that he worked late, after hours, when he had fulfilled his obligation to look after Gertie. Harriet made it crystal clear that, in future, he would have to clear it with her first if he wanted time off from looking after Gertie.

'Remember, I asked you and Mum to look after Gertie together. I know what she's like.'

'Who – your mother?'

Harriet looked at him askance. 'No, I was talking about Gertie. She can be a handful, and you guys are not getting any younger.'

'Gee thanks for the vote of confidence.' John said sarcastically. He thought he was doing rather well looking after a two-year-old considering he was doing it all on his own. Of course, Harriet didn't know that.

'Sorry, Dad, but I feel much more confident knowing she's being looked after by *both* grandparents.'

John swallowed hard thinking of Barbara. Harriet only ought to know that at this moment Gertie wasn't being looked after by *either* grandparent.

'Working on your column for the magazine *and* looking after Gertie won't be a problem for you, will it? Otherwise . . .' Harriet picked up the contract John had just signed.

'No, not at all,' John said, trying his best to keep a reassuring smile plastered on his face. Unbeknown to Harriet, it wasn't Grandpa that was the problem. John still couldn't believe that on the day he needed Sylvie to step in and look after their grandchild, she hadn't turned up.

John was thanking his lucky stars for Barbara when the shrill sound of a mobile phone ringtone cut across his thoughts.

'Aren't you going to answer that, Dad?'

'Oh, er, is that my phone?'

'Well, it isn't *my* mobile pho—' Harriet's sarcastic retort was interrupted by the sound of her mobile phone ringing.

John glanced at Harriet reaching for her mobile phone as he opened his briefcase. John found his phone and looked at the number, expecting it to be Sylvie calling to apologise for forgetting about their arrangement today. It wasn't Sylvie.

John's heart leapt in his throat when he saw who was calling. It was Barbara. She was only meant to ring him in emergencies. This was exactly what he was afraid of, that when he left Gertie with someone else something might happen when he wasn't there. *Christ!* He had only been gone an hour.

John answered the phone, trying to remain calm. 'Hello.' He glanced across the desk at Harriet.

Harriet checked who was calling her mobile before answering. 'Hello, Dominic. Why are you calling me at work?' Her husband *never* called her at work. Harriet's brow furrowed. Something was up.

'Barbara, you're going to have to slow down.' John was starting to panic because Barbara was in such a state. He didn't have a clue what she was talking about. 'Now, tell me again what's happened?' John listened as Barbara repeated herself.

'What do you mean – a strange man turned up at the house?' John's heart was racing. From what he could understand, Barbara had opened the front door to a man she didn't recognise who then barged into the house, threatened her, and took his grandchild.

'What do you mean,' said Harriet, talking on her mobile phone, 'you turned up at the house and some woman you didn't know answered their door, then refused to hand over Gertie?'

John was just about to ring off and call the police when his attention was diverted to Harriet's phone conversation. Suddenly, he knew exactly what had happened. Even so, he needed to be sure. 'Barbara? Listen to me. Can you describe this man, and can you tell me exactly what he said?'

Barbara did as she was asked. 'He was quite tall, over six feet, slim build, dark wavy hair, in his early forties—'

John didn't need Barbara to add anything further to that description; he knew exactly who had taken Gertie. *Oh, God!*

'John, he said he was Gertie's father, but I don't know who her father is. I just panicked. I didn't want to hand her over to a complete stranger. He was so irate. I tried to calm him down but he just flew up the stairs, grabbed Gertie, and left. I think he said his name was Dominic.'

John heaved a sigh of relief. 'It's all right, Barbara. Don't you worry,' John reassured her. 'What he said is true. That was Gertie's father. Everything is fine.'

John wasn't actually thinking everything was fine. It wasn't fine. Not. At. All.

Barbara rang off with the parting words, 'I need to go home and have a stiff drink.'

John needed a stiff drink too. He put his phone back in his briefcase and stole a glance across the desk at Harriet. He quickly averted his gaze. She was staring right back at him, her face like thunder. Bloody hell! He was in trouble now. She had overheard every word of his conversation. And she was still on the phone to Dominic. 'Yes, I know you only popped round there in the afternoon to—'

John could feel himself sliding down in his chair under her angry gaze, wishing he could slide right under the table and disappear into a big black hole. It would be a darn sight preferable to this. God almighty, how did he get himself into these fixes?

'No, I don't know who the hell Barbara is.' Harriet shot John an angry look.

John closed his eyes and wished he was anywhere but here.

'Dominic, I know where Dad is. He's sitting right in front of me . . . My mum? How do I know her whereabouts? Yes, Dominic, I know they were meant to be looking after Gertie . . . Pardon? . . . Are you saying it's *my* fault that she was left with a complete stranger? Yes, I do know they're *my* parents . . . Well, I thought they could be trusted too . . . No, please don't do that. I don't want you to call *them!*'

John's eyes shot open. He stared at Harriet. John knew exactly who Harriet meant by *them;* they were the in-laws. If Dominic was going to call *them* it meant only one thing: they'd be coming down to London to help out with Gertie, for a few days, until all this blew over. And that meant something else: they'd be staying with Dominic and Harriet. *Christ!* He'd done it now. He knew how much Harriet hated her in-laws.

Harriet ended the call with, 'Leave it to me, Dominic. I'll sort them out.'

John watched Harriet as she calmly put her mobile phone down on her desk, leaned back in her chair, and folded her arms across her chest. She threw John a look that said he better put his tin hat on because he was about to get a piece of her mind.

John looked at the contract he had just signed, and said in a small voice, 'Am I fired?'

27

John wasn't fired. He was pretty sure Harriet would have taken great pleasure in tearing up that contract, but she could not let her personal life interfere with her professional responsibilities. That didn't mean she was happy about it – far from it. He could tell she just wanted to fire his ass after pulling off a stunt like that, telling her bare-faced lies about Gertie.

In his defence, John pointed out that he had not told any outright lies; he had merely answered her question about Gertie by telling Harriet, quite truthfully, she was at home. He had just omitted to tell Harriet exactly who she was at home with.

Isn't hindsight a wonderful thing thought John as he traipsed out of her office to find the assistant editor, whom he would be working with from now on because Harriet didn't want anything more to do with him. John shook his head. He was an idiot. He should have brought Gertie along and told Harriet the truth: Sylvie didn't turn up to look after Gertie as she had promised. She had let him down. It was Sylvie who should be getting it in the neck and not him. After all, it was her fault he was in this mess – wasn't it? Then again, he risked blowing their whole arrangement wide open which would only make matters worse.

Harriet slammed the door behind him, making John jump.

People busy working at their desks, in the open-plan office, looked over in his direction.

John put his head down and sidled up to the secretary's desk to ask her where he could find the assistant editor; Harriet wouldn't even tell him the assistant editor's name. Yes, thought John, he was definitely in her bad books. Although, surprisingly he didn't get the rant he was expecting. In fact, Harriet was remarkably restrained. She hadn't said an awful lot to him after she got off the phone to Dominic.

John guessed that was because she was at work. Consequently, she couldn't fully lift-off and vent at her father in front of all these people. Her office was not soundproof. Her office had very large windows looking out on to the big open-plan office beyond, and there were no blinds to pull for moments when one might need some privacy to give someone a right rollocking. John guessed she was going to save that for later. He wasn't looking forward to it. But what he *was* going to do was make sure Sylvie received her share. After all, they were in this together.

Later, John discovered there was something far worse than getting a right rollocking from Harriet when he found out just what they stood to lose as a consequence of Dominic's incredibly ill-timed visit . . .

Dominic, John's son-in-law, had a rare afternoon off work and had decided to pop around Sylvie and John's house, unannounced, to collect Gertie; he wanted to spend the afternoon with his daughter. He thought it would be a pleasant surprise for Sylvie and John because, as much as he imagined they loved spending time with Gertie, they had been landed with the responsibility of looking after their grandchild full time. Dominic felt they would appreciate an unexpected afternoon off.

Dominic had been impressed at how they had handled the situation; from what he gathered had been going on in the Baxter household, over the last few months, it sounded as though they had really got their act together for the sake of Harriet and Gertie. Dominic was extremely pleased to hear they had put aside their differences to look after Gertie together. It was what Harriet and Dominic wanted.

So, imagine his surprise when he called around their house and discovered not one, but two absent grandparents, and a complete stranger looking after his child. Dominic hit the roof. He took Gertie home and phoned Harriet at work telling her he had had it up to here with her parents. Harriet had been banging on about their living arrangements for months. He never heard the end of it. Then there was that blasted blogger who had stolen her column. If it wasn't for Love on the Rooftop, maybe his wife would still be doing some freelance work from home, and his child wouldn't have been left with a perfect stranger.

This was the last straw. He was calling his parents from up north to help them out with Gertie. Not only that, he was withdrawing all contact between Gertie and her grandparents in London until they sorted out their domestic issues, once and for all. As far as he was concerned, they were not fit to be grandparents. Until they proved otherwise, he was pulling the plug on either Sylvie or John seeing Gertie.

Dominic ended the call to Harriet with, 'If you don't tell them, I bloody well will.'

After slamming her office door shut, with John on the other

side, Harriet had sat down at her desk and stared at her mobile phone in dismay. She couldn't tell Dad at work but tell them she did – both of them – later that day.

It was not what either grandparent had expected. It wasn't a slap on the wrist, and then things will blow over, kind of telling off. It was more serious than that. Harriet and Dominic had issued an ultimatum: *Until you get your house in order and stop playing games with us, and with each other, we don't want Gertie to have any further contact with either of you.*

Sylvie and John were shocked by this turn of events. They wouldn't do that, would they? They wouldn't take their grand-child away from them? They couldn't just withdraw all contact without so much as a by-your-leave.

After the discovery that Gertie was being looked after by a stranger, Harriet wanted to know *exactly* what had been going on while she was at work.

John didn't waste any time filling Harriet in with all the de-tails. John didn't want to lose Gertie. He didn't deserve this. Over the past few weeks, he was the one who had been conscientiously looking after Gertie for the majority of the time. It wasn't fair. So John had been quick to share with Harriet, in front of Sylvie, how Sylvie had left him looking after Gertie all on his own, apart from Fridays.

Harriet wasn't interested to know how Sylvie was spending her time, which was incidental, all she was interested in was the fact that Sylvie had not been there for Gertie as promised. Harriet concluded that Mum could not be trusted with her child.

Sylvie was quick to implicate John as a co-conspirator, com-plicit in the deception, reminding Harriet that he had plenty of opportunities to tell her what was really going on, but he chose not to. Harriet concluded that Dad could not be trusted with her child.

They both pleaded with Harriet not to do this, to give them a second chance. Harriet couldn't do that because it wasn't just up to her, it involved her husband too, and his mind was made up. Sylvie and John then turned on each other with recriminations, accusations and insults, eventually degenerating into petty name-calling.

Harriet stood there listening to Mum and Dad blaming each other. They were behaving like two school children arguing in the playground. Harriet wondered what had ever possessed her to think it was a good idea to leave Gertie in the clearly incapable hands of her parents.

Dominic was *so* right: under the circumstances, it had been too much to ask them to look after her. Harriet blamed herself for not seeing that. Her parents had enough issues going on between them, without throwing a grandchild into the mix and expecting them to take care of a two-year-old. Something was bound to go wrong. And it had.

Harriet slipped out of the house unnoticed. She could still hear their raised voices as she walked down the path towards the front gate. She shook her head wondering how long they could go on like this. When were they going to stop avoiding each other and face the real issue: were they getting back together or splitting up for good?

Harriet didn't think that decision would be coming any time soon; by the sound of it, they were heading for a massive falling out. They were blaming each other for this situation with Gertie when, quite frankly, as far as Harriet was concerned, they were both equally to blame. Harriet sighed. At this rate, they wouldn't even be talking to each other, let alone sorting out their relationship and making fundamental decisions about their future.

Harriet walked through the front gate and closed it behind her. She stood on the pavement and stared up at the house.

An old couple were walking along the street, out for an evening stroll together. They momentarily stopped next to Harriet and glanced up at the house. All three stood listening to the heated exchange that could be heard quite distinctly from the street.

Harriet exchanged a look with the two strangers standing beside her. They hadn't seen her walk out of the house, so must have assumed she was just another passer-by pausing to take in the sound of a car wreck that was once a marriage.

'Doesn't sound good, does it George?' said the old lady, turning to the gentlemen beside her.

'That depends, Ethel. Inside that house are either two people who have grown apart, and really have no business being together . . .'

Harriet nodded in silent agreement.

'Or . . .?' said Ethel.

George looked at Ethel. 'Or what?'

'You said that inside that house are either two people . . .'

'Oh yes I did, didn't I,' he guffawed. 'My memory is not what it once was.' George tapped his temple under his dark brown fedora hat.

'Well?' said Harriet interested to know his opinion. She couldn't help staring at the fedora hat he was wearing; that wasn't something you saw every day.

George answered, 'I suppose the other possibility is that inside that house are two people who are still very much in love.'

'How do you figure that?' said Ethel, wrapping her black fur coat more tightly around her to keep out the cold.

Harriet frowned at the coat hoping that wasn't real fur she was wearing.

'That's quite easy, my dear,' he said jovially. 'So far neither of them has just given up, packed their bags, and walked out that front door.'

All three swivelled their heads in the direction of the house and watched the front door. Nobody came out. And the row inside continued.

'It's easy to walk away, is it not?' George commented. 'So why doesn't one of them just leave and be done with it? I'll tell you why, because it's no easy thing to walk away from the person you love.' He smiled at Ethel.

Harriet looked back at the house, deep in thought.

'Well, we can't stand here all night gawping,' said George. 'Lord knows if anybody had passed by our house and stopped to listen, over the years, they'd have heard some lively exchanges.'

'Not to mention some choice words that would make your toes curl,' added Ethel laughing.

Harriet turned to look at them both, standing there arm-in-arm in their overcoats, leather gloves, and funny hats; old-fashioned attire they had probably owned for decades. They looked as though they were off to an evening out at the theatre, not just taking an evening stroll in the cold night air. She guessed they must be in their eighties.

'So how long have you two been married?' asked Harriet, looking from George to Ethel.

Ethel and George exchanged glances. George said, 'Oh far, far too long, can't even remember.' He guffawed.

'Well, best be off,' said Ethel.

'Good evening,' said George, holding the rim of his hat between two fingers and nodding his head once in Harriet's direction.

'Oh, er good evening,' said Harriet absently, her attention drawn to her parents' house and the row still going full throttle inside. She glanced at the old couple as they shuffled off down the street. The streetlights above them flicked on, one by one, above them as they walked by until Ethel and George disappeared from view around the corner.

As soon as they were gone, one by one the streetlights flicked off. 'How odd,' remarked Harriet wondering what was wrong with the street lighting?

Harriet shrugged and turned back to the house. She didn't recall seeing Ethel and George around Penfold Street before. Harriet wondered where they lived. Perhaps they were visiting relatives? Unfortunately, that thought reminded Harriet about her own visitors at home. She rolled her eyes and resolved not to speak to either one of her parents, for the next few days, until she calmed down. Not only was she angry with them over Gertie, but to add insult to injury she now had the in-laws staying at her house, and they were already driving her mental.

Harriet took one last look at her parents' house and thought of the old couple who happened along; it was unusual nowadays to find anyone out at dusk just taking a stroll unless they were walking their dog. People were simply afraid to walk the London streets after dark. Afraid of the things they'd heard on the news, or read in the newspapers, even though this was a relatively safe neighbourhood.

Ethel and George had made for a pleasant distraction from

the heated exchange still going on between her parents behind closed doors. They had made some interesting observations that Harriet wanted to think about on her way home. She fancied walking to give herself a precious half-an-hour thinking time and mull over the conversation between George and Ethel before she arrived home to the in-laws. However, something was wrong with the street lighting. It was pitch dark. Harriet was about to hail a taxi when all of a sudden the streetlights came on.

'That's more like it,' said Harriet as she started for home. Harriet's thoughts turned back to her parents. Mum and Dad might be living in separate apartments, but the fact remained they were still living under one roof and, as George had rightly observed, neither one of them had walked out that door. Surely, that counted for something.

Before she turned the corner, into the next street, Harriet couldn't resist a quick glance over her shoulder at her parents' house. Perhaps George was right: maybe they still had a future together. They just didn't know it yet. Harriet walked home hoping that she could find a spare moment, away from the in-laws, to phone Chloe and Jess; she needed to talk to them about Mum and Dad.

Meanwhile, for Sylvie and John things had finally come to a head. Losing access to Gertie had been a terrible shock and a huge wake-up call for the both of them. Harriet and Dominic were absolutely right when they said they couldn't go on living like this; it was time to sort out their domestic situation, their relationship, their marriage, once and for all. They both knew that. And they both knew what they had to do. It was time to sit down like two mature, responsible grown-ups and calmly talk things through.

So, when the dust had settled on their blazing row, they both went into their respective apartments and slammed their doors shut – vying with each other who could slam theirs the loudest – each deciding not to speak to the other ever again.

28

Sylvie sat at the kitchen table with Alfie at her feet. She glanced at her dog. He was whining softly, sensing something was wrong. Sylvie plucked another tissue from the box of Kleenex on the table and wiped her nose.

It was Friday, the day after they had lost access to Gertie, and the day Sylvie would normally be spending with her grandchild if she hadn't stupidly forgotten to write down in her diary that she had agreed to look after Gertie yesterday afternoon. To make matters worse, she had been having lunch at The Rooftop Café with Bertram when she should have been looking after her grandchild.

Sylvie threw the damp tissue in the bin. Although she had half a mind to go into work today, just to take her mind off things, Sylvie couldn't bring herself to do that. This was Grandma Day. Even though Gertie wasn't here, and it was probably making her feel a whole lot worse moping around the apartment feeling sorry for herself, she still couldn't imagine going into work and pretending everything was all right.

Sylvie's phone rang. Bertram had already left two messages regarding that lunch date they were going to arrange. Sylvie wished she hadn't given Bertram her home number. Now she was avoiding the phone because, after this, she very much doubted there would be another lunch date with Bertram. When the answerphone kicked in, for the third time that morning, Sylvie got up from the kitchen table to walk upstairs. She didn't want to hear the sound of his voice again.

Sylvie stopped on the bottom stair and turned around at the sound of Julia's voice on her answering machine. Julia was apologising for missing their lunch date yesterday. She had finally arrived home late last night and was hoping they could get together very soon. She was just ending her call by wishing Sylvie a lovely day with Gertie when Sylvie picked up the phone.

'Sylvie?'

'Sorry, Julia, I thought you were . . . someone else.'

'Someone else – as in Bertram?'

Sylvie sighed heavily.

'Has something happened? Did you meet him again?'

'Julia, anyone would think you've got the sixth sense.'

'Well – did you?'

Sylvie really didn't want to be reminded.

'Well?'

And Sylvie didn't want to have this conversation because, if she did, she thought she might break down again and need to open another box of Kleenex.

As usual, Julia was persistent.

Sylvie gave in and answered her question. 'You were right about Bertram. It's not what I thought. The young woman who left a message on his answerphone was his daughter.'

'That's great news – isn't it?'

Sylvie went quiet.

'Sylvie, what happened? Is it Bertram?'

'Yes. No. Oh, Julia,' Sylvie exhaled. She wiped the tears from her eyes with a tissue. 'Harriet has forbidden John and me from seeing Gertie. I've lost my Gertie.'

Now it was Julia's turn to go quiet. 'I don't understand, Sylvie. I thought we were just talking about Bertram?' She paused. 'Hold up, isn't this the day you normally look after Gertie?'

Tears started to well up as Sylvie told Julia what happened yesterday. 'John left her with a stranger – well Barbara actually – while he was off gallivanting with some other woman.'

'Another woman?'

'Yep. He didn't even deny it. But the thing is, Julia, it turns out that I'm no better than John. When I was supposed to be looking after Gertie, instead, I was having lunch with a man.'

'You mean Bertram.'

'Yes.'

'Is that why you weren't answering the phone?'

Sylvie nodded.

'At least tell him what happened. It wasn't his fault you didn't write it down in your diary. He wasn't to know.'

'Oh Julia, what am I going to do?'

'Hang tight. I'm coming over. In the meantime, why don't you phone Bertram and tell him what happened? It might make you feel better.'

It would certainly make Julia feel better to know that Sylvie was on the phone chatting to a friend, while she was on her way over, and not sitting alone in her apartment with nothing but the dog for company.

Sylvie took Julia's advice and rang Bertram. She wished she hadn't. He couldn't have been less sympathetic if he tried.

'Maybe it's for the best, Sylvie.' said Bertram, sounding not in the least bit empathetic. 'I must admit I was disappointed that you had to go straight home from work every evening and we couldn't meet up for a drink. To be honest, all that was just getting in the way of us.'

Sylvie couldn't believe what she was hearing. '*All that* is my daughter and granddaughter you're talking about!'

'I know,' continued Bertram, in his infuriatingly even tone. 'But let's face it, we raised our children, we've done our bit. Now it's our turn.'

'Well, you would say that wouldn't you because you're not seeing your grandchild.'

Bertram wasn't seeing his daughter or grandchild because he had *chosen* to cut them out of his life. Little wonder he wasn't sympathetic, thought Sylvie. She shook her head in dismay. 'Wait and see what it feels like Bertram, when the boot is on the other foot. When your daughter stops coming around and decides she doesn't want anything to do with you – and doesn't want you to see Rory.' Sylvie slammed the phone down.

She opened a kitchen cupboard, found another box of Kleenex tissues, and made her way back to the kitchen table followed closely by Alfie. Just as she sat down the phone rang again. Sylvie didn't bother answering it. Instead, she opened the box of tissues and stared forlornly at the phone, waiting to hear Bertram's lame attempt at another apology.

Alfie sat quietly at her feet.

Sylvie looked down at her dog and managed a smile. 'You know how I feel, don't you Alfie.'

Alfie wagged his tail as Sylvie gave him an affectionate pat on the head. Satisfied she was all right, Alfie plodded over to his basket and settled himself down for a snooze. Sylvie turned her attention back to the phone. She wasn't all right. After speaking to Bertram, Sylvie felt more upset than ever, and the apology wasn't helping matters.

'Look, Sylvie, I'm sorry about what I said. That was completely out of line. I just . . . I want to see you, but it just seems to be one thing after another; first, it's my daughter, now it's yours—'

Sylvie sighed heavily. 'I know.'

'Will you meet me then?' he asked as though he had heard Sylvie's voice. 'When you can. When you've sorted things out with your family.'

Sylvie looked at the answerphone and shook her head. 'I don't know, Bertram – maybe.'

'I'm in London for a few more days. I'll be at The Rooftop Café for lunch every day until I leave. I want to make it up to you. Please, just give me one more chance.' Bertram signed off with another apology.

Sylvie left the answerphone beeping with Bertram's message and took herself upstairs to sit on the sofa and wait for Julia.

When Julia arrived, Sylvie took one look at her and burst into tears; the enormity of losing Gertie hit her. 'Oh Julia, I've made a terrible, terrible mistake. I wish I'd never met Bertram.'

'Now, now, darling.' Julia gave her a hug and then drew back to tell her firmly, 'It's not your fault or Bertram's fault. It's that idiot upstairs. If you couldn't make it home, whatever the reason, John should not have left Gertie with Barbara. Need I remind you that it was John who left her with a stranger – not you?'

Sylvie nodded even though she knew she wasn't entirely blameless.

'Darling, let's go downstairs and make a nice cup of tea.' On the way down the stairs, Julia tried to convince Sylvie that taking Gertie away from them was just a knee-jerk reaction and it would all blow over, come the weekend.

Sylvie wished that were true. Julia didn't really know Harriet all that well – or her husband; they made quite a formidable team. Once their minds were made up . . .

Sylvie's bottom lip quivered. 'I might not see Gertie again.'

'Oh Sylvie, it can't be as bad as all that.'

Sylvie didn't want to sound patronising, so she didn't tell her best friend what she was really thinking. The trouble with Julia's rather limited perspective on her situation was that she'd never had children of her own; she couldn't really put herself in Harriet and Dominic's shoes. They must have felt sick to their stomachs when they discovered Gertie was not with her grandparents but with a total stranger.

Unfortunately, Sylvie could put herself in their shoes all too easily, and the fact that she was partly to blame made it all the more painful. The worse part was that she had no idea how to put things right.

'I don't know what to do, Julia.' All Sylvie could do was burst into tears again.

Julia could tell that nothing she said would make any difference to how Sylvie was feeling right now. Perhaps it was better to try and take her mind off it. In an effort to change the subject, Julia handed Sylvie a hot mug of tea and asked how the phone call went with Bertram.

Sylvie repeated that unsavoury conversation with Bertram

before she cut him off by slamming the phone down. She then mentioned the apologetic phone message which swiftly followed. The message Julia replayed before Sylvie could stop her.

'Are you going to see him again?' asked Julia, once she finished listening to the message.

'What do *you* think?' Sylvie threw back sarcastically.

Julia took that as a *no*. 'Is it because of yesterday?'

Sylvie sighed. 'It's not just about what happened with Gertie. Honestly, Julia, I don't really know if Bertram is *the one*. I've been having second thoughts about where this relationship is going.'

'Second thoughts?'

'Well – doubts actually.'

'How come?'

Sylvie confided in Julia that she had started to have doubts about how this relationship could work. She was thinking about his jet-set lifestyle and the time he spends in cities all over the world. Although it sounded glamorous, it wasn't the life for Sylvie. They had talked about how her job was a perfect fit for this kind of lifestyle. She was a writer, and thanks to modern technology she could create her articles anywhere in the world and just email them.

That was true, but the writing was only one part of her life. Sylvie would miss the buzz of the office, and the team of fellow journalists whom she worked with and counted as friends. She would miss her family, her dog, her apartment. Even, surprisingly, her irritating neighbour upstairs. Sylvie had a life here in London. She wasn't sure a long-distance relationship was what she, or Bertram, wanted.

Julia shrugged. 'Who knows, perhaps he'll stay in London.'

'I doubt it.'

'But you never know. Hasn't he got an apartment in London?'

'Well yes, but—'

'I wish you'd reconsider, Sylvie. By the sound of things, you two get on quite well, and need I remind you that you *did* meet on The Rooftop Café.'

'I know,' said Sylvie half-heartedly. Losing Gertie was still painfully at the forefront of her mind. All the same, at Julia's prompting Sylvie divulged what she had found out about Bertram during that ill-fated lunch together yesterday.

'It turns out that his wife abandoned him, leaving him to bring up their daughter alone. Apparently, she did well at school and was on the cusp of going to university when she fell pregnant. She chose to abandon her studies and have the child.'

Julia nodded. 'Go on.'

'I get that it was tough. He thought she would be off to university, making her own way in the world, and he would be free. Instead, he found himself with a responsibility again – well, two actually. He made a lot of sacrifices for his daughter, and now he wants his life back. But these things happen. I just wish he'd see his daughter and realise what he is missing by not having a relationship with his grandchild.'

'Yes,' agreed Julia. 'It's Amy I feel sorry for.'

Sylvie looked at Julia and furrowed her brow. 'Who's Amy?'

'His daughter, the one you were just telling me about.'

'Yes, but I never mentioned her by name. How do you know Bertram's daughter is called Amy?'

'You must have mentioned it.'

'That's not possible, Julia. He refused to speak her name.'

Julia pursed her lips. 'I think we need another cup of tea, don't you?' Julia got up.

Sylvie caught her arm. 'Sit!'

Julia slowly sat back down under Sylvie's watchful gaze.

Sylvie studied her best friend.

Julia nervously glanced her way.

Sylvie's eyebrows shot up. 'You know him – don't you. You know Bertram!'

'Look, Sylvie, I wanted you to have the opportunity to meet someone, like I met my new partner, Tom. He's one of Tom's friends, actually. When I was first introduced to Bertram, I thought – why not? You were looking for love, for romance, for the one. So, I kind of set it up that he would be at The Rooftop Café the day I cancelled our lunch date.'

'You did *what*?'

'Bertram thought he was on a blind date. He had no idea his date was sitting right behind him at another table. I had this crazy idea to plant you both there and see if something happened – and it did!' Julia threw her arms in the air theatrically. 'It worked.'

'Oh. My. God.' Sylvie stared at her dumbfounded. 'I can't believe what I'm hearing! You used my dream, Love on the Rooftop, didn't you? And to think, I told you all about meeting Bertram on The Rooftop Café, under the illusion that my dream had come true. I can't believe you manipulated me like that.'

Sylvie thought back to that first meeting when Bertram invited her to join him at his table because, apparently, they had both been stood up. Her immediate instinct was to say no. Not because she didn't like him. Bertram seemed very nice. It was the fact that she was cautious by nature, and she had a lot going on in her life with work, with Gertie.

However, there was something else that stopped her in her tracks. Sylvie had taken one look at Bertram and liked what she saw – very much. She was attracted to him. Sylvie had not experienced that feeling for years. It took her by surprise. Would a chance meeting with a stranger blossom into something more? That's what Sylvie was really afraid of. She didn't see the harm in joining him for lunch, but she couldn't see where she would fit a new relationship into her complicated life. It's not that she didn't want to find the one. Sylvie wanted exactly what Julia had. She wanted romance in her life. But things were complicated. She still hadn't sorted out her issues with John. The timing was all wrong – she knew that.

On the other hand, she remembered thinking that she hadn't eaten lunch, she was starving, and it's not as though she was committing to anything more than sitting with him to eat lunch together. Even so, she would still have said no if it wasn't for one thing, and one thing alone, she had met him on The Rooftop Café. That's what had intrigued her. Julia knew it would. If it had been anywhere else, Sylvie would have walked away, and that would have been the end of it.

'I still can't believe you set me up on a blind date without my knowledge!' Sylvie glared at Julia.

'I'm sorry,' said Julia, not sounding one bit sorry.

Sylvie paused. She thought back to that first meeting with Bertram when she discovered they had something in common: they both had a friend who liked to play cupid. Bertram never mentioned the name of this friend. Sylvie stared at Julia. 'He wasn't in on it, was he?'

'Of course not. Look, I just thought that if you knew you were on a blind date, straightaway you would be on your guard because it's something you were coerced into doing. This way, you *chose* to spend lunch together – that's completely different, don't you see? It turned out even better than a blind date because I threw in the element of chance. You were just two strangers who had supposedly both been stood up. And then something happened. It was fate.'

'No, Julia – it was *you*.' Sylvie shook her head. 'I can't believe you did that. I told you a secret and you used it to manipulate me into going out with Bertram. I get it now. That's what the little pep talk was all about.'

'Pep talk?'

'You told me to seize opportunities, remember?'

'Yes, well I may have mentioned something along those lines.'

Sylvie gave her a look. 'You had an idea that something might happen at The Rooftop Café when you didn't turn up. You knew there might be the possibility that Bertram would ask me to join him.'

'But he wouldn't have if he didn't like what he saw, Sylvie. That was nothing to do with me.'

'I know that. But that's not the point. Meeting Bertram on The Rooftop Café wasn't a sign that he was the one. You had engineered the situation.'

'You can't wait for a dream to come true,' Julia said in exasperation. 'I don't want life to pass you by, all because you're waiting to find love on a rooftop.' Julia sighed. 'I don't think all my talk of *signs* and *the one* has helped.'

'But I thought you believed in all that.'

'Only because I happened to meet Tom who lived on a houseboat too. I wanted to believe it was a sign that he was the one, but perhaps it was just a lucky coincidence – that's all. Maybe it was fate, or destiny, or just happenstance that led me to him. Honestly, Sylvie, I don't know. All I know is that I wanted the same thing to happen to you. It's just your stupid dream was getting in the way.'

Sylvie stared at Julia. 'But I thought you, of all people, would understand. Now I wish I'd never ever confided in you about my dream, love on the rooftop. It wouldn't have given you any ideas.'

'You're right, it's true,' admitted Julia. 'When you told me, it gave me the most marvellous idea, darling.'

Sylvie grimaced. 'You call setting me up with Bertram on The Rooftop Café *marvellous?*' Sylvie shook her head in dismay. She really didn't have anything more to say to Julia.

'Look, Sylvie, that dream – it's nonsense. It's going to spell the death knell for any second chances on the romance front – don't you see that?'

When she didn't respond, Julia continued, 'Sylvie, I'm your best friend, and I promise you I've only got your best interests at heart. So please listen to me when I tell you that you are going to miss opportunities like this. I'm not sorry I did it if I can make you see that.'

Sylvie had enough on her plate right now without finding out her best friend had lied and manipulated her. Sylvie got up from the table and walked over to the french doors leading out into the garden. She opened one.

Julia swivelled around in her chair. 'Where are you going?'

Sylvie ignored her. 'Come on, Alfie, let's go for a walk. When we get back, hopefully Julia will be gone.' Sylvie glared at her not-so-best friend.

'Oh Sylvie, don't be like that. Please talk to me. Say something.'

Sylvie turned from the door and eyed Julia coolly. 'I still can't believe what you did. Stop interfering in my life, Julia. I mean it. I don't need your help to find the one. What if I hadn't found out your little game and things had got serious with Bertram, and as a consequence I missed meeting the person I was meant to spend the rest of my life with – all because of my interfering best friend? What about that?'

Julia hadn't thought about that. She held out a placating hand. 'I was only trying to help.'

Sylvie marched across the kitchen and found Alfie's lead in the kitchen drawer. She then marched back to the french doors, followed by a bouncy excitable spaniel. Sylvie stepped outside.

'Oh Sylvie, please don't go.' Julia rose from her chair. 'Look, I'll do anything to make it up to you, really I will.'

Sylvie stopped and turned around. She looked at Julia a long moment. 'Anything?'

29

John was sitting in his kitchen staring at the redundant calendar stuck to his fridge door, with all Gertie's activities pencilled in for the coming weeks.

It was Friday morning, the day he normally had off from grandpa duty, and almost a week had gone by without seeing his grandchild. John was feeling depressed. He had spent so much time with Gertie, over the last few weeks, that to suddenly withdraw all contact with his grandchild was breaking his heart. It was like losing one of his own daughters. The last time he felt this way was when their daughter, Jess, moved to Australia and there wasn't a damn thing he could do about it.

John sighed. He knew what Dominic meant by getting their act together. They couldn't carry on like this, as though living apart together under the same roof was normal – it wasn't. Evidently, Harriet and Dominic didn't think so either. John suspected there was more to withdrawing all contact with Gertie than just the mistake he and Sylvie had made over their grandchild's childcare arrangements that afternoon. That's why they had issued an ultimatum: either get a divorce or get back together. They were probably past caring which one.

John doubted Sylvie would have him back even if he prostrated himself on the floor in front of her and kissed her shiny designer shoes. There was too much water under the bridge. So much had gone on since she moved into her own apartment, too many changes driving a wedge between them. What John was really thinking about were the changes in Sylvie.

She was an independent woman now with her own income and a good one at that. Since she moved downstairs, John noticed she was taking better care of herself. Sylvie had lost weight, and she was looking terrific; the way she dressed, her new hairstyle, the makeup, even the way she carried herself. To John, she looked like some sort of celebrity. He could almost imagine a braying crowd of photographers and fans gathering around Sylvie to secure her autograph. But John knew it was more than the change in her appearance that had surprised him. There was something about her he couldn't quite quantify. He wondered if it had something to do with her new job.

Whatever it was, the Sylvie he saw today was a very different person to the one he had married nearly forty years ago. The fact was she didn't need a husband to take care of her. She didn't need John anymore – that much was obvious. What she needed was to meet someone new. Someone with whom she had something in common, more than marriage, more than children, more than sharing the roof over their head. And more than the man she had married. Someone like Bertram thought John miserably.

John realised they owed it to themselves, and their family, to conclude this silly affair and finally bring up the D word; after all, wasn't that where all this was leading – to a divorce? Why prolong the inevitable? There was just one problem. Since that almighty row over whose fault it was that they had lost access to their grandchild, neither John nor Sylvie would back down. They hadn't uttered a single word to each other since that day. Even when they passed each other in the hall, they both acted as though the other wasn't there. They were strangers, like ships passing in the night, but without even the courtesy of a greeting to acknowledge their presence as they pass each other by.

John had no intention of backing down. Why should he? It wasn't his fault that Sylvie had reneged on her promise to look after Gertie because she forgot. At least he didn't do that; at least he didn't forget about his own grandchild. John told her as much.

Sylvie blamed him. As far as she was concerned, he was the one who had left Gertie with a stranger. It wound her up even more, the fact that he wouldn't tell her what was so damn important that it couldn't wait another day. He knew what she was thinking because during their heated exchange Sylvie didn't hold back voicing her suspicions. The way he was dressed, the way he was taking care of himself, the new spring in his step, the renewed sense of purpose; Sylvie concluded he was seeing a woman, and that's who he was with on the afternoon he had left Gertie with Barbara.

John made no effort to correct this misconception. In fact, he riled her up even more by saying that it was true – he *was* with a woman; but just neglected to add that it was work-related and had a job interview with the woman in question – their daughter. John didn't feel he owed Sylvie an explanation. It was a stand-off. The rug had been yanked from under them, the plug pulled on their grandparent duty, and there wasn't a damn thing they could do about it apart from blame each other.

John sat there staring into space. He didn't realise just how much he looked forward to seeing Gertie until it all suddenly stopped. The only thing John could console himself with, was the fact that Sylvie still left Alfie outside his door every weekday morning, with a note that said, *walk me.*

It was a small consolation for what he had lost. John was lonely. John was craving some human company. His apartment was so quiet, so extraordinarily empty, without Gertie around and only the dog for company. Even on Fridays, when Sylvie used to look after Gertie and John had a day off, he would hear them downstairs; the sound of Peppa Pig on the television or Sylvie singing Gertie a lullaby in the afternoon before her nap.

It brought back vivid memories of times past when their three girls were Gertie's age, and the house was filled with the background noise of small children. But today, just like the Friday before, there were none of those familiar sounds emanating from the apartment downstairs. However, Sylvie wasn't moping around at home feeling sorry for herself; she had gone to work. John was standing at the window in his lounge, drinking his morning cuppa when he saw her walk out of the house dressed in a smart business-like suit. She got into a waiting taxi. It made John wish he had somewhere to go too.

Thinking of Sylvie off to work brought to mind Harriet's suggestion. After he'd signed the contract with the magazine, she said he could come into the office to write his *Dear John* column. Of course, Harriet only offered him that option on the basis that he worked in the office, after hours, in the evening because he was meant to be looking after Gertie during the day.

Now that little ruse had been blown wide open, he had no reason to hang around at home. The thought of being surrounded by people, and the buzz of an office, was infinitely preferable to this – moping around his apartment all day, feeling lonely and depressed, with only the dog for company. He could well understand why Sylvie had got out of the house and taken herself off to work. Almost as soon as John considered going into the office, he realised it was a bad idea; the possibility of Harriet spotting him at work, and then getting another earful about Gertie, did not appeal to John one bit. Besides, he couldn't imagine the offer to come into work still stood. In fact, John thought she was much more likely to fire him if she saw him there; better to keep a low to non-existent profile.

John stood up from the kitchen table and walked through the lounge into his study. He sat down at his desk and switched on the laptop. Once again, John found himself staring into space thinking about Gertie and what happened almost a week ago. For some reason, John's thoughts drifted to Sylvie and the new man in her life, Bertram what's-his-face. Another sore subject that made him feel lonely and depressed.

John turned his attention back to the laptop screen and the blinking cursor taunting him on the empty page. He hadn't written a single word since he lost access to Gertie – not a word. Writer's block had never happened to John before. It got him thinking about another writer no doubt sitting at their desk, somewhere in London, at this very moment. He bet they were happily tapping away on their computer, writing their next article, probably not troubled by writer's block.

'Love on the Rooftop,' John said out loud to the empty room. He grimaced. John wanted to meet her, this mystery woman for whom LAT living had worked out tremendously well. He wanted to ask her how she did it; how on earth did living apart together cement her relationship rather than tear it apart?

John reached across his desk and picked up two magazines, the current issues of which he always had on hand. One magazine had the words *Love on the Rooftop* plastered across the front cover, along with the page number of her next article inside. The other magazine was the one John wrote his column for. The words *Dear John* adorned the front cover, reminding him that he was one of their most popular columnists and the deadline was already looming for his next article. The pressure was on for him to write something for the next issue.

John opened the magazine containing Love on the Rooftop's column and flicked to the front. He was looking for the address of their head office where, presumably, he might find the writer. John saw what he was looking for and noted down the address. Then it occurred to him that it was more likely he wouldn't find her at the office because, like him, she probably worked from home. The magazine would hardly give him her home address even if he did mention that he was the writer, Dear John, and he really wanted to meet her. John was beginning to think that turning up at the office in Hanover Square, to see Love on the Rooftop, might turn out a complete waste of time.

He stared at the magazine in front of him and then glanced at Alfie lying on the floor beside his desk. He had already walked the dog first thing this morning, but John always liked to fit in a lunchtime walk too. It was an excuse to get out of the house and remind himself there was a world out there beyond his study.

John's world had shrunk considerably since losing Gertie. The calendar on the fridge door, with all her activities, reminding him how much his day, his week, his world revolved around looking after his grandchild. Soon after he lost access to Gertie, the modelling agency had phoned John with more auditions. Not wanting to acknowledge this might be it, he might never see her again, John had asked if they could take a break from attending any up-and-coming auditions while he sorted out some family issues. John wouldn't go into any details. The agency had been really understanding and agreed to keep Gertie on their books. They hoped she returned very soon.

So did John.

John closed the lid on his laptop and listened to it powering down. It was no use. He still hadn't written a single word. He looked at Alfie, and said, 'Walkies?'

Alfie's ears twitched at the sound of John's voice. He yapped excitedly and raced out of the room.

John had barely got out of his chair when Alfie returned with the lead dangling between his jaws.

'Good boy!' John knelt down and attached the lead to his collar. In the lobby, John put on his shoes, grabbed a coat and opened the door to his apartment, at which point Alfie forgot his manners. As soon as the door opened, he belted out of the flat and raced down the stairs, his lead trailing on the floor behind him.

John was busy tucking the piece of paper into his wallet on which he had noted down the address of the magazine offices in Hanover Square. He thought the writer, Love on the Rooftop, was most likely not going to be there, but what had he got to lose? It wasn't as though he was going to be productive, sitting at his desk, staring at a blank computer screen. It might well prove a wasted trip, but perhaps getting out in the fresh air at midday would give him some inspiration and clear his writer's block.

John popped the wallet in his coat pocket and looked about him. 'Alfie?' He heard a familiar spaniel's yap coming from the communal hall downstairs. John shut his apartment door and walked down the stairs, eyeing Alfie. The dog was running around in circles getting excited. John shook his head and couldn't help but smile. It was the same routine every time he took Alfie out for a walk. Dogs were so uncomplicated and easy to please – unlike some he could mention. John frowned at Sylvie's door as he passed by.

'Come on, you,' said John, picking up his lead. 'Let's go for this walk.' John opened the front door. 'And if you are very, very lucky,' John added, trying to ignore the fact that, for lack of human company, he had resorted to talking to a dog, 'you might get to meet the writer, Love on the Rooftop. What do you think about that?'

'Yap, yap, yap!'

'You think it's an excellent idea?'

'Yap!'

'Well – let's go and introduce ourselves.'

30

Sylvie was sitting on a park bench in Hanover Square on her lunch break. After spending last Friday moping around at home feeling sorry for herself, Sylvie decided that come the following Friday – assuming relations had not improved with Harriet, which they had not – she would force herself to go into work. It turned out that Sylvie had other reasons, besides work, to be in Hanover Square on Friday.

Sylvie picked up the binoculars. She was spying on a gentleman sitting alone at a table up on The Rooftop Café. Sylvie put the binoculars back on her lap, satisfied nothing had happened – yet. She picked up her sunglasses and put them back on. Sylvie was aware she looked like some sort of celebrity, trying to disguise her identity in a headscarf and large dark sunglasses, but she had her reasons for going incognito. Sylvie was on a stakeout.

Sylvie finished one half of her ploughman's sandwich while she sat thinking about the set-up and waiting for things to unfold on The Rooftop Café. With a little help from Julia, Sylvie had everything planned.

As part of Julia's penance for setting her up with Bertram on The Rooftop Café, Sylvie insisted Julia told Bertram the truth:

she was a mutual friend, and she had been very naughty and set him up on a blind date with her other friend, Sylvie.

On hearing Julia's confession, it turned out Bertram didn't give a fig about that. He told Julia to pass on the message that he still wanted to see Sylvie and make it up to her. This had given Sylvie an idea. She decided to borrow a leaf out of Julia's book and set him up again.

Sylvie picked up her binoculars once more and spied on Bertram. He was still sitting alone at the table. Bertram was under the illusion that Sylvie would be meeting him for lunch. Sylvie put the binoculars down and looked at the other half of her sandwich. She had lost her appetite. Sitting on a park bench in Hanover Square Gardens, Sylvie was starting to feel nervous about setting Bertram up. She crossed her fingers hoping this worked.

It had been up to Julia to arrange everything. It was Julia who had to cajole Amy into seeing her father. It turned out that Sylvie's fears were not unfounded; Amy was on the verge of throwing in the towel on her relationship with her father. Apparently, going to see Bertram at The Grand Hotel had been a last ditch effort to resume relations between them. She had a life now, and she was done with wasting her time.

Julia found out that soon after Rory was born, Amy had started night school, re-awakening her dream of one day becoming a lawyer. It was something she wanted, not only for herself but for Rory too. More than anything, she wanted him to be proud of his mum. Resuming her education was made possible because Amy had met someone. She was in a steady relationship with a young man who was supportive and encouraged Amy to achieve her dream. Not only that, two years into her law degree Amy had secured a job as a part-time paralegal. She would gain some valuable work experience and increase her chances of getting an all-important training contract with a prestigious firm of solicitors when she finished her law degree.

Amy was aiming high. Sylvie had every confidence that she was well on her way to a bright future. The problem was Bertram didn't know any of this about his daughter. He was about to find out. Sylvie had written it all down in a letter, about how she was working hard to achieve something in her life for herself and Rory, and that he better give her one more chance before he lost his daughter and grandchild for good.

Sylvie picked up the binoculars and watched the maître d' deliver the letter to Bertram. He opened the envelope. Sylvie thought about what she had written inside. It may have sounded harsh, but Sylvie needed to get her point across . . .

You're the grown, up and yet you've still got a lot of growing up to do Bertram. Amy is only twenty years old. She was left with a child to bring up on her own just like you were, but the difference is she was just starting out in life. She is so much younger. You were more than twice her age when you were left to raise Amy alone. Think about that, Bertram. She needs your support. I'm not talking about money. You have to let her know that you love her, and you are there for her – no matter what. We all make mistakes. This might not be the life's path you would have chosen for Amy, but for heaven's sake get over it and see your child.

You are probably wondering what all this is about, why I've

written you a letter. I wrote it in the hope that by the time you read this, you're ready to meet your daughter. I'm sorry I tricked you into coming to The Rooftop Café today when I had no intention of meeting you for lunch.

I don't know whether there's a future for us after this, but I think that before you embark on a new relationship, you need to sort out your relationships closer to home. I didn't do that and look what happened to John and me! Please don't make the same mistake and lose your precious daughter and grandchild. The people we love are all that matter in this life.

Sylvie watched him fold the letter and put it back in the envelope. He suddenly got up from the table, out of her line of sight. For a split second, Sylvie thought he had left. Her binoculars darted this way and that, trying to locate him. Sylvie sighed in relief when she spotted him. He was standing on the other side of the table, pulling out a chair. Sylvie quickly adjusted her binoculars to see who was taking a seat at his table. A young woman dressed in black, with short spiky hair, sat down opposite Bertram. Sylvie smiled in relief. Amy had arrived.

Sylvie was avidly watching them when all of a sudden her view was obscured by a dark shape. Someone was standing right in front of her. Sylvie slowly lowered her binoculars and blinked in surprise.

A young man, pushing a toddler in a buggy, had stopped along the path. He was standing in front of Sylvie with his back to her. He appeared to be looking up in the direction of The Rooftop Café.

Sylvie quickly put her binoculars out of sight. 'It's new,' she said to his back.

He turned around. 'I'm sorry, what?'

'The café up there on the roof – it hasn't been here long.' Sylvie looked at the little boy in the buggy. He looked about Gertie's age. 'Isn't he adorable! What's his name?'

'Rory.'

'Rory,' repeated Sylvie, glancing up at The Rooftop Café. What an incredible coincidence if he was—

'Do you mind if we join you? All the benches are taken.'

Sylvie took a cursory glance around the gardens as she moved along the bench to make room. He was right. It was lunchtime. Surprisingly, for this time of year, the gardens in the centre of Hanover Square were full of office workers braving the damp and cold to eat their lunch outside. Sylvie smiled. She always used to eat her lunch in the gardens until she started meeting Bertram at the café.

Sylvie stole a glance through her binoculars at Bertram and Amy, still seated at their table.

The young man sitting beside her was busy unstrapping the toddler from his buggy.

Rory demanded, 'Snacks!'

The young man shook his head at the little boy. 'You'll have to sit back in the buggy while I find your snacks.' He tried to put him back in the buggy, but Rory wasn't playing ball.

'Here, let me,' said Sylvie, holding out her arms.

'That's really kind of you,' he replied, passing Rory over to sit on her lap.

Sylvie watched the young man rummage through his rucksack. Out came some nappies, talcum powder, wet wipes, a spare set of clothes, and a toy car. 'I could have sworn I packed—'

Sylvie glanced at her lunch. 'Does Rory like bananas?'

The young man looked up.

Rory was already reaching for the banana in Sylvie's hand.

He nodded. 'Sorry. This isn't like me. Believe it or not,' said the young man, piling the stuff back in his rucksack, 'I'm normally quite organised. It's just been one of those mornings.'

'Has it indeed,' said Sylvie. She unpeeled the banana and eyed the young man. He kept anxiously glancing in the direction of The Rooftop Café.

Sylvie was about to hand Rory the banana when the young man intervened. 'Here, let me take him. You don't want sticky fingers down your coat.'

Sylvie smiled. 'It's all right. I've had worse, believe me. I've got a grandchild about the same age.' She looked down at the little boy in her arms, and a wave of sadness engulfed her as she handed him the banana. She missed Gertie terribly.

Rory sat happily on Sylvie's lap, eating his banana, while the young man sat next to them watching his every move with a wet wipe at the ready.

Sylvie turned to the young man and offered him the other half of her M&S sandwich. 'They're very filling. I can't finish it.'

'Oh, I couldn't possibly—'

Sylvie smiled. 'Don't be silly.' She handed it over and watched him unwrap the other half of the sandwich. He took a bite and looked up at The Rooftop Café.

Sylvie asked, 'Are you waiting for someone?'

'My girlfriend.'

Sylvie glanced at Rory munching on his banana. She was dying to find out whether this little boy was Amy's Rory.

'Does your girlfriend work around here?'

'Uh no. She's meeting her father in the café up there.' He nodded in that direction and then turned to Sylvie. He lowered his voice. 'I don't know who arranged it. She thought she was meeting a friend. Then I got a text to say that when she arrived her father was there.'

'Really?' said Sylvie innocently. 'Well, fancy that.'

'Yes. They've been estranged, you see. The trouble is I feel really guilty. I've kept on at her about how important it is for her to build bridges for Rory's sake. But every time she approaches her father, he rejects her. It was breaking my heart to see her so upset and hurt—' He stopped abruptly. 'I'm sorry. I'm sure you don't want to hear all this.'

'No – do go on.'

'Just the other day she told me enough was enough. She said, "If he doesn't want Rory in his life then that's his loss." I got the impression she had decided it was time to move on.'

'Move on?'

'Yes. Amy had made up her mind she wasn't going to see him again.'

'Oh dear.'

'Who could blame her? She's tried so hard to reconnect. There's only so many times you can try before you have to face the fact that they're just not worth it.'

So it was true, thought Sylvie, Bertram was almost certainly on the verge of losing them for good.

The young man finished his sandwich and checked his mobile phone. 'To be honest, when she texted to let me know who she had met at the café, I thought she'd tell him to get lost.'

Sylvie nodded, not really surprised by that remark.

'I was quite taken aback when she said she was giving him one last chance. I hope he doesn't blow it.'

So do I, thought Sylvie.

They both turned to look in the direction of The Rooftop Café.

31

John walked into Hanover Square Gardens looking for a lady wearing a headscarf and dark sunglasses. He had just paid a visit to the address in Hanover Square written down on his scrap of paper. It was the head office of the magazine where he hoped to find the writer of the column, *Love on the Rooftop*. As expected, the receptionist on the front desk in the foyer of the building had fobbed him off. She couldn't let John go upstairs to the office unless he had an appointment with the editor, Marcia Hunt. Apparently, John didn't have an appointment.

He was on the verge of walking out the door when the receptionist, a dog lover, spotted the cute cocker spaniel accompanying John. 'Isn't he the sweetest thing?' she gushed.

John glanced at Alfie sitting by his feet. The dog was looking up at the receptionist and wagging his tail. John rolled his eyes. For some reason, Alfie made friends wherever he went.

Alfie yapped – loudly.

John pointed a finger at Alfie. 'Quiet!'

Alfie cowered under John's pointy finger and gave the receptionist his sad brown eyes – *nobody loves me* – routine.

John shook his head at Alfie, unmoved. He'd seen it countless times before. The receptionist had not. Those sad brown puppy-dog eyes instantly melted her frosty exterior.

She lifted her gaze, and said, 'Look, if it's any help, one of the journalists from the office upstairs popped out about ten minutes ago with her lunch. Most everyone nips across the road to sit in Hanover Square Gardens during their lunch hour.'

'Really? Even at this time of year?'

She shrugged. 'Yes. I'm sure you'll find her there. I don't know her name. She may be the person you're after. She may not. But either way, perhaps she can help you find who you are looking for.'

'How will I know who to look out for?'

'Oh, that's easy. She was wearing dark sunglasses and a headscarf.'

'Dark sunglasses and a headscarf – right you are.'

And that's how John found himself in Hanover Square Gardens looking for a lady wearing a headscarf and dark sunglasses. He spotted her almost immediately across the square. You couldn't exactly miss her; she was the only person sitting in the gardens wearing sunglasses on a dull December day. The next thing he noticed was the toddler balanced on her knee eating a banana. The woman in the sunglasses was having lunch with the young man sitting next to her. She offered him a sandwich as they sat together chatting amiably.

John stared at the happy familial scene guessing the writer's son and grandchild had met her for lunch. He didn't feel inclined to intrude. John's thoughts turned immediately to Gertie. A wave of unhappiness engulfed him at the thought of losing his only grandchild for good.

John slunk off to take Alfie for a walk. It didn't occur to him that this writer, who may or may not be Love on the Rooftop, might be meeting somebody for lunch, least of all her family.

Alfie started to bark and pull on the lead in the direction of the lady sitting on the bench.

John kept a firm hold on his lead. 'Sorry, chum, but I don't think we're going to meet Love on the Rooftop today.' John turned in the other direction and headed off to take Alfie for a walk around the outside perimeter of the gardens.

Sylvie turned her head at the sound of a dog barking. It sounded like a cocker spaniel and an awful lot like Alfie. Sylvie shook her head; what a silly thought. She turned her attention back to the young man sitting beside her who had been telling her all about his girlfriend, Amy, and her father, Bertram.

'It's been difficult for her. She wants him in her life, but I think she's got to the point where she's had enough. When she arrived at the café and found out it was her father waiting for her, she was going to turn around and walk straight out.'

Sylvie wasn't surprised. That's what she was afraid of.

'I texted her back and told her to give him a chance.' He looked up at the café. 'I hope I did the right thing.'

Sylvie saw her opportunity and stole a glance through the binoculars once more. Bertram and Amy appeared deep in conversation. Then something wonderful happened. Bertram reached across the table and took her hand.

Sylvie lowered the binoculars and smiled. 'I have a feeling things are going to work out just fine.'

Rory finished his banana and reached out for the young man sitting beside her.

Sylvie placed Rory in his arms. 'He's such a lovely little boy.'

'I know. I wish . . .' he trailed off.

Sylvie touched his arm. 'What is it?'

'I want to propose to Amy and not only that I'm hoping she'll let me be his dad. He's not mine, you know. I wish he were. His real dad . . . well, he was a complete waste of space. As soon as he found out she was pregnant, he didn't stick around.'

Sylvie looked at Rory cradled in the young man's arms. He was happily playing with his toy car. 'I think Rory would be a very lucky boy to have you as his dad.'

'You think so?'

'Absolutely.' Sylvie smiled at the young man. She also thought Bertram would be very fortunate to have him as his son-in-law.

'I would like to adopt him – make it official.'

Sylvie nodded. 'I'm sure Amy would be very hap—' Sylvie was cut off by the sound of a mobile phone.

'Excuse me, I better take this.' He glanced nervously in the direction of the café.

Sylvie guessed who was on the end of that phone.

'Hi, Amy. How's things?'

Sylvie waited with bated breath.

'Great, that's great news.' He glanced at Sylvie and smiled happily. 'He wants to see his grandson? Oh sure, sure. I'm still in the square. I'll bring him right over. Pardon? Your father wants to see me too?' He frowned. 'Why?'

Sylvie caught his anxious expression.

'You did? He does? Crumbs, I don't know what to say.' He looked taken aback.

'I take it,' said Sylvie, as soon as he got off the phone, 'that he wants to see his grandson?'

'Yes – and me too. Apparently, she told her father I was "the one". I'm not exactly sure what she meant by that.'

Sylvie grinned. 'It's a girl thing. It means she wants to spend the rest of her life with you.'

'I hoped that was it. There's more. She told her father she wants me to be Rory's dad – can you believe it?'

'Most definitely,' said Sylvie, not at all surprised. In the short time she had known Amy's partner, there was no doubt in her mind that he would make a terrific father. Anybody could become a dad – being a parent, now that was the hard part.

Rory reached for the mobile phone in his hand.

'Oh all right.' He handed it over.

Rory took the mobile phone and gave him the sweetest smile in return before he dropped it.

Sylvie picked it up. 'Oh dear.' There was a crack in the plastic casing.

The young man sighed. 'Ah well, I'll never learn. Amy told me not to let him play with it.' He hugged little Rory close, and said to him, 'But who could resist that smile – eh?'

Rory reached for the phone again.

'Sorry, Rory, you can't have it. It's broken – look.'

Rory wasn't smiling anymore. 'Phone!' he wailed.

'You don't want to cut your finger – do you?' He tried to show Rory where the phone was cracked, but Rory just lunged for the phone.

Sylvie found the toy car and handed it to Rory.

'NO!' He threw it on the floor in disgust.

'Rory!' The young man admonished him. He said to Sylvie, 'Sorry about that.'

Sylvie looked at him in surprise. 'You don't have to apologise.'

She watched him bounce Rory on his knee. When Rory had calmed down, Sylvie handed him the toy car. This time he took it with no objections.

The young man sighed in relief. 'I can't wait to get the terrible-two's out the way.'

'Hmm.' Sylvie didn't comment. In her experience, the so-called terrible-twos didn't magically disappear when they turned three, thirteen, or twenty-three. Sylvie watched him surreptitiously slip the broken phone back in his pocket.

There was something else in his pocket. He turned to Sylvie with it in his hand. 'I've been carrying this ring around in my pocket, like forever.'

Sylvie stared at the ring. 'It's beautiful.'

He looked down at the ring and shook his head. 'I can't seem to find the right moment to pop the question. The problem is I wanted to do things properly and ask her father for her hand in marriage before I proposed.'

'Oh.' Sylvie could see the problem. She glanced at The Rooftop Café. 'What about now?'

'Now? As in, when I go and meet her father?'

'Why not? I think this is the perfect opportunity,' said Sylvie encouragingly.

She watched him put Rory back in the buggy and head off through the gardens, in the direction of The Rooftop Café, with a beautiful engagement ring in his pocket. Sylvie smiled. There was a man who was about to make a young woman very happy.

Sylvie saw them cross the road and disappear inside the building. She waited a minute or two and then looked through her binoculars. Rory was sitting on his grandfather's knee. By the look on Bertram's face, it was love at first sight.

Seeing them together brought a tear to her eye. Sylvie lowered the binoculars and found a tissue. She wiped her eyes dry and found herself thinking about John, of all people. It had taken her by surprise when she saw all the time and effort he put into looking after their grandchild. John wanted to be part of Gertie's life – that was a given. He didn't think twice about agreeing to look after her. Not all grandchildren were so fortunate to have grandparents who wanted to be part of their lives.

Unfortunately, seeing Bertram with Rory was a harsh reminder that they were no longer part of Gertie's life, and they had nobody but themselves to blame. They had made a mistake, a *big* mistake, leaving Gertie in the care of somebody else. But John wouldn't have left her with someone he didn't trust.

Sylvie wasn't excusing his behaviour, gallivanting off with another woman when he should have been looking after Gertie. She was still angry with John, but also with Harriet for not stopping to consider how fortunate she was to have such willing hands-on grandparents. Harriet should have cut them some slack. After all, no parent, or grandparent for that matter, was perfect. Bertram was a case in point. There he was getting to know his grandson all because his future son-in-law had persuaded Amy to give him a second chance. Bertram didn't realise how lucky he was.

Sylvie took one last look through her binoculars. She saw the young man on bended knee in front of Amy. He was holding the ring aloft. It glinted in the winter sunshine. This meant only one thing: he had asked her father for her hand in marriage and Bertram had said yes.

Sylvie breathed a sigh of relief. Her ruse to bring father and daughter back together had worked like a dream, and to top it all a young couple in love had just got engaged. 'How romantic,' Sylvie whispered as she watched him propose on bended knee. A moment later the young couple kissed.

'Love on the rooftop,' commented Sylvie, smiling wistfully as she put her binoculars away. Her smile faded when she realised what she'd said. Did this mean her dream about finding love on the rooftop wasn't about her at all?

Something Julia said came to mind, ". . . that dream – it's nonsense. It's going to spell the death knell for any second chances on the romance front – don't you see that?"

She saw that now. Sylvie sat there deep in thought. She still wanted some romance in her life, and to find the one. Sylvie stared in the direction of The Rooftop Café and wondered if, thanks to Julia, she had already found him.

John had done several circuits of the perimeter of the gardens with Alfie and was getting mightily bored walking around in circles. He was about to head off home when he spotted the lady in the headscarf and sunglasses still seated on a bench in the square. She was alone. John saw his opportunity.

He was just making his approach when he heard a mobile phone ringtone. The lady on the bench answered her mobile phone. John came to a halt, undecided what to do. He couldn't very well interrupt her phone conversation. However, there was now a vacant spot on her bench. John didn't see the harm in taking a seat next to her while he waited for her to get off the phone.

John was making his way towards her when he glanced down at Alfie. What if she didn't like dogs? She might well get up and walk off as soon as he sat down. Ditto if she didn't want a stranger sitting on the park bench next to her overhearing a private conversation. If she left and he followed her, then he'd look like a stalker.

Up ahead, across the park from the woman on the phone, a young couple got up from a bench and tossed their rubbish in a nearby bin. John spotted them and changed direction, quickening his pace. He was intent on nabbing that bench. It offered the perfect vantage point from which he could sit and wait for the woman to finish her call.

Alfie tried to dart ahead, so John paused to let him off the lead. 'Good boy, fetch the bench.'

Alfie yapped excitedly and raced ahead.

Sylvie momentarily looked up at the sound of a dog barking but was quickly drawn back into the conversation with Julia.

Julia had phoned Sylvie on her mobile because she couldn't stand it any longer. She wanted to find out what was happening, whether the plan was working.

Sylvie told her the plan had gone like clockwork. As far as she was concerned, Julia had scored extra brownie points for getting the boyfriend involved and making sure he was here with Rory to see his grandfather. Then Julia nearly lost all her brownie points for letting it slip that Bertram had told her all about the apartment he had offered to buy Sylvie with a rooftop garden.

'Why on earth did he tell you that?' asked Sylvie.

'Ah . . .well . . . it might have something to do with the fact that I er told Bertram the reason I arranged a blind date at The Rooftop Café.'

'You told him about my dream didn't you!'

'It just came out – sorry.'

Sylvie frowned. Julia didn't sound particularly sorry.

'Bertram said that it did explain why you asked him whether he had a rooftop garden when you visited his place.'

'Ah, so that makes it all right then.'

'Well, I guess it does if your boyfriend then offers to buy you an apartment with a rooftop garden . . . '

Sylvie rolled her eyes. 'Julia, for one thing, I don't know if Bertram and I . . . if we're an item. And besides, the last thing I want, after forty years of marriage, is to be a kept woman. I love having a career and my own autonomy.'

'He knows that. I think that's what he loves about you, Sylvie. You are independent. You don't want anything from him – financially speaking.'

'So he knows I don't want him to buy me a flat – right?'

'He knew you'd say that. That's why he said, if you insist, he'll charge you rent.'

Sylvie laughed at the joke. 'Okay, enough already.'

'Seriously, perhaps you should consider moving into your own place.'

Sylvie frowned. 'I already did that.' She heard Julia sigh heavily down the phone. 'What?'

'Darling, you moved *downstairs* . . .'

'Into a self-contained apartment.'

'But you're still living under the same roof.'

'I know that,' snapped Sylvie. 'So?'

'Have you read your column, lately?'

'Very funny,' said Sylvie sarcastically. 'What of it?'

'Don't you see? You're not your alter ego, Love on the Rooftop. You and John, you're not really living apart together, or LAT living – as you call it. The fact is you are no longer together. Your relationship – it's over.'

Sylvie fell silent. Finally, she said, 'What are you suggesting – that I move out of the house altogether?'

'In a word – yes. Perhaps it's time to get out from under John. Bertram told me all about the evening he tried to have coffee at your place and the resulting shenanigans with your neighbour upstairs.'

Sylvie rolled her eyes. 'Don't remind me.'

'So he asked me to tell you to think about it.'

'Think about what?'

'Moving into the apartment.'

'What apartment?'

'The penthouse apartment, with the rooftop garden, he just purchased.'

Sylvie stopped short. Her mouth dropped open. 'You're pulling my leg.'

'He said to tell you that the landlord – that's him – has no problem if his new tenant wants to bring her dog.'

Sylvie managed a smile. Talking of dogs, Sylvie heard a dog barking again. It was a familiar yap that sounded an awful lot like a cocker spaniel. Sylvie knew she was being paranoid, but her eyes darted around the gardens, looking for any sign of Alfie – and John.

'Are you going to think about moving into the penthouse apartment?' asked Julia. 'You would still have your own place, and John would finally get what he wanted – to rent out the garden apartment.'

Sylvie was listening to Julia when she spotted a dog, which

looked remarkably like Alfie, sitting on the opposite side of the square pulling on his lead and yapping excitedly at something – or someone. The man sitting on the park bench, holding the dog lead, was engrossed in his newspaper.

Sylvie grasped her sunglasses and pulled them down a fraction to peer over the top. She watched the man fold the newspaper and tuck it under his arm. He bent down and admonished the dog that looked an awful lot like Alfie; the dog that was, in fact, Alfie and had recognised Sylvie even in her dark sunglasses. The moment she pulled them down, to peer over the top, he went berserk.

The man sitting on the bench got up and looked in her direction.

Sylvie gasped. It *was* John. 'Shit! Crap! And hells bells all rolled into one!'

Julia started to laugh down the phone. She had never, ever heard Sylvie swear before. It was very entertaining.

'Julia – gotta go. Bye.' Sylvie put her sunglasses back on, threw the phone in her handbag and got up from the bench.

John was already striding across the gardens. Alfie was pulling on the lead. They were heading straight towards her.

'What in god's name was he doing here?' said Sylvie under her breath. The only explanation she could think of was that John wanted to talk to her. He knew that she had lunch at The Rooftop Café, so Sylvie guessed he had turned up here again on the off chance he might see her.

Sylvie grimaced. She did not want to talk to John. She wasn't done being angry with him over Gertie. And she certainly didn't want John to find out where she worked; that was all she needed. Sylvie had to think quickly. Her lunch break was over, but she couldn't very well have John follow her back to the office. Sylvie needed to lose John before she made her way back to work.

Sylvie hurried out of Hanover Square Gardens. She took a quick glance over her shoulder. John was still in pursuit. Sylvie quickened her pace. She turned left, in the opposite direction to the office, bolted up a side street and dived into the entrance of John Lewis department store. Sylvie made straight for the perfume counter. She doubted John would find her in the throng of lunchtime shoppers. That's assuming he managed to step foot inside the store with a dog.

As soon as she walked into the store, Sylvie had to remove her sunglasses. Next came the headscarf. Sylvie had broken into a hot flush, brought on by the sudden exercise in her bid to lose John.

'Would madam like to try a fragrance?'

Sylvie tucked the scarf and sunglasses into her bag, did up the clasp and held out her wrist.

The young lady was about to spray the expensive perfume when someone backed into Sylvie, bumping her sideways and nearly knocking her over. Fortunately, she caught herself in time, but the scent missed her wrist and was accidentally sprayed into the face of the gentleman who had bumped straight into her.

Closing his eyes just in time, John got a spray of perfume full in the face. As he stepped back in surprise, a doggy yelp could be heard as he accidentally stepped on Alfie's tail.

Sylvie watched from behind a mannequin as the drama at the perfume counter unfolded. The shop assistant holding the perfume bottle started to apologise. Then she spotted Alfie. She curtly told John that dogs were not allowed in the store.

Sylvie overhead John asking the shop assistant if she had

seen a woman wearing a headscarf and dark sunglasses pass this way. Sylvie narrowed her eyes. She couldn't believe John had followed her. It was one thing putting up with John's shenanigans at home. He could be a royal pain in the behind if he had a mind to. But at least when she went to work, she assumed she could get away from him. Evidently not. Thoughts of Bertram's penthouse apartment, with the rooftop garden, floated into her consciousness.

Sylvie watched as John and Alfie were escorted from the store by a security guard.

Sylvie, who was still hidden from view behind a mannequin, caught the pungent fragrance of women's perfume as John passed by.

John smelled lovely. Sylvie imagined the looks he was going to get, on his journey home on the bus, smelling of expensive ladies' perfume. Served him right, thought Sylvie wickedly.

Sylvie bought the expensive perfume before she headed back to work.

32

John always made sure he had showered, dressed and breakfasted each morning by eight o'clock, so he was ready to walk Alfie. At least he had a reason to get up in the morning. Since he stopped looking after Gertie, John started to feel depressed. He thought about adding a bottle or two of Drambuie to his weekly shopping list. That was not a good sign.

John had even contemplated phoning up Barbara and inviting her and her friends over for a party at his place to cheer himself up, which he knew was a really, really bad idea. He always hated those parties and had no idea why he thought they would cheer him up.

John was on the verge of slipping back into bad habits. There were only two things that stopped the spiral downwards. One was his weekly column, which he still worked on late in the evening. It was a routine he had grown accustomed to when his days were filled with Gertie and having fun together. Even though there were times he felt too exhausted to write, after a day spent with a two-year-old, John would give anything to rewind the clock and have Gertie back.

Then there was the other reason he got out of bed in the

morning; the reason he was ready by eight o'clock every weekday, come rain or shine. John had another important job to do besides write his weekly column and update his blog. His second purpose in life was to walk Alfie.

John opened his apartment door at eight sharp, and called out, 'Alfie, walkies!' He stopped dead. Where was the little dog that was always waiting outside his apartment door to greet him with a wag of the tail and the little note attached to his collar that said *walk me*? His first thought was that Sylvie had a day off work and was walking her own dog. That was plausible. It was also likely that she hadn't bothered to tell him. John didn't need reminding that they weren't exactly on speaking terms.

He glanced across at the bannister where he expected to see Alfie wagging his tail, looking pleased to see him. John depended on seeing that happy little chappie first thing in the morning because, right now, it felt like the whole world was against him and Alfie was the only friend he had. Certainly, the only friend he had in this household, thought John miserably.

John was standing outside his apartment door, at a total loss, when he spotted something. He raised an eyebrow. There was a piece of notepaper sellotaped to the bannister where Alfie's lead was normally tied. John managed a smile. Sylvie might not have left him the dog to walk this morning, but she *had* left him a note; at least that was something. Perhaps she left a message to say she had the morning off work and was going to deposit Alfie outside his apartment door this afternoon? He hoped so. John never thought he would see the day when he would miss having that hairy, slobbery mutt around.

John walked over to retrieve the note. He peeled away the sellotape and carefully unfolded the paper.

It began, *Dear John . . .*

John's eyes went wide in shock. 'Oh God!' He immediately crumpled up the note into a tight paper ball and tossed it over the bannister. He stood there watching it fall to the hallway below. So, this was it. The day he was dreading had finally arrived. He didn't have to read the note any further. John knew what it was. He had got his Dear John letter informing him that she had found someone else and their marriage was over. John shook his head, turned on his heel, and walked back into his apartment, slamming the door shut behind him.

John had just found his wallet and slipped it into his back pocket, intending to go to the corner shop and get himself a bottle of booze, when he heard the unmistakable sound of a dog yapping outside in the street below.

'Alfie?' John rushed over to his lounge window and pulled the curtains. He stopped dead, stunned. 'Well, you don't waste any time – do you?' said John bitterly as he watched his wife load two suitcases and an overnight bag into the back of a taxi. She then climbed into the cab with Alfie in her arms.

John had the sudden impulse to run out of his apartment in order to catch the taxi before it left, hoping to make her stop and reconsider. But reconsider what? She had made her choice; she'd written that letter, hadn't she? John's shoulders sagged in defeat. There was nothing more to be said. She had written *Dear John,* and that said it all.

Thinking of that note, John's sudden impulse dissipated. He slowly turned around and slumped on to one of the upholstered chairs by the window. The sudden urge to buy the bottle of booze had also taken flight. He had the column to write for next week's magazine issue. The deadline was fast approaching, and he *still* hadn't written a single word; he was up against the clock. He couldn't afford to waste any more time getting shit-faced and then dealing with the aftermath by trying to write the article drunk, or worse nursing a hangover. It just wasn't worth it.

Getting plastered wasn't going to change a thing. Sylvie had left him – for good this time. She packed her bags and walked out that door; he had seen it with his own eyes. Nothing was going to change that. And losing his new job as a columnist, because he failed to meet a deadline, wasn't going to help his situation either. He could imagine Harriet was just waiting for him to slip up and give her an excuse to get rid of him. His job as a columnist was all he had left. He couldn't afford to lose that too.

John took the wallet out of his back pocket and tossed it on the sofa, on his way out of the room. He shut himself away in the study to write the final article for his *Dear John* column. There wouldn't be anymore. He knew this for a fact because he had finally received his Dear John letter. John thought of the crumpled up note lying on the floor in the communal hall downstairs. As soon as he read those two words, he knew it spelled the end of their marriage and the end of his blog about their life, living apart together.

He hoped the end of the *Dear John* column wouldn't mean the end of his new writing career. Perhaps his current popularity might go some way to influencing Harriet to keep him on to write about something else, but he couldn't guarantee that. Besides, that really was the least of his concerns right now; his wife had left him. John's world had been turned upside down in one of the worst ways imaginable. He had lost the only woman he'd ever loved.

By late afternoon John was starting to feel restless. He had worked through the day, without a break, to keep his mind off buying the bottle of booze he still craved. The upside was that he seemed to have recovered from writer's block.

He was about to submit what might turn out to be his last article for the magazine when he received a phone call from the assistant editor. John didn't want to hear that he had missed the deadline and Harriet had decided to fire him. It was enough that he was going to have to beg them to keep him on once they realised the end of *Dear John* was nigh.

'Hello John.' The young assistant editor sounded cheerful.

John frowned. He wasn't sure whether to take it as a good sign that everything was fine, or a bad sign that he was trying to sound upbeat because he was calling with bad news. He never called John at home.

John waited with bated breath. So far, everything in his life had rapidly gone south. Why should this be any different? John had already resigned himself to the fact that his new career was over. He waited for the assistant editor to tell him so.

The assistant editor said, 'We've had a tip-off that the other blogger, the anonymous writer Love on the Rooftop, is on their way to New York as we speak.'

'So what?' said John glumly. He wasn't in the mood to hear about the success of his arch rival.

'There are rumours that she is going to reveal her identity on live television.'

John shook his head. He really couldn't care less.

'So, we had this totally crazy idea.'

'Idea?' John yawned.

'Yes. What if we could get these two in the same room to-gether, on live television?'

'These two?' repeated John, rubbing his forehead. John was feeling tired and irritable. He was finding it hard to concentrate. It wasn't to do with the hours he'd just spent writing. It was everything else in his life. As soon as he finished writing his column, the note from Sylvie that he had crumpled up into a ball and tossed down the stairs came back to haunt him. He knew he should go and retrieve it, and actually read the damn thing. But what good would that do? She'd gone. There was no point rubbing salt in the wound by reading the Dear John letter she had written before she left.

'Did you hear me, John? We thought, wouldn't it be a crazy but brilliant idea if we could get these two together in the same room on live television?'

John didn't have the first clue what he was talking about, let alone what it had to do with him. John said, 'I'm sorry, but I have no idea what you are talking about.'

'You John, we're talking about *you* – the writer, Dear John.'

John was still in the dark as to the purpose of the phone call. 'You mean you're not firing me?'

There was a pause on the end of the line. 'No, John, we're not firing you. We're offering you an all-expenses-paid trip to New York.'

'Pardon me?'

'We're talking about you and Love on the Rooftop meeting for the very first time, in front of a live studio audience, in New York!'

It took a moment for John to fully grasp what he was saying.

John was glad he was sitting down. *New York*. Were they serious? They wanted John Baxter to fly all the way to New York and appear on an American television talk show?

'I realise we have no right to ask you to drop everything . . .'

'Drop what?' blurted John. He had absolutely nothing going on in his life right now – apart from work. He missed Gertie. He missed Alfie. He even missed Mouse, the cat he had bought in the heat of the moment to prove to Sylvie that he too liked pets – the cat that had, incidentally, also left him.

John shook his head. That wasn't entirely true. Mouse was probably asleep in a sock drawer, or at the back of his laundry cupboard, but John was feeling sorry for himself with a capital S. He couldn't get the image of Sylvie loading her suitcases into the back of a taxi out of his mind.

The fact was that despite everything, despite their major falling out over Gertie, he was missing his downstairs neighbour already. He would miss the tap of her heels walking across the wooden floor when she came home from work. He would miss the faint tinkle of cutlery when she ate her evening meals on the sofa in the lounge downstairs. He would even miss the sound of the television on into the early hours when she was catching up on those old black-and-white late-night B-movies she loved so much. It felt so lonely knowing that the apartment downstairs was empty, that Sylvie was gone.

'John – are you still there?'

'Oh, yeah – sorry.' John was so preoccupied with Sylvie and that blasted Dear John letter, he had all but forgotten the phone conversation. 'You did say "New York" didn't you?'

'Yes, John. Are you okay? You sound a bit—'

'I sound a bit *what?*' snapped John. His wife had just left him

– what did they expect? John quickly apologised, 'Sorry.' They weren't to know that. It wasn't the assistant editor's fault he'd caught Dear John at a bad time – or had he?

John raised an eyebrow. *New York.* Perhaps this was just what he needed: an all-expenses-paid trip to America, to cheer himself up before the shit really hit the fan and divorce papers started winging their way over to him to mark the official end of their marriage. John didn't want to be around when that envelope plopped through the letter box.

John sat bolt upright in his chair. 'I'll do it – I'll go to New York!'

'Really? For a minute there I thought you weren't interested.'

'Oh, I'm interested all right.' If Sylvie thought he was just going to sit around waiting for the divorce papers to come through, then she was sorely mistaken. You wait, thought John, she was going to find out he had a life too. He might not walk out the door each morning, like Sylvie, off to a high-flying career – or whatever the hell she did dressed in her drop-dead gorgeous designer clothes – but he *had* made a success of himself in a second career.

John smiled. She would get the shock of her life if she knew a magazine was flying him business class all the way to New York to meet the famous writer, Love on the Rooftop, on live television – no less. It was all he could do not to ring Sylvie's mobile number and tell her the news. John had eventually found Sylvie's mobile number when he wasn't looking for it, tucked in his little black book. Even though he was no longer looking after Gertie, for some reason, John had decided to keep the phone number on his person, specifically in his wallet, just in case.

He would have liked nothing more than to phone Sylvie and

tell her all about his blog and how he had become a successful columnist. However, as much as he wanted to introduce Sylvie to the real John, the man who many moons ago secretly wished he could ditch his accountancy career to become a writer, the fact of the matter was he couldn't do that. Not now. Not after what he had been writing – those witty and entertaining articles about living apart together, which his readers lapped up. John knew if he told Sylvie all this, then he would have to tell her *everything*. He would have to reveal that he had written about Sylvie in his blog, and then moved on to writing articles all about how living apart together had destroyed their relationship and ended their marriage.

John sighed heavily. He got up from his desk and wandered over to the study window. John looked down at the street below. The taxi ferrying his wife god-knows-where had left hours ago. All afternoon he had sat in his study keeping an ear out for the sound of a car pulling up outside the house. He thought perhaps she might change her mind and come home.

John turned from the window and stared at his laptop. The cursor was blinking at the bottom of a page of writing; the next article for his column was ready to wing off to the magazine. John frowned. 'What was that saying?' He scratched his head. 'Ah yes,' John remembered. 'Be careful what you wish for.'

John slowly shook his head from side to side. When he was forced into early retirement, all he wished for was to be able to do something more with his life and prove he wasn't over-the-hill, passed it, redundant – financially speaking. He had no idea that converting the house into two apartments would eventually lead to a successful writing career as a consequence of living apart together.

John had got exactly what he wished for, but at what price? He was thinking about that Dear John letter he had crumpled up and tossed over the bannisters into the communal hall downstairs. It was still on the floor outside the door to Sylvie's apartment. Was that the price of his success – losing his wife?

John returned to his desk and stared at the page of writing. His final article for the magazine, in the saga of Sylvie and John Living Apart Together, was all about the shock of receiving that Dear John letter and seeing his wife leaving him – for good this time. John forced himself to read the whole sorry affair one last time, checking for typos, before he sent the email submitting his article for publication in this month's magazine. He'd just made the deadline.

Sitting reading the article made him wonder what Sylvie would make of his new career as a writer. Even though he had disguised his wife's identity by using a fictitious name in his column, it was bound to happen sooner or later; Sylvie was going to find out he had been writing about their personal lives – about her. If John was going to reveal his identity as the writer, Dear John, on a live television show, then he was going to take the opportunity for that to happen in New York, thousands of miles away from his wife. John was a coward. He would much rather Sylvie found out what he had been up to when he had the whole Atlantic Ocean between them, than telling Sylvie face-to-face and ending up having another almighty bust-up.

New York. John still couldn't quite believe he was really going to America. He was itching to tell someone. There was no point phoning Harriet; she wouldn't be at all surprised by this news because she would have been in on the idea from the start. Harriet was looking forward to finding out the identity of the anonymous writer, Love on the Rooftop, just as much as anybody else.

John wondered why Harriet hadn't phoned him herself; after all, it was probably her idea to send him to New York to meet his nemesis. John reached for the phone, intending to get in touch with Harriet and thank her for the trip. Under the circumstances, the timing couldn't have been better. It was an excuse to get away from the house, for a few days, and try not to think about a future without Sylvie.

John hesitated before he made that call. The fact that he was still dealing with the assistant editor told John she didn't want to speak to him. The last thing he wanted to do was jeopardise the trip. Perhaps it would be better to err on the side of caution and steer clear of Harriet for the time being. That left Jess and Chloe.

John chose to phone Chloe. She was closer to home, and he needed someone to care for his cat while he was away. He could take his cat to a cattery, but he had to find her first. John had enough experience of living with Mouse to know that he would only be able to find her if she wanted to be found; more often than not, she seemed to go out of her way to make John's life difficult by doing exactly the opposite of what he wanted.

Mouse, John soon discovered, was complicated. His pet was not at all like Sylvie's easy-going, easy-to-please pet dog, Alfie. John wondered if that was because Mouse was a cat, or because Mouse was a female. Sometimes John wished he hadn't bought a *female* cat - maybe *that* was the problem.

Chloe was very excited to hear John's news and not at all phased by John's request to look after his cat.

'Are you sure you don't mind?' queried John, aware that it was extremely short notice to ask her to drop everything and come over to his apartment right away to collect his house keys, so she could pop in and feed his cat while he was away.

'You'll come right now?' John was surprised she had agreed without hesitation, and not only that she even offered to drive him to the airport. This was quite unlike Chloe. John was familiar with his youngest daughter's modus operandi; Chloe only did a good turn if there was something in it for her.

John put the phone down and thought nothing more of it. He had other things on his mind like, for instance, 'What on earth did I do with my passport?'

By the time Chloe drove up and parked outside the house, John had packed for his trip to New York and was ready to go. He walked down the stairs carrying his suitcase and an old British Airways shoulder bag he had found for the flight. John hadn't been abroad or flown for years. In truth, he was feeling a bit nervous.

He opened the front door to find Chloe standing on his doorstep.

'Got everything, Dad?'

'I think so.'

'Did you remember to pack a fresh change of clothes for the show?'

'Yes.' John had that covered. He wanted to look the part and make the right impression – smart but casual. It wasn't difficult because that's the way John dressed these days. He was wearing jeans, a flannel shirt, and a blue blazer. John had packed a pair of chinos, another flannel shirt and a tweed jacket for the show.

He didn't dress like an accountant anymore in those stuffy starched suits. John looked and felt more comfortable with his new image, with his new life as a writer and columnist. The trouble was, John wasn't feeling particularly relaxed right now. He had the strange sensation that he was missing something. John glanced at the suitcase in his hand and frowned. He couldn't for the life of him think what he may have forgotten to pack.

'Dad, what's the matter?'

'My passport!' John left his suitcase and shoulder bag in the hall and scooted back upstairs.

Chloe stepped inside the house and watched her father rush back upstairs. She bent down to pick up his suitcase, intending to take it to the car, when something caught her eye; there was a crumpled up piece of paper on the floor outside the door to the garden apartment. Chloe reached down and picked it up.

She was just unfolding the notepaper when John, who was walking back down the stairs with his passport, spotted Chloe with his Dear John letter.

He hurried down the stairs towards her. 'Give me that!' He snatched it out of her hand before she had a chance to read it.

'What is it?'

'Never-you-mind,' said John, stuffing the note into his blazer pocket. 'Let's go. I've got a plane to catch.'

The story continues in

Love on the Rooftop

Paperback and Kindle eBook available to buy from Amazon

For further details about the author and her books visit

www.elisedarcy.com

And finally . . .

If you enjoyed this book, and have a spare moment, please consider leaving some feedback for other readers by writing a quick review on Amazon. Great reviews spread the word and help readers like you choose books they enjoy.